The Rainbow Rim

a novel
by Michael Just

Giddings Street Press, Mancos CO

2026

The Rainbow Rim

ISBN: 979-8-9940195-0-4

Giddings Street Press Mancos, CO

Additional publications may be found at the following websites: just mike just.com, for fiction and nonfiction spanning several genres, just mikejust.substack.com for his blog, *The Accidental Naturalist*, and at canyoncallsthebook.com, for Canyon Calls, a collection of short stories related to the Grand Canyon, as well as essays of nonfiction with nature-related themes.

Praise for *The Rainbow Rim*

What you'll get with Michael C. Just's "Rainbow Rim" is an explosive, no-holds-barred road trip, peopled with bizarre, colorful characters. Our heroine, so to speak, is a faded drug addict/prostitute/low-life who looks for the newborn son she abandoned 17 years ago, Martin, to confront him with the painful truth, that she is his mother. Patsy and Martin--who is a somewhat guileless Bible-reading young man--set out, leaving Illinois for points West.

"Rainbow Rim" is dark in mood, exposing the demi-world of the mentally ill and their institutional life and giving voice to a pervasive anger present in much human interaction. The reader is, throughout this black comedy, in the company of unrelievedly unpleasant people. As I began reading, I was reminded of William Carlos Williams's introduction to "Howl," the Allen Ginsberg long poem about the institutionalized insane. The warning lines from Williams can serve as introduction to the world in "Rainbow Rim" as well: "Hold back the edges of your gowns, ladies, we are going through Hell." And, it's unrelenting. The characters in the novel endure constant yelling, shouting, punching, and hitting out. They live in a miasma of pain.

Yet this darkly comic novel is in the hands of a writer's writer, Mike Just, and he humanizes the work: he creates a vivid cast of characters, employs dialogue that is believable, and creates a wonderfully crafted narrative line. Despite all the dysfunction, the characters and story are nuanced. For instance, as they drive through Kansas, Patsy stops so Martin can pray at a church. She disparages him, sneering, "I've been to outhouses that were bigger." He tries to convince her to pray in the tiny chapel, and tears come as Martin tells her she'll be ready for religion someday. "You has a beautiful heart," he says, "One day, it happens for you."

It's worth noting here at the last, that Just is also a nature writer nonpareil, and he ends the novel in a quiet and beautifully redemptive natural setting. Patsy and Martin are at the Rainbow Rim; they've left the urban sprawl and "walked together out to a headland surrounded by cubic miles of air." It feels to her that they, with the aspen and the ponderosa around them, are in a citadel. Finally, they are together. Unassailable.

~Jo Gibson, Adjunct Faculty, Department of English, Cleveland State University (retired).

A visceral family tale, a vivid road trip story, The Rainbow Rim kept me up past my bedtime many nights. Michael Just is a master wordsmith and has created wonderfully flawed characters and unforgettable places. He takes us on a physical and emotional journey as, against nearly all odds, a mother and son hope to find their way toward each other.

~Jenna Hawkins, Screenwriter, Actor, Editor

Rainbow Rim is a wild journey to connection between a long-separated mother and son. Both are misfits in their respective lives, unable to find where they fit within their worlds, due to their respective challenges. Through their helter-skelter journey, they discover the beautiful and difficult things they have in common. Mike Just weaves an intricate and stunning story of difficult lives changed for the better through love and determination.

~Bea Sorelle

DEDICATION

To my Mother and my Father,
my truest teachers

Their van squeezed through sandstone spires veneered with badland finish on either side of the road. She wondered what her boy thought of this raw plateau. She was his age when she'd first seen mountains. For her, an MDA trance transmogrified Sleeping Ute Mountain into a warrior god raised up on behalf of his people. While she'd watched, he vanquished an army of giants made from nearby mesas that had been raised to destroy his people, the Utes. And she knew that this god had fought for all peoples and won. That had been a primeval ecstasy, but she hadn't earned the right to the experience.

This time she'd earned her right to it.

ACKNOWLEDGMENTS

This book would not be possible without my consultations of the fol-
lowing books: *The Navajo*, by Clyde Kluckhohn and Dorothy Leighton;
Coyote Stories, by Mourning Dove; and *The Navajos*, by Peter Iverson.
I also thank the Navajo people, Amtrak, the *National Park Service*, the
U.S. Department of the Interior, my first editor and mentor, Kathleen
Anne Fleming, Sheila Wilbur and Gert Just, proofers extraordinaire, and
AnnaBeth Davidson, my editor, agent, and professional partner in all
my work.

1.

She posed like a Sphinx in a cheap office papered with the dark and perceptive art of those in psychosis. Outsider art, they call it. Art therapists all over the earth had wallpaper like this: images preoccupied with eyes and hands and dark swirls of night and an occasional scream.

Patsy's legs hung long and bruised. At the end of them, she wagged a set of pedicured toes cradled in high-heeled pumps crossed over her knee. The insides of her stiletto heels were lined with mirrors. To hide the fact that her hair was thinning, she combed it to one side, cropping it just below her ears. Even though she was past her best head-turning days, anyone could tell how beautiful she must have been. She had so much of that quality in her shimmering hazel eyes and flawless bone-colored complexion, that Ms. Pringle still got her way much of the time. That way consisted of hitched rides, free drinks, a few bucks when she felt her belly empty.

An older man, especially, may have said she was still a beautiful woman at 34. All six feet and ½ inch of her. She liked to say it was the fact that "Most girls with boobs as big as my own have big butts. I think what guys like about me," she'd opine with well-thought-out words, "is that my butt's so damn tiny." Sometimes, she wished she could just take her bosom off and leave it in a drawer somewhere. She called her beauty her blessing. She blamed everything on it.

Sandy, the intake coordinator, sat across from her. An equal sign in the colors of the rainbow decorated her desk, next to a picture of Sandy and her partner. Sandy was out and she didn't care who knew it.

"It says here that a voice told you to take off your top. In a church," Sandy said. She scanned the Petition for Involuntary Commitment, a form half-faded from being photocopied so many times.

"You have," Patsy said, "the sexiest chestnut hair. The way it teases your shoulders."

Patsy rose from her chair and slid her cellulite over the corner of Sandy's desk and sat right there so Sandy could get a good look. Patsy prided herself in her superpower: she told everyone she could smell which way someone blew, whether they were randy, even whether they'd gotten any the night before. But the rainbow equal sign was a dead giveaway.

"I usually don't do this with my clients," Sandy said.

"Do what?"

"This sign on my desk. Know what the equal stands for?"

"Yeah," Patsy smiled. "I think I do."

"Doesn't stand for idiot."

Patsy's smile dropped to a frown.

"*Ding ding*," Sandy sang. "The captain has just turned on the fasten seat belt sign. Please return to your seat, fasten your seatbelt, and return your tray table and chair to their upright and locked positions."

"Worked before," Patsy said. She decamped from her perch and sat back down in the metal folding chair. She liked Sandy. She reminded Patsy of herself.

"So, what do your voices sound like?"

"Mother Theresa sometimes. Eighties hits, mostly," she said in her southern Illinois drawl, from a region they called Little Egypt.

"Do they ever tell you to hurt yourself?"

"When you're sick enough to hear voices, they don't pay compliments." She pulled out a strand of hair. "Under this black bark, I'm a redwood, too."

She showed Sandy the rusty root that tapered to Clairol black. Sandy nodded and checked SUICIDAL IDEATION on her intake sheet. *The Cat in the Hat* doubled as her clipboard.

"Do you have any plans to hurt yourself?" Sandy asked.

"That affect where you put me?"

Sandy jotted down a note: MALINGERING?

"Do you ever have beliefs that God is talking to you, communicating to you through the TV or radio?"

"Yeah, He tells me to turn it the fuck off and do somethin' useful."

"No, I mean do you believe that you're special, chosen, or damned?"

"Hell yeah, I'm all three. Whaddya think I'm doin' here?"

"No — do you have any delusions?"

"Sure, if I got enough money, I can buy freedom. If I pick the right guy,

I'll have enough money. I don't know why I still entertain that one —"

"Patsy, a delusion is a belief system not grounded in reality."

"Those qualify. But you're talkin' about the Mistress Witch who planted that video card in my head." She leaned forward and whispered: "Makes me see humans, when really we live on the Planet of the Penguinoids." She sat back. "That do?"

Sandy shook her head.

"Have you ever been hospitalized for psychiatric reasons before?"

"Let's just say I been to places where they don't screw bulbs into the lamps so folks don't break 'em and let their arms breathe with the jagged pieces."

"How long ago, Patsy?"

"When I was 16."

"What for?"

"Swallowed too many oysters."

She glanced at the vertical tracks on Patsy's wrists. Vertical scars marked a serious attempt.

"Where were you hospitalized, Patsy?"

"Here."

"Here? This isn't a hospital."

"No, I mean here in Illinois."

"Oh, okay." Sandy scribbled on her intake form. Patsy looked around the faux-paneled office.

"You ever been in one a those new McMansions they build nowadays? You know, with the three-car garage parked out front? I was. Won't tell you what for. Had this walk-in closet attached to the master bedroom suite. The closet was 'bout the size of this office. Jehesus. You'd think people had better things to do with all that money. Then they gotta go out and buy all that Armani and Gucci just to stock the damn thing. Shit." She shook her head.

The southern Illinois summer made everything cling to every other thing. Sandy's muddy coffee mug stuck to her stack of progress notes. The damp weakened the tape that held the outsider art in place for a few more days until it fell and was thrown away.

"Where were you hospitalized?"

"At the state hospital. In Lincoln."

Patsy lit a hand-rolled Bugle Boy. Tarred fingertips stood out against perfect, oval nails that alternated from finger to finger with the American flag, or a single blue star with red and white stripes as background.

"There's no smoking. They don't take minors at Lincoln."

"They sure used to." Patsy knocked the cherry off her cigarette and hasped it back under her bra strap. "Know what Vitamin H is?"

"Vitamin what?"

"Haldol. They shoot you up with that, say once a month. First few days it's like wearin' a lead tiara."

"We use atypical anti-psychotics now."

"Like me: Atypical. Anti-psychotic."

"And you checked here that you have Native American ancestry?" Sandy's clinical voice connected only to Patsy's words, not to the wry sadness behind them.

"I'm a quarter Cherokee from my mother's side. Can't you tell? The olive stirred into my skin, the high cheekbones. People've made me everything from Italian to Lebanese —"

"— Do you have any children?"

"I do. A son."

"Do you have any contact with him?"

Patsy pulled out a guitar pick and nibbled on it, picking stained but perfect teeth.

"Is he part of your support system?"

"He never had a chance to be."

"Have you —"

"I'd just like to see him once, know what I mean?"

Sandy managed a soft smile. "Yeah, I think so." She glanced up from her obsolete, maroon-covered version of the Diagnostic and Statistical Manual of Mental Disorders. In the diagnosis box of her intake form under AXIS III, she wrote 'problems with primary support system.'

"Have you ever been convicted of a felony?"

"Oh, once every sunspot cycle." She winked at Sandy. "That's about every eleven years, I believe," Patsy yawned.

"Okay, what about financial resources?"

"Now if I had cheddar, I'd be outta this jack-o-lantern gallery so damn fast." She tossed her head back.

"Job history?"

"I was a Playboy Bunny. In the L.A. Mansion."

"No, I mean, in the last ten years."

"Just what do you imply?" Patsy's back snapped straight up.

"It's 1996. Not 1976."

She crossed her arms and legs, wiggling her foot in a huff. She didn't like Sandy anymore.

"Okay then, how long did you work there?"

"The other rabbits got jealous."

"How long, Pats —?"

"Two weeks."

"Do you have a fixed abode?"

"Nope. Haven't had time to fix it up yet," she said. She didn't feel like cooperating anymore.

"No, what I mean is: 'are you homele —'"

"Yes. I know what you meant. Can't you take a joke?"

"Okay, Dr. Hope has to sign off on this," Sandy said. She left.

As soon as the door closed, Patsy leaned over the desk and pored over the intake papers.

"'Grandiose'?" She read on. "'Histrionic'? 'Rule out borderline personality disorder.' 'Flight of ideas.' None of my ideas ever flew. 'Dysthymic.' I don't even know how that one's s'posed to come outta my mouth."

The door swung open. In strutted a pale man with hairless arms and rumpled skin. Pallid blue eyes shimmered in a white-coated smile behind gold-rimmed glasses from another decade. After a quick scan of Patsy, he scanned the intake papers.

"Hiii," Patsy cooed.

"Patsy, is it?"

She nodded as the man knocked the intake papers into a neat stack. She couldn't take her eyes off his toupée, piled up high and black, threatening to decouple from his scalp at any moment.

"Well, Patsy, I think you're faking," he said, crossing his baggy arms.

"Dr. Lug-wig, is it?" she teased, patting down her hair.

Sandy slipped back in. He leaned over the desk, propping his jiggling torso up with meaty fists.

"My name is Dr. Hope. And I own this place."

"Then you should be warned that anything you say can and will be used against you, Doctor."

Sandy hid a delicious smile. Hope flourished his arm toward the door in the fashion of a maître d'.

"Thank you for applying." He smiled.

Patsy smiled too. She peeled up the edge of her spandex shorts and massaged the inside of her thigh.

"Do you really think I'd fall for that?" he asked.

"No, not without a little blue pill, I s'pose," she replied.

"I don't care what the court says. You don't meet the criteria for admission. Out," Hope ordered.

"Lord, ain't it close in here?" Patsy said. She crossed her arms and reached down to the hem of her tank top, flipping it up over her face.

Out in the hall, one of the residents, Red Beard Roy, coaxed a mop past Sandy's office.

"That is inappropriate!" Hope shouted from inside.

Roy peeked through the door, caught a sight he hadn't seen in years, and grinned.

2.

Walter's pipe smoldered in a pewter ashtray. CHAIRMAN, H.H.S.TEEN SUICIDE PREVENTION TASK FORCE — the ashtray was christened like His Majesty's Ship, overloaded with ash.

Tongue-in-groove, white pine lightened the windowless cellar. Walter's dainty fingers held a model paintbrush tipped with cobalt. He highlighted an HO gauge model train car, an Amtrak Superliner. A dust filter hummed in the background.

"Is that how you think God works?" Walter asked the boy in baggies moping in his corner rocker.

"Shit, yeah."

Walter stared him down with a good-natured smirk.

"Hell, yeah," the boy said, with a little less conviction.

Walter kept the smug smile burning.

"Heck, yeah," the boy said, his voice diminished. Metalwork crowded his eyebrows. His hood engulfed his crew cut. He pulled a soft pack of Marlboro's from his sweatshirt and packed them down.

Walter eyed the smokes in an obvious way and that was enough for the teenager to slip them back down inside the hand-warmer where hidden things didn't bulge.

"Well, maybe God works through coincidence and maybe He doesn't." Then he looked the wannabe baby banger square on. Walter's gaze could burn or illuminate whatever it trained itself on. "What I do know is that He works." His voice held an aridity that was a mark of middle age.

Walter was a fine-looking man at 46. His eyes were the faded blue of a winter sky and they stood out against thick breakers of white hair and a manicured, silvering beard. Tiny red vessels climbed like spiders across his narrow nose and cheeks, but it made him seem perpetually tan. Until he took a wife last year, Walter Tallman had been one of the most eligible bachelors in Ukiah.

"So you're saying I shouldn't ask the Ouija board whether I'm gonna hook up with Marla."

"I'm saying you should ask God to direct your sex life. Ouija boards can fail you. God can't."

The boy's face scrunched in thought. Walter scored a point and he seemed to know it. He set the Superliner down on the tracks in the middle of the little town he'd made. The train station said it was Ukiah — *you-ky-ah*. The people who lived there said it like that. A drug store, a police station, and a restaurant were nestled in among the thin wafers of ante-bellum shops that made up the downtown. At the end of Hickory Street, a pristine white church presided over Ukiah. A tiny minister in white hair and beard, and a lanky, red-haired boy welcomed folks at the front door.

Walter glanced at the grandfather clock in the corner meting out tocks at a peaceful pace. "Next week?" he asked.

The boy thought about it. "I guess," he said.

The teen let himself out the back door. A phone jangled upstairs. "Virginia!?" Walter called out.

It rang again. Walter plunked his model brush in a water bowl and ran upstairs to answer. By the time he reached the kitchen, a very pregnant woman twenty years his younger had beaten him to it.

"Hello? Oh, hiiii, Dr. Hope," she said, holding an envelope up to Walter.

It was addressed in a woman's hand to YOUTHFUL RESIDENT. Walter nabbed it. His wife laughed over the phone. Her pasta steamed on an induction stovetop on the far side of the kitchen. It was all very stainless and hi-tech and big.

"I'll be skinny again any day. Crash diet," she giggled.

Walter reviewed the rest of the day's mail that Virginia had set down.

There were some papers from a lawyer and Walter opened them. A petition for guardianship. IN RE THE MATTER OF MARTIN TALLMAN, the caption read.

"He tried to run away again?" Virginia gasped.

That drew Walter's attention. He pattered through the foyer and into an oak den. He scooped the phone off the cherry-wood desk.

"Ted, this is Reverend Tallman," he said in his mellifluous phone persona.

"I'm so sorry to bother you on a Saturday, Walter. He only got as far as the fence. You know, we've got pretty good security here."

"Oh Lord, he's doing just like he did when he lived with us," Virginia said. "Well, that's the reason we had to do it."

Walter sliced open the envelope addressed to Youthful Resident as Dr. Hope explained in detail just how good the security was at Hope House. Walter unfolded a letter written on a page torn from a notebook.

Dear son, it's been a while since I broke open a Bic and sent missives your way. I gave you my number, but you never called, the letter began.

Walter wiped the gleam from his nose with his hankie. "Have you finished his evaluation? Walter asked.

"Yes, he's uh, exhibiting some homicidal ideation regarding his mother. He thinks he can read others' thoughts, stays up for nights on end," Hope said. "Those are symptomatic of a psychotic disorder, not just MR, uh, mental retardation."

I'm going to be out your way on some business, the letter went on.

"We're lucky he's involuntary. He can't sign himself out now. Not with these findings," Hope said.

In the kitchen, Virginia's pasta boiled over her ceramic range with a hiss. "Oh no. Ted, I'm ruining another dinner. Can you talk to Walter?"

"Sure."

She hung up.

"Walter, did you get those guardianship papers?"

"Yes."

I was thinking maybe I could pay you a call and we could visit, Walter read from the letter.

"It would be better if he signed them to avoid a hearing. But he doesn't have to anymore. We have grounds for commitment now," Dr. Hope said. "It's just that it'll save you the time and expense of a contested hearing if he waives his rights."

"Sure thing," Walter said. "We'll be by to see him for his birthday. Ted, I've got another call."

"Not a problem. God bless." Hope signed off.

"You too. Bye-bye."

Walter hung up.

"Was that another one of those letters for Martin?" Virginia wondered from the kitchen.

He unlocked a strong box and buried the letter at the bottom below a mound of cash.

"Just junk mail," he said.

3.

The TV in the corner was an old Zenith, one of the first to have a Space Command remote, back when remotes were cutting edge. Jerry Springer possessed the cathode ray tube now, to be followed by Montel and Maury, then Pat O'Brien on *The Insider*. Other days it was the parade of judges and their pageant of plaintiffs and defendants. It was the same every day. And the same people soaked it in, or were soaked in by it, in the long and wide day room of Hope House.

Eric, a chubby paranoid schizophrenic with a wild, white beard who'd gone as far as pre-med before his break, melted into the couch. Marcum, an older man who'd been a machinist before booze blew out his brain, liked to play Uno but he couldn't remember the rules no matter how many times he played. Enedino, a gentle, 35-year-old psychotic who spoke no English, went wherever anyone told him to go. No one knew where he came from, or how the wind blew him to Little Egypt where the Hope House net snagged him. Rumor was he'd been an indentured servant in the deep south of Mexico.

Jack, a hunched man with jet hair who darted around the day room like a sidewalk pigeon and rattled his words out like a Gatling gun, divided humanity into Goobers and Gomers. If you were a Gomer, he didn't like you. He bummed smokes or scabbed butts from the ashtrays. Both were Hope House No-No's, so Jack was barred from the smoking porch most of the time.

Rhonda was a TV fixture, too. With only one leg, a manual wheelchair bound her. She loved to give away the teddy bears her family sent her. At the birthday parties Hope House threw every month, Rachel, the music therapist, would double as DJ and play old Madonna dance numbers. Rhonda would punch her arms back and forth in a twist until her wheelchair danced too. She did spins, wheelies, figure eights. No one could dance like Rhonda.

Rhonda was MR, DD, mentally disabled, intellectually challenged — there were so many terms for someone with an IQ below the borderline. She wasn't MI — mentally ill. The state was supposed to make places like Hope House segregate the mentally ill from the mentally disabled from the just plain old. In theory. In the real world, the MR got dumped in with the MI, the psychotic with the psychopathic, and the young with the old.

Red Beard Roy hovered at the edges of the television zone. Water terrified him. He fought the shower so ferociously that staff just gave him weekly sponge baths and he smelled like it. But his dirty hands were always holding a mop or a bottle of Windex or a dust cloth. At a glacial pace, his self-appointed calling was to clean Hope House — 12 hours a day, 365 days a year.

Dr. Hope decreed that the TV had to go off a half-hour before dinner. Then they'd listen to top 40 or MC Hammer on the crackly stereo or maybe to talk-radio. Sometimes they played Uno or spades on flaccid cards smudged by finger oil and snot.

But Skinny Steve never played cards. He'd sit in a motionless gaze at one of the long, folding tables. He was 44, but with his long, blonde hair in greasy strings, he never lost the air of a pot-smoking adolescent. He'd zone to Black Sabbath on the old Walkman that you could never be sure was on, even when he had his earbuds in. He told anyone who would listen that he was here because he OD'd on acid. Partly true. But Steve heard voices even before he dropped LSD. The acid just nudged him over into decades of frozen watchfulness, decades in Hope House. He always sat next to Leela, an old Austrian woman who was a wet-brain alcoholic. Between her shuffling rounds, she and Steve were like paired cats, side-by-side but miles away. They never talked but they were inseparable. Once, when Steve got scabies and had to be quarantined,

Leela refused to eat until staff let him back in the milieu.

Every forty minutes or so, she'd walk a circuit around the dayroom and shout, "I am Leela and nobody else!" or "Vake up and smell za Gott damned coffee!" Staff couldn't get her to stop saying that no matter how many Hope Hints they gave her. Hope Hints were index cards with suggestions for "replacement" behaviors. Hope was a behaviorist, a true believer in reward and punishment, in reinforcers, in fading and extinction. He had faith in that and in drugs.

If you didn't need drugs you didn't belong in Hope House. And you didn't need drugs unless you were psychotic. Everyone in Hope House was diagnosed with schizoaffective disorder whether they had it or not. So everyone in Hope House was on anti-psychotics whether they needed them or not. Medication management sessions were had. Medicaid was billed. The universe stayed in balance.

These were the easy residents — the neurovegetatives. Drugs kept the harmony for them. The others weren't so easy. Benjamin towered over everyone, lorded that size over them. As a child he'd twice cut the ears off cats with scissors. He fancied himself a concert pianist once a day at 3:30 when Hope House dozed on the edge of oblivion, yanking everyone back with his concerto of "All Along the Watchtower," full on the sustain pedal.

Anthony had been a high school quarterback before his break. Still dripping with muscle at 27, he obsessed over his once-handsome profile in mirror fragments he smuggled in, a Hope House No-No.

"I'm decayed! I'm fucking decayed!" He'd shout. He'd fling his mirror against the wall and storm off. "I used to be good-looking."

The TV people would glance up, but Judge Judy would summon them back with a shaming, pointed finger. They'd seen it all before.

By now, even Martin didn't flinch when Anthony blew. Martin, the tall beanpole with frizzy red hair, glanced up at the shards of Anthony's latest broken reflection. He beamed the intense emeralds in his eyes back into *Interpreting the Revelation with Edgar Cayce*, balanced on a boney knee. Martin, the Kid. That's what they called him. He scratched the freckle on the tip of his nose, scratched it and scratched it and then looked at the tip of his finger like he was looking to see if it'd finally come off. He scratched it raw and pink but the freckle remained.

He was the youngest Hope Housemate. That's what some people in town called the residents. Nobody else even came close to 17. At that age, he shouldn't have been here, but housing for the mentally ill was scarce in this part of Illinois and his father wanted him close. Dr. Hope owed Martin's father for all the business the Reverend had kicked his way over the years. And Reverend Tallman's church made Hope House, technically a not-for-profit, a favored charity, receiving everything from cases of applesauce to an old zither. In a month, Martin would be 18 anyway. Then Martin Tallman would officially belong.

"Anthony, clean that UP!" Peter said in a tin voice.

He was the old-timer on staff. With eyes dim like a floor waxed too many times, Peter had seen them all shuffle in and shuffle through. He was the RN who injected the Haldol that Hope ordered when Anthony got too rowdy or Leela wouldn't shut up or Red Beard Roy started getting his personality back.

Anthony eyed Peter with some high school QB defiance recaptured for a moment, but then slunk to the water-damaged armoire and gripped its sides and kept his face hidden in it until he recovered his erasure face, his medicine face. That's what Hope, MD wanted to see, or it was the Clozaril closet or dis-Abilify. Then Anthony grabbed the broom and dustbin from Roy and started sweeping. It had all happened so many times before. Hope House afternoons were like dreamy innings in a scoreless baseball game that went on long after anyone cared.

Patsy was the newest on the floor. The first thing she'd do when she got someplace new was learn the players and the plays — who was top dog, who was dog shit, and the difference between the rules you could bend and those you could outright shatter. She leaned back in a broken La-Z-Boy in the corner and thrummed her beat-up Yamaha, blanketed with bumper stickers from every conceivable place and every political point of view:

WHERE THE HELL IS WALL DRUG? One said. I MAY BE STRAIGHT, BUT I'M NOT NARROW, spoke another. THE MOST

IMPORTANT THINGS IN LIFE AREN'T THINGS next to THE ONE WHO DIES WITH THE MOST TOYS WINS.

Martin was a good-looking sort, she thought as she studied the intensity in his semi-Biblical study. He seemed to pick up on her watch. He shot his high-beams up and practically blinded her. But it lasted only a moment. He was too shy to match a woman's gaze.

She got familiar with the layout — important in case she needed to make one of her emergency exits. The dayroom, or milieu, as those in the business called it, was the biggest room in Hope House, a state-licensed Institute for the Mentally Disabled. The creaky old Victorian had once been a funeral home. Besides the dayroom, the main floor held the dining room, the smoke room and coffee area, an enclosed front porch, and a front office with a Plexiglas window where the custodian, Miomir, was supposed to check on who came and went. Balkan born, Miomir shattered his English. He'd been a high school math teacher back home but his credentials wouldn't transfer Stateside.

Staff offices were upstairs. That included offices for Rich, the recreational director, whose job description seemed to include Budweiser and afternoon naps on a cot next to the boiler in the basement.

Rachel had her office upstairs too. Filled with the ideals that poured from her coffee eyes, she was slender and porcelain, a vase unbroken. Her cocoa hair wouldn't curl and it spilled well over her shoulders. It seemed to Patsy that Rachel was the only one who hadn't given up around here. Patsy noted her post-sorority face and shoved Rachel into one of her thumbnail files — she was daddy's little girl come to save the world. Patsy couldn't stand her.

The dorms were on the third floor. Three to a room, no opposite sex residents allowed in rooms. Ever. That was the most unbreakable Hope House No-No. A chest at the foot of each bed housed all the personalty any resident was allowed to own. Benjamin was Martin's roommate. He picked Martin's lock the first night.

There wasn't much funding for IMDs. Most of them were in private hands. The government mailed each resident a disability check once a month. The IMD was the bank. It gave the resident a few bucks for cigarettes and pop and kept the rest. IMDs like Hope House tried to spend as little as possible on things like fieldtrips, so no one got out much.

The constant was the sweet, pickled musk that lingered like a watchful spirit, an admixture of BO and urine and the frantic fear that stalks the severely mentally ill. Watered-down coffee and cigarettes, compulsively consumed, stoked the anxiety but kept it at a constant temperature. Beyond C & C, there wasn't much else to do.

4.

The dining room was crammed. Mealtime was the main event and everyone looked forward to it. It made life worth living. Dinner was broiled Atlantic salmon and rice pilaf with cheesy broccoli.

Martin scooped his applesauce and let the water drip back on his plate before he spooned it in. He sat across from Palindrome Bob, balding, looking a little older than 50. He seemed wizened in his John Lennon specs and his Mona Lisa lips just added to the countenance. His shoulders were brittle and stiff and he sat unnaturally erect. A tiny hole nearly pierced through Bob's cheek.

"Hey, Martin, you mad at your mom? Mad at your mom. Madatmomtadam. M-O-M. Mom. Know what a palindrome is? Mom. Pop. Dad. Stits," Bob rattled out in his tin voice.

Patsy pattered up behind Martin with her food tray. She stood there for a few moments and held him in proud eyes.

"That last one's made up," Bob went on. "Know the world's longest palindrome? 'A man. A plan. A canal. Panama.' Same forward as backwards. Try it out. Makes sense too. Teddy Roosevelt."

Martin slid down the table but Bob hounded him.

"I don't think you belong here, son. I think you'll be getting out soon. I really do. Really. Yllear. I. 'I.' I wonder if a one-letter word can be a palindrome. Naww, geez goddamnit, that's too cheap," Bob said, disgusted at himself for even proposing it.

Patsy took a deep breath and sat down across from Martin. She held out a slender, dove-like hand with a slight tremble. "Hi."

Martin looked at her, looked at her hand.

"Well, don't just stare at it like it's an alien relic," she said.

Finally, he shook it. Really, it was she who shook his arm, shook it like a Slinky.

"Wonderful, manly grip there," she said with a wink.

"I is a man. I is 18 soon," he said in words that lacked cadence.

"Shakin' hands like that's all good. It's what the Navajo do. On the Rez, strong grip's bad manners."

She took a few bites of the salmon and fluttered her fingers to her chest. "Dame Patsy Pringle," she said in the Queen's English. "I'm a potato chip heiress. Ha ha ha!"

She cued him with a finger that ended in a starry nail. "What's —"

"Martin Tallman," he said.

"What the man gotcha in this itty bitty shitty little grin bin for, Martin?"

He stared open-mouthed at her cleavage, at the hint of tattoo across her breast. She nudged his chin until his mouth closed.

"Why you —"

"I hypnotize peoples," he finished.

"You —"

"I hear into peoples' minds."

"Oh. Oh, well, that ain't a crime. But they'll install you in one of these motherboards if you admit to it. This place? This place ain't nothin'. You ever been to a state hospital? You ever get sent there, boy, I'll tell you: run."

She sampled her lentil soup and made a sour face. Few meals passed her taste test. Her eyes glanced off his floppy ears.

"I got a read on people, too," she said as she tongued the applesauce. "That's why I'm here."

"Because you is different, like me?"

"Sure. They downloaded me to this lady factory. Come in one end a dirty li'l girl, come out the other a First Lady demo."

Dr. Hope, who had a habit of chatting up his clients during the dinner hour, swiveled like a figure skater between the tables. He'd been listening.

"It doesn't look like the process of maturation took hold," he said to her.

"Yours either," she said, eyeing his crotch.

"Your records finally came from the State police. We had a hard time fitting them through the door, Ms. Pringle. Or should I say, Ms. Amst —"

"If you had a long enough straw, I'd just ask you to bend down and blow yourself, you…"

"Martin, remember I told you to be careful about a certain kind of resident?"

Martin nodded and spooned in rice pilaf.

"Well, she's that kind," Hope said as he crouched eye level. "She wants something from you."

"Just your friendship," she said.

"She's a thief. That's how she landed in prison." Martin's wide eyes bulged even wider. "She's a con artist. That's how she wiggled her way in here."

"I ain't tryin' to con you, Martin."

"And, she's a prostitute."

The boy's shoulders recoiled. He eyed her with horror. She stood up, three inches taller than Hope.

"Don't you go bringin' me down in front of him, Dr. Strangehair."

"Martin, Reverend Tallman wouldn't want you associating with her."

"Oh, the Reverend chooses our companions, does he?" she said.

"The Reverend is his father."

She glared at the gold crucifix around Hope's neck.

"Guys like you, you think a little dyin' Jesus gives you the right to cast stones, you phony freak." She turned to Martin. "Your daddy ain't the friend he pretends to be, boy, or he'd stop by for a social now and then."

"He is busy," Martin said.

"What about your mother?" she asked.

"That is none of you business."

"Stay away from him," Hope said.

"Who put you in here? Your daddy?"

"He is a good man."

"Why did he put you in here? You ain't crazy like me."

"He has his reason."

"A reasonable man wouldn't jam his own boy in this 501(c)(3) brain-yard."

His jaw clinched. Martin slid down the table as far from her as he could.

She followed him down. "Hun, listen. I didn't have the right to utter that moral choral."

He once-overred her and ate his applesauce. Then he just looked through her like she wasn't even there anymore. Hope smiled victorious.

"Now ain'tcha just sippin' soup with a fork again, Pats?" She smacked herself on the head.

"Now now. Remember, no self-harm," Hope said.

"Ya know, I've had about enough of you."

She reached out with her fork and snagged his toupée. She flung it into an urn of lentil soup. Bob pointed and laughed. That made it safe for everybody else to laugh too. Hope rushed over to the bowl, fished out his rug with the ladle, and wrung it out.

"Okay, Ugly Room!" Hope said.

He snapped his fingers, summoning Miomir.

"Illinois law may not allow me to restrain you, but it doesn't say you can't be placed in isolation for unsafe conduct. Put her in the Ugly Room," Hope ordered.

"The Ugly Room is not really unsightly," Miomir whispered to Patsy with an unshaven smile.

"Not on my ship, Ms. Pringle," Hope said as he blew on his toupée. She stopped at the dining room door.

"Oh, but I am good at rockin' boats, Doctor. Sometimes, I even tip 'em over."

5.

She stood alone in the Ugly Room. She'd been here before, when she'd done her intake. It was Sandy's office. At first she thought it was too good to be true. The files — they were all in here. Then she spotted the one-way glass on the far wall. She was on the mirror side and couldn't resist a good preen, rearranging a curl that dangled too close to her eye. She crept up to the mirror and cupped her hands over her face. In the next room, Miomir dozed with his feet propped on the desk.

"I take it you're s'posed to be watchin' me," she whispered. "Sweet dreams." She snuck to the file cabinet and tugged at the handle.

"Locked, of course."

She scanned Sandy's desk, grabbed a jumbo pink paper clip, straightened it out, and fished it into the lock. In a few seconds, she had the 'T' drawer open and yanked Martin's file. She closed the drawer and spread the file all over Sandy's desk. There were psychological evaluations, Individualized Education Plans for special ed, progress reports, case notes.

"'Wants to kill his mother…'" It was highlighted.

"'Father (adoptive): Rev. Walter Tallman'… 'Chronic run away'… 'Top end, borderline intellectual functioning — IQ 84,'" she read. "'Rule out Intermittent Explosive Personality Disorder.' Can't rule that one out with anybody."

She heard a noise and glanced up.

"Screw it, if they tag me, what're they gonna do? I'm already locked up. 'Homicidal ideation…Attempted assault on step-mother…with knife!?' Jesus, Martin," she murmured.

"'Expressive Language Disorder.' Alright, what the hell is that? 'Delusional Disorder.' Here we go: 'Medications: Ritalin – 30 mg/2x day, Risperidone – 3 mg/day PO, Lamictal – 200 mg/day PO, Fluvoxamine – 300 mg/day, PO.' That's enough to keep Pfizer in business through the end of their fiscal year. Okay, what's it say about his mother? What's it say about his mother?" She shuffled through the pages.

She came across a psych evaluation, five years old.

"'Background,'" she read. "'Martin was born nine weeks premature with Fetal Alcohol Spectrum Disorder suffered as the result of repeated possible exposure to alcohol during pregnancy and also due to an acute alcohol poisoning episode suffered by his 16 year-old mother. Blood tests revealed the presence of barbiturates in his mother's blood, apparently as the result of an attempted suicide. She was not prosecuted, ostensibly due to her age.'"

She stopped reading. Patsy didn't need to read what she'd almost not lived through. Back then, Walter was still a youth minister. It was summertime, and he was on break from divinity school. How many times, lying in a crap motel room in the middle of the night on the outskirts of some meth town had she wished he hadn't come back from St. Louis that summer…

6.

…She was 16 again. She faded in and out, mostly out at first.

"Ann, I know you're groggy, but it's very important you tell me what you took," the delivery room doc said.

"Percs," she whispered, swallowing slow. "Whiskey." Her eyes fluttered. "Ludes." She lost consciousness again.

The doctors injected her with epinephrine and naloxone. They intubated her and dosed her with activated charcoal. They'd flown her out from Ukiah to the Prez Medical Center in Lincoln, and she'd aspirated twice on the helicopter. Doctors whizzed around her, prepping her for delivery. It was a big deal for them — they were trying to save an unborn not yet to term.

She felt herself float up above them and watch them work. *How can I keep from singing, how can I keep from singing*, an old folk song her daddy taught her, kept playing in her mind. At first, she thought they were playing it over the loudspeaker. But then she thought maybe she was dying and going to heaven. She drifted out from the curtained stall and over to her mother, Ann, who huddled with Walter, slim and dark-haired at 28. They stood by the nurse's station.

Mother Tallman strutted in with her other son, Chadwick, the ex-high school football star in his mid-twenties, wearing his starched sheriff's uniform. What a forceful woman, Annie saw, against the bony diminution of her own mother, who whispered prayers with Walter.

"Mother, you shouldn't have come all the way out here," Walter said.

"Oh, yes I should have," Mother Tallman said, glancing at Momma. "Hello, Ann. I wish I could say it was good to see you."

Mother Tallman turned to her eldest boy.

"So when the hell were you going to tell me you impregnated a goddamn child?" she whispered, then slapped Walter so hard he fell into a garment cart. Everyone turned and watched.

"Ma," Chad said.

Walter raised himself, pressing a bloody lip. "I'll do the right thing by your daughter," he promised Annie's mother.

"Shut your goddamned mouth. You owe that little tramp nothing," Mother Tallman said.

"Now wait a minute. My daughter might be a disappointment, but she's no tramp," Momma said.

"She tried to destroy an unborn child. That's immoral. And illegal," Mother Tallman said, towering over this small woman who'd possessed her own countenance up 'til now.

"Don't you lecture me about morals," Momma said. "One or another of your boys've gone through half the girls in Ukiah before they turned 18."

"You keep your trap shut, we keep ours shut. You know what I mean, Ann," Mother Tallman said.

"No. Some fool's to own this mess."

"Oh, don't worry. I've got just the fool," Mother Tallman said, sneering at Walter.

Walter tried to rebel. "I make my own decisions."

"And you've been doing such a great job, son." She turned back to Momma. "We'll own the mess. We'll take the baby."

Momma didn't expect that. Her eyes darted around, searching for the right reply.

"You can't just take a child away," she said.

"The mother's unfit," Chad said.

"You people own this town, but you don't own us," Momma told Chad.

"Your girl should already be packing her bags," Mother Tallman said.

"Who are you, so high and mighty?"

"The mother of the Deputy Sheriff of the City of Ukiah, where your daughter possessed and used illegal drugs. The sister of the State's Attorney in Logan County, where your daughter tried to murder her unborn child."

"Stop it! This is my mess!" Walter said. Chad elbowed him to shut up.

"Walter Tallman?" A nurse interrupted. "She wants to see you before she goes in. Quickly."

Behind the curtain, Annie faded in and out. They'd pulled the tube out of her throat. A bearded OB/GYN pulled up Annie's eyelids and looked in with his penlight. Walter slipped into the stall and made sure he closed the curtain full behind him.

"You ain't mad, are you?" she asked Walter. He squeezed her hand.

"I'm not mad." He sniffled.

A young nurse ran in with the results of the blood draw.

"Don't know how I got so goofy," she slurred to the doctors. "Let 'im be with me 'til it's over."

Walter kissed her hand. She closed her eyes.

"I just didn't wanna feel," she muttered before she drifted off…

Patsy thought she remembered it this way. But the shrinks always told her she'd made it all up. She couldn't have remembered that much detail, doped up like that. She was too far away from Mother Tallman and Momma to overhear all that anyway.

Still, when she came to after Martin was born, it played out exactly the way she'd imagined it back in that Lincoln ER. Chad delivered the 40 pieces of silver to her, backed by the threat of jail and an order terminating her parental rights entered in the Circuit Court of Logan County. Annie Amstead had acquiesced to the court's finding of her unfitness. As to the father? UNKNOWN, the court papers said.

The only ones who knew who the father really was were those people at the hospital that night. And Lincoln was too far away from a small town like Ukiah for word to get back. Back in Ukiah, only Momma knew the truth. Momma and the Tallman clan. And they rode right over Momma, didn't they?

7.

Martin hunched over the Book of Jeremiah along with a Concordance. Patsy picked her guitar in the corner, catching his eye with a glance now and then. Finally, she laid down her instrument and tiptoed over like a runway model. He pretended not to see her.

"Want me to read your palm?" she asked.

He craned his long neck even further into Jeremiah, where his Lord was set to punish the prophets and priests who cheated others without shame.

"Martin?"

He ignored her.

"Day after day goes by and you don't say a word. You just keep that peely nose of yours buried in the pages of a book that gives you the rules, but not the experience. Sergeant Daddy used to say that the map ain't the territory." She pointed to her chest. "The lay of the land's right here, boy."

He turned a page.

"Ain't polite to ignore a woman like that. Ain't natural, either. You —"

"I is not crazy," he interrupted.

"Now that is just the thing about you. You finish folks off before they got a chance to do it to themselves."

"Not crazy," he repeated, never looking up.

"Then you shouldn't be in here, should you?"

She took hold of his giant but underfed hand. He drew it back.

"'Member how you said you could read folks' minds? Well, I'm a mutant, too. 'Cuz I read hands."

She gathered up his hand again. He stared at her stars-and-stripes nails. "I believe in America, don't you? You ever see glove holders like mine?"

He shook his head. She traced her calloused fingertips along the clean furrows of his palm.

"Well, says here…you never been with a woman. With wolfish eyes like yours? So soulful and serious?"

He tried to hide the hint of a grin. Then his lips re-hardened. His eyes stayed away.

"I am not a heartthrob anymore!" Anthony wailed as he pounded a table.

"Mmmm," Patsy soothed as she traced Martin's palm. "Says here, you're gonna meet somebody real important soon."

"Who?"

"Somebody from your past," she whispered. "Looks like…your mother." He yanked his hand away.

"You do not know. You should not talk about my dad like you do to Dr. Hope."

"And Dr. Hope should not talk about me like he did to you."

He glanced up to make sure Dr. Hope wasn't around.

"Do you really go to jail?"

"Never for more than a year."

"Is you a con artist?"

She shook her head.

"I'm here 'cuz I did somethin'…" she straightened her arms and legs and levered them up and down like a robot. "…in-a-ppro-pri-ate."

"What do you do?"

"Oh, got somethin' off my chest." She picked up her guitar. "So, you mad at your —"

"Yes."

He went back to his Bible as if he'd never known her. Her eyelids fell into a coy droop and she strummed "Fire and Rain" like she'd written it.

"Why you mad at 'er, boy? You even know what she's like?"

The stairs groaned under the weight of someone heavy and Dr. Hope marched down. He stopped at the foot of the stairs and scrutinized Patsy with his browless eyes, incongruous against his grassy, jet-sheen wig.

"I should not talk to you," Martin whispered.

"Why, 'cuz ol' Dr. Hopeless says you can't?"

Hope stared at her for a moment and whispered something to Miomir, who played solitaire on his old Mac in the front office. Then Hope walked out. Patsy strummed wandering notes and watched Hope slip into his blue Mercedes and drive off toward town.

"I bet she did somethin' pretty awful," she sang as she played.

Martin's owlish eyes rolled up to hers while his face stayed buried in the Bible.

"I am Leela and nobody else!" Leela pierced the air. She shot up from her seat, then sank back down.

"I'm gonna guess your momma ran off," Patsy said.

"How do you know?"

She grabbed his palm to show him how she knew.

"I know you ain't crazy," she said as she went back to strumming. "Well, I know you can't talk to me. Bye."

She stood. Martin's eyes darted around to see if anyone was watching.

"Is you crazy?" he asked.

"Folks used to say I was."

"Because you hypnotize them in they hands? Is they scairt of you, too?"

"You just gotta know howda use your crazy. I mean, yeah, I hypnotized folks. Men mostly. It was only their women that were scared of me." She set her guitar down. "So, you're in here 'cuz you went after your step-mom with a knife?"

"I do not."

"Martin, I read your palm."

"You could not read peoples' hands."

"Then howda you expect me to believe you can read their minds?"

"I told her, Martin." It was Palindrome Bob, who'd crept up behind.

Martin looked out through the latticed picture window that showcased the Hope House picnic grounds.

"Why'd you go after her like that, honey?" she asked Martin, leaning in.

"Do not call me 'honey.'"

He stared out the window with a face flat from meds, pretending she wasn't there.

Just when she was about to leave, he spoke up. "She says I is supposed to be a bortion."

"An abortion?" she said.

"I has a plan for her."

"For who?"

"Wait a minute. 'A man. A plan. A mom,'" Bob palindromed. "No, no, no."

"You mind, Bob?" she said. "This is private."

Bob clenched his rotten teeth in a skeletal smile, ear to ear. It turned her head.

"Do you know who I am?" she asked her boy.

"Dr. Hope says you is a no-good prostitute."

"And that's what you think?"

He nodded and plugged back into Jeremiah.

"My daddy used to say even a gutter drunk was somebody's little boy once. Well, I was somebody's little girl too, once." She picked up her guitar and walked away, her belly sinking when she realized that brain damage, the destruction she'd wrought and could never heal, blocked him from knowing who she really was to him.

"'A man. A plan. A mom, momma.' Shit on this, man! I hate this!" Bob cursed and stormed off.

8.

artin's room was close and crammed with three beds and that was two too many. Still, he had the window bed. Usually that went to the resident with the most seniority, but Benjamin shook down so many Hope Housers for cigarettes and SSD money that Hope withdrew his window-bed privileges. A false ceiling dropped down from the 10-foot Victorian lathe plaster and a coat of sunny paint had just been splashed on the walls last fall, but like everything else in Hope House, the room aged quickly. Half the ceiling tiles were cracked. Benjamin would poke them with a crutch, checking for the bodies of dead dictators that Staff stowed up there.

Martin stared out the scratched, plastic window crosshatched on the out- side with rusted cyclone. Outside, Miomir trimmed the lawn on a ride-on, priming the grounds for spring.

Martin moped in bed, photos spread across his chest. One was a close-up of him with his arm around his father, and Martin held a medal in his hand. Everything was sun and smiles. Walter Tallman was in his 40s, already silvered, his eyes penetrating the camera lens with wisdom and his smile wry with victory over the world.

He flipped another picture from face down on the bed — his legs were just a blur in this one. He was at a track meet, conquering a hurdle with a single-minded frown.

It was a strange game of solitaire and he got bored. He pulled a framed photo of a perky, auburn-haired woman from the drawer of his nightstand. She was an older woman and seemed to come straight out of *Better Homes and Gardens*. In fact, she did. Patsy popped her head in the door.

"Happy Mother's Day," she sang.

He jammed the picture partway between the mattresses, rolled over and showed her his back.

"You more of a Good Friday kinda guy?" She swung herself in around the doorframe.

"Go away please."

She plopped down in the corner chair, a second-hand Danish-modern upholstered with orange Naugahyde.

"That mother of yours. She, ya know, far off?"

"No ladies suppose to be in here."

"There ain't."

He watched out the window as Enedino and Rhonda planted impatiens in the picnic grounds. They were part of the Garden Club. Rich stood over them, suffering a bad hangover.

"My mom might as well be dead. She tells everybody I am," Patsy said.

Every once in a while, Rich meandered over to the garden shed, sipped from a Coke can, and returned. Through the glass, Martin could hear Rich speak. He rattled off made-up Spanish to Enedino, who couldn't stop laughing.

"But if she were here on this day of hers, I s'pose I'd try to be all sweet and nauseous like she always looked for in me. Kinda like Dawn, my sister. Dawwwn." She drew the name out like it was royalty. "Shiiit."

He rolled over and faced her.

"Do you miss her very bad?" he wondered.

"Dawn, not at all. My mom, you bet."

She snapped up the photo of the red-haired woman from between the mattresses.

"Give it back!"

"Why, this woman don't look like your momma at all. 'Cept for that flammable hair you share."

He took it back from her and pined over it.

"That's your stand-in, huh? What would you tell —"

"Is it because I is messed up she runs off? Does she hate me? Does God punish me, like Job?"

"Punish you for what?"

"Original sin. Everybody is guilty."

"Don't you for one minute chomp into that line of ham bone. 'Cuz you are perfect."

His face wrinkled, confused.

"Yes. You are just as God intended, right on schedule."

"Do you have babies somewhere?"

"I do. I have a boy."

"Do you miss him today?"

"Not today."

Outside, the more Coke Rich drank, the happier he became as Garden Club boss. His Spanish became more florid and Enedino had to put down his spade he laughed so hard.

Martin brooded over the picture of the red-haired woman. "She should not have run," he said.

"No, she shouldn't've. That was the worst mistake she made in her whole rotten life," Patsy said.

"If I could talk to her, I would say I hate you for running away and making my life a mess."

"Hun, maybe we could go out and find her, and you could tell her —"

"She is the reason I is in here. She is the reason I is special ed, why I hypnotize peoples. I wish she is dead."

"'— And I could show you the world outside this rotten place." He slapped the picture face down on the bed.

"Please go away"

"Think about it, okay?"

She picked up the red-haired woman. It made her sick to look at her. She looked like Betty White. Every woman who never turfed a street corner looked like Betty White and Betty White was one thing she could never be. Betty White was someone she squandered away by the time she was 14 and she wanted her back more than anything, but she could never ever have that back. And she hated herself and she hated Betty White for it. That's what came up in her throat — that hate. That's when she spotted them — Martin's meds on his dresser, scheduled in little plastic pill boxes. She knew what they could do to a man over time. They were solid chloroform and they could peel his lips inside-out and bare his teeth in a permanent wolf's grimace, and give him tics he'd never shake no matter how long off the drugs he'd been. So she lifted them and left.

She took them because she knew he didn't need them. It took until 3 a.m. to convince herself she didn't either.

9.

"Alright everaybutty, pleasa comma to attention," Rich blasted through the cheap karaoke PA. He'd set it to maximum reverb.

The electric echo distorted his Lawrence Welk imitation which vacillated along a continuum from Prussian to Italian. The Hope Housemates crammed the day room for the weekly community meeting. In the corner, Red Beard Roy cleaned the ferret cage. Hope House always smelled like a pet shop no matter how clean Roy tried to keep the ferrets.

Rachel snaked through the back of the room, lithe and airy. She crouched next to Martin, who laughed at Rich along with everybody else.

"Martin, are you ready?" she asked.

She smiled sweet but not saccharin and her words were crisp but not erudite. Rachel framed her porcelain face with long, straight hair she kept in a partial braid.

"I think he is drinking," Martin whispered.

She seemed to walk on air and he followed her feathered footfalls into the sky, up the stairs to her office. There, the air brightened. The Hope House smell left behind in favor of spring. Stuffed bears and wide-eyed monkeys smiled from shelves. Inspirational messages cheered from the walls. A panoramic seascape stretched the length of one wall. Adorable kittens and near edible wolf pups leapt from frames. LIFE'S TOO SHORT TO BE SMALL, it said under one kitten that gazed into a mirror and saw a lion. She'd hung a watercolor she'd painted of a sunset over the Mississippi with the Gateway Arch in St. Louis on the far bank.

Rachel kept candles afire. Her office always smelled like lavender which she'd read had calming effects on the brain. But more than anything else, the four walls made music. Songbooks lined the shelves. A 12-string guitar leaned in the corner. There were steel drums from Puerto Rico and handmade ones from Israel. A wooden recorder rested in its case on her desk. A dulcimer lay prone on an ottoman. The walls themselves made melody — piano drizzled with rain from hidden speakers.

She closed the door and Martin took his customary perch on the velour loveseat, the one laced with a hand-knitted afghan she'd brought from home. Rachel sat in her old stuffed chair.

She had Martin's scrapbook out — his life from when he was a baby until he came to Hope House. Dozens of happy photos: Martin at Bible camp; Martin winning the Radio City Christmas Spectacular Church Choir Competition. They were Martin and Walter mostly — fishing, water skiing, playing soccer. She wanted to help him create a narrative. Rachel believed adopted kids needed that.

"What should we do today?" she said. "Hey wait, did you get a haircut?"

"Yes." His smile reached out to her but his eyes stayed to the floor.

"Are you going to be shy with me again, Martin?"

"No." He blushed.

"Okay."

She pulled a table harp from under her desk and set it between her legs. She plucked a few notes from "Clair de Lune."

"Want to work on your scrapbook?"

"No."

"Do you want to sing today?"

"No. I sang in church on Sunday."

"Hey, I heard," she said as she downshifted to "Greensleeves," "I heard you've been talking about your mother again."

The smile evaporated. He shook his head.

Her words were soft over the angelic pitch of the strings. "You're not thinking about running away again, are you, Martin?"

He stared at the cinnamon throw rug she'd brought in to cover the hole in the carpet. She played on, waiting for him to come out on his own. It was a couple minutes before he did.

"Sometime, I wish she would die." She stopped playing.

"Sounds like you're pretty angry."

He nodded in his resolute way, holding a reservoir of tears in the corners of his eyes.

"You're safe now. It's okay to let it out in here."

He sunk his head in his hands, dug his palms into his eyes, let out deep, throaty chokes. She reached out and massaged his shoulder. His head shot up and she flinched.

"That is why I go after Virginia new mom with the knife."

She nodded.

"But I run out of the house and stab the snow-woman instead, I is so mad," he said. "I is so ashame I do that to Virginia new mom."

He lowered his head and cried more. Rachel reached for one of the tissue boxes that were everywhere. The tears, heavy and old, fell onto his new jeans. He ripped some tissues off and wiped his snot.

He hung his head and mumbled into his mitts. The words were garbled but she understood. He'd told the story before — about how he stabbed the snow-woman he and his father made, how he ripped its nose and sliced through its eyes; toppled its head and kicked through its middle. From the start, the snow-woman had been his mother. Walter had helped him build her. It was Walter's idea to roll her into balls and stack them three high. He said the two of them should make her because Martin had never known his real mom, and this way he could maybe talk to her and work things out, and then maybe he wouldn't want to run away and find her anymore. Martin hadn't wanted to make a snow-mother but he didn't want Walter to think he was angry at his real mother anymore. Then maybe dad would let him out of Hope House and he could come back to live with dad and Virginia new mom. But it all backfired.

"What would you say to her if you could?" Rachel said.

"I would just want to know why she goes. Why she takes the alcohol and drug to make me special."

"Mmm." She nodded.

"Why. Why why why why why why why!" He said it between white teeth as he punched a heart-shaped pillow squeezed between his legs.

He didn't say anything the rest of the session. Rachel took out some clay. He liked to work with his hands when he was like this. It calmed him. Together, they built a new snow-woman from the putty. And then the hour was up.

"I'll see you next week, Martin."

He nodded and turned toward the door. In an unexpected rush, he turned into her and hugged her hard. She patted his back.

"I wish she is like you."

He wiped his nose and left.

Rachel took a moment, took a breath and closed her eyes, preparing herself mentally for her next client. Then she stepped out into the hall. Patsy waited downwind near the staircase.

Patsy smiled at Martin as he passed her. He didn't even know she was there, she thought. *What'd that woman just do to him?*

"Patsy?" Rachel said.

She tossed Rachel a reluctant glance, swallowed and held her breath to let Rachel know just how little she was looking forward to their first session. She made the death march toward her latest healer.

She stepped into the office. Her eyes shot around. Her mouth gaped in mock horror. Dolls? The Talking, Feeling, Doing Game? *My Body Is Private* on the bookshelf?

"Lass, I don't mind tellin' you, I think I just walked into Michael Jackson's grooming closet here," Patsy said.

Rachel giggled. "Make yourself comfortable." Patsy stared at the 12-string in the corner.

"Do you play?" Rachel asked.

She didn't answer. She winced as her elbow caught the tip of a candle flame. She rubbed it.

"What is it exactly that you do?" Patsy quizzed.

"I'm a music therapist," Rachel explained, smiling, picking up a fresh legal pad.

"I guess they'll call anything therapy nowadays."

"Well, I'm thinking, since this is your first session, we can talk about what your goals are?"

Patsy laughed. "Goals," she said, scratching her scalp and checking for dandruff under her nails. "You ever been to a hockey game, Rachel?"

"Yes, I have. Up in Chicago."

"Me, too. Corporate suite, actually. With Fortune 500 execs. I was on the entertainment committee. Anyway, did you see how the guys with the sticks on the ice shot the little black goober into the net?"

Rachel nodded.

"And when they did, you see how the flashing red light behind the net went off with a siren, like a fire truck?"

"Uh-huh." Rachel's nods were eager.

"That's a goal. You're engagin' in the wrong sport here."

Rachel laughed. So did Patsy. She didn't want to, it just came. She didn't want to like Rachel so she tossed a grenade.

"Let's get very clear. I've talked to more head shrinkers, and PhDs and PsyDs, and LCSWs and LCPCs, and guidance counselors and POs who tried to be my best friend. And they're all gonna help you. And they're in your life for about two minutes before they pawn your ass off on some other 'helper.' At best, you get some born-again virgin, some tight twat who hasn't been outta social work school long enough to know the difference between psychodrama and a psycho drama mama. At worst, you get a jaded bitch who ends up writin' a report to the court that says you ain't treatment compliant, and you get violated and shipped back to County to finish out your term. So I ain't gonna give you shit, little girl. Got that?"

The air between them froze and the moments hung like icicles.

"You've been around the block. That's what you're saying," Rachel said.

"Thank you, miss." She crossed her legs and wagged her pumps.

After a couple minutes, Rachel reached for the guitar and strummed some chords.

Patsy got an idea.

"Actually, there is somethin' you could do for me."

Rachel set the guitar aside.

"That boy who was just in here," Patsy said.

"I don't want to shut you down, but I can't talk about another client. HIPAA," Rachel explained, pointing to a federal confidentiality notice that hung on her door.

"Will you let me finish?"

"Sure."

Patsy grabbed the guitar and picked the opening riff to "Classical Gas." Her fingers weaved the strings like strands in a loom and her tapestry filled the room and wafted down the hall.

"Wow," Rachel said.

"He, uh, disturbed me the other day. Told me he was hearin' voices. Hurtful voices," Patsy said over the music. "He talked about hurtin' somebody."

Rachel nodded and grabbed her notebook.

"But, HIPAA," Patsy shrugged.

"You can tell me what you know. You're not bound by confidentiality, Patsy. Only I am."

"And I will tell you," Patsy said. She stopped playing. "If you tell me your read on his situation."

"I can't, Patsy."

With a pained look, Rachel gestured toward the confidentiality notice.

"Okay, I understand. But when I was in the bin back in California, I heard about this court case called Tarasoff. Hockey players like you got a duty to warn other folks if one of your patients is threatening them."

"Yes, I know about the Tarasoff case, Patsy."

"Yeah, I'd imagine they train you about all that CYA stuff in hockey college. So, if you wanna know what I know..."

"What I can tell you about him is very limited."

"All I wanna know is what he's in for. He threatened somebody to my face."

"Martin has several diagnoses but his condition's difficult to categorize. I'd say what comes closest to a true diagnosis for him is borderline intellectual functioning. His IQ is about 84. I don't think that's any big secret."

"But I mean, is he really, ya know, crazy? He smacks his lips a lot and makes these faces."

"Oh that's, no, that's tardive dyskinesia. Facial tics can be a side effect from some of his meds. I don't feel he's psychotic."

"But he says he can suck up my thoughts."

Rachel was careful with what she said next. "He does have an un-canny ability to pick up on what others may be feeling or thinking. I think it's intuition mostly."

"But is he dangerous? I got a right to know. I live with 'im."

"He has impulse control issues when it comes to anger. That's all I'm at liberty to say."

Rachel sunk into her chair. Her brown eyes withdrew, faced inward, and reviewed what she'd just been made to reveal. She was only 25. She'd never been with a pro before.

"So, who did he threaten?" Rachel asked, readying her pen.

"Me."

She handed the guitar to Rachel and walked out.

10.

Air conditioning chilled the air like wine but fouled the air like wine gone bad. Martin stared between the diamonds of cyclone that fenced his window. Elm, sycamore, and white oak hemmed the Hope House picnic grounds. On the far edge where the trees began, a couple dozen seasick headstones marked graves no one bothered to keep up anymore. The trees' boughs joined into archways and through them soy and cornrows melted into the slurry sky like runny colors. He could make out a farmhouse, just a white smudge on the horizon wedged between navy blue Harvester silos. He dozed into a Seroquel sleep.

Two shadows blurred his doorway and snuck into the room. The man bore a gift wrapped in gold foil and a boat seat cushion under his arm. The woman cradled a child, Walter, Jr., who'd been in the world a precious six weeks. Walter Tallman had come to see his adopted son.

"*Happy birthday to you! Happy birthday to you!*" Martin rolled to face them. "*Happy birthday, dear Martin! Happy birthday to you!* Happy birthday!"

"Thank you."

"Get your coat, 'cuz you are coming home for the weekend!" said Walter.

Walter handed him the gold-gilded gift. He grabbed a brush and tried taming his son's electrified carrot top.

"This is your baby?" Martin asked Virginia.

"Of course, Martin," she said.

"He is beautiful."

"How did you know it was —"

"Blue," he interrupted, feeling the silky swaddle between long fingers.

"You just put two and two together," Walter said in his soft drawl. "Nothing more."

"What is his name?"

"Baby Walter," she said.

"Could I hold him?" Martin said.

"Oh, I don't think so, sweetie," Virginia said. She stepped back and eyed her husband.

They fumbled their way through a stuffy silence. "Open your present," Walter said.

Martin undressed the gift, folding the wrapping paper along its original creases so as not to waste it. It was a leather-bound Bible, old and cracked but fresh with oil.

"I already has one," he said.

Patsy waltzed in. She couldn't back out fast enough but they hadn't seen her. "Oh, but this is a special Bible. It is a Tallman tradition among the men that when the first son turns eighteen, he gets this Bible," Walter said.

"But I is not born to you."

"It doesn't matter. It's our rite of manhood. It's the Tallman way."

"I get to move out on my own now!?"

Virginia glanced at Walter, who straightened the collar on his son's blue polo shirt. When he was nervous, Walter did two things — cleaned and sweated.

"Has Doctor Hope spoken to you?" Walter inquired. Out in the hall, Patsy leaned against the wall and heard it all.

He handed Martin a sheaf of court papers and smoothed out Martin's bed. "Doctor Hope says you have a mental illness," Walter said as he flipped the boat seat cushion onto the next bed and sat down.

Martin stared down at the court papers. Baby Walter started to cry. "I'll explain what these mean because you could read them all day —"

"You's want me in here for good," Martin said.

"For your own protection," Virginia said.

"For you protection," he said.

"Martin that's enough," Walter cut in.

Out in the hall, Palindrome Bob stood over Patsy with his bad teeth grin. A shatterproof mirror played with his image on the opposite wall. Patsy waved him off but he winked.

"You is scairt of me because I hear what you think," Martin told Virginia.

"Honey, that's why you need to be here. You don't understand what people mean as well as average people, so you pretend you hear what they think," Virginia said.

"You want me away. You would only be a mom to you own baby."

"And it's not my fault your mother ran off, either."

"Things is okay here until you come along."

"You don't talk that way to her," Walter said.

Martin got up to leave, but Walter clasped his shoulder.

"All these mean," he said, holding up the papers, "is that I get to make the same decisions for you I did before your birthday."

"He'll just do the things for you he's always done," Virginia said.

"If you sign these waivers, I'll be that person for you."

"When a boy turns 18, he is in a right manhood. You just say it." Martin was firm.

"It's not automatic," Walter countered.

"Peoples is just scairt of me because I can tell when they is sick, where the pain be in they bodies or they minds."

"No one could do that but Jesus," Walter said.

"I can. I do not know how, but when I run my fingers up and down they spines, I feel hot and cold. Hot and cold!"

"That's why Doctor Hope knows you need to be in here. 'Schizoaffective,' remember that word he taught us?" Walter said.

The baby wailed. Virginia walked him up and down the room.

"I is not that word," Martin said, twirling his own hair into knots.

"Stop that, please," Walter said. "You went after Virginia with a knife."

"It is only made of white plastic."

"And then you went out on the front lawn and sliced that woman to shreds," Virginia said.

"You — you tried to run away on some crazy vendetta against your mother. And you don't even know where she lives," Walter said.

"The letters say she is in Los Angeles."

"But there's never a return address," Virginia shrilled.

"I could take care of myself. I know how."

"I had to go all the way to Alton after you and I found you picking your breakfast out of a dumpster. That's not someone who can take care of himself, son."

"I just want to meet her."

"No, you want to get back at her. I'm afraid what you'd do if you did find her."

"She needs to pay," Martin said. He held up his Bible. "That is what this says."

"You're reading the wrong chapters," said Walter.

"She needs to pay," he said, scowling at Virginia.

"If that's what you believe, then I've failed you. As a father, and as God's teacher." Walter shook his head.

"She is bad. You even say. She makes me so I hypnotize peoples."

"For God's sake, you can't hypnotize people!" Walter held his chest, breathed from his belly, held it for a two-count, like his cardiologist taught him.

The baby quieted down. Virginia approached Martin from behind, stood over his shoulder as he looked out at the picnic grounds.

"You're going to give this man another heart attack," she whispered.

He twisted his neck over his shoulder and studied his father. Walter panted and mopped his sweat with a cruciform-embroidered hankie.

"Then you won't have a real dad, either," she said.

Martin turned back toward the window. He looked at the floor. "Remember what he looked like after open heart surgery? After you ran away?"

"Honey, not like this," Walter said, reaching out a hand to quell her.

She checked her husband's pulse with two red fingernails on his throat. Martin watched his father's reflection in the window as Walter popped a pill from a silver case. He glanced at a photo on the windowsill: he and dad at a track meet.

The only sound in the room was Virginia patting her baby's back.

"Where do I put my name?" Martin said.

Walter rose up with the papers and took a seat beside him, handing him a gold pen.

"Right here, and here. And here." Walter had the signature lines flagged with tiny crosses.

Martin scrawled his name in deliberate cursive on waivers of notice and a waiver of the right to contest guardianship. He tossed the pen on the bed. His half-brother started screaming again. Walter folded up the papers and slipped them in an envelope. In the hall, Patsy dashed to her room.

A Navajo blanket hung on her wall. That's all there was to her chattel except her old Yamaha guitar. She filched a pen and some purple stationery from her roommate's nightstand. She sat down at an old wooden school desk that faced the window. She pelted the page:

> *You are cordially invited to meet the mama. After eighteen years! Limited engagement.*
> *Act now! Offer expires soon!*
> *You deserve an explanation. You deserve more than that. You deserve justice, and you're ready for it. Ask, and ye shall receive. Seek, and ye shall find.*

She laid on paragraph after paragraph. Out her window, Martin, Walter, and Virginia snaked between cars in the lot. Patsy shoved the letter along with an Amtrak train table in a mauve envelope as the Tallmans loaded into Walter's black Escalade. She made out the envelope to Martin at Hope House. She wrote ANN AMSTEAD in the corner, along with an L.A. return address.

She'd never be sorry she sent the letter, but she'd come to regret ever letting him know where she lived.

11.

It was bigger than Christmas and Halloween put together. There'd be big-ticket prizes, baby spareribs and corn-on-the-cob with melted cheddar, live bluegrass, the wild dance of children, and the laughter brought by clowns. Staff planned it for weeks. Denizens giggled around its edges as the day drew near. Families made the pilgrimage from five counties away. It was the Fourth of July, the annual Hope House picnic.

Dr. Hope claimed the grill as his exclusive right. He bobby-pinned the high chef's hat to his wig so it wouldn't slide off and take his hair along with it. Walter's church loaned him two giant Webers and he stoked them like locomotives.

Rich set up his karaoke PA on one of the picnic tables and turned the reverb up as high as he could. Red, white, and blue streamers fluttered with the tablecloths on rows of picnic tables. Jack, the cigarette bandit, wandered from table to table, bumming smokes.

Kids darted between the tables and blew sooper-dooper soap bubbles. Old men belched Old Style and cigars as they sat around a hollowed rain barrel. The VFW man onstage finished "Beer Barrel Polka" on his squeeze box. Rich went onstage and did his best Ed Sullivan.

"Thank you, Mr. Presley, uh, Mr. Preston. Excuse me, excuse me," he said, then dropped his shoulders and puffed himself up like a fight announcer as Patsy and Rachel took the stage. "And nowwww, all the way from Ukiah, Illinois. Iiin thiiis cornerrr, in the tight, black jeans, weighing in at 89 pounds, Raaachelll WAGNER!!!!

"In this corner, weighing in at 110 pounds and wearing even tighter bluuuuue shorts, Paatsy PRIIINGLE!! Together, they fight as *La*-aa Chiquitas Insanitas!!!!!!"

No one knew whether Rich was done, whether to expect a fight, so no one knew to applaud.

Patsy picked a bluegrass standard, "Rocky Top," on Rachel's banjo. Rachel tried to keep up on guitar but Patsy rattled it off like a Gatling gun.

Peter, the nurse, handed out raffle tickets — the big prize this year was a trip to a gospel festival down in Branson, courtesy of Walter's church. Families clogged the lot out front as Anthony showed them where to park. He'd polish their side mirrors over and over, arguing with his reflection about faded football glory. Rhonda kept the pop cold and made sure everybody had some. Benjamin organized the softball game. Eric handed out plates and napkins whether people wanted them or not. Leela waited tables and Marcum bused them.

Onstage, Patsy and Rachel finished.

"Alrighta!" Rich squealed into the mic as he channeled the Italian Lawrence Welk. "E-va-ree-buddy havin' a gooda time-a?"

They all shouted and clapped. Patsy scanned the crowd but couldn't find Martin. She wandered over to Bob who'd taken to lining up any related series of objects in palindrome equations. He put up two tomatoes then three onions followed by two more tomatoes on a picnic table.

"The more I do this, the more it helps keep things from getting out of control on the Security Council," he said.

"So if they spoke fluent Palindrome at the U.N., there'd be no more war," she said.

"You got it! You understand this. You're the only one who gets me."

"You see Martin around anywhere?"

"Uh-uh. Hu-hu."

"Which'll it be? Uh-uh, or hu-hu?"

"Uh-uh."

"You know if he talked about gettin' any mail lately?"

"Uh-uh. Hold these." He handed her five wedges of watermelon he'd stolen from Miomir's cooler.

"I was talkin' with Rachel, you know, his therapist? She seemed to think Martin could get kinda violent. You seem to know 'im pretty well. What do you think?"

He took the melon slices from her one by one, arranging them in a 'CCD- CC' line.

"No, that's not right, thgir," he muttered. He gathered up the pieces and tried again. "Well, word has it that he stabbed a white woman in his front yard last December. That's why he's in."

"Yeah?"

"Yeah. Some albino chick. Spread her guts all over the lawn. It was grisly, ylsirg."

"Yuck." She grimaced. "I heard about that. What about this ESP shit? He delusional, or what?"

"Well, all I know is his nickname in Ukiah is," Bob put his hand in front of his mouth and leaned to her ear, "the Lie Detector."

He lined up the slices like DDCDD.

"No, Bob, like this," she said. She set them in two smiles, one frown, and two more smiles.

"How very obvious. Thank you, Patsy."

She maundered off into Hope House and spied Martin from the front porch. He watched a Cubs game in the dayroom, all alone. He rotted away a little more each day, blending in more and more with Eric, Marcum, and the other TV people until all their faces caved into one composite stare. He vacuumed up the same pureed *Jerry Springer* reruns no matter how re-ran they were. When she was his age, she'd broken a needle off in a psych attendant's arm when they tried to give her ECT. The kid was way too young to give up like this.

Patsy trod up to him on the stained shag. His eye twitched. "You a big fan?" she asked as she sat on an ottoman next to him.

"They win, one of these years."

"You're missin' all the fun out there, child." She clasped her knee in her fingers. "Lotsa family outside. Where's your daddy today?"

"Apaculpo."

She giggled. He gave her the hard stare.

"Spanish can be tricky," she said.

His eyes went back to the commercials. "Rachel's out there," she said.

He perked up, then pretended not to care.

"Her name stands for being pure," he said. "In Jewish."

"Certified organic, pasture-raised and pasteurized, vegan, gluten free," she scoffed. "You really got a thing for the virgins, dontcha? I know what that's like."

The dreamy confines of Wrigley Field siphoned off his gaze.

"Ever tell 'er how you feel?"

"She has a boyfriend." The game came back on. "His name is Jesus. We go to a ballgame together."

"Really, his name's Jesus?"

"The way they say it in Spanish. I always say it bad."

"Oh, Hey-zeuss," she said, but he'd already forgotten she was there.

Patsy bit her lip and looked around the dayroom for another way to reach him. At the far end, through the window in Miomir's office, she spotted the mail in a letter bin on the wall. Her purple envelope was unmistakable.

"Grand slam," she whispered.

But the office was locked. She strutted through the dayroom and pulled two American flags from the planter on the porch. Using the flag handles like chopsticks, she threaded her arms under the security window. She fished the envelope from the bin and walked back to him. She cleared her throat. He hadn't noticed she'd been gone.

"Uhm, Martin?" He dozed. "Honey?"

His lids fluttered. "Yes," he stirred.

"This just came for you."

She presented him with the letter like it was an Oscar envelope. It bore a Ukiah postmark, but he didn't know about such things. He sat up and opened it with his finger. He unfolded it and mouthed the words inside. Resolve pumped his posture back to life. He read that single page over and over. When he finished, he trembled and nodded to himself. He stood and marched to the staircase and up the stairs two at a time. She bit her cuticle as she watched, not knowing what magic she'd unleashed. Things rumbled in the ceiling where his room was. She put her fingers to her mouth.

"Oh please God, help me not to screw this up."

She went outside for some air, but it was torrid and gluey and still before noon so she took some shade under an oak. Dr. Hope and Sandy supervised Bob as he dipped a sponge in a water bucket and dabbed graffiti off the raffle board — POP DID MOM DID POP in purple marker.

The scorch of the sun shot off the glass doors to Hope House as they swung open. Martin tramped down the steps. He clutched a duffel bag and a windbreaker.

When he reached the flagstone walk, he surveyed the crowd with grim lips. He hunched into the start position for the 100-meter dash, his spine arched high, his fingers pawing the pavement. Patsy's heart fluttered. No one else had spotted him.

He sprung like a cheetah in strides longer than Patsy had ever seen — the strides of a sprinter, the strides of a hurdler. No one could stop him and she knew it. She ran inside.

He zoomed past picnic tables, ripping the crepe-paper banners into wind-bitten flags in his wake. He picked up speed as he blurred past Hope and Sandy. People twisted to see what had flown by like a horse on fire.

"Martin!" Hope said.

"Where are you going!?" Sandy yelled.

"To get my mom!"

"'A man. A Plan. A ma.' No no no," Bob said.

"You can't do that! You're involuntary now!" Hope said. Martin slowed and spun around.

"I is old enough to leave this grin bin."

"Security, Code Yellow!" Hope barked.

Martin vaulted rows of picnic tables in single strides — one, two, three sets. But Anthony stood between him and freedom.

"'Ma, I am dam mad ma. I am.' That's it! 'Ma, I am dam mad ma. I am.' Oh baby!" said Bob.

"Anthony, get him!" Hope bellowed.

Anthony lined up between two elms, the only thing blocking Martin from the sky deep with miles. He dove for Martin's ankles in a mow down tackle, but Martin sailed over him in an open field run.

12.

Patsy exploded into her room and packed like a professional. Hope, Sandy, and Peter flooded Sandy's office and Sandy pulled Martin's chart. She and Hope huddled over it while Peter grabbed the intake sheet and made a call. "Reverend Tallman, please."

"Has he signed the papers? Find the papers!" Hope said. Sandy ripped through the file. "His father hasn't sent them in yet."

Peter twisted the receiver away from his mouth. "His assistant says he's at the parade."

"Well then call the damned parade!" Hope shrieked.

Patsy whooshed by, drawing their eyes for a moment, her psychedelic guitar strapped on mariachi style. She flew down the stairs, ran past the front office, and knocked over business cards stacked by the window. She grabbed a handful of Rachel's cards as an afterthought.

She blasted through the double doors and jogged past the raffle board. Hope popped his head out a second-floor window, knocking his chef's hat and wig off on the frame.

"Where do you think you're going!?" he said.

"To make amends!"

Bob grabbed his wash bucket and sponge and followed her.

"Now you get back there and finish that chalkboard!" Hope told him.

"Nein!" Bob said.

The picnic broke down to confused chatters.

Over the PA, Rich did his W.C. Fields, which wasn't any good even when he was sober. "Don't worry folks. They never get very farrrr. The cornfield you see to your west is laced with claymores. BOOM! Whoa, do you know where your child is? Yah yah yah yah." He swigged his Coke.

Nobody noticed the graffiti somebody scrawled over the face of the awning over the doors to Hope House:

ABANDON HOPE ALL YE WHO ENTER HERE.

13.

The two-lane county road twisted like a ribbon over an undulating blanket of leafy corn and remnant patches of ash and maple. On one side, the corn gave way to a rock-dotted pasture. A few cows grazed under a lone oak in the corner by a green pond. The field turned up to a red milking barn with white fencing.

Up ahead, he clarified from a willowy mirage. He kept a steady pace. He'd won trophies for sprinting, but his body was built for long distance. It was a half-hour before she closed the gap to him in a noon sun that made everything drip. She speed-walked along the shoulder.

"Martin! Martin wait!"

She ran to catch up, the guitar flopping on her back. With a sponge in one hand and a water bucket in the other, Bob followed a few paces behind her. She caught up to Martin about the same time Bob caught up to her.

"Oh! Bless those cigarettes. Martin, where are —"

"La," he cut her off.

"La la la. La la la. La la la la la," Bob hummed to the tune of "Chicago."

"Never heard of a place called La. Heard of Shangri-La," she said.

"Los Angeles," he said, trucking under a string of willows lining the highway.

"Ohhh, L.A.," she said. "L.A. may be a lot of things, but it sure as hell ain't no Shangri-La."

A tractor on the opposite shoulder kicked up smoky gravel and they coughed in its cloud. A crow shimmered in the sun, piercing the dust like metal.

"Sure is a beautiful day, ain't it, Mr. Raven or Senorita Crow or whatever you are? God made today. Yes, He did," she said. It was good to be free again. Martin picked up the pace. Bob matched him, slopping suds from his bucket.

"She write you," Patsy panted, "from Los Angeles or somethin'?"

"Yes."

"She invite you —"

"She says I is ready."

"I'm ready for some booze, man," Bob crisped like the pages of an old book.

"You're respondin' to internal stimuli, Bob. Go home."

Martin trekked on past a farmhouse set with field stone.

"You got endurance, boy," she gasped. "A pair a lungs…to rival my own."

Up ahead, the green sign marked the city limits: UKIAH.

"Population: 4,000," Bob read. But it was less than that now.

"I can get us to L.A., but we'll need cash," she said.

"You is on you own."

"I got a motorcycle. In town."

The heat didn't seem to faze him. He didn't pant. He didn't even sweat. To Patsy, part of him seemed inhuman. No, that wasn't it. Part of him seemed beyond human. He seemed wise to her, this 6'3" freckled face kid with eye-stones mined from jade. She couldn't lay her hands on the kind of wisdom he had. It wasn't something you acquired. Oh, she knew that everyone was born with the guilelessness he still wore on the outside. But she'd covered it over with what the world told her about herself. Things like: *Sometimes I wish I could just trade you in at the used daughter lot,* or *Someone oughtta send you back to blow job school.*

In most people, the wisdom Martin had but didn't know he had was enameled over by 9th grade, she thought. It was split off by a slap on the face or the idea that touching yourself in the wrong place was bad even if it felt good. By the time she ended up in a place like Hope House, she'd poured so much leather over the welts from the whippings that'd been meted out as a punishment for her innocence that she couldn't feel what she was trying to protect anymore. There weren't many people who survived high school wearing their souls as skin. He hadn't learned that he needed to keep his walls up, and so his outsides still matched his insides. And she made up her mind, as she watched his arms sway like windmill blades in that diamond-making heat, that she'd do anything to make sure he never lost track of his insides the way she had.

"Look, honey, I got a confession to make."

"I is not you honey."

She nabbed his hand and stopped him. She waded into his hungry eyes. Bob took off his flannel shirt and gave himself a liberal sponge bath.

"I am she for whom you search."

"You lie."

"Alright. Hypnotize me." She closed her eyes. "Go on."

"It do not work that way. It come when it come."

"Well, let's try and make it come."

She splayed her fingers on his face and did a Vulcan mind-meld. "What is you doing?"

"You never seen *Star Trek*?"

He shook his head.

"Just focus."

"Uuuuuuooooooohhhhhmmmmmmmm. Uuuuuuuuooooooohhhhhmmmmm," Bob chanted.

"Gettin' anything?" she asked.

"No."

"Worked for Spock." She dropped her arms.

"You is a fraud, lady," he said, and strode on.

"What happens when you find her?" Patsy asked.

"I should murder her."

"Murder her?"

"She tries to kill me when I is born," he said. He stopped and pulled the Tallman Family Bible from his duffel bag. "Eye for an eye. Life for life."

"She better have some good insurance," Bob said.

The land flattened and the road straightened. Ukiah bulged like a bell curve out of the cornfields, peaked by a crescendo of oak and maple that walled in Hickory Street, the main drag. The three of them eased into forgiving shade that grayed white frame houses with cold porches for winter apples. An antique fire engine rusted in an open field. A psychedelic white bus from Murphysboro New Bible Church leaned on two wheels on the front lawn of a pink cottage. As the speed limit wound down to 30 then 25, downtown came into view. The trees gave way to a row of shops embedded in brownstone facades on either side of Hickory. It was the town Walter Tallman built to keep the company of his model trains. There were more taverns than an outsider would expect — a couple of them still hung faded signs for Hamms and Schlitz.

Where Hickory curved up ahead, a humble, white-steepled church held the ground, ringed by meticulous turf. Patsy squinted at the marquee's message: ALMOST ALL OF OUR FAULTS ARE MORE PARDONABLE THAN THE EFFORTS WE MAKE TO CONCEAL THEM.

"True that, Reverend," she said.

They walked past the Red Owl, Ukiah's only supermarket, and the Plaza Theatre. It played second-run movies you could get at Blockbuster, but that never mattered since there was no Blockbuster. God cast Ukiah far off the interstate, so Wal-Mart and Denny's and La Quinta Inn all passed it by. The railroad did pass through, and the Chamber of Commerce, headed up by Walter Tallman, convinced the Amtrak Board to let an occasional cross-country train stop in on its way to St. Louis or Chicago. Beyond the tracks, she squinted at gathering crowds. Floats staged for the Independence Day parade.

"Just what I need: Publicity," she said.

They passed the old storefronts — an under-stocked resale shop, an antique "mart" that sported the looms and wheelbarrows of farmhouse attics, and a couple diners that never heard of pesto or latte.

"Honey, we should maybe stick to the alleys," she said.

He cast wary glances at his reflection as it glided past storefront glass.

"Marty!" a voice called from one of the doorways.

He froze.

It was Mr. Kantwell, well into his seventies now but still fixing lawn-mowers in summer and snow blowers in winter. He shuffled over and shook Martin's hand, lifting his Cardinals hat for Patsy.

"Well, chivalry ain't dead. It's just snoozin' under bumps in the high-way like this," she said, curtseying.

"How are you, Marty?" He was the only one who ever called him Marty.

"Good."

"Didn't I hear you were in a…home somewhere?" he asked. Martin stared without an answer at the wheezy old man.

"Are you here with your family?" Kantwell quizzed, sniffing something was amiss.

"They is in Apaculpo," he mumbled and looked away.

"You wouldn't want to break your dad's heart and run off again, would you?"

"We're here for the parade," Patsy said.

She figured Kantwell would buy that. But then he got a load of Bob. She tossed Bob a "get busy" look and he did, soaping up the plate glass with his sponge.

"You look a little familiar," Kantwell said to her.

"I have one of those bodies."

"When my hands were a little steadier, I used to sketch portraits. You know, for a hobby. I never forget faces. Attached to bodies," he said.

"Especially when those faces happen to be attached to female bod-ies."

"Just what do you imply, ma'am?" He kept his smile on her.

She crossed her arms. She remembered him. He'd picked her up hitching from Lincoln early one Sunday morning after a party, but then he wouldn't let her out of the car. She remembered alright.

"They haven't been able to replace you in the choir. Not a soprano around like you Martin," Kantwell said in his wet voice.

"I is baritone," Martin said.

"Ah, I could never get those I-talian words right. Your father's Grand Marshal again this year. By default, I guess," Kantwell said. "He's done so much for so many."

"Mmmhmm," Patsy agreed.

"I is late," Martin said.

"Will you tell him something for me?" Kantwell asked, draping his arthritic arm over the boy's shoulder. "Thank him one more time for seeing Mrs. Kantwell before she passed. It meant the world to her."

"I will, Mr. Kantwell."

Kantwell patted his cheek.

"We miss having you around. Everybody always asks about you."

"Thank you." Martin smiled and moved on.

"I'll remember you. Five minutes after you're gone, I'll remember," Kantwell told Patsy.

"Don't let it keep you up at night when you do," she said. "C'mon, Bob."

Bob shook his head and grinned. She walked back to him with a plastic smile and dug her nails into his arm.

"Ow Wo!"

"You know your s'posed to be savin' that water for the parade cars," she said.

"I'm coming if you don't squeeze so hard, Miss Harlot," he said. She escorted him down the sidewalk.

Kantwell shook his head and stepped back inside to the conundrum posed by his latest ride-on mower.

Ukiah flashed with chrome and glass and drowned with sound. Boys from just outside town flaunted muscle cars that thundered thrash metal or thudded what came to be known as hip-hop. Moms and dads pushed strollers, the hands of toddlers wrapped like clay around their fingers. Bandana'd bikers slanted their cruisers in front of Bad Moon, their unofficial church. Beyond the crowds, bands and floats lined up at Echo Park: 4-H, the Jaycees, Amvets, the VFW.

Martin stopped. He spotted something he couldn't make sense of:

his dad yakking with Mayor Blume over where the floats staged.

"I thought he is in Mexico," he whispered.

He looked for a place to hide but a horn honked at him. A girl in a cheerleader outfit waved from a Mustang with the top down. "Martin!" she shouted.

He threw her a distracted wave.

"It ain't safe out here, honey pot," Patsy said. She stood between him and the staging ground.

Then she spotted her iron up ahead, cluttering up the parade route all by itself. It was feathered with parking tickets. A tow driver hoisted it up to his flatbed with a machine-driven chain. A well-built lawman disguising his baldness with a crew cut wrote another ticket for the jet black Chopper, painted with gods of war. She recognized him — Walter's brother. Ukiah's Sheriff. The man who'd paid her off and booted her out of town eighteen years before. Chadwick Tallman. He glanced up at the hours posted on the NO PARKING sign and copied the California plate in his citation book.

"Maybe you were right about that original sin thing," she said to Martin. Martin spotted Chad and ducked into an alley and she and Bob followed.

Chad hadn't seen them, and he'd left his radio in the squad. He hadn't heard the crackle of bulletins about three psychiatric escapees from unincorporated Logan County running loose in his fief.

14.

The one-room Amtrak Station was a toaster oven. A sign on the wall told people to buy their tickets on board. Martin scanned the rack with the train tables, whispering the names to places he'd never heard of. Bob took a stack of schedules and crammed them in his flood pants. He announced the names of far flung routes.

"'Texas Eagle.' Sounds like a Green Beret unit."

"Hun? I was thinkin' maybe Los Angeles wouldn't be best. They'd be lookin' for us there," Patsy told Martin.

"'City of New Orleans,'" Bob went on. "No thank you. I prefer my corpses dry."

"We could go to San Francisco. It's a suburb of Los Angeles. Least it will be soon," she said.

He tried to make sense of the schedule she'd put in with her letter.

"Don't you wanna see the world first, sweetie? God, when I was your age, I was flyin' through the Ozarks on the back of a Hog on my way to everywhere."

"You is not going."

"But why?"

"You is hiding something. I can tell when peoples is lying."

"Like you lied to me when you said you didn't go after Walter's wife with a knife?"

"How do you know my dad's name?"

"Maybe I hypnotized him."

"Do not make fun of me."

"Do not distrust me."

"You steal from old men who is you boyfriends. Dr. Hope says."

He smirked and that burned her up. She pushed her nose out until it nearly collided with his.

"Don't you play high 'n mighty with me. You're a runaway just like me."

"I is no stealer."

"You may not be…"

"Do not say bad things about my dad."

"I didn't say a word."

"You is thinking them."

"Thinking what!?"

"That he steals me from my bio mom."

"What if he did?"

"He picks me up off his doorstep. He takes me in."

"Did that — did he tell you you were adopted?"

"My dad loves me so much he chooses me. He is the best there ever is."

He shook with awe and ire and a dash of spittle pooled in the corner of his mouth. She simmered for other reasons, reasons she wished she could just spit out right now. But she knew that to tell him what Walter really was, she'd have to tell him who she really was. She remembered what he'd done to that albino woman on his front lawn. So she backed down.

"That's what you think, huh?"

"Everyone thinks that."

"Okay."

"So do not tell lies about him."

"Alright."

"'Empire Builder,'" Bob read. "That sounds a little arrogant." She turned, gathered Bob's collar in her fists and reeled him in.

"Will you go back where you fucking came from!?"

Bob unleashed his breath and she let go. Martin studied his Texas Eagle schedule. Los Angeles was the final stop and the next train would leave out at 1 p.m.

The station clock read 12:50.

"I hear you didn't do too good by yourself last time out," she said.

"Because I has no money."

"Can you get some this time?"

"You leach," he said, taking in her whole life in one long glare. That hurt and she knew how to get him back. She eyed his duffel bag and grazed it with her fingers.

"Wonder how much you got in there. Bet a leach could get pretty far with it."

He brandished a pen like a knife. "Stay away!"

"You wouldn't use that."

"They had to pull him off his stepmom. Mompets," Bob said.

"That is not the truth!"

He stormed out of the station, down the steps and into the scope of Sheriff Tallman's gaze. Chad leaned against his squad, his arms crossed over a firm but spreading belly. He'd been chatting up the cheerleader in the Mustang, the one who'd honked at Martin. Her boyfriend didn't seem to like the Sheriff talking to his girl, but the braids on Chad's uniform outranked the braids in her boyfriend's hair.

"Hello, Uncle Chad," Martin said.

"Oh, my God! Martin!" The girl leapt from the curb.

"Hello, Cammy."

She gave him a peck and bundled his arms in her own like pipe cleaners.

"You are so dead for not signing my yearbook."

He hyperventilated into a queer sigh. Bob stumbled out of the station.

"What're you doin' out here, Martin?" Chad drawled as he eyed Bob.

The train schedule quavered in Martin's hand. Patsy popped out the door and relieved him of the evidence with some practiced dexterity. Chad's radio squawked out a fresh dispatch about escapees from Hope House, but Patsy slipped the guitar off her back and made a big deal about setting it on the curb. It threw off ghost chords that echoed around its insides, masking the radio call.

"Damn thing always comes loose," she said and retied the guitar strap.

"Martin, your dad didn't say anything about you out on pass. Who are you to this boy, ma'am?" Chad said.

"His music therapist. We're on a fieldtrip."

"Oh, going to the Ukiah Symphony?"

"No, to see the parade," she said, a little indignant. She thought he recognized her.

"So, where's the rest of the class?" Chad wondered as he inspected Bob.

"Well, Martin and Bob are in a music group that I facilitate. They asked if they could come out and see the high school band." She smiled and produced one of Rachel Wagner's music therapy cards.

Cammy pulled Martin away and made him sign her yearbook. Bob decided the train station needed cleansing and swabbed the windows with his dry sponge. Patsy's eye caught the tow truck clattering by with her Hog.

"You like motorcycles?" Chad asked.

She shook her head. "Too dangerous in big cities like this."

He looked over her tight blue shorts and matching tank top, stopping his eyes on her tummy ring.

"You don't look an awful lot like a social worker. Not like the kind I'm thinking of anyway."

"Music therapist," she said. "How are we supposed to look, like nuns? I mean, come on. I'm an artiste."

"Well, enjoy the parade, artiste," Chad said. "Cammy, you better get going or you'll miss your spot."

She nodded, kissed Martin long and sloppy on the cheek and squeezed him like a puppy. A big scarlet dot blushed between his eyes. Patsy knew that Great Red Spot. That's what the man who turned her out used to call it. When she was raging or shamed, it would rise between her eyes, too. The Great Red Spot. It was the first real sign Martin had her genes. She'd begun to wonder.

Cammy hopped back in the Mustang. Before she even slammed the door, her boyfriend squealed toward Echo Park. Chad stood in front of the train tracks and folded his arms like Superman. When the train came past at 1:00, he'd hold up the parade. Patsy took Martin's palm and nodded for Bob to follow. They had to stay for the parade now, at least for part of it. They headed for the thickest part of the crowd.

She and Martin could finally agree on something — not wanting to be seen. But that wouldn't be easy with Bob. He'd tied his shirt over his shoulders like a '50s college frat boy might his squash sweater, and flexed his saggy pecks for the young moms. It didn't matter anyway. Martin couldn't hide. Every few feet, somebody would stop him and give him a soupy hug or shake his hand.

"You sure as hell are popular," she whispered as they took a spot three rows from the curb. An old couple dawdled by, each wearing a pair of giant sunglasses. "What we need is shades."

"Ann?" the man addressed her from behind.

She ignored it.

"Excuse me, I think I know you," the man said again.

He came around to her side. It was Mr. Nicholson, her music teacher from Lincoln Township High. She'd transferred there in sophomore year after they kicked her out of Ukiah High for sleeping with the gym teacher. Toby Nicholson, in his sixties with a winnowing shock of long white hair that sprouted from his crown, smiled a crooked smile. He was with his wife, Juanita.

"Ann Amstead," he said, igniting a smile on his wife's dry lips. Patsy shook her head and smiled as if she didn't get English.

"Toby never forgets one of his students," Juanita nodded. "He remembers little else."

"You took guitar from me. Classical guitar," Toby said. She shrugged.

"I can't believe you're not remembering this," Mr. Nicholson said.

"I get mistaken for a lot of people," Patsy said.

Toby plunked the fingers of her left hand into his hand and unfurled their length. He ran the calluses of her fret fingers in his palm.

"You don't get fingers like this from the piano," he said. "You were so promising. We tried to get you into Juilliard, but they didn't even have a guitar program back then. Then we tried Northwestern. Don't you remember? You were that good. You were the best I ever had. Then you just disappeared."

She pulled her fingers away and wiped them on the strap of her top.

"I think you're all wrong," Patsy spat out, acidity welling up alongside the fear that she'd been made. She didn't want to be reminded of the life she'd left roadside.

The train horn bayed. Her eyes and Martin's eyes shot back toward the station. They both leaned that way, but Chadwick Tallman stood between them and the railroad crossing, his rusty mustache riding a suspicious smile. He looked right at them.

She tugged Martin's sleeve. "Let's get a better look." They twisted through the crowd, leaving Toby and his wife bemused.

They found an open spot in front and martial music doused them. An ADM float rode by. Behind it, Cammy and last year's pompom squad cartwheeled across the pavement. Then a red Cadillac El Dorado, vintage 1970 with a white, leather interior, inched past. The Grand Marshal, his deliciously thin wife with eyes that bled cleanliness and caution, and Walter, Jr., perched on the back seat. Walter and Virginia waved like marionettes. Walter was decked out as Uncle Sam, replete with a stiletto beard. Ray-Ban Predator sunglasses endowed him with an unintended psychedelic appeal. Virginia dressed as Lady Liberty in a sleeveless gown, her shoulders untouched by daylight before today. They'd clad Baby Walter in a one-piece Stars and Stripes jumper. They were a family in the fullness of their mythological alter egos, the ones they slipped on every Independence Day. The Fourth was Walter Tallman's Fat Tuesday.

The crossing gates went down and the parade lurched to a stop. Warning bells clashed with marching brass and threw off the rhythm of the band. The Amtrak slowed and shuddered and rocked to a halt on Hickory. Walter's car stalled in front of Martin and the smile drained from Walter's jaw when he looked Martin's way.

"Duck," she said as she turned away.

She dunked his head down and they inched their way to the rear of the crowd. Bob followed.

Cymbals crashed. The train hadn't pulled out yet so they could still make it. They headed for an alley. A pair of black boots blocked them, attached to khaki pants, a gun belt, crossed arms.

"Parade over?" Chad asked.

"We have to get back to the Hope House picnic. Martin's singing," she said. "But he forgot some sheet music at his dad's house."

The train sounded its horn three times for the parade and a high school bugler trumpeted back three times. The train started out of the station.

"Why don't I drop y'all off at Martin's house?" Chad said.

She'd walked right into that one.

Patsy, Martin, and Bob crammed in back of the prowler like delinquents. They glided down Magnolia Street to the Tallman home. Elms shaped the boulevard into a church's nave. She hated churches. They reminded her of jails...

15.

…A banner proclaimed YOUTH IN CHRIST. Above those words, Jesus was cut out of felt, ringed by little people holding hands. The church cellar was clean and organized. Bookshelves lined the walls, bricked with King James Bibles and red hymnals frayed at the spines' edges. A foosball table stood in the center of the room. A tacky green couch from the sixties took up one wall. It would find its way to the Hope House dayroom years later. Out the cellar window, snapdragons bloomed over a bed of red and violet coleuses that shuddered in a late afternoon breeze.

Annie Amstead was 16, with sunset hair set ablaze a second time by sun shafts that cascaded through the windows. She crouched in one of the play chairs around a preschool table. She sobbed. Walter stood over her.

"I'm scared," she sniffled.

"I'm scared, too," he said, dangling a Kleenex for her. He was only 28.

He tightened his jaw around the news she just handed him. He sat down in one of the tiny chairs. He grasped her hand in both of his own.

He swallowed. "Do you trust me?"

"Of course," she said, wiping her nose.

"Then there's someone I want you to see."

She looked to him for clarity.

"Kind of like a doctor, but he's not 'official.' He doesn't have to tell your mom."

"Please don't ask me to do that. I don't know if I can do that."

"What else can we do?"

"You know. What we talked about?"

Walter didn't get it.

"You know. You 'n me."

"Annie, I'm the youth minister. I'm in line for pastor here once I finish school." He squeezed her palm. "I've prayed for that my whole life."

"I really love you."

He nodded, stroked his beard, prepared a sermon in his mind.

"People — everyone needs someone to look up to, you know; an example they can follow. It makes them feel like they can do it, too. They need someone they can look up to and believe in. So they don't fall down. That's what I do for people. I bear the burden of example for them. People need that," he said, as if to a child.

"I need you, too. You love me."

He let her hand go and looked away.

"What we had wasn't love. It was lust."

She socked him in the mouth. She cried.

"I'm thorry, I'm thorry." He mashed the words, fingering his molar to check for blood.

He stroked her hair. "We'll find a way," he said.

She laid her head on his shoulder and bawled.

"In the meantime, you can't tell anyone whose this is," he whispered.

"I won't tell. I promise."

"I can't ask my family for money. But I can get some, if that's what you want."

She hushed. She disengaged. She straightened out her shirt.

"Okay. Fine," she nodded.

"Is that alright?"

"Yeah, sure. Fine," she said, and smiled shallow...

16.

She hunched forward in Chad's squad. His salmon eyes ricocheted off the rearview mirror and through the cage. Another patrol car, behind more wire. It reminded her of the cyclone on her window at Hope House and a couple dozen hospitals and county jails before that. After she'd kicked, she thought this part of her life was over.

She could hardly stand Bob's B.O., squeezed in next to him the way she was. But it was the big house they approached that made her stomach clench. Her heart drummed and she shivered and burned at the same time. The closer they got, the worse it got. It was the way she felt when the bus would stop while they raised the jail gate.

"Right here," she exhaled.

"I think I know where my brother lives," Chad said, pulling down the U-shaped driveway to the Tallman house. The brakes squeaked and Martin opened the door.

"Hope I made your day easier," Chad said.

Martin and Bob stepped out and she followed. The train table fell out of her bag as it swung. She bent to pick it up and her guitar strap came loose.

"Don't move," Chad said.

She froze. Chad launched out of the prowler and tightened her strap.

"There. Y'almost lost it," he said.

"I sure almost did." She stepped on the schedule.

"You and me, we should go out for a drink sometime," Chad said.

"I'm glad you asked."

"I didn't ask."

"Call me at Hope House," she said.

Chad smiled and watched them step through the grand double doors. He ducked back in his vehicle, drove a half-block down, pulled a U, and staked out the house.

17.

She closed her eyes until her stomach crawled back down to where it usually was. She breathed slow. *There.* Breathed deep. *You're gonna be alright, Pats, even here.* She yanked the curtain up from a foyer window and peeked out front. No law that she could see.

Bob preened over his profile in a hand mirror and came up to her.

"People depend on this side of my face for comfort," he said.

"Oh, shut up."

She swiped the mirror away and knocked a wedding picture of Virginia from the bureau. She picked it up and shook her head.

"Bet the gown came with a chastity belt," she said. "Bet she's still wearin' it, too."

Martin pattered down the stairs, stuffing a pair of underwear and socks into his duffel bag.

"And old enough to be your sister," she said.

"Put that down."

"We missed our train," she said.

"You is not going."

"We don't need to 'cuz, well 'cuz, I could be your mom. I could… pretend, ya know?"

"You could not be a mom. A dad would not marry you."

He turned into the den.

"Yeah, well, a whole lot of 'em have tried," she said.

"Were they paying customers?" Bob said.

She threw Virginia's picture at Bob and huffed into the kitchen. It opened up into a sunroom where a breakfast nook was built into a giant turntable. From there, the family could face the sun all morning and watch the deer that sometimes browsed the yard. There'd been an in-ground pool there when Patsy had been here as a teen, but Virginia had it filled in. She didn't want her child drowning or picking up an earache. Everything matched — the stainless convection oven; the undermount stainless steel sink; the pewter coat hooks where designer jeans and a brass-button blouse had just been delivered by the cleaners.

"Who sends jeans to a dry-cleaner?" Patsy was mystified.

She yanked the buttons off the blouse and sent them down the garbage disposal. She made a call from the stainless steel phone. She played with the cord.

"And who uses phone cords anymore, Mrs. Flintstone?" Then she read the headline taped next to the phone: CORDLESS PHONES CANCER RISK? "Got any Lysol chewing gum, mom? Jesus."

Bob wandered in, checked into the fridge, and made himself a sandwich. He stacked a whole package of salami with pimento and crumbled goat cheese onto a cold English muffin and scarfed it as fast as he could. He found the liquor cabinet and washed it down with room temperature Jägermeister.

"Bob, don't, okay?"

He stole a Marlboro from her purse and lit it.

"Will you just re-admit yourself?" She went for him but he stood beyond the reach of the phone cord. He smiled, showed her what a half-chewed 16-pack of salami and pimento looked like.

Finally, after about ten rings, a scratchy voice answered Patsy's call:

"Shut up, Wilhelmina!" the man said to a barking dog. "Nitty Gritty Dirt Bag Spittoon Magoon Saloon."

"Why you always answer like that?" Patsy said.

"'Cuz Ink kicks ass when I dain't," the man said.

"He there?" she asked, almost not wanting to know.

"Yeah, he's workin' somebody over. Who's this?" he shouted over the juke, the dog, and a crowd of people trying to jabber over it all.

"Milt? Can you hear me?" Patsy said.

"Ink! Phone!" the man yelled and slammed the phone down.

The Nitty Gritty Dirt Bag Spittoon Magoon Saloon was a one-story cinderblock grogshop that could have doubled as a bomb shelter. That was why Ink bought it.

"Solid construction," he'd brag as he tapped the walls.

But probably just as much, he bought it because he got it for $20,000 at a county tax sale. It sat in skid row on the edge of downtown L.A. The whole place smelled like stale beer and puke no matter how many times Ink bleach-bombed the johns in the morning.

A blind man sat across from Milton, Ink's bartender and telephone receptionist. A weathered man with thick, horn-rimmed glasses, Milton looked ten years older than his 55. He was a doctor, of philosophy, in philosophy. Like half the people here, he owed a lot to Ink. Milton was one of the first people Ink worked to get sober after Ink cleaned up himself.

The blind man's seeing-eye dog perched on the stool next to him. The man poured half a mug of beer from a Tyrolean stein onto the bartop. Wilhelmina lapped it up then barked for more. Her eyes were yellow from jaundice.

The place was packed with hoppers and piss artists, with flatbacks who laid their trade out in the porta-johns and wherever else they could. They were Latino and Anglo, African-American and Russian and Vietnamese, drawn from the corners of the earth to Ink's El Dorado.

"Ink! Phone!" Milton shouted again as he bagged a brick of Richards Wild Irish Rose for a shaky carryout customer.

At the back of the place, a man nudged a black curtain aside and stepped out, surveying his domain. In his late forties, he stood with a flowing, gray biker's mane. His anvil chin was clad with a long, ashy beard he braided and kept rolled up in a black leather pouch that matched his vest. His Navajo skin was rucked by twenty years of work as a roofer, and the hot kettles and buckets of cold tar he'd tended left him with deep crows' feet that punched commas around almond-stained eyes. His heavy iron hull was a tapestry of war — Samurai subduing on his right arm, conquistadors chasing on his left. A sleeveless whitey let the world see the slaying horde of Mongols on his back and the band of ambushing

Navajo on his chest. Warriors conquered his surfaces and nearly jumped off and slew. He'd never tell who it was that etched him with such religious ferocity over every inch below his neck. And just like Bradbury's *Illustrated Man*, Ink's shoulder blade was left empty. He told people that whatever they saw in the unrendered region would be their own fate. It kept people at bay and that was fine with him. But that wasn't why they called him Ink. It was because of what he did behind the black curtain.

Ink looked at Milton. Milton pointed to the receiver hung on the bull-nose of the bar. Ink strode up in his snake skins with steel toes that could have cut glass.

"Yo," he barked into the phone.

"Ink? It's me," Patsy said.

"You find him?"

"I did."

"You say what you needed?"

"Well, things got kinda complex on me."

"They always do. What happened?" He spoke deep, monotone.

"Well, I brought him with me," she said.

In the kitchen, Patsy grimaced as Ink's voice exploded in low frequency booms. Even Bob noticed when Ink's voice took hold of the receiver.

"Ink, you didn't see. They had him sewed up in this piss ward. They got 'im convinced he's crazy, and he ain't," she said, a little broken up.

"You got any idea how to raise a kid!?"

"I can teach 'im to be on his own," she said to the man she called the second coming of her father.

"How do you know he can?" Ink said.

"He can. They told me I was crazy, too."

"Prove you're not right now."

Ink's storm attracted more attention than usual. His trigger was shorter than he might've liked after fifteen years clean and sober. Dean Dealish, a runt in biker rags with thick Coke-bottle glasses, hustled pool in the back corner. When he heard Ink nuke, he peered around the ceiling post. He watched as Ink whipped a switchblade again and again into the bartop, whittled with old knife scars and wood graffiti.

"Ink?" Patsy said as she bit into her nail. "I kinda…misapplied your bike."

She flinched. Ink's sonic boom rocketed all the way from L.A.

"It got towed," she said.

The blind man's hand wandered too close to Ink's blade, but Ink didn't see.

"Ahhhhhh!" She heard the scream.

"What was that?" she asked.

"Never mind. I want my damn bike!"

"I'll get it. I'll get it. If you wire money."

"I got zip, zilch. Shit is what I have. And if I did have any goddamn money, I sure as hell wouldn't waste it on you. I am tired of bailing you out," Ink said as Milton stretched a Band Aid over the blind man's knuckle.

Ink surveyed the derelicts and tweakers that crowded his universe. Half of them ran tabs they'd never pay. The other half owed him money for treatment or half-way houses or Greyhounds out of town to cool off from meth.

"I run a mission here, not a business," he said.

"You should see 'im, Ink. Tall and handsome. And quiet like you. About to burst with ideals," Patsy said.

Car brakes squealed out front of the Tallman home.

"You'll see 'im when we get to town," she said, and hung up.

In the den at the front of the house, Martin stood behind Walter's cherry wood desk. Everything seemed too big to fit him — the high walls sheathed in Tudor panels; a five-foot fireplace; an icy portrait of Mother Tallman, matriarch of the clan. Long departed, her visage glowered down as her illegitimate grandson wrestled with his father's strong box. He'd look up at her, look at the strong box. Finally he turned his back so she couldn't see. He picked the lock with a plastic letter opener, compliments of Logan Furniture & Funeral Home. He inspected the sharp, white tip. It was just like the one he'd used to slice and dice the snow-woman last winter. He slipped it in his back pocket.

Bob wandered in and lifted a brass plaque from the wall. It named Walter "Ukiah Person of the Year." A dozen other awards congratulated the man.

"Your dad is kind of an ass kiss, isn't he?" Bob concluded.

"Martin, somebody's out front," Patsy said from the foyer.

18.

In his squad a half-block down beneath a dying elm, Chadwick flipped through a Victoria's Secret catalog. He glanced up as Walter, still decked out as Uncle Sam, dashed from his Escalade toward the house. Chad flicked on his gumballs. Walter got the signal and pranced over to the driver's side. Chad held up the magazine.

"You 'n the wife want to go in on some of these with me?" Chad said.

"Put that away." Walter pushed the magazine down.

"He's in the house."

"Well, let's go."

"You know who he's with, don't you?"

"I haven't a clue."

"Your old girl. Ann Amstead," Chad said, delighting in his older brother's subtle excruciation.

Walter wiped his face with a new hankie and popped a tablet.

"You don't want this in a Logan County court or a Ukiah newspaper. Wait'll they're out of town. Way out," Chad said.

19.

Walter buried them at the bottom of his strong box, so Martin had never seen them. He found them while he'd been looking for the guardianship papers he'd signed. He laid out the letters from Patsy on his father's desk.

"He lies to me. He says he in Apaculpo, so he can ride in the parade." He said it to himself like he was still trying to believe it.

He joggled the guardianship papers into a perfect stack and ripped them in half. She leaned in the doorway and spotted the only thing in the strong box he hadn't touched — a thick wad of cash. Walter had scrawled CHURCH FUN FAIR RECEIPTS on a Post-it note on top.

"We'll need that money," she said.

"It belongs to the church."

"You wanna gouge mother's eyes out? There's only one way to get there."

"No! My father looks guilty then."

"Then his outsides'll finally match his insides."

"That is good peoples' money."

She walked up, grabbed the wad and jammed it down into her cleavage. She knew he wouldn't dare. His infuriated glare backed her into the bay window that opened onto the side of the house. He had her cornered.

"Give it back." He held out his hand.

She slipped the guitar from her back, unlatched the window and pulled it open.

"Guess you'll have to fight me for it," she said.

She climbed out, blowing Mother Tallman's portrait a silky kiss.

"Didn't think I'd be back, did ya?"

Martin looked back and forth between the window and the empty strong box.

"You're already a fugitive. Might as well get some mileage out of it," she said as she threaded her guitar and bag through the window.

The sound of a far-off siren made up his mind for him. He folded himself in half and slipped out past the baby blue drapes. That left Bob.

"You have a very loose face, ma'am. Madam. Ma'am," Bob said to Mother Tallman. "Doog, I, Man, am I good!"

He crawled out the window.

20.

The parade was long gone. Just a couple streamers trembled in the gutter to remember it by 'til next year. The windshield of Chadwick's patrol car was stained with last week's rain and they watched the sun set through it on the Amtrak Station. Walter and Chad were staked out behind some old lumber piles across from the tracks. Three grain silos stood on their side of the street, white and peeling. Tall weeds embroidered the tracks on the other side of the street. Chad and Walter, back in his civies, hadn't passed a phrase between them in the last hour. They were brothers in blood only. Chad drawled. Walter didn't. Walter disdained what Chad did with his free time. Chad may have gone over into Tazewell County to do it, but Walter still couldn't abide it. He despised Chad's sarcastic mien, couldn't stand the way his brother swaggered or chewed his meat. Mostly, he loathed the secret that bound him to his brother.

A quarter-mile or so down track, the four yellow headlights of the Amtrak locomotive, set like the eyes of a spider, burned through the dusky heat. Patsy, Martin, and Bob slunk through the milk thistles and popped out along the tracks as the blue-gray train eased in next to the planks. Coats of beige paint enameled the station, peeling just like the grain elevators. The Chamber of Commerce wanted the station converted into a trendy restaurant, but no one bit. Trends didn't crest as far as Ukiah.

Patsy shoved an empty envelope into a crack in the platform where it fluttered in the locomotive's diesel gasp. Shrill warning bells chimed over the engine's shudder as the conductor hopped off the train before it stopped. He scowled at his three sojourners, as if resenting the imposition of having to stop in a blip like Ukiah. It was the smallest stop from Chicago all the way to L.A. Other Amtrak men stepped off their berths along the idling Superliner. There were three coach cars, a dining car, three sleepers, a lounge car, a baggage car, two freight cars, and the sleek triple engine, shaped like a bullet nose. The train dwarfed the station.

Bob followed Patsy and Martin aboard. Patsy froze.

"Oh, my Lord. That envelope," she pointed, but Bob looked the wrong way.

"No, over here!" She nudged him. "I just dropped the world's newest, longest palindrome in that envelope." She was horrified. "It's the lyrics to my new song."

Martin looked at her like she was crazy.

"I just finished writing it. Bob, could you go fetch it for me?"

"Oh si si si si si. Sho!" he said, giddy at the thought.

He stepped off the train backwards, doing everything in reverse.

"He just came to see us off," she told the conductor as Bob made for the envelope.

The doors closed just as Bob picked the envelope from the planks.

"We'd like a sleeper," she said. "Deluxe."

The engine raged up a cloud of soot and trembled with a legion of spirits waiting to be unleashed. The conductor showed them to a sleeping compartment with a bathroom and a view out both sides of the train. Through the window, Bob jumped up and down, pointing to an old billboard that advertised a CD from ABBA. The train stammered into movement.

"That is not fair, what you do to Bob. You trick him," Martin said.

"He wanted to be tricked."

She stretched her arms and fell back onto the lounge seat. The wad of cash popped from her bosom to the floor. Martin raced her for it and beat her to it. He jammed it into his duffel bag with a snide smile.

"Give that back, you little shit."

"It belongs to my father's peoples."

"What about you? Ain't you entitled to somethin' for all that time cooped up in Hope House?"

"Two wrongs do not make right."

"But the second wrong'll help you forget the first one. For a while anyway," she said as she leaned back in the seat and crossed her arms.

She spied the tip of the envelope she'd sent her last letter in sticking out from the top of his bag, minus her letter. She swiped it.

"That is mine!" he said.

"Anything's yours. For a price."

"This is not fair!"

"Ain't a question of what's fair. It's a question of what we can negotiate."

He pulled out his plastic letter opener. She held the envelope up in a threat to rip it up. He re-sheathed the letter opener in his pocket.

"Neither one belongs to you. Not the letter. Not the money," he said.

"Don't be so sure they both ain't mine."

They hadn't flipped on the cabin lights yet. That was fine. She didn't want the car attendant to be able to identify her when he came along. She had the idea their descriptions were broadcast all over by now, maybe with an Amber Alert. Maybe the Man would post their vitals on those electronic billboards all over the interstate. She'd always craved fame, but infamy?

She figured a woman in spandex shorts and a skimpy halter top with a belly ring was an easy make. So she bent into her roomy carpet bag and pulled out a copper paisley blouse. She stood and slipped it on. Outside, dusk dissolved into night. Streetlights along the road flitted by, silhouetting Patsy's lithe profile every few seconds as she buttoned the long shirt midway down her thighs. Her silhouette drew Martin's eyes as he dropped into the seat opposite her, clasping the duffel bag close. She caught him peeking and he looked away.

"We could put that in the train's safe," she said, but he latched his fingers tighter around the handles. "Didn't think so."

She tried the bathroom door, but the attendant hadn't been by to collect their fare and unlock it.

"I gotta step outta these shorts. Close those eyes."

He clenched his eyes as she showed him her back and peeled off her black spandex. She was down to her panties. He peeked at her reflection in the window. The outline of a half-naked woman was enough to widen his eyes before he clamped them shut again. But she noticed.

"Your daddy ever tell you 'bout girls, Martin?"

He denied it with a head shake, his eyes buried in a clinch.

"That's probably 'cuz he don't fully know yet himself."

She squirmed into a pair of ripped jeans that were a little too small for her now. She pulled her Navajo blanket from her carpet bag and hung it from the fasteners that kept the top bunk folded into the wall. Patsy hung that blanket everywhere she went, no matter how long or how short she stayed. Ink said it would protect her.

"That school wet nurse this afternoon by the train station — she your girl?"

"I is not ready."

"The only way you get ready to do some things is to do 'em before you're ready. For some things, that's the only way."

She caught a glimpse of herself in the window. "Oh, Jesus Christ, I'm the Bride of Frankenstein."

She pulled out a brush and teased what was left of her hair.

"S'pose your real mom ain't like you think."

He opened his eyes and stared out at the impenetrable night.

"Maybe," she said as she plucked her eyebrows, "lost people are like landscapes in the night. When you never get a chance to see 'em, you make up what you think they must be like."

"I do not make things up," he informed her.

"No, I mean, just say your mother was different than you imagine. What if she was more…like me?" she ventured as she presented herself with a flourish of her colorful fingernails.

"She should be dead."

"You really wanna kill her."

He nodded.

"Now that's against God's commandments. 'Thou shalt not kilt.' Even I haven't busted that one."

"'Everything that happens in this world happens at the time God chooses. There is a time for killing.' Ecclesiastes."

"Then what happens to you? You end up in the hospital at Menard 'til you're 40. Nope. Over my dead bod —" she stopped herself.

She flipped on the lights and smoothed on some lip gloss. "No, you gotta think of some other way to get back at her."

He crossed his arms, shook his head, and stared out the window. His sad, angry eyes, as big and shiny as silver dollars, gazed back at him from the glass. She looked him over. It didn't seem like he'd ever thrown a punch in all his life. Still, he'd gone after Walter's wife with a knife. And she shivered over that albino woman he'd stabbed in his front yard.

She crouched down and met his eyes in the reflection in the window.

"We're not gonna kill your mother, got that?"

Her stare gave way to his glare. She gave up, collapsing in her seat. Her slumped shoulders contrasted with the straight line of his back. She wondered how he could keep such a posture for so long.

"You wouldn't have really used that knife on your dad's wife."

His gaze, icy and simmering at the same time, pried a sigh from her.

"Well, I'll help you find her. I know L.A."

He mulled it over, pursing his lips between his teeth.

"I could help you hide the body," she suggested.

He grudged her a nod.

"All this vengeance makes me hungry for a good, bloody steak. How's by you?"

21.

The dining car was almost empty. Two booths of older couples sat at the far end. White linen tablecloths capped by ice water goblets dazzled off the ivory incandescence. The flatware was painstakingly polished. Patsy was surprised at how the glasses stayed in place. Even the ice didn't swirl as the dining car careened through the black at close to 90 miles an hour.

The dining car attendant, a gracile African-American man in his sixties with a radiant face, handed Patsy her menu.

"Thank you," she lilted.

"You're just in time for the last supper," the attendant said in a soothing voice.

"Let's start with your best bottle of," she said, perusing the menu, "Chardonnay. That won't argue too much with the porterhouse."

"Very well," the attendant said as he left them.

She smiled at Martin. His stare steered her smile right back on her. He seemed to know the mixed motives behind her grins and winks. Was he really able to read folks' thinking? Or was it a delusion, a bluff to compensate for his lack of sophistication? She didn't know. He seemed to know something of her, something he shouldn't know. But if that was true, why didn't he know she was his mother? She was usually able to read people pretty well herself, in a more calculating way, looking for tells. Yet what he really knew about her remained inscrutable.

The attendant returned and broke the boy's gaze, and she was glad. He showed the bottle to Patsy, who nodded like the connoisseur of things edible and drinkable she was. Patsy had educated tastes, even if she could seldom indulge them. The attendant poured her a glass and set the bottle down.

"A few more minutes before we order?" she asked.

Patsy waited until the man left. She poured Martin a glass and slid it across the tablecloth like a stack of poker chips.

"No," he said.

"C'mon. Ever tried it?"

"I take the pledge."

"Oh, I can see you're gonna be a blast for the next six states."

"I is not old enough," he said, staring out the window.

"A man's appetite's one route to his God, hun. Your good don't mean much 'less you go bad first."

"There is no shortcut to feel good."

"My wine'll outlast your whine," she vowed, holding up his glass. She swished a mouthful like a taster.

"Is you supposed to be drinking?" he said, eyeing her with a knowing that froze her wine-swelled cheeks.

It was a moment of decision — one of those knife edges the AA's told her would come. How could she let it get this far after all she'd worked for? All those detoxes, that final one where she thought she'd die down on the Rez in Shiprock. And she hadn't even thought about any of that this time.

Fuck it. You'll be okay now. It's been way over a year.

She looked across the table at green eyes with irreducible flecks of gold that could bore through lead. The eyes of this handsome young man would allow her to choose, but they knew the best choice. How did he know? If he didn't know who she was, how could he know what she was?

She spit it back out into the wine glass, then spit some more, drawing over their waiter with a wave of her hand.

"Is the wine alright, ma'am?"

"No, fine," she gasped, grabbing her water goblet and rinsing out her mouth, then spitting that back. "Just remembered I'm allergic to grapes.

Oh boy, close call," she sighed, gripping Martin's hand. "Thanks, honey."

Martin begrudged a slight smile. He scanned the train car, watching everyone else in the car drink. He resumed his study of the countryside at night.

Her urges re-marshaled themselves in her palate. She ended up ordering half the dishes on the menu, the expensive ones. After all, they had money now. Why not spend it? That's what money was for. It never served its purpose going stale in a bank or a duffel bag, she thought. She talked on about her first trip out west after she'd run away at 16. She fancied herself a flower child back then, even though she'd missed the sixties.

"My first time out, I hitched a ride with this band that called themselves The Pussy Posse. You don't remember them. Before your time. They did that song, 'War Clown.' They were big in the sixties. 'Course, by then, the sixties were the seventies. That was before your time, too. I'll never forget — they had this clattery old school bus painted up like the Partridge Family bus. You remember that bus? From the Partridge Family?" She had to omit the part about being a groupie and what was expected of groupies.

He looked out the window, though there wasn't much to see.

"Don't you ever blink?"

He looked at her. That made her blink.

"*The Partridge Family* was this show in the seventies about a family who were also a rock band. Hey, do you know who Hutton Smith is? Or was, I should say. He died a while back. Unsolved murder. He was Captain Xenon, from *The Skinnypigs*. You remember that show, dontcha? Was a sitcom."

Captain Xenon didn't seem to register in his austere look, but then again, who could tell? It prodded her to yak on, out of frustration, out of desperation that this distant young man was sliding even farther away.

"He was a lot older than I was. He introduced me to Hollywood."

She omitted the part that at the time she met Hutton Smith it was through an escort service.

No matter what she talked about, he seemed nonplussed. He just gazed out the window, at nothing. A floodlit gravel quarry drew his eyes. In a blip, it was gone.

"Ever see the Grand Canyon?"

She waited the appropriate time for a response.

"Storms roll in, crash into the rim, your shadow cast over the side like a giant's shadow, wreathed in rainbow. It's a gorgeous tear in the world too gloried for human eyes."

She figured she'd catch him with her poetry. Men didn't expect that from the ditz they thought she was. But he seemed to look right past her poetics, too.

"But if you can behold such awe, you must be Grand, too. Everyone born should have a chance to see the Grand Canyon. Even the blind."

He didn't seem to hear.

"I'll take you there sometime. And we'll walk down the Rainbow Rim Trail," she promised, nibbling her thumbnail.

He looked out at the occasional farmhouse, its lone light a torch against the night.

"Don't say much, do you?"

"I like quiet."

She glanced down at all the untasted dishes she'd ordered for him. "And you don't eat either."

"I is on a diet."

She burst out laughing. "Spartan Martin."

"This is a waste," he said, waving his hand at the food.

"Life goes fast, slim. Do what you wanna do. Do it now."

"The peoples of my father's church has to pay for this."

"You know how many times I spilled for twice as much as you got in that pitiful little gym bag in one lousy night? I been to the top suite in the Bellagio. We rented half of friggin' Catalina Island for a weekend just to toast the release of a new album. For the Eagles."

"You talk and talk and do not say anything."

"Yeah, well you do not say anything and do not say anything and that's why I talk and talk."

"Peoples who stuff theyselves with one thing is starving of something else."

"Anything you take to the grave's a damn waste."

"You put the wrong things inside you that just make you hungrier."

"And you're too afraid to put anything inside you at all!" she shouted, drawing the looks of the guests at the other end of the car.

He left in a huff. Halfway down the car, he stopped, pulled a couple twenties from his bag, marched back, and threw them down in front of her.

"I want to see the change," he said.

"I don't know if this'll be enough."

He left the car, abandoning her to the wreckage of just one more public scene. She wanted to run away, again, but her mind took her back to why she'd embarked on this crazy ride…

22.

…Ink stopped at a place called Parasawampitts, one of the Vista Points along the North Rim of the Grand Canyon, so they could camp for the night. She asked him what it meant, Parasawampitts.

He shrugged. "How the hell should I know?"

Patsy felt dragged along with each yellow dash on the road since they left Shiprock. She was sober now, but still precarious.

"Ink, I think I wanna be alone for a while," she said, almost as if now were the time of her confinement to end. And he seemed to know, nodded just once.

She walked away, with no water, no compass. She hiked along the trail, the Rainbow Rim Trail, until the rim became a montane forest as it meandered in from the canyon. The winds gale force, they seemed to moan a lamentation, seemed to want her to let go. That is what she hadn't done back in Shiprock, let go of what she'd confessed to Ink's sister. The tempests were telling her to let go.

She thought of each one of her transgressions: There was bad daughter. All that running away. Causing Momma grief. Pawning Momma's cranberry glass collection for a teenth of glass. Rolling johns for Dean to culcock. One by one, as the gale force slammed her thinning hair, she let them go.

She walked miles, more than she ever remembered walking, as the side chasm wandered back out to the Canyon, always holding to the Rainbow Rim. It was a trail that wandered in and out along the North Rim, canopying her in towering ponderosa as she leaned out over the rim for one leg of the trek, blanketing her in oak and aspen as it cut into the mainland the next.

But there was one transgression that just wouldn't go, wouldn't let go, lodged so deep and hard inside her craw. It was the boy. Of course, which other one could it be? If there was one she didn't want to face. If there was one person in the world she never wanted to have to see, it was the one she'd left behind. And yet, beneath the fear of facing him was her hushed hope, her greatest yearning: to see him, to be with him once again. That was when she knew what she must do. Maybe not now. Maybe the time wasn't ripe.

Winds roared like jets, never stopped blowing. Forty miles west by southwest, mountains called the Uinkarets rested on the straight horizon line of the North Rim, miles and miles away. The wind strafed everything, twittered every branch and limb, driving the flies and bees alee. Talus slopes of island mesas were carpeted lime with oak brush and cliffrose in bloom. She knew the names of some of the monoliths, but most she didn't. She peered down, and the inner chasm wound its serpentine channel. The broad tables of the Esplanade north and the Tonto Platform south poured cliffs that formed the final rim of the inner gorge.

From the Esplanade and the Tonto, plains spread in all directions. Every surface jade, yet all topology red as well. Cloud shadows stained scarps and buttes near black with a fleeting finish.

She rested in a bivouac of dirt under the shade of a piñon, her berth necklaced by fragments of Kaibab limestone. Concave cones in the loose dirt, far out on the headland of Locust Point, formed perfect circles. She didn't know what could've made them. She looked it up when she left. They marked the traps of ant lions.

She couldn't summon up another soul all that afternoon, ant lion or human. At first, she found it unnerving, her mind chattering, wanting to go back to camp and talk to Ink. But something inside, the impression of a voice, told her to stay put. She nestled in on a dimple, a dry kettle in the limestone, crossing her elbows on the outsides of her knees. Only herself and the ferocity of gusts that shaped a dead juniper trunk into a boney filigree which blended to the limestone broken at the base of the bole. Wood petrified to stone.

She became aware that what really was, what really lived, never died. It was unborn. Birthless. Deathless. And this unborn wind in its desolation broke hard across the cliffs, filled its own breaking heart with dervishes of dark soil that spit in her eyes, wailed through the endless stands of ponderosa across the side canyon, a cataract of wind 50 miles wide. The sage and piñon, the Gambel oak and Mormon tea, the fiery claret cup in bloom beside the paintbrush and dandelion, surrounded her at the tip of the promontory. In recline here at this dry cape — sometimes inspired, at other times bored or thinking of the three plus mile slog back to camp, as the squall paid her no heed. Only that one thought kept returning, refraining like the gnats that'd come back to her ears between blasts of wind.

Is love as intense and uncompromising as the wind?

I let go! I let go! she cried, but the gusts wouldn't cease, letting her know what she must do.

Then, in a softer mien, *I let go.* Yet the squalls kept on. Surrender must be utter, she concluded, or it's just another compromise. And she knew that compromise just got you back into bed.

Dust from the mistrals, which blew across the world, filtered the sun a half-blood hue, and she could look at it head on as it descended to the tops of the northern Uinkarets, a Vulcan line that stretched dozens of miles from the North Rim. The knives of the mountains pricked the sun's yoke and it bled, releasing its cytol into the atmosphere, a divine oblation to itself. How fast the full circle of the sun became a yellow sliver as its pallet shifted like the skin of an octopus, wafting just above the summit. Then the rich gloaming seared as the sun dropped its blood, engorging the earth. Each day goes the way of night, she thought. And each day dies its own death. Crags and spires slackened into the flax light, their supple shapes unified with sky and shadow. The world all one thing.

The soft peaks dissolved into sky at their summits, sky into light, light into penumbra. Every precipice in the canyon the gentle bend of a Goliath's knee. Ridgelines stacked in selfsame platforms that merged with the fog of dust. A vague and dreamy gulf dissipated in its final or-ison into the ocean from which it calved.

All is dust and all is darkness, she understood. She walked back to camp in darkness, unafraid of what she had to do. The scour of the wind drove its whip all night, finding its way into the corners of her dreams.

23.

She knew what soothed and that was soft strumming from an aged guitar.She leaned back in the corner of the bottom sleeper with her legs folded into a lotus and massaged the tense strings until they relented with a sad, velvet melody. It was the intro to "How Can I Keep from Singing." Martin sat in the window seat as far from her as he could. He read the Tallman Family Bible, incongruously large on his thin lap. She felt she had to start all over again, like she was taming a skittish, feral dog she'd tried to get too close to, too quickly.

She sang the opening lines in a raspy voice cut down by Marlboros and blonde Lebanese hash.

My life flows on in endless song;
Above earth's lamentation,
I hear the sweet, tho' far-off hymn
That hails a new creation;

She coughed. Without looking up, he picked up the words where she'd relinquished them.

Thro' all the tumult and the strife
I hear the music ringing;
It finds an echo in my soul
How can I keep from singing?

When he'd finished the verse, he glanced at her for a moment. She looked back as if she'd just dropped her scarf and he'd picked it up and handed it back.

"That is the voice of King David himself," she whispered. His white smile took up half his face, eyes down.

"With fiery hair and a smile to make night the day," she said.

She got up, walked over and ran her fingers through his hair, combed to one side in a tsunami. "You sing one of my favorite songs so beautifully," she marveled. She was intrigued that he knew it.

"I sing that song since before I is born," he said proudly. She wondered about this declaration, but didn't want to ruin the moment by asking him how that was possible.

"There's somethin' you need to know you ain't ready to hear, but it'll free you. Once you own it," she said.

His shoulders drank up her touch, but his nerves snapped his head back, banging it against the wall. He stood up and backed to the other side of the compartment, bumping against her guitar. He picked it up and handled it for the first time, almost as a way to keep her at bay.

"You play?"

He shook his head, trying to regain his aloofness. He smoothed his pants as his father would have done for him.

"Well you just sit down, and we'll have us a lesson then."

He sat down with the guitar in his lap, holding it like a bird gun. She sat down next to him and adjusted his hands and arms so he cradled it. She draped her arms around his. His limbs were stiff as coat hangers, but they relaxed as she shaped his left fingers to the frets to form a simple chord. He strummed out of rhythm. He closed his eyes. His nostrils flared as they sucked in her Chanel No. 5.

He bolted up, banging his head on the top bunk. He grabbed his duffel bag and slid open the door.

"Where you goin' at this hour?"

"F-for a walk."

"On a train? With all that cash?"

The Fantastic Four played on the observation deck. It was loud and

Martin shied away from volume. The lounge car below was his only refuge. A small kiosk down there sold coffee, snacks, and alcohol. Martin and Patsy stepped into the shop. Their kiosk attendant, a Filipino man in a starched shirt and bowtie, waited behind the register.

Martin's eyes weaved in methodical rows, scanning shelves jammed with sandwiches, cans, and bottles. She watched his eyes as they kept returning to the beer and chasers. Laughter from the lounge drew his eye for a moment. The car was dark and empty except for one booth with a svelte blonde, an executive, and two young men in stiff-brimmed Stetsons. They seemed thrown together just for the trip. They clinked drinks and flirted. Patsy watched him peer over at their laughter while he tried not to seem nosy.

"I pour the drinks and then I stir. May I help you, skinny sir?" the attendant said.

"Bar poetry. I used to do that," Patsy said.

The man nodded and waited for Martin to make a selection. "What they is having?" he said with a confused look.

"You sure 'bout this, honey? You just stopped me from shootin' myself a little while back. You ain't doin' this to prove anything to me, are you?"

He shook his head, glancing at the cowboys and the woman. The attendant waited for Patsy to give the okay. She held up her fingers, gesturing just a splash. The attendant got busy mixing a weak Seven & Seven. He handed her the drink. She couldn't wait to get it out of her hands this time.

"Drink it slow, babe. It's a little industrial the first time down."

He gripped the cup with both hands like it was nitro, and held it eye level. He sniffed at it. Finally, he offered it to heavy lips as Patsy and the attendant witnessed. Then he gulped half the glass. Cheeks swelled. Lips puckered.

A shadow crept behind them. He swiveled his head to see who it was.

Reverend Walter Tallman stood with his arms crossed. Martin's eyes bulged and his cheeks emptied, streaming whiskey in his father's eyes. He threw down the cup and ran for the stairs. The train banked into a curve and he stumbled. Walter lurched after him. Patsy stuck out her foot and tripped him. Martin spiraled up the stairs and disappeared into the movie dark. Patsy stepped on Walter and ran after him.

He grabbed her ankle, tried to drag her down. "You gave up your claim to him a long time ago," he shouted.

"More like you stole him!"

She tried to kick free. The cowboys wanted to help, but no one seemed to know who the good guy was.

"You ran away from him," he said, dodging her heel.

"And you paid me to do it."

"Don't make this harder on yourself."

She spit in his hair. He shrieked and let go of her leg. Germs were Walter's weakness. He ran after her but slipped on the ice from Martin's drink, falling face-first in the blonde woman's lap. Patsy escaped up the stairs. The train braked into an urban rail yard. They'd made St. Louis.

Upstairs, she stumbled through the end of *The Fantastic Four*. She had to guess which way he'd gone. She headed toward the rear of the train. She wound down the steps and flew through the corridor to their sleeper. Empty. She grabbed her guitar and bag and headed for the coach cars. She spotted him through the window to the next car. He grabbed a bucket hat from the luggage rack and pulled it down over his hair, Gilligan-style, as the train glided to a stop.

Martin twisted politely through the passengers as they stood to grab their baggage. She just shoved them out of the way. He found an open sleeper in the next car and made a sharp turn in. She followed him in and slid the door shut. A windbreaker swayed on the door hook. She fished through it and came up with a wallet. It was Walter's. She snagged his Ray-Bans from the other pocket and handed them to Martin. Their train eased into the last berth in the station. Their car was up against the station wall.

She scanned the instructions on the window: EMERGENCY EXIT PULL HANDLE REMOVE RUBBER

She yanked the handle, stripped the rubber molding around the window. She wrestled the window from the frame.

Walter and Chad ran sideways through a sleeper corridor. Chad dragged Bob behind, his hands manacled in a cruel tightness.

Martin stood on the sill and grabbed hold of the roof over the window. He hoisted himself to the roof, reached down his hand for Patsy and pulled her up. Walter slid the compartment door open just as Patsy's heels disappeared. He and his brother faced the wind from an inrushing train. It blew Walter's jacket into his face.

"I didn't know those windows opened," Bob said. "I imagine they lose quite a few children that way."

Walter fumed.

"You were the last one out, Chad. You were supposed to lock the compartment."

"They don't have locks, Walter."

"They have my wallet!"

"Most people sit on their wallets."

"Most people don't have sciatica!" He whipped his jacket against the wall.

Patsy and Martin hugged the roof of the double-decker. Police flashlights broke the dirty dark under the train and along the sooty station wall. The platform bubbled with passengers getting on and off, mixing with late-night commuters streaming toward the suburban lines. Martin climbed down between two sleeper cars and hopped onto the platform. Patsy dimpled the steel panels of the sleeper with her high heels as she slid down the side of the car. "Ow. Ow. Ow!" Her skin squeaked against the metal and she slid down onto the platform. A Red Cap helped her up. She scanned the crowd but he'd dissolved into it. She clambered up the Red Cap's luggage cart and spotted him.

"Martin!"

He whipped around and she waved a hand. "Martin!" another woman shouted.

Rachel waved her hand. Patsy jumped down from the luggage cart and squeezed toward him, but Rachel beat her there. Rachel clasped his arm and tugged. Patsy caught up and grabbed his other arm.

"Let go of him!" Patsy said.

"It's not too late, Patsy. If you give yourself up, we can all talk this out. Come with us now. Please!"

Patsy couldn't afford the attention so she rolled her arm around Martin's shoulder. "Let's go, sweetie."

"Martin, remember what we talked about? About how the hardest thing about growing up is doing what you have to do, not what you want to do. This is one of those times," Rachel said. "We never did write that song together." She tugged again and Patsy felt her boy succumbing.

"Martin, I can be the mother you always wanted. You 'n me, we can travel the country together. I can show you things you can't even imagine are out there, just waitin' to be tasted and tried. She just wants you back in Hope Hell forever," Patsy whispered.

He shook them both off with a fury neither woman could have gauged. "Stop, both of youselfs!" He turned to Rachel. "I is not going back." He looked at Patsy. "And you is never ever my mother." He talked to a gathering crowd. "I is myself, alone."

He spotted Walter coming for him with two Amtrak cops in tow. Martin parted the crowd with his long arms and dashed into the station.

"He's my kid. Back off," Patsy warned Rachel, shoving her into a garbage can.

Patsy ran through the automatic doors after him.

24.

Chad unlocked the cuffs from Bob's bony wrists. "Siddown," he said. "Sheriff Tallllman. Sheriff Tallllman," Bob chanted.

He'd been repeating that ever since he caught the name on his badge back in Ukiah. If he didn't stop saying it, Chad had threatened to lock him in the trunk as they raced the train for Alton. They were lucky Rachel agreed to come with them, for a few reasons: she explained that Bob's meds were wearing thin. He'd decompensate as time went on.

Chad and Bob stood in the glass-walled Amtrak waiting room. He'd picked Bob up at the station back in Ukiah and hadn't had time to drop him off at Hope House. Besides, they didn't know what Patsy had told Bob. He might have information about her plans. So Bob went along for the ride. Chad needed to liaise with the Amtrak police, the local transit cops, and search for Patsy and Martin all at once, so Bob had to be parked.

"Sheriff Tallllllmaaaaaan. Sheriff Tallllllmaaaaaan."

"Shuddup. Put your hand on the armrest."

Chad relocked the manacle over Bob's wrist and battened the other cuff to the chair.

"Now you stay put. If anybody comes and asks you what you're doing here, hand them this," Chad said as he jammed one of his business cards into Bob's hand.

He'd written a note on back: Bob was a fugitive who should be kept in temporary custody until Chad came back.

"Sheriff Tallllllmunnnn, munnnn, munnnn," Bob intoned. "Notice how it's…evowwlving, Shhhhereeeef Tallllmoooond. Ahhhhhhhhhhh-hoooooooo-hh-hhhhuuuuhhhhhmmmmmmmmmm."

Chad glanced around with an apologetic smile. They were the only entertainment for a handful of travelers.

"He's an escapee from a mental institution. If any police comes to claim him, make sure you tell them a lawman locked him down and that I'll be back," Chad said as he flashed his badge around the room.

But all his witnesses cleared out as an announcement crackled over the PA that the train to Chicago just came in. Chad left as an African-American woman walked in with her grandchildren. Bob stuck Chad's card in his mouth and chewed. The grandchildren watched. He winked.

"Mmm-hmmm." He swallowed. "I eat glass, too."

25.

"Because it's more polite for a lady to be in a men's room than the other way around," she whispered.

Patsy balanced her high-heeled clogs on the rim of the toilet. Martin sat on the toilet seat, still sporting his white bucket hat, Gilligan style. With one size-14 Converse All Star gym shoe, he kept the latchless door to the crapper closed so no one could see that a woman straddled the porcelain with shaky ankles. He peered up at her.

"How long we stay?" he murmured.

Just then, a pair of blue polyester pants and tan wingtips appeared under the door.

The man rattled the door. Patsy took one hand off the side of the stall to put her finger to her lips. She lost her balance. Her eyes bulged. She fell against the door and slid to the floor.

"Ow! Aw!"

She pulled herself up and rubbed her bum. Martin opened the door and snaked around her, slipping past the man, bowing in shame.

"I is —" He couldn't finish.

The old man in the out-of-favor three-piece suit seemed stunned. Patsy smoothed her blouse and followed Martin out.

"Oh quit gawkin', ol' man." She squinted at his open fly. "And zip up the barn before the horse chokes, will ya?"

She left the bathroom.

Along the main concourse, Patsy waltzed as if in a graceful pageant, her arm hooked into Martin's. She'd donned a pair of beach glasses with

little alligators on the corners that she'd picked from an old woman on
the train. Martin kept his face down as they moved in lockstep.

"Just move slow. Move slow. You got the hat on, honey. Nobody's
gonna make us," she said with a phony smile.

They passed by the waiting area where two transit cops stood over
Bob, one with a pair of bolt cutters.

"What're you doin' here?" one of the cops said to Bob.

He shrugged and raised his free hand like he was swearing an oath.

"It was a practical joke," he testified.

"Well it's no joke," the other cop said as he clipped the chain to the
handcuff.

Bob fluttered the fingers of his freed hand and examined them like
he'd never seen them before.

"I've never known what to do with my hands. I've never felt comfortable with them, do you know what I mean? I never know where
to put them or how to hold them. Should I put them in my lap? When
they're in my pockets, it makes me feel like I'm hiding something. When
I fold them, or play with my fingers, I feel kind of silly and dithering, a
little like a sissy or a tiny boy. Sometimes I'll look around a room to see
what other people are doing with their hands. As an example, you know.
They don't seem to know what to do with them either. That's why people
buy so many trinkets and baubles, so many pens and combs, I think. So
they'll have something to do with their hands. It's why people smoke,
really. The only time I've ever truly felt comfortable with them was once
when I was a little buzzed. I just set them down on the bar. They felt so
right, like they really belonged at the end of my wrists. I think this all
bothers me because my fingers are dainty. I've often thought they'd have
played the piccolo nicely. But it's too late for that now."

The Black kids giggled. The cops glimpsed each other.

"You have an ID?" the first, a bald man with a grey pencil mustache,
asked.

"Neither an ID nor an address have I," Bob said.

"Get the hell outta here," said the mustached cop.

"Oy!" said Bob.

He spotted Patsy and Martin as they strolled past. "Yo!"

"Aw, Jesus," Patsy moaned when Bob synced in alongside her.

"No, just Bob," he said. "You must have a religious fixation."

He hooked his arm in hers. Three abreast, they headed toward the escalator and escaped into downtown St. Louis.

26.

Chad's fist worked a gnarly, green stress ball as he paced the platform. He'd combed the whole station. Walter, Rachel, the Amtrak cops, and local transit police rounded out the circle. Walter snorted the diesel from his nose into a hankie. He stared at Chad like the whole thing was his fault.

"What're you looking at? You lost them on that train, not me," Chad said.

"You even let Bob get away. Please, enlighten us all as to how you let a psychotic man in handcuffs escape you," Walter said.

"Find 'em yourself," Chad said, and sulked away.

Rachel followed him and nabbed his shoulder with her soft hand.

"He's lost his son. Wouldn't you be upset?"

"Why should you apologize for him? Let the ladies' man apologize for himself," Chad muttered as he cast a wounded glance at his older brother.

"He can't do this without you. He doesn't even have his wallet."

"Y'all don't know him like I do. He's had a spokeswoman ever since he was eight years old. I'm tired of all the women in his life bailing him out. Let him stand on his own for a change."

But Rachel only knew the version of Walter with which she'd fallen in love. That version was eloquent and steady. It was selfless and sagacious. She'd fallen for the earnest devotion he had to his calling. Walter Tallman, the man, and Walter Tallman, the ministry, were collapsed into one personage. He once responded to a frantic, 3 a.m. phone call by driving 75 miles in a blizzard to talk the young wife of a habitual drunkard out of keeping her appointment for an abortion later that morning. That level of dedication was routine for him. It became his brand. It was who Walter was. He knew that. Everyone did.

Rachel had been his student at Lincoln Christian College where Walter served as adjunct faculty. He'd taught her course in pastoral counseling, playing the lectern the same way he did the pulpit — as if it were an instrument he'd carved himself. And then there was his resume. He'd founded the largest Bible school in Southern Illinois. He led a Bible camp each summer for two weeks in Shawnee National Forest. That was where, in fact, he'd impregnated the infamous Ann Amstead. As Ann had been lulled by it before her, Rachel, too, was drawn to the Office, indistinguishable from the man himself.

They'd been intimate for about eight months now. Rachel had even cast aside her promising, pre-med beau, Jesus, in favor of a man twenty years her senior. Right now, she'd do anything for him, especially if that anything included helping him rescue his son and her favorite client from a dangerously unstable woman.

As much as Walter's presence calmed Rachel, Chad's made her shiver. Chadwick was different than the other three men who bore the untarnished Tallman coat-of-arms. Forrest Tallman had become an attorney and taken over their father's law practice after he died. Now he sat as a federal judge in Peoria. Dennis, the youngest, moved away to Murphysboro and became mayor. Mother Tallman bred all her boys for office of one kind or another. But Walter had remained the centerpiece on her mantle. She was most desirous that one of her boys stand as a man of God. "No one's bigger than the Lord," she used to say. "You better curry His favor."

She selected her firstborn for ordination and then raised her second son to watch his back. Chad had been groomed to look out for Walter ever since Walter had accidentally-on-purpose snipped the taunting fingertip off Rickie Severenson with a pair of hedge clippers. Mother Tallman suspected that Walter would need an occasional bailing out, and her instinct had been right. Walter was no different than the other Tallman boys. They all suffered the sting of the flesh. In Walter's profession, that was both an occupational hazard and an occupational death sentence. How such a popular minister in such a small town managed his many affairs while at the same time keeping his reputation unstained remained a family secret. Usually, he chose well — women who were honorable enough to walk and discreet enough not to talk. But everyone made mistakes, especially the young. Ann Amstead had been Walter Tallman's great miscalculation.

27.

That night, three fugitives crossed the bridge back into Illinois and slept in a riverside park. Patsy calculated that Walter would never suspect they'd backtrack. They spread out beneath a canopy of catalpa trees. It was a clear night, and the breeze off the river left a pleasant chill on their skin. They each nodded off into their own private dreams, except for Bob who transmitted flight vectors to the bats from the control tower of his mind. Before his break, he'd studied aeronautical engineering.

The blare of a morning car horn broke the night's peace. The sun glaring off of downtown St. Louis glass cracked their eyes like sunrise eggs. Patsy woke first. She sat up in the grass, stretched her arms and aired out a yawn. She looked at Bob who chattered voiceless commands to a ghost of gnats. Downriver, a floating casino docked on the East St. Louis side. She pointed to the riverboat about a quarter-mile south.

"See that boat, Bob?"

"Uh hum muh hu."

"I want you to wait about twenty minutes, until Martin and I are way gone. Then, I want you to walk over, find a guard, and tell 'im who you are. Got that?"

"Ya. Ay."

Martin sat up and wiped away his sleepers.

"Tell them last you saw us, we were hitchin' to Chicago on I-55. That's Interstate Fifty Five," she said as she flashed two fives with her hand.

"Yes, ma'am, sey," he said, standing like a private with his arms at his sides and his chest pumped out.

"Okay, now make sure you give us twenty minutes," she reminded him. "Bye, Bob."

Bob stuck out his cheek, the one with the divot, for a goodbye kiss. She held her breath, bent over, and pecked him on the forehead.

"Martin, let's go, babe."

She walked north toward the bridge over to St. Louis. Martin shook Bob's hand.

"Goodbye, Bob. You is my funny friend. You make the world laugh."

"Just because I'm crazy doesn't mean I'm not also a fool," Bob agreed.

Bob watched them go toward the bridge as the first rumbles of rush hour rolled out over the Mississippi. Patsy glanced back; Bob was just matchstick size by now. He stood watching them. He hadn't moved a muscle. They walked the hill to the bridge and Martin stopped.

He planted himself in some dirt under the heavy shade of a maple. "Martin?" She turned toward him.

"I is not going," he said, barely audible.

"But going to L.A. was your i—"

"Unless Bob goes too," he finished.

"But he can't. He's dead weight. They'll find us easy with him. He's crazy. What'll we do with him once we're in L.A.? Believe me, it's better for him —"

"He has no family that wants him. He tells me."

"But we're not a clinic. We don't have what it takes to care for him," she said.

"I know what it is like to be 'bandoned."

She didn't have the words for that one.

"Hope House is like Egypt," he said.

She had no idea why it was like Egypt.

"A place for slaves," he said as he confronted her with unwavering eyes. "Bob comes with us, too."

She sighed.

28.

They shot out of the used Harley dealership like a tank shell, fanning through the stultifying steam of St. Louis. Jane's Addiction's "Caught Stealing" pounded out from the woofer and the tweeter. Patsy throttled it as they hit the street. Martin sported his Gilligan's hat and Walter's chic Ray-Bans. He wired his fingers onto the Hog's handholds so tight the blood squeezed out of his joints. Bob was cradled in the sidecar with a Rushmore face, his silver helmet shooting back the sun bolts.

It wasn't full blown custom, but it would do. It was an FL Series and it burned in a bright copper two-tone that bled into red bronze on the bottom end. Bob's sidecar was hand-laid fiberglass with a third-wheel disc brake, a carpeted interior, and its own fairing. It came with a tonneau cover, but there'd be no place to keep that on the road, so she pitched it back to the dealer for Bob's helmet. Her voice squealed over the pipes' wail.

"Did you know, Bob, that Harley-Davidson is the only major manufacturer that makes its own sidecars!?"

Bob just smiled into the wind. He didn't know that the interior of his sidecar was decked out in the ultra-classic style, and that the sound system that barreled "Caught Stealing" was also custom.

"This thing carries fourteen hunnerd cc's and electronic sequential port fuel injection!" she screamed with pride.

She knew that the cagers rattling down the expressway in their four wheel contraptions had to be jealous. Who wouldn't be? Her machine had a custom chrome exhaust and foot pedals. She felt a little awkward riding three-up, and knew her lockable saddle bags made her look a little granny out here, but still, she didn't mind saddling a dresser. A fat-ass touring bike was less of an outcast than it was back when the one-percenters used to call it a garbage wagon. Besides, when you're riding 2,000 miles, you can't have a bike just be naked. You need a fairing.

"There's foreign bikes that are faster, but nuthin's more adaptable. That's why a Harley's the best machine ever made!"

The wind curled Bob's overgrown, ashy eyebrows over the small circles of his John Lennon's. As the riff for "Caught Stealing" squalled, Patsy ramped up I-70 and floored it past the Gateway Arch. Martin took his eye off the hearse in front of them as a fleck of sunlight off the Mississippi snagged his eye. Patsy caught his glance in her rear view.

"Ever see a river that big, boy!?" she shouted.

"No!" he shouted back.

"I'll show you a river that's longer! The River That's a Road!"

She sliced into the hammer lane and torched the motor as a cop exited for downtown. She glanced over at Bob who looked like a field marshal in his gray helmet. He ignored the Arch and didn't seem to notice the river. It was the undersides of the semis that got him going. He pointed at the mud flaps.

"Rainwater!" he screamed.

"Where you from, Bob!?"

"Effingham!" he said in his old man's voice.

"You can do all kindsa things with that name! Just use your imagination!"

"Rainwater!" he pointed with long, custard nails at a Peterbilt mud flap.

They rode due west, flowing with the current toward Kansas City. Missouri shook off the concrete with deep sighs of green, hints of the Ozarks farther south. Dense oak crowns shaded unpainted barns, brittle and gray. Swollen clouds would congeal into thunder-banks farther east.

They passed billboards for *The Adult Superstore* and for *Passions: Where Lovers Shop*, sandwiched between *Love Your Babies: Born and*

Unborn. From Our Lady of Guadalupe for Life. Then a corrugated metal barn painted pink along with a sign: *EXIT NOW! EROTICA!* The naked outline of a woman crooked her figure. That one caught Martin's dead-ahead focus. A half-mile later in big black letters on another metal barn: *NO GOD, NO PEACE. KNOW GOD, KNOW PEACE*. Mother Mary held out her hands.

"Gettin' confused!?" Patsy turned and asked.

"Yes!" he replied.

"Sometimes, I think God speaks to me through the billboards!"

Bob pointed to a billboard for road safety: *THE MAN IN THE HARD HAT IS FIRST AMONG EQUALS!* He knocked on his helmet.

"'Course, Bob, guys like you take that idea a little too far!"

Missouri had a helmet law, but Patsy took the pledge and never wore a dome, under penalty of excommunication from the Helmet Law Defense League. She was a card-carrying member. She wanted one for Martin, but they didn't have one in XXL.

They crossed the Missouri into Kansas City, the tale of two cities — the big brother in Missouri and the smaller one in Kansas. After K.C., they left the forests behind. Kansas seemed one field with a lone tree. Deep furrows cut by water foreshadowed the rending the land would take a thousand miles west. They cut across the yaw and pitch of the Osage Plains into the stubborn limestone of the Flint Hills, pierced like jewels into the belly of Kansas. The land smoothed. Rows of grain elevators stood like chalk cliffs against the breakers of wheat and soy. She always thought someone should write a book on the architecture of grain elevators — one of those books that sat like a brick on a coffee table in a house like Virginia Tallman's.

They breezed by other billboards: *EVERY CHILD IS A PRECIOUS GIFT*; *CHOOSE LIFE*; *IT'S A CHILD, NOT A CHOICE*.

She watched her boy scrutinize the admonitions. They flitted by another for an Adult Superstore, and right after that, another warned — *The eyes of the Lord are in every place, beholding the evil and the good.*

Legions of caterpillars gambled across the highway. And even at 65 mph, the three riders could hear the whistle of the locusts, mile after mile. No one spoke for long stretches. It was easier than arguing with the headwinds. Rolling wheels and still sky quieted Patsy's mind. She felt like she was riding in place, as if the universe flowed around her like the wind. Busy stalks of corn surrendered to simple shafts of wheat. The world loosened its grip. Martin did too, she thought. He'd take his hand off the safety bars long enough to screw down his white hat.

Maybe this thing's gonna work, she thought. Maybe we've both finally come home.

29.

It was a wayside pit. She knew places like this. She could feel the grime rising up from it a mile before they even stopped. A hissing streetlight dangled from a termite-pocked pole on the two-laner. Moths swarmed anything that wasn't black. Heat lightning fluttered on the horizon.

A broken-down diner carved out of a rusty Santa Fe boxcar flanked the county road. Down the way, a pink motel flashed like a giant firefly under ruby neon. The strip bar past the diner didn't bother her as much as the motel. There were lots of people in that club. In the club, you didn't have to worry about what might happen next. The girls had muscle there. But motel rooms had no protection built in. You were on your own.

Patsy and Martin scissor-stepped off the saddle and their soles stuck to the gummy asphalt. Bob pulled himself out and popped off his helmet. His oily skull shimmered under the pumpkin halo of the streetlamp. Martin slapped the dust from his windbreaker and exhumed his duffel bag from the side car. He stepped into the booking office before Patsy.

"You stay here," she told Bob.

"You stay here," he mocked her.

Inside, Martin took off his hat. His Brillo Pad was piled high in an orange ziggurat. Patsy grinned and tried to pat it down.

"Quit it," he said, slapping her hand away, staring at the moth mired in her scalp.

The clerk, a hunched man, was hypnotized by the Fox News Channel on an old Sony on the counter.

"A room with two singles, please," she said.

The clerk unglued his eyes from Bill O'Reilly and plunked them onto Patsy's bosom. So she ogled his bosom through his sweaty, yellow tee shirt.

"A hundred bucks, smokin' only," he said.

"A C-note? Shit, I coulda paid that much along the innerstate," she said.

"Then go there."

They'd already used one of Walter's credit cards to fill up along the interstate. If Walter traced the charges up 'til now, he'd still think they were headed west on I-70. But if she used his card here, the cops might have them by morning.

"Your money, honey," she said to Martin. He shook his head.

"I sleep outside," he said, and walked out.

"What about me?" She followed him as the clerk's grin followed her. He made his way for a weedy culvert outside. She chased after.

"You ever heard of chivalry?"

Bob watched Martin dissolve beyond the jurisdiction of the motel's stammering neon. She stood under the sign and whipped out the envelope she'd wrote to him. It rippled in a breeze from a passing flatbed.

"Momma's bein' held hostage right here. A hunnerd bucks," she said.

He resurfaced under the sign for the CHATEAU RITZ, suffocated in red.

30.

Two lumpy doubles were made up with lime-green bedspreads. It was the kind of place where they changed the sheets after every other guest. No cable. At a table by the window, she used Liquid Paper to doctor her motorcycle registration from Ann Amstead to Ann Ams. But she blotched the VIN on the line above by mistake.

"Shit," she said, crumpling the registration.

Martin sat on the edge of the bed and sneered. "She is like you. She is Mary Magdalene."

"Howda you know? You ever met her?" she said, flattening out the certificate.

"I could not. She is dead in Palestine."

"No. Your mom. If you never met her, howda you know what she's like?"

"My dad tells me about her."

"Hope he didn't gush too much," she said, searching for tissue paper.

She walked into the bathroom and shrieked. Martin rushed in. Bob lay in state in the bathtub, naked, wrapped in a see-through shower curtain. He crossed his arms over his chest like a vampire. A bar of hotel soap stuck out of his mouth.

"What the hell you doin', boy?" she asked.

He ejected the soap part way with his tongue. "Thleeping," he said then chomped back down on the bar.

"You don't gotta sleep in the tub. Use the floor," she said, yanking some toilet paper and dabbing the VIN on her certificate.

He tongued the soap half out again.

"I uhm undeadth. Thith ith my coffin," he said, and bit down on the soap. Martin looked to Patsy for a translation.

"A vampire," she sighed.

"Why you have soap in you mouth? Is you 'fraid of swearing?" Martin said. Bob spit the bar out all the way this time.

"It's in lieu of salt. To keep me from killing again."

Martin nodded and put the soap back in for him. She shook her head and walked out, slipping the registration in the middle of a phone book and pressing down. Her plan was to smear the printing ink from the phonebook addresses over the doctored parts on the title certificate. But when she opened it back up, the Liquid Paper streaked instead.

"Goddamn it, I hate Liquid Paper! Why do they make shit that don't work!?"

She looked at him for an answer.

"Huh, Martin? Why do they do that?" she asked in a way that made light of her feud with the Liquid Paper people.

But he glanced at the violet envelope that stuck out of her bag, the one with Ann Amstead's all-important return address.

"Hey," she said, nodding toward his duffel bag. "Wanna trade? Your money for your mom's address."

He scoffed. "Dad says she leaves me for money. Some man who gets her pregnant, he pays her to go away, and she takes it."

"So you figure she kinda sold you, huh?"

He nodded.

"Maybe your dad was that man. Maybe he paid your mom off with the church's money."

"You lie so I do not trust him."

"No, he lie so you do not trust her."

"So you can steal the money."

"I'd rather be Mary Magdalene than a damn Pharisee."

"He is an honest man."

"A man's honesty lasts about as long as his dick and stomach hold out. You ain't much different than most men, bein' as it is you got a stomach. And a dick, I guess. I'm goin' out to eat." She left.

31.

Walter, Chad, and Rachel tunneled through the I-70 darkness, hopping from island to island along the archipelagoes of midnight semis. The dashboard glimmer painted the faces of the Tallman boys green.

"Therapists can be great sex offenders," Chad observed out of nowhere. "There was one up in Peoria a while back — pretty girl, about 26 — who helped her client break jail then put him up at her house. She'd send text messages to him about how much she wanted him to make love to her legs and how that'd make her cum all over. And when she broke him out, I guess he did her that way." He glanced at her backseat shadow in the mirror. "Yes, ma'am, when they finally executed the warrant on that one, she'd wiped down her whole apartment with goddamn bleach. Her client was 15."

Walter served his brother a contemnible stare.

"Therapists aren't supposed to sleep with clients, I know that. There's a law against it in Illinois. But it's not in the criminal code. It's a civil law. Still, it's law. But what about a therapist being sexual with someone in her client's family? There an ethical issue with that? I mean, I'm not talking about me 'n you. I'm not making a play for you. But people might ask about why you're out here with Walter on this —"

"I'm here because Martin trusts me," she said.

"But if things get to court, and now it looks like they might, it'll look like a conspiracy if it turns out my brother had both you and Dr. Hope in his pocket to have his son committed," Chad said.

"I'm not in your brother's pocket."

"But, is he in your pants?"

"Shut up. Just shut your dirty trap and drive!" Walter said. "And Martin's not committed."

"Okay. Just thought it would be important to know what you know," Chad said.

The air between them sunk like swamp water. Walter's allergies didn't tolerate air conditioning and he insisted they keep it off.

"It's just that…I saw you two sharing a little intimate moment when I busted in on you in the sleeper compartment back between Alton and St. Louis," Chad said with sardonic deliberateness. "You know, that kiss. On your cheek."

"We're friends," she said.

"That did look a little friendly, yes it did," Chad said.

Walter turned to her and shook his head slightly. Chad pursed his lips into a smug grin and winked at her in his mirror.

"My brother is trying to stop you from presenting me with evidence by which I might infer he's having an affair with his son's social worker," Chad said.

It *felt* like the AC flowed out from the backseat.

"I'm not a social worker," Rachel said. "I'm a music therapist."

"That's funny. You're the second music therapist I met lately," Chad replied. "The first one was a real looker. Used to be anyway."

"Stop," Walter said.

"She used to live in Ukiah."

"Stop."

"In case it comes up, Rachel, you'll need to know —"

"No more!" Walter bellowed.

Chad quieted for a while. But he was just circling.

"Just look at his social history," Chad finally said. "That's what you guys call somebody's past, right? The key to how something ends up is usually in how it begins. Just look at the boy's early history. That's all."

Next to her, a thick file with IEPs and evaluations and tests regarding Martin Harmon Tallman trembled on the spongy seat. She had miles of reading to catch up on.

32.

The crickets kept a beat to the faint melody of porn jazz wafting over from the strip club downwind. Martin pocketed his hands and kicked gravel in front of an old diner. In the window, Patsy yakked with a local in his 40s with a mullet haircut and a dusty CAT hat. Martin moped as he watched her gather the man's hand in hers and graze her finger over his palm.

They giggled, and that did it. Martin marched into the diner and homed in on their booth while Patsy fondled the lumps on her customer's pitch-stained palm. Martin glowered over them. She didn't look up but she knew it was him. She rubbed it in by rubbing that palm.

"Why is you holding his hand? You do not even know him."

"Gypsy girls read palms," she said, winking at her patron.

"You is no Gypsy." He addressed the man: "Stay away from her. She steals from her boyfriends. She —"

"That's enough, Dr. Hope."

The customer stood up and stretched with an amused yawn.

"Well, I wouldn't wanna move in on yer gal there, boss," the man said.

"She is not that," Martin said.

He patted Martin's shoulder.

"She ain't much of a fortune teller either," the man said as he tipped his brim to both of them.

He clacked off in his dried mud boots and stopped at the register to snag a toothpick. Patsy scowled. Martin had queered her deal with the local. That hand had been worth $20 maybe. It'd been her chance to show her boy she didn't need his money.

The man tipped the waitress and strode out. The waitress seemed confused. She was about 18, pretty and wholesome. For a girl like that in a place like this, Patsy knew high school prom might have been the top of the roller coaster. Her tag ID'd her as Nancy. She walked up to Patsy holding two lukewarm waters in plastic glasses.

"Will you be wanting another seating?" she asked, switching her glance from Patsy to Martin.

Patsy waved Nancy off. But she took interest when Martin went soft as Nancy bent in front of him to set the waters down. She handed them menus.

"Anything to drink?"

"Coffee. Sludge. Give 'im a beer."

"Chocolate milk," Martin corrected her.

Nancy smiled at Martin, who grinned askance.

"She's your type," Patsy said after Nancy trotted off.

He ignored her, perusing the menu. She leaned into him.

"So when she comes back, just smile the way you do, tell 'er your name ..."

"Mind you own business."

"She likes you. You're a nice lookin' kid, only you don't know it."

"Shush," he said in a way that meant he wanted her to go on.

"That's good. Girls like a guy who don't know what he's got."

Nancy came back with their drinks.

"There you go," Nancy sang.

He gazed out the window, ignoring her.

"I'll have the tuna melt deluxe. I hope that's albacore. Martin?"

"A pickle," he said.

"A pickle?" Nancy repeated.

He nodded, jostling in his seat. He studied the menu upside down.

"He's in training," Patsy said. "Martin was a track champion."

"Really," Nancy gushed.

He nodded to get rid of her.

"Well, that's just... great," Nancy said, a little perplexed.

She jotted their orders and left.

"You're blowin' it. She thinks you don't like her. She —"

"Will you mind you own damn business?" he whispered.

"Ohhh, he swears. Just like a regular fella. I'll bet he shits too," she said. "When she comes back, tell 'er you got a motorcycle. See what time she gets off."

"I know how to talk to girls on my own."

"You can have the hotel room."

"Take my pickle back to the room!"

He shot up and left. She pinched the bridge of her nose and sighed. She knew she'd blown it. Why was she pushing it with him? He already figured her as a whore and a thief. Sure, she needed to show him there was a world beyond the membrane that sealed Ukiah in. But she'd just lanced his ego, coaching him the way she did. You didn't do that to a guy. Then to offer him the room? That wasn't something a mother did for her son. She felt shame chill up her spine like she hadn't felt since her mother found her in bed with Fred La Framboise back in sophomore year. She peered out the window. A hideous face grinned from the other side.

"Ahhh!" She jumped back.

It was Bob, made out in her lipstick and eyeliner like something out of *The Rocky Horror Picture Show*.

33.

Martin squatted down on a railroad tie that marked the end of a parking space. He'd moved down toward Headliners Strip Club. They didn't have places like it in Logan County. He watched the traffic in and out. Men would go in worn out or wound tight. He'd see the same men pop out later, relaxed, rejuvenated. Mostly, there was laughter.

Patsy emerged from the diner, toting a dill pickle in a sealed baggie. Bob curled up his lips and hissed at her. He tried his best to make his eye teeth stand out like fangs.

"Go back to the room and take that shit off," she said. "Makeup's expensive."

He raised his arms like wings and flew back toward the motel. She saw Martin's silhouette hunched at the edge of the lot. She meandered over, hovered, waited for him to come out of himself.

"I can be kinda pushy sometimes," she said.

His eyes tracked the laughing, tipsy parade in and out of the club.

"It's an awful lonely feeling watchin' other people have fun," she said.

He looked up at her as if he agreed. She scooted in next to him, the warm creosote from the railroad tie sticking to her shorts. She kicked off her heels. "I remember what it was like, tryin' to talk to the boys. Of course, I was a little younger than you at the time."

"Really?"

"Yeah, girls mature quicker than boys. Plus, they don't have to do the approachin'. That's easier. And, that's harder," she said, swirling her toes in the gravel.

"Do you has a boyfriend when you is my age?"

She didn't have the heart to tell him what she had back then.

"Is they girls in that place?" he asked, nodding toward the club.

"Not the kind you're lookin' for, I'm afraid."

He peeked at her with needful eyes.

"Can you get a girl impregnant by kicking her? In the stomach?"

"Who told you that?"

"Uncle Chad."

"You know, some boys, the first time they're with a girl, they go with a different kinda girl," she said.

"Like you?"

"Kinda. But closer to your age."

"Is they girls in that place who is my age?"

"Most likely, but I don't think you'll be any less scared of them than you were of Nancy back there."

"I is not 'fraid of girls."

"Most boys are," she assured him.

"I is not a boy."

"I know, I know. But there's an extra 50 miles between Boy's Town and Manhood the map don't tell you 'bout."

"What do you mean?"

"I mean," she sighed, "you're gonna hafta walk just a few more miles before you'll be a man."

"I is 18. I has my dad's Bible. I is a Tallman," he said, standing and jabbing his thumb into his breadbasket. "I is not scairt."

He stalked toward the club to show her just how unafraid he was.

"Martin, you don't wanna go in there." She followed him. "I can hook you up with a real nice girl once I meet one."

"I do not need you to help me get a girlfriend. Stay out." He pointed at her.

"If you're gonna get the band clipped off your cigar in a place like this, you'll need a guide."

Outside, there were two bouncers, both beer gut bikers. One wore sunglasses. The other man, minus a pinky, pressed a fleshy hand on Martin's sternum, putting him to a dead stop.

"ID," Sunglasses said.

"You go to Sturgis last year?" Patsy asked him.

"Nobody real goes to Sturgis no more," Sunglasses said.

"I do. I'm a one-percenter," she said, raising her thigh, showing off a faded mama tattoo on the inside. COYOTE, the brand said.

"That's some dusty ink ridin' up there, maw maw," Sunglasses said.

"I was in, back in the day," she contested.

"Yeah, back in the day a Sonny Barger." Sunglasses bumped Pinky's shoulder and he and Pinky laughed. Barger was a Hells' Angel legend from the 60s.

She stood her ground and flashed four twenties.

"Where do you get the money?" Martin said.

Pinky didn't care where she got it. He ripped it from her fingers.

"Enjoy the ride, son. No touch the merch," Pinky warned with a finger wag. He stood by to let them past.

Martin pulled open the screen door. His face, taut with trepidation, reflected back the neon. He stepped onto an empty porch littered with cigarette butts. Patsy slipped in front to lead the way. She opened a second door.

They walked inside. Their eyes shut down in the black. Synthetic jazz broke over them in deafening waves. It was a pornographic ambient that looped round and round with no beginning or end. The reek of cum and cologne drifted out from the bathroom whenever a man went in or out. There was no ladies room.

He searched for his senses. "I has to use the bathroom."

He followed the light from the door that opened and closed, opened and closed. He stepped inside the men's room, clear of the black jazz blasts and queasy liquor smell. The Hollywood bulbs that lined the mirror blinded him. A reedy man wobbled at the urinal, his privates exposed. Martin's nostrils flared, vacuumed in the strange new smells. He stared at condom machines along the back wall. He scrutinized himself in the mirror. The freckle on his nose was peeling again. He tried to rub it out like he had a thousand times before, only now it seemed more urgent. He turned on the faucet and tamped down his crazy hair. He dried his hands on his pants. Walter taught him not to use those cheap, roll towel devices. Too many germs.

A cologne machine was next to the towels. He had his choice of six fragrances to make him smell like *Lady Bait*, but the coin slot demanded 75 cents for *irresistvirility*.

He sniffed his armpits and waited until the other man stumbled out. He whispered the cologne dispenser directions to himself and dropped in three quarters. He chose Brute, the only cologne he knew. The Tallmans didn't concern themselves with such sweet smells. Nothing came out of the spigot. He had to pump it out. He put his eye to the cologne teat and pumped. Brute squirted out all over his eye.

"Ahhhh!" He splashed his eye with water.

A couple minutes later he stepped out from the bathroom with a ruby eye, half-closed.

"You get mugged in there," she sniffed him, "or kissed?"

"My eye fall asleep."

She followed him into the meld of men. They were dried-out farmers with dried-out skin from too many years of dryland farming at depression scale. The men hunched at tiny round tables while naked girls, some fresh but some used up and cracked around the eyes, dallied at the tables and dangled their breasts like fishhooks over eager smiles that wanted to be caught. They weren't beautiful women. Some were downright plump and saggy, Patsy observed. She cataloged some as meth monsters, others as skin poppers, depending on whether their faces were scratched and pawed or whether they hid their teeth when they smiled. Patsy's eyes swept it up with sick compassion tinged by faint superiority for the body she still had, and for the genuine gentlemen's clubs she'd worked.

It wasn't even pretend happiness on their faces, but impassive, frozen duty caked over layers of practiced apathy. At a good club, the girls would be smiling and those smiles, that pretend wanting, would earn them money. But these girls were baked and their bodies didn't belong to themselves. They strutted in stilettos like animatronic dolls. On stage, a black-haired girl bleached blonde with dumpling cheeks and a cellulite bottom spun around a fire pole and made love to it in derived gyrations. Patsy knew what the girl felt — she felt nothing. The men's stares sucked everything out of her, and at the same time, that vacancy was how she survived their eyes.

Martin spun in a circle, overcome by bourbon fumes and smoke and musk. His eyes were drilled on the murky backroom, where crude red stalls with red benches seasoned with glitter paint separated one lap dancer from the next. A tasteful club, like one up in Windsor, wouldn't let the backroom seem so lurid. But in places like this, where Bibles were slapped on the billboards, the forbidden nature of the draw was spray-painted onto everything.

Patsy took his hand and squeezed. She felt bad for him. She'd wanted to protect him from all this. It was a mother's job, wasn't it? But she also knew she couldn't protect the prince from the world outside the palace once he decided it was time to splash into it. She barely made out the scarlet figures of the men in the lap stools swooned over by the dancers and tickled by their hanging hair. A short, squat man in Outlaw rags patrolled up and down the lap stalls like he was walking the bowels of a slave galley. Martin teetered. His terrified, enticed eyes ricocheted off everything. He drew the watch of the girls, some even younger than him.

He ripped his hand from Patsy and bolted. She chased him. He tried to yank open the slow door, but it was reluctant to let him escape. He piled into three young guys in the anteroom. Patsy saw him in the arms of one of the clean cuts who smiled amused, smiled embarrassed. Martin pushed himself off and yanked at the screen door, but it would only open the other way. He kicked it open. He stumbled outside, fell past the bouncers, and Sunglasses peeked over his dark specs like a curious professor. Patsy grabbed Martin's shoulder and stopped him from walking out into the night beyond the stinging neon. Would-be gentlemen on their way inside eyed him as he coughed up the black gas of the club and choked in air, his hands on his knees. She rubbed his back.

"Honey, it's gotta be sometime," she said.

"No! There is no love in a place like that. It just bring pain in the end."

He puked. She kept her hand on his shoulder.

"I shoulda warned you. I thought you knew. I thought you had ESP."

"It does not always work." He spit.

"What'd you think that place was anyway?"

"I thought it is like a Chuck E. Cheese." Drool dangling from his lips. "For grown-ups."

"It is, kinda."

"It is for evil, sinful peoples," he wheezed, "like youselves."

He glowered at her sideways from his hunch, from another plane. A switch flipped inside her. Who the hell was he to tell her how to live, after all she'd been through? He was her boy — her bent, puking, violated boy — that was who. The switch didn't flip over all the way this time. He sleeved his mouth and leaned into her.

"You should go back inside. Go. Go on, make some money. Like the money you make from the man in the restaurant."

Her twitching eyebrows gathered the Great Red Spot that stormed between her eyes, as red as the spot between his own eyes right now.

"You know why you say that?" she began, low and throaty.

"Some things need be between peoples who respet each others."

"'Cuz you wanna hide all your lusts in the cellar where they just fester and come out sideways."

"I do not has lust in my cellar. I has a lawnmower."

"Those men in there are the walking wounded of the gender wars and they need absolution and TLC and that is what they get. That ain't wrong!"

"It is wrong. Those girls is lost."

"And you're just scared."

"I will have a good woman when God says," he said, pointing to the sky glittered with moths.

"Now I remember why I left Ukiah. You people sell your souls to stay small, then call it salvation."

"I know the difference between what is right and what is wrong!

You do not, Patsy! That is why you is all used up!"

She looked away. "Touché," she said.

"What does that mean?"

"Means you win."

"I do not want to win. I want you not to go to hell for you sins."

"Aw, don't you spit your village virtues at me. Don't try to save me, and don't you warn me 'bout hell, 'cuz I already been."

She shook her head, trying to rid herself of the feeling he'd betrayed her.

"Ask Jesus to forgive you," he said.

"I never did nuthin' to Him in the first place."

"He forgives Mary Magdalene."

"She didn't need His forgiveness. She needed her own."

"My dad has to forgive you too."

"For what!?"

"For stealing his church money. And his sunglasses."

"He needs my forgiveness. And he ain't never gonna get it!"

He turned away and shook his head.

"You go to your church and read your goddamn Bible. I'm goin' in there and read some palms."

"And what else?"

"Believe what you want." She headed for the club.

34.

She conned the bartender into sliding her a glass of club soda. No sense in paying 10 bucks a pop for booze that would bake her black mood decidedly worse.

"Spoiled rich kid. He's got no idea what my life was like when I was 18," she bitched under the music.

She gulped down the seltzer and felt the steam give off.

"Sittin' on milk crates in basements of abandonment buildings, burnin' trash for heat!"

The bartender looked over, watched her talk at herself.

The only thing her boy and her had in common was Walter Tallman; Walter and that Great Red Spot. She'd belch if she had to. He'd swallow the bad taste instead. His God inspired him through the Beatitudes. Hers spoke to her through the Billboards. She thought about bringing him back to Ukiah and copping a plea. But would Hope House be the best thing for him? It was the only thing worse than what he had right now, the only thing worse than the way her life had been back then.

She chewed on the ice from a glass that tasted like bar no matter how many times they washed it. A club girl's eyes knifed her with suspicion. Patsy was competition, and there was no way the management would let her bark with the consumers. She knew how a place like this operated, knew how many other outlaws were around, how a man in a backroom counted cash and cut himself in before the runner came to pick up the proceeds and ride them on to Topeka.

She knew how they got their girls into a place like this, how they turned them out or bought them from a missionary who'd already broken them in, how they rotated them from town to town so no john could get sorry for one and try to steer her straight. Patsy knew how bloody the competition was to operate a place like this, how big city gangs, operators from Mexico and other clubhouses made runs for the operation, and for the meth labs, too. But the rural biker gangs still held their own out here, for now. No, she knew she wouldn't read any palms in here tonight — not without a broke nose. She just needed a place to let the Great Red Spot fade before she faced Martin Tallman again.

A middle-aged townie came by, a gooser. In an intentional, unintentional act of frottage, he pressed his pelvis into her for a moment as he stumbled past the bar on the way to the bathroom.

"Got it. Want it. Whip it out. Pull it. Hide it. In you. Over at the hotel," he chanted, stoned, half-hard.

She knew some of the other girls would go over to the motel. She gave him a wait, pretended like she was considering his offer.

"Buy me a drink," she counter-offered.

He held up his paw for the bartender to pour her another glass, and he did. She sipped on the soda. When she knew the wait had made him horny, hopeful, delusional, she spoke:

"I think bein' a man, that's gotta be hard. I mean, God gives you two heads, but only enough blood to make one of 'em work at any given time. When the little head gets big, the big head, it gets little. It must be difficult wanderin' through life, decidin' whether you wanna think or fuck."

"Well, I don't feel like using my brains right now," he smiled as he looked down into his glass and swirled the ice.

She laughed.

"Is that so?" She sucked her soda through the straw. "See that man over there?" she said, tilting her head toward one of the bouncers, Sunglasses, who'd reconnoitered inside so he could spy on her.

Her consumer glanced over at Sunglasses and his brindled, ZZ Top beard.

Sunglasses could've been staring back at him from behind electric blue.

"That man has a cattle prod he lifted from a feedlot down by Ulysses. Put a man in boot hill with it, I swear to fuck he did. If I hold up my finger and twirl it around like this," she said and swirled it, drilling it into his breastplate, "he is gonna come over here, haul you into the john, and ram that prod up your bumpin' and grindin' ass for a few volts until you're shittin' out your side into a bag 'til the end of days. You want me to do that, Bones?" she said as she raised a finger.

"No, no, no!" He pulled her hand down and stumbled back into a barstool. "It was just a joke. Just a joke." He held up his hands and surrendered.

"That's usin' your head."

He sidled through the crowd, newly sober. She laughed and shook her head. Chances were, if she took the man up on his offer and edged in on their market share here, she'd be the one who'd walk out of the club a little funny.

Her smile faded as she stared at the new number onstage. The girl danced to repeating bars of cheap jazz as she wandered a Ninja sword between her legs. She couldn't have been 21, and she had red hair, seeded with glitter...

35.

…"Momma, am I a good girl, too?" Annie Amstead wondered over the phone.

She stood next to Doris, the girl who'd end up getting a four-year degree at SIU, moving to Chicago, and marrying a lawyer.

"You're my daughter, honey. That's all that matters," Momma told her 13-year-old child that June day.

Annie was calling Momma for permission to stay out past curfew, or to stay overnight at her friend's house, whichever she could negotiate. Momma had just said what a good girl Doris had always been. And Annie longed to hear those words that Momma never seemed to be able to say to her own flesh.

Annie craved a different answer. So she tried to be more like Dawn, her older sister. She tried not to be any trouble, not to come home drunk. But some girls just need a father as bad as a boy does.

Over the last six months, the boys had been paying attention, and she was thrilled, even though she didn't fully understand why she'd become so damned interesting. In that time, she'd gone from a skinny kid to a kid in a woman's body. Dawn tried to fill the hole for Annie left by Daddy's passing. But then someone, a boy who Dawn wanted, wanted Annie instead. He called Annie "Marilyn Monroe with red hair," and asked Dawn if Annie had a boyfriend. The boys Dawn dated were always looking over her shoulder trying to snare a look at her little sister. Dawn stopped trying to teach her how to catch baseballs or catch boys. Annie didn't understand why her big sister wouldn't hang around with her anymore.

Even the teachers at school thought Annie was interesting now. Coach Demhoefer gave her the privileged position of volleyball team captain even though she was always late and had a lousy overhand serve. But she didn't need to serve. She didn't need to be good at anything. She tucked in her tee shirt during practice and caught Coach looking. It was curious and wonderful and frightening. She needed an interpreter for it, but Momma seemed afraid of it too. Friends of her father who used to tousle her frizzy hair stood back now, some eyeing her with a smile and telling her how she's changed. She began to grasp the power she had over grown men, even at 13. And Annie could tell some were so bugged by it, they hardly talked to her at all anymore. What was wrong?

Daddy had died last December from cancer. She'd fit with him like Dawn fit with Momma. Momma worked all night at the glass factory, the only big employer in Ukiah. She wasn't there to hold her younger daughter on nights when the sobs fluttered broken-winged from the other room. And in the daytime, Momma didn't have the energy. She had her own grief she pushed down, private and guilty because hers had been a marriage frayed by overwork and debt.

Annie felt the hole that fed on itself, aching for Daddy. Years later, after she cleaned up, she realized she went into puberty overdrive right after Daddy died. Maybe her body did that all at once on purpose, so she could rely on the affection, and the protection, of men who pretended to be like Daddy.

Momma didn't know how to handle a girl grown up so quick, so Momma clamped down.

"You think those boys want a thing more than to fiddle with you, Ann?" she said in her heavy, Kentucky drawl one Saturday night before Annie was summoned from the house by a horn honking out front. "They won't even do you the courtesy of coming to the door."

Inside a year, Annie Amstead, later trademarked into Patsy Pringle by a sporting-girl's manager who said he was a Hollywood talent agent, discovered more than just boys could make happiness. Boys wanted certain things, like "it ain't sex" in the back seat, and even more in the basement when the folks left. And if a girl was, well, resistant, they could groom her with Budweiser or with Long Island ice teas or red dragons that tasted just like Hawaiian Punch. Drugs worked even better. First weed, then acid, tick, coke, eight-balls, and a bunch of drugs that aren't around so much as they used to be, but that were just as good as molly: rock, ludes, black beauties and white crosses, 'shrooms, blotter and purple microdot; anything to change the way she felt. Anything to make her feel normal, so that her insides felt like other people's outsides looked to her. That's when the rounds of involuntary admission began at Lincoln State Hospital.

Momma didn't know what to do. She was helpless against the drugs. So she resorted to locking Annie in the hospital where Annie learned about other drugs and picked up other habits from the inmates, like how to take it out in trade. After that, everyone — inside and outside — they marked her down as damaged goods. The football players wouldn't date her anymore and she didn't know why. It was something she couldn't get back, but didn't know she lost until it was already gone. Life could be so cruel that way.

She remembered waking up in the cellar of the Victorian the Marks family had abandoned outside of town. It was early Sunday morning. She touched a sore eye. She felt her legs. Her pants were gone. She was only 15. The house was boarded up and she was alone. The last thing she recalled, three boys from Litchfield were talking to her at a party the night before.

She had to wear a towel home. The shame that leaked from her private places, all sticky and soiled. She felt that as she gimped home barefoot between pebbles and broken glass on the hot road, hot even at 7 a.m. She snuck through deserted Ukiah alleys. She crawled through the downstairs kitchen window. Momma was still at work. Annie caught her face in the mirror and saw the hideous black eye for the first time. She gasped, terrified she'd never be beautiful again, but almost wishing she wouldn't be anymore. Upstairs, she slipped on clean panties and sobbed. She couldn't sleep. She remembered a couple cans of Bud she'd stashed in her windowsill on Friday night. She slugged them down one after another, stopping just to let the burps up. Years later, she still believed that somehow, if she would have wished that eye never to have healed, she would have been led to a different life.

Momma had been trying to get her to talk to Walter Tallman for weeks. Momma believed in the saving power of Jesus, believed just as much in Deacon Tallman, the youth minister. At 28, he was already Ukiah's budding personal savior.

"You ought to talk to Reverend Tallman," Momma said one hungover morning.

"He ain't a Reverend yet," Annie said as she laid on their old couch, clenching a pillow to get the sick off.

"No, but he'll be that soon," Momma said from the dining room, where she folded bath towels cut from an old tablecloth. Momma was always busy folding or mending something so she didn't have to think, Annie thought.

"You just want him to marry Dawn," Annie yawned.

"I want no such thing," Momma said without looking up.

Momma's always so cold to me, Annie thought. *Am I that bad?*

"I just think he might be able to show you a road. He is the youth minister. You're a youth. In some ways," Momma added under her breath.

But Annie heard those last words. *I am that bad.*

By 16, Momma had her locked up in Lincoln State Hospital three separate times. Annie had made two suicide attempts. She was a cutter — she went at her arms with broken glass even when she wasn't trying to kill herself. They sent her to one of those tough-love camps in Utah.

Three days out of that place, she was stoned with the bikers at Gretta's, a pukish dive on the highway just outside Ukiah. They wanted to pull the train on her. She managed to get away and stumbled back to town, holding steady to the white dash in the middle of the road. It was Momma's night off, so Annie couldn't go home. She'd go see Walter Tallman.

The Tallmans resided on Magnolia Street, a boulevard with a leafy parkway up the middle. The Tallmans had one of the grandest homes on grand old Magnolia, a Plantation house with a black, wrought iron lamp suspended over the entrance from a chain that could have borne a ship's anchor.

Annie swayed down Magnolia that Friday night after she escaped from Gretta's. She'd never felt right on Magnolia. She came from the Glass Factory Houses near the old Foster Forbes plant, from a one-bedroom cottage the size of the Tallman's garage. People from Magnolia Street and Glass Factory Road only mixed at church.

But Annie found the desperation to knock on that unassailable white door to the Tallman manse. Walter answered. He seemed surprised, but receptive. He hardly recognized her anymore. He said he remembered when he taught her in Sunday school years back when he himself was just a high school boy, but Annie had steered clear of anything to do with the Bible since Daddy died.

He took her to the back yard where dogwoods and catalpas in bloom turned the ellipse into a cloistered green. An emerald, oval swimming pool lit from below glimmered like a cat's eye at the center of the ellipse. There they sat, side-by-side, on the swing painted with dozens of coats of spring green to hide the perennial stains from the mulberry tree under which it swayed.

That first night with Walter she sobered as the hours unfolded one from another, unafraid of Momma's "where have you been all night" wrath this time. She could tell her she'd been talking to the future Reverend Tallman, handsome in his blondness and blue-eyedness, funny in his application of anecdotes from the gentle Book of Ruth, desirable in his pedigree. The Tallmans were as close to Camelot as one could get in Ukiah.

As she sobered that starry night, as the mosquito whine in her ears turned to birdsong, she remembered Walter Tallman making so much sense. He paid attention to her in ways no man had since Daddy. He didn't come on to her. He didn't avoid her out of fear of his own impulses. Walter didn't talk about God, not directly. He didn't talk about what she needed to do to avoid the abyss in the next life. He asked her what she wanted to do with her life today. He didn't treat her like an errant child, like Momma did. He didn't condescend and pretend to connect, like the staff at the State hospital did. He spoke to her like a friend, like Daddy did. He didn't want anything from her, not even her obedience.

And like Daddy, he made her laugh. Even now, as she recalled that magical night, she believed Walter had sincerely wanted to help her by carrying a message of forgiveness. How terribly twisted God's word could turn out of the mouth of a man.

She blamed herself for a long time for what went wrong after that night. She wondered how she'd led Walter on. And she blamed Momma, too, for letting her believe he could redeem her.

36.

But now, as the last of the ice thinned in her glass, she thought about Martin. Patsy wanted him to forgive her. Why shouldn't she forgive her own mother? As the headline act strutted onstage, a young stripper in a tight nurse's uniform, Patsy broke a bill and found the pay phone. She made the call. "Momma, it's me."

She was 13 all over again.

"I told you not to call here anymore, Ann," her mother reminded her in an icy drawl.

"I know, I know. I missed you on Mother's Day, that's all."

"Mother's Day's for the mother, not the child."

"I was busy celebratin' my own."

A brittle silence crackled over the line. Patsy didn't know whether to tell her, whether to suck her into a problem that Momma had had enough of years ago. She didn't want to implicate Momma in an obstruction charge, if she gave her evidence the elder Ann Amstead would be forced to withhold upon questioning. Still, she hoped Momma would show enough interest in her daughter's life to ask the obvious question in reply to her boast. That's what Patsy hoped for during that shaky silence. But the question never came.

"How's Dawn?" Patsy finally asked.

"Still married. Still has a job. Still has two kids and a regular address."

"Blah blah wee, I get it already. My anti-matter opposite," Patsy said, then inhaled deep and closed her eyes. "I just got to thinkin', maybe you 'n me could build a bridge —"

"I followed you out to California twenty years ago and tried to do that with you, and —"

"— by maybe me stoppin' in to see you sometime."

"What would you be needing this time, Ann?"

"You only got this one daughter you gave your own name to."

"As you much remind me."

"I just want you to know that I think I know what you went through with me. That's all." Patsy felt her voice about to crack but patched it up and let the cracks shatter her face instead.

"If you say so."

"What is it with you? I mean, are you all ice in there, or what?" Patsy wondered.

"What should I be saying?"

"What should you say?"

"Mmm-hmmm. What should I say?"

"How 'bout, 'That's a start'?"

"No, that's another false start."

"Alright, I need a place to stay," Patsy paid her off bitterly.

"That's more like it, Ann."

"It's not about me this time, Momma."

"It's always about you."

"Yeah, and how I shattered your little china heart by stealin' away with the boys while you slaved away for us in the glass works."

"Maybe I rode you too much, but there's never any excuse for a woman to turn out the way you did," Momma said.

"You didn't even stick up for me!" She slammed the phone down.

She drew the cautious eye of another young stripper, another girl who didn't seem quite old enough. This one had freckles and braces. Some of the men, they'd like that.

37.

The screen door wouldn't let her out at first, stuck to its paint frame in the grimy Plains night. Sex clubs were like pitcher plants, she thought. They let women in but wouldn't let them leave. And the men? They were slaves as much as the women. Even the outlaws who ran it were stuck to its insides somehow. A place like this took on a spirit of its own. She'd been pulling at a door that opened out just like Martin had. She kicked it open and punished it with a slam as she stepped outside.

She walked past the lone one percenter, Pinky, who squinted into a copy of *The Tibetan Book of the Dead*. She scanned the parking lot. Martin was nowhere.

She went back the motel. Their room was empty. "Martin? Bob?"

His jacket was gone. A ceiling tile tilted out of place where he'd hid his duffel bag. The envelope with the L.A. address? She'd left it in her bag. The envelope was gone, too.

"Shit."

She stepped into the bathroom. Bob's shower curtain was folded neatly on the flush box.

She dumped her stuff in her bag and flew out. She hustled over to her motorcycle. She'd parked it out back in case a LEO came along. It was gone, too.

She hurried to the front office of the motel. The door was locked and the man wasn't there, but the TV droned. WANTED: DEAD OR ALIVE, a Crime Channel show, hyped itself in a red banner.

WANTED!

A photo of Martin above the banner. Patsy's mug shot next to him. She wore a delicious black eye where a cop had punched her for resisting and her hair stood up Don King style. She'd done six months for extortion after that shot was taken.

"Fuck!" She kicked the door. "You answer my prayer to be on TV now? It's twenty years too late!" She glowered at the sky. "Least they coulda done was get my look right. I look like goddamn hair cancer."

The TV asked anyone with information to contact the Ukiah Sheriff's Office and the Illinois State Police. Below the red banners, Patsy caught a phrase on the crawler: AMSTEAD GUILTY OF MULTIPLE SEX CRIMES.

"Sex crimes!? They were for soliciting, for chrissake."

Panic welled up. She ran to the road. She guessed they'd headed west. She jogged past the diner and the strip club and the acid jazz. She picked up another sound: a faint drone like a lawnmower or a weed whacker. Weeds obscured a pinkish glow in the ditch up ahead. She ran faster and faster.

"Oh no, please God," she said, swallowing gnats.

She neared the glimmer and whine. It was her Harley alright — on its side. The back tire spun like a berserk potter's wheel. Martin crouched by the handlebars and tried to pick it up. Bob sat in the upended sidecar, his helmet on and his wind visor still down. She rushed over and spun Martin to her. Just a scratch over his eye. No road rash.

"Goddamn it, Bob! You put 'im up to this!"

"He do not!" Martin protested, squatting to lift the bike again.

She had to hurry — they were chum in the water as long as that bike was down.

"Bob, get out!"

Bob pulled himself out of the car and landed on his head. She grabbed the sidecar with both arms.

"On three, lift! Got it? One, two, three. Go!"

The sinews strained in Martin's neck and they righted the bike. He was a lot stronger than anyone probably ever gave him credit for, she thought. Just like no one ever gave her credit for an IQ of 150. That was fine with her. She liked it when they holed her as a ditz. She roped the mark that way. That was how she smoked them.

"Get on," she said as she mounted the front seat.

Martin walked down the road instead.

"Please?"

Bob slid in behind her and hugged her waist.

"Not you!" she said, slapping his hands off. He jumped in the side car.

"Motor bike. Ekib rotom. Scrotum rotor. Rotor rotator," he said into cupped hands like a police radio.

She idled up alongside Martin.

"Ya know, I don't think you're gonna find what you're lookin' for in L.A."

He kept a pace no one could keep for long.

"Maybe she don't live so far. Maybe she lives real close by."

"Lies."

"Howda you know?"

"The envelope says L.A."

"People don't always tell the truth even when they write it down."

"You talk sideways."

"Alright, then let's talk straight."

She punched it, turned into his path, and cut the pipes. He seemed startled and stopped. Bob jumped from the sidecar and ripped off his helmet. He snagged a lightning bug and spread its goo on his eyelids like glow-in-the-dark eye shadow.

"What if I was your mother? Would you still wanna kill me?"

He nodded.

"Then you just turn right 'round and go home. She spent too long survivin' to let somebody off 'er now."

"She tries to murder me with drugs."

"That's what you were told? That she tried to get rid of you on purpose?"

He nodded.

"Lies," she said.

"How do you know so much 'bout her?"

"Maybe I knew your mother, alright? Maybe I was there."

He grabbed her by the collar. "Lies."

"Then how come I knew your daddy's name? How'd I know to tell ol' Uncle Chad which house was yours back there in Ukiah?"

"Okay, I test you then. What does a boy has to do in Ukiah to get to become a man?"

"The rite of passage of every red-blooded Ukiah high school senior?"

He nodded.

"That's easy. He's s'posed to take off all his clothes and run up to the top of the Ukiah Jumbos, then run down the other side," she said. "On New Year's Eve."

The Jumbos were weedy slag heaps from the old coal mines just outside town.

"If you're the lie detector, you know I ain't lyin' now."

He let her go.

"How do you know my mom?"

"I was her friend, okay?"

He started walking at an easier pace. She kicked up the Hog and puttered alongside him.

"The first thing you gotta know is that your mom didn't try to kill you on purpose."

"She takes drugs so I be a bortion."

"No, she didn't."

He shook his head. She cut the motor again and rolled to a stop. He walked a few more yards and stopped too. She hopped off and strode over to him. She took his hands in hers.

"It didn't happen on purpose. I promise."

He looked at her as if he believed her, she thought. And he should. It was the truth.

"She just didn't want to feel. That's why she got high."

The meat around his eyes creased with grief.

"But she runs from the mess she leaves behind. She needs to be punish."

"I agree. I've wondered about how she should be held to account; for years I've wondered that." She snapped her fingers. "Now this is an idea. Martin, howda you think she should be punished? Given that she didn't try to make you an abortion?"

"Make her go on *Jerry Springer* and letting people yell at her face?"

"Hmmm. Humiliation," she said. "She might like that too much, drama queen that she is. Besides, then you'd have to go on, too. What would your dad think?"

He mulled it over.

"And my family has to go on and be a shame."

"Then sue 'er," Bob said, batting his glowing eyes.

"She has no money. My dad says she takes money to leave town," he replied.

She pointed at Martin. "The best revenge is to put your enemy right in your shoes. Then they know how it feels."

"Lock her up?"

"You got it."

"She makes sure I is locked up in Hope House."

"That might do it. But there'd have to be a crime."

"Well, she runs away from the mess. That is what she does."

"Abandonment and Irresponsibility," she accused.

"That is a crime?"

"The worst kind."

She went to the bike and pulled out a scrap of paper from a saddle bag. She flattened it on her seat and asked Bob to flick her lighter on for her. Bob stood like a green-eyed Statue of Liberty and Patsy drew up an arrest warrant with some fanfare. Martin hunched over and whispered the words one-by-one in fractured syllables:

"WANT-ED. ANN AMSTEAD. FOR A-BAN-DON-MENT AND IR-RE-SPON-SIB-I-LI-TY."

She presented it to him and Bob clapped.

"I could arrest her with this?"

She nodded, and he folded it carefully into quarters twice. He fit the square in his wallet.

"She should get skid row with this."

"She already has. Why skid row?"

"That is where peoples wait to die."

"Then you mean 'death row.'"

"I know."

"They can't execute somebody for runnin' away."

"On Devil's Island they can," said Bob.

Martin nodded. "That is right — on the Devil's Island in hell where she is ending up after they execute her."

"But it was a mistake."

"A mistake is an accident. She takes the drugs on purpose."

"But not to kill you!" She stamped her foot.

"It is still a crime."

"Maybe she was crazy and scared and mixed up. You don't know. I know it's hard, but you don't know." She tried to make his eyes meet hers.

"If she makes a mistake, then I is a mistake. She does not want me to be born."

"No. No, that's not what I meant."

"It would be better if I would not be born."

"She felt the same thing 'bout herself. Maybe that's why she overdosed."

"She is hurt maybe."

"Yeah. Maybe she felt she was all alone and nobody would help."

"What 'bout her Navy boyfriend who makes her impregnant?"

"What?"

"The seaman that makes her impregnant!"

"Semen. What if he was the one who told 'er not to have the baby to start with?"

"She is confused?"

"Exactly. She wasn't grown up yet herself. So she felt like she couldn't be a mom to nobody."

This was fantastic. She had a toehold into him for the first time.

"She was 16 years-old. That's two years younger than you are now.

Would you have felt grown up enough to have a baby when you were 16?"

His eyes bulleted around, then turned red and clinched, ready for tears. But he wouldn't let them go.

"She is the one who runs away."

"She loved you, Martin. She still does."

"She has a nice way to show it."

He picked up rocks and winged them at a STOP sign ahead. They clanged against it, timed to his words:

"I will *kill* her! And *kill* her! And *kill* her again!"

She ducked the salvo and held back her own tears with a fierce bite. She gathered a quiver of sharp stones.

"Attaboy! Knock 'er dead!" she cheered.

She picked up some gravel, let a barrage fly against the sign like buckshot, and rung it like a circus bell.

"Congratulations! The lady wins death by stoning!" Bob shouted.

38.

The next room was worse. It had just one double bed. Martin had folded the topsheet into a flawless rectangle and bivouacked on the indoor-outdoor carpeting.

Patsy painted her toenails in alternating shades of red, white, and blue. A skimpy robe crept halfway up a bruised thigh when she sat down. He smoothed out the wrinkles in his sheet. Then he sat in the chair and watched her work the tiny brush.

His eye caught the 'Coyote' ink on the inside of her thigh.

"Why do you has that name on you body?"

Her brushwork was patient and smooth.

"You been lookin' in places you shouldn't?"

He looked away with a sheepish shrug.

"It's just a decoration," she said.

"The dancing ladies at the hall has them."

"Somebody wanted to know that I belonged to him."

"Like Virginia belongs to my dad?"

"Not exactly —"

"It means she was somebody's asset, Martin," Bob echoed from the bathroom.

"Bob, don't you start in," she said.

That quieted things for a while.

"Has you ever been in love?" Martin asked.

"Yeah, I was. Once."

"When?"

"When I was 16."

"With who?"

"Some pearly man I could never have."

She spilled polish on the sash of the baby blue robe. "God damn it, I can never keep anything nice."

"Why could you never have —"

"Look, I don't wanna go back to the good ol' days 'cuz to tell you the truth, there weren't many."

He thought that over. Then he took out her letter and mouthed the words in a prayerful whisper:

> *Maybe you're mad, mixed up, loving and hating me at the same time. If you want to find out why I left, come on down to Los Angeles and see me, and I'll explain it all for you. Some things need to be face-to-face.*

"Never make that mistake, Martin. Never love beyond your station," she said.

She walked to the bathroom, then froze before she walked in.

"Bob? You decent?"

"I have been for many years, Patsy. I paid taxes for a time, as did my father before me."

She stepped into the bathroom. Bob stretched the naked length of his bones in the tub.

"I thought you said you were decent."

"I prefer the free ranging of the testicles. It makes for a higher sperm count."

"Didn't your family believe in circumcision?"

"I was born in uncircumcised Europe. Royal blood, you know." His voice bounced around the tub.

She threw a towel over him, pulled a leg up to the rim of the old porcelain sink and rinsed the stain from her robe. She had to lift her robe to do it, and Martin spied the bottom of her panties through the doorway. He swallowed. She came back to the room and finished rubbing out the stain with a damp washcloth.

"There, got it," she said.

"'Beyond you station.' What does that mean?"

"Means lovin' somebody you can never have 'cuz they got the same blood type as the Christ clan," she said. "Some of us can't be ministerial even if we pray on it with all our hearts."

A fragile ice cracked around her eyes as she let the words drift like acrid smoke. She didn't want him to see this side, but she couldn't stop it from coming up.

"Is I you station?"

"They used to call us the Untouchables. Us who lived in the stick-built cottages over on Glass Factory Road. When I was a real little girl, we didn't even have hot water. Know what that's like?"

She peeked at him as she flipped a Marlboro between sandy lips. It didn't seem to register, what life was like without hot water.

"No, I thought not." She fired the smoke and finished her little toe with a blue stroke. "Judgin' from that castle your daddy lives in, you 'n me ain't even on the same railroad line."

"That is not true. All peoples is created equals."

She cackled, unsettling the skin on his forearms.

"But they don't stay that way long," she told him. She propped up her other foot for a paint job. "I mean, I ain't the kinda woman you'd wanna have as a mother, right? That's what you said."

He shook his head.

"What would it take for you to change your mind, Martin?"

"You could never be that."

"No, but what kinda mother do you want?"

"Like Rachel."

Her lips clenched.

"What does she got that I ain't got? You tell me. I'm as pretty as her or Virginia, I know that," she said to herself, her voice wandering off into a field of oft-asked questions. "I'm smart, talented. I can make guys laugh. I play six instruments, speak Spanish, Italian —"

"It is not on her outside," he explained. "She does not try to be what she is not. She is kind."

"Geez, is that all? I got a heart the size of — You know, I won 20 grand in Vegas once playin' blackjack. Swear to God. More money than I ever had at one time in my whole life. More money than my mother saved in thirty friggin' years. You know what I did with that money?"

Her face stilled as she thought about it.

"So I'm headed down the Strip with all that cash, struttin' like I just went from a double-D to triple-D cup. And I run into this man. Least I think it was a man. The skin was melted off his face. He didn't even have any flesh on his cheeks or his nose. No lips. I mean, a skull was all there was left of 'im."

He winced.

"And he was out there beggin', man." Her words shivered as she re-called it. "I handed that 20,000, minus the few hunnerd I'd blown on craps and drinks, to that man." She swallowed the memory back down again. "You didn't register that one on your little polygraph machine, didja?"

She studied his distant introspection. She assumed she was getting through, letting him know who his mother really was.

"Rachel is pure," he said. "She does not curse."

"Yeah, yeah, and she shits chocolate eggs on Easter too," she said, worrying at her worry lines in the mirror. "Look, what I'm saying is: even Rachel isn't Rachel. No one's that good, hun. Not underneath."

"She knows how to make apple pancake breakfast. Her office is clean and smells like sweet soap always. She grows tomatoes in her garden and green peppers, and she gives them to me at lunch." A wistful look said he was back with her in Ukiah. "She sews my pants for me once. When they rip. With no machine."

"Would you settle for Eggos, and maybe those little iron-on patch-es?"

39.

L ater that night, she knelt by the bathtub and washed her hair under the faucet and over Palindrome Bob's grimy toes. When she finished, she counted the hairs that clung to her palm. The roots were getting rusty, Martin's shade of red.

Van Morrison's "Domino" came on the radio in the other room. She wrapped her hair in a towel and belly-danced into the room. Martin read the Tallman Bible, undistracted. She danced up on the bed and held out her hand.

"C'mon, let's swing."

It took her the next three songs, all danceable, catchy tunes, to lure his eyes away from scripture. Finally, he rose up, let the music make him move.

They danced around the table. They danced around the bed. The cheap clockradio played "Walk Like an Egyptian" but she danced a combination belly dance/salsa. She oozed through the air like oil in a lava lamp, the backs of her fingers cast across her face in alternating, horizontal sweeps. He jerked his arms and legs in an unintentional robotic dance. He wore a death mask.

"They ever call you Smiley? I think we should call you Smiley."

She gripped his fingers in a banana bunch and taught him to spin, turn, and swing under her arm. She unwrapped the towel from her hair and wedged it between her teeth as she would a rose. That made him smile.

"There ya go. You're feelin' better."

The song ended, and Procol Harum's "Whiter Shade of Pale" bayed out next along with a static hiss. It was a perfect number to teach him to slow dance, but he backed away.

"Now, now. You ain't never gonna step out with the ladies, 'less you know howda 'tew' step."

She grabbed his hand and pulled him into a slow number. She led. Over his shoulder, she peered at the Tallman Family Bible opened to the Book of Revelation.

"You still think Tom Cruise is the Antichrist?" she asked.

"That man who is in *Mission Impossible*?"

"Mmm-hmm."

"How do you know I think that?"

"The palm of your hand," she said, holding it up and mirroring it with her own. "S'pose readin' over your file had somethin' to do with it, too."

His arms and legs were all angles and straight lines.

"You go to prom?" she asked.

"No."

"Homecoming?"

"No."

"Ever dance with a girl before?"

He shook his head.

"You ever dance at all?"

He looked away, too ashamed to answer. His feet lost the tempo.

"That's alright. That's what I'm here for," she said.

She re-engaged him in the rhythm.

"I'm leadin' now. But boys usually lead. Ya go like this." She did a simple two-step. "One two, one two, one two, One. Got it? One two —"

"— One two, one two, One," they said together.

He looked down at his feet.

"Nah nah. Never look at your feet. Just…feel the movement with your body." They moved in sync.

"That's it. There's a rhythm to everything," she said. "Even murder."

They closed their eyes. Bob came dancing out of the bathroom wearing the shower curtain like a toga. He tried to make it a threesome. She knocked him onto the bed with a clothesline shove and didn't miss a step. Martin inched closer.

40.

Long after the dance hall closed down, Martin laid on the floor clutching a blanket and pillow. He rolled over in the dark. He was used to sleeping every other night. It was one of the things about him that scared his father's bride. He just didn't need as much sleep as everybody else.

On nights when he didn't sleep, he'd close his eyes and pick up stray thoughts. That was one of the reasons he hated crowds. Crowds flooded him with thoughts. At night, there was peace. And reception was better at night because there was less chatter out there. Sometimes, he'd snare a wayward AM radio beacon, CB talk, even animal calls. Those were hard to decipher. They were more like impulses instead of thoughts. When he told people that he could tell a dog was lost a few farms away or that he heard a shortwave radio broadcast from a program called Radio Earth, they'd just give him more Seroquel. That helped him sleep every night. But tonight there was no Seroquel, so there was no sleep. Patsy read these things about him in a report Hope wrote for the guardianship hearing.

She heard him roll over and sigh. A bed bug climbed up the side of his face. He bolted up and slapped it. Half asleep, she flung the covers back and made space for him on the bed.

"Get in."

He laid still.

"Don't worry. I ain't gonna jump your bones," she muffled into the pillow, groggy.

He pulled the sheet tight over his shoulder.

"You're too skinny for me."

"I is not."

"Too talkie."

He watched a roach meander across the floor. He climbed in beside her. He hugged the edge of the mattress, putting as much space between them as he could.

"Slept in beds half this size with double the folks," she mumbled, dozing.

His eyes were wide in the dark. He edged his foot closer to her. Closer. Almost touching.

He slung his foot over her ankle. Her eyes sprung open.

41.

"**M**agic Carpet Ride" thundered. She let the collar off the two-stroke engine. Martin perched on the pillion pad, his hand on the sissy bar. He slipped on his shades, inadvertently cool, as she wheeled the Hog in a donut and smoked the lot, tires gripping the asphalt like leopard's paws.

They'd have to stick to the state roads from now on. Out on the slab, there were troopers and turnpikes, Amber Alerts and just plain A-holes. Once they finished with Kansas, they might have to chance the interstate since state roads would be harder to come by.

They'd be alright when that time came. She knew the I-way. She knew the truckers, the lots, how to make money. She laid plans. When they hit the pueblos west of Albuquerque, she'd drive through as much reservation as she could. Those were vacant lands unperturbed by Anglo. And in New Mexico and Arizona to come, there was a lot of rez to ride.

That was somewhere in their future. This was still Kansas. She took 281 south toward Great Bend. They passed a bird sanctuary along the flyway called Quivira. Gulls by the thousands shrieked as the flock sank into the horizon.

Martin yelled in her ear. "I do not know there is an ocean nearby!"

"There ain't!"

A smatter of guano slapped Bob's visor.

She laughed. "Oh, Bob, that is so apropos!"

A dropping plastered her forehead. Bob pointed and laughed.

"It ain't funny if you don't got a helmet, asshole!"

They drove the morning and burned the afternoon hanging low in a state park. The bison hypnotized Bob. He watched them for hours. She had a real thought about leaving him here. But she knew Martin wouldn't stand for it. Besides, who'd take care of him?

She planned to take her time now and wait for the media hunt to die down. They could hide in these Kansas towns. They motored into Great Bend, scooting in along the main drag — Tenth Street. It wasn't like she remembered. The chains had all swooped in: Holiday Inn, Bennigans, Wal-Mart, and even a convention center. Tenth Street went on and on until it was tired. You couldn't ask a small-town road to shoulder this much mall. The Plains were emptying. Towns shriveled up into dryland corpses. But the sprawl only seemed to get worse.

A Toyota sign with free-standing letters towered in the open air.

"'A TOYOTA!'" Bob said, pointing at the letters in front of them.

He turned around as they passed the sign. "'A TOYOTA!'" he read again. "We should stay here!"

She took a side road out of town and a dusky sky settled over them. Clouds in the corner of the sky, cured amber and auburn, seemed to have been there as long as the loamy earth had been. White cirrus streaks reached north in fingers. Crimson splashes, like a painter's mess, exceeded the fingers' grasp. A wisp of cloud turned out to be a flock of geese instead. Clouds didn't honk. But Bob did when he saw them.

The last of Great Bend's subdivisions gave way to a seascape of wheat and milo. They approached a small cemetery, nearly treeless. Wheat lapped up to it on three sides. She dropped the engine, coasted to a close, and stepped off. Bob rose and flipped up his visor. He and Martin watched her proceed to a grave in the last row where a lawnmower had beaten back the wheat. She stood at the grave and paid her respects. Her crew stood off, glancing at each other, wondering what alien god the captain of their spaceship had come to worship.

"He tried to help me," she said. "I mean, he tried to fuck me, but he tried to help me."

The gentle pitch of the Plains threatened to swamp this small isle of memory. The gentleness reminded her of the man beneath the grave marked with no name.

"God knows his name," she whispered.

When it was time to go, she led them back to their sled. They waited for her to raise her leg over the leather and then got on themselves. It was time to move on. She knew she'd never see Great Bend again.

42.

They reached Hugoton in southwest Kansas the next day. People in Hugoton bragged you could put a marble on the road and it wouldn't roll anywhere; things were that flat. They passed a prowler lurking in the dip of a median, and Patsy thought it prudent to take the next offramp. Only the next exit was as close to non-being as a town could get — no paved roads and no trees out here in the flats. The only things that made it a town besides a few frame houses were a tiny post office, a co-op that looked like a feed store, and a trio of grain elevators that stood out like skyscrapers against the chalk sky. There'd been rain, so they splattered mud all over themselves as Patsy inched up and down the ruts that covered the few square blocks of town.

Martin gawked at a woman who stood out in her yard and gawked back. In a town like this, there were no visitors, ever. Patsy got a kick out of seeing the wandering, wondering eyes of her boy scan streets that rode off into nowhere. They passed through tiny Ukiahs where grain elevators — six-packs or even twelvers — might be painted with a giant sheaf of wheat, the name of the high school football team, or a long extinct brew of beer. Bob announced the name of each town as they rode in.

"'Sublette.' There must be many apartments in this little town."

They were out of town almost before they rode in. A few farms later, they passed another Welcome sign.

"'Kismet,'" Bob read. "Destiny, or fate."

Every day, usually in late afternoon, Martin made them stop in an out-of-the-way place. The people of Ukiah knew him for long walks in the woods. Walter had to go looking for him more than once at church picnics, and he'd find him sitting in the middle of the trees listening to the quiet.

Patsy would stop and Martin would find a church and have a quiet time. One day, they stopped in a town that advertised the smallest chapel in the world. She waited outside for him. She hadn't prayed inside a church in years. It was a mutual arrangement she'd made with Walter's God.

"I been to outhouses that were bigger," she said as he came back out.

He glared at her.

"God's house is not an outhouse."

"Sorry. Sometimes the tongue slips into gear without permission. I gotta overhaul my transmission."

"You could go inside," he said.

"Afraid it's a little late for that."

"It is never too late."

"I parted with prayer 'long time ago. I can't change the past."

"But you do not has to repeat it."

She nodded and sized up the tiny wooden A-frame.

"Maybe I'm not ready. Not just yet."

"One day, it happens for you, I know. You has a beautiful heart after all."

"Thank you for noticing."

As they headed out of town, a clear, salty drop spattered his cheek from just a foot ahead of him. But it wasn't rain.

43.

South of Dodge City's feed lots, the shortgrass prairie relinquished its hold on the exhausted earth.

"'Plains,'" Bob read as they passed the town sign. "The town fathers might have opted for a more creative nomenclatural notion."

Thunderheads southwest were slanted like cuestas. Anvil clouds staggered in sea cliffs over the Oklahoma Panhandle ahead.

"'Liberal,'" Bob read as they passed through another city's limits. "I thought this was a red state."

The first panhandle town was Hooker. They slowed past the sign. Bob looked at Patsy and started to speak.

"Mention me and that name in the same breath and you'll be hitchin'," she said.

They sliced through the panhandle, splitting a storm that trended north and south of them, riding a dry furrow that plowed up its middle. The lightning struck again and again, the pedipalps of a great spider. They drove the back roads until she figured it was dark enough to chance the interstate. In east New Mexico, they made I-40 and took it.

They drove through the night until only the semis abided with them.

"Rainwater!" Bob cried and pointed to the apron of every truck they passed.

The headlights of eastbound cattle trucks gathered in convoys that mimicked the lights of a small town. Crooks of lightning fractured the horizon.

"You is going too fast!" Martin said, his voice slipping like spit back into the east.

She ignored him even though she felt the frame shaftjack as they breezed the hammer lane.

"She is going too fast!" he yelled to Bob.

Bob nodded.

"It's places like this," she shouted, "that the sheer size of this land of ours becomes apparent! You can drive all day and barely make it through one state! The Texas Panhandle alone, the skinniest, smallest part of that state, takes an afternoon to beat!"

"The reason it takes so long to drive out west is because they made the states too big!" Bob screamed over the wind. "If they pulled the borders back a little and made states like New Mexico smaller, we'd be able to cover more ground! That's why the Founding Fathers made the thirteen colonies small! They didn't have cars back then! Those guys who wrote the Constitution! They knew what they were doing!"

"Bob, you is a brilliant genius!" Martin said. "He is smart!" he told Patsy. She crouched into the tuck and became one with the wheels.

Storms waited ahead. Shards of plasma raked the range, frazzling the night like a shorted circuit. There was a blameless indifference to a storm's violence, she reflected. But no evil. And if there was no evil, then the devil died out here decoupled from any made thing. Most people couldn't take that kind of indifference. They thought it left no room for God. But to Patsy, it took away the fear of the Lord and left just the Lord. A good storm made her feel alive. But it sure sucked when you were riding.

The pungent scent of ozone fixed in the air. The first bullets of rain came. She throttled it through the rangeland, riding the stitch line as fast as she could. No sense in suffering through a night of soaked underwear. Patsy always had it that cops were like cats — they didn't like to get wet. She figured they didn't want to risk lightning or a sideswipe while they stood by the driver's side and waited for a license in a downpour. And then there was her Tale of the Taillights theory. You fly low as hell, as long as somebody else goes just a little faster. You let them pass you and watch their taillights. As soon as they throw on the reds, you know there's a bear ahead. But her ace was that cops never stopped motorcycles because bikes were too damned fast. And if all that failed, Patsy had flirted her way out of enough movers to keep her license dry.

So she pushed it as hard as the rain let her. Marble-sized drops gouged their faces except for Bob, ensconced behind his visor with an unknowable expression. She ripped through an underpass. A New Mexico prowler snoozed underneath, dry as a dune. On went his dance lights. Out sprung the cat.

She slowed to a stop in a rage of rain as the lone trooper made the long, slow walk from his car. He wore rain gear, rubber-soled boots against the lightning, and parked his patrol car halfway out in the right lane so he wouldn't get hit. Oh, and she'd forgot that her three-wheeler couldn't outrun shit.

She kept it in gear with her boot on the sidecar brake. The cop checked her temporary tag on the rear plate.

"Ya know you were doin' 95 in a 75, right?"

"Oh, no, I sure wasn't aware, officer. I am so new at this." The rain slapped her hair into a pitiful part.

"The speed limit higher where you come from?"

"Would you believe this is my first time out on one of these beasts? My son was teaching me how to drive."

"At 11 p.m. In a rainstorm," the cop said.

"I wanted to learn in all weather conditions. I believe a person should be prepared. Like they say in the military, ya fight like ya train," she said in his West Texas drawl. She always tried to sound local.

"Your license and registration, please." He held out his hand and gathered rain.

"I feel so guilty 'cuz it's his motorcycle and he'll get the ticket, won't he? I was goin' for my license tomorrow."

"Tomorrow's Sunday. License and registration, please."

"Show him your license, honey."

"I don't —"

"Well go on. Go on," she said.

"You bought —"

"The officer doesn't have all day!" she insisted as the rain punished them.

"License," Martin muttered.

He pulled out his juvenile, stitch wallet, the one he'd made in Crafts class at Hope House. He handed the trooper his Illinois State ID. The officer's eyes bulged as if he recognized the name from an APB. Bob flipped up his visor and scrutinized the trooper's badge: NOONAN.

"Officer Noonan. Na Noonan."

"Disengage your engine. Dismount —"

"Yahhahhhhh!" she let out the warrior cry.

She snapped her fist out like a switchblade, popped the brake and throttled up.

Her tire flattened the trooper's boot and left him writhing in the mud. He gripped his boot and drew his sidearm. Martin ducked but the shots never came. She leaned into the machine, pushing it to the limit, sucking a soggy tumbleweed into her wake. Thunder crackled like a gunshot. Bob pumped a fist to the sky and screamed.

"Rainwater!"

44.

A juvie tout trolled for tricks in the Oklahoma City terminal, pimping out a runaway looking to get low. Every once in a while, the pimp would eye Chad, trying to get a bead on where the uniform was from. Chad stapled posters of three fugitives to the message board. Walter plugged his free ear against the bus noise and plugged his nose against the diesel fumes with his other hand. He spoke to Virginia with his cell crammed against his shoulder.

"I'm putting a stop on all your credit cards. Whoever this woman is, she's ruining our financial history," Virginia said.

"Honey, where are the charges from?"

Mrs. Tallman leaned over the island in the center of her kitchen and studied faxed credit card statements.

"Clinton, Elk City, both in Oklahoma. A gas station in McLean, Texas. Oh my Lord, they bought a Harley Davidson in St. Louis."

A tide of agony rolled across Walter's face. "How much?"

"$18,000," she gasped.

"Alright, get daily updates of the charges on all my cards."

"We should cancel them. We have $30,000 limits on these."

"Money I can get more of."

Walter watched Rachel talk up an Amish family waiting for a bus. She handed them photocopies of Martin and Patsy.

"There's talk," Virginia told him.

"What talk?"

"That she knew you."

"There's always talk in a small town. You're from the city. I wouldn't expect you to know that."

"I'm canceling the cards."

"It happened the way I've always told you. She was a kid in crisis like half the ones I minister to now. When she overdosed, her mother asked if I'd look after the baby when he was born. I was youth minister back then. Of course she knew me."

"I'd just hate to see her smear you…"

"Oh, c'mon. She's just one bad apple with an ax to grind."

"I miss you."

"I'll be home in a couple days. Keep praying we find him."

"Love you."

Chad walked up to Walter and waited for him to finish.

"Love you, too," Walter said.

Chad puckered up and kiss-kissed the air. Walter beeped the call dead. He pulled out a highway map from his back pocket.

"They're in Texas, on the panhandle. They're driving a motorcycle," Walter said.

45.

Early morning sun dried up the old rain and soaked her with fresh sweat. She camouflaged the Hog with sagebrush and plastic bags. Martin paced back and forth behind the last standing wall of an old house that hid them from the highway. A window framed them against the road.

"Why you not give the man you license? Now we is in trouble!" His fists throbbed.

"We were already in trouble."

"I is going to jail!" he screeched.

"No, I am. You'll just get sent back to Hope Hell. Trust me, I was right where you are when I was your age."

"I would never get like you!"

"We're both borderline, babe — just in different ways."

She popped Bob's helmet off his head and tossed it in some weeds.

"Hey!" Bob said. "I could hear the sea in that thing."

Martin stormed back toward the road and she followed.

"Sweetie, listen. It ain't safe near the road. That cop's got litter-mates."

A rusty pickup clattered by. She flashed a thumb and the blowback plastered her hair to her ear as it swooshed past. Martin stretched his legs, walked in circles, readying for some great migration. His eyes fixed on a distant point. His lips drew down. Then he started west on the shoulder, marching in strides she couldn't match. She ran after him and Bob ran after her.

"Honey —"

"Do not call me that again!"

"Forget about 'er. She ain't no good. You said it yourself."

He tramped faster.

"Maybe she's got a life of 'er own. With a husband, and new kids!"

He loped. And she knew his legs would hold out longer than her voice.

"I can get us a ride!" she promised.

A Jeep came up. She hailed it but it screamed past.

"Bob, I'd a' snagged that one if it wasn't for your funny farm face. Get behind that sign," she said, pointing to a billboard.

"I have to water myself."

"You shoulda thought a that before."

"But it came about unexpectedly like a micro-burst."

"Get!" She stomped her foot and Bob skittered off the shoulder behind the road sign. She turned up road. "Martin, maybe you should lay back, too. Let the girl do the thumbin'. The drivers like that."

Another truck came up, a flatbed semi hauling portable toilets. Patsy waved and the driver slowed.

"See?" she said.

He passed her up.

"Misogynist."

The rig slowed some.

"Wait! Wait, wait!" She ran to catch up.

It swerved onto the shoulder and the passenger door swung open. Tall gold letters painted the side: HELMER OLSON – PROUD TO BE NORSE & HUNG LIKE A HORSE.

"Fuckin' great," she groused. "An Independent."

The jetblack Kenwood cab, polished like a new leather shoe, hailed out of Macon, Georgia. The truck worked its jake to a stop. She mounted the step and turned to Martin.

"C'mon baby," she said.

"I is not you 'baby.'" He kept slogging.

"Fine. We're done."

She jostled her hair and smoothed out her shirt, then hoisted herself up. She wished she could just shut her eyes, gulp in a breath and hold it in until the ride was done.

Patsy looked down on truckers for more reasons than one. They made one percenters eat more asphalt than the cagers ever did. Over-the-road truckers called themselves 'drivers,' they called cars 'four-wheelers,' and they'd have called Patsy a lot lizard in the old days, a troubadour whore. She had her own name for them — the Lost Boys Club.

Suspicion hung between her kind and theirs. Each vied for position, trying to climb over the other on the food chain. Both species lived in a veldt of terminal migration. They leapfrogged each other from truck stop to rest stop, from motel room to sleeper cab.

The drivers were the lions. They shoveled in chicken fried steak and grits and hobbled around on feet murdered by the pedals and backs bent by the cockpit. Mostly, they were road-warped. They trucked on asphalt lives of isolation, on and on with nobody but each other to reach out to on Channel 19. Dispossessed males cast from the relatedness of the pride and destined to wander the periphery, searching for territories of their own but never finding them. That was the sore all those adult superstores were made to salve.

The clans of hyenas sucked on that wound, drew blood and cum and poison from it. They'd evolved to feed off the lions. They fooled the lions into believing they were kings. But on any given night, a clan could turn on a prideless male. It all depended. Sometimes, State Patrol would find a lot lizard beaten beyond recognition, folded into a dumpster. But every once in a while, they'd dig up a driver from a mountain pass after spring thaw, his pants to his knees, still sporting a red-hot poker preserved by bloody ice and Viagra. She shivered. The drivers scared her more than any pimp ever did.

Bob scrambled out from behind the billboard. She nodded for him to sneak aboard the trailer. Instead, he swung under the chassis and cradled himself in the empty tire carrier.

"Rainwater!"

She slammed the door. A garlic cloud knocked her back. On state-of-the-art sound, the intro harmonics of "The Rooster," a lurid Alice In Chains ballad, wailed like cave wind. Helmer, thick-armed with a matte of yellow hair going white, leered at her with a side glance. He'd twined a Campbell's soup can around his neck with a broken old rosary. He dipped a finger in the can and came up with a pinch of garlic, popped it in his mouth and wedged it in his cheek like a hunk of chew.

"Good thing Bob didn't come aboard," she whispered.

"Eh?"

"Nuthin'."

He shoved it in gear and crackled out from the shoulder. The only thing missing was the Viking helmet, she thought.

"Howdy. Name's Helmer," he said in a weird mash of Norwegian lilt and Georgia drawl.

"Patsy." She forced a smile.

The truck rumbled up alongside Martin as it gathered power down a grade.

"See that kid here? He hates my guts right now. But he needs me so."

"I didn't bargain fer no boy, ma'am."

"Package deal."

He screeched to a stop.

"Outtie!"

"I'll make it worth your while."

Helmer watched Martin as he walked ahead along the shoulder.

"I mean, look at 'im. He's harmless," she said.

Helmer nodded. She opened her door. "Martin!"

Helmer rode the brake and his tractor groaned up next to Martin. "It's gotta be a hunnerd ten degrees out there," she said.

He looked straight ahead, mowed on.

"That Los Angeles, it's 'bout six hunnerd miles down the pike."

She stepped out on the running board and leaned out. She offered her hand, but he batted it away. She lost her balance and swung on the door with one hand.

"Stop! Stop!"

Helmer hit the jake and the truck rumbled to a stop. She fell, landing on her ankle.

"OW! Oh! OmiGod! I think I broke my ankle! Oooh, oh, oh, oh!"

Martin rushed over, knelt down, and slipped off her shoe. He cradled her head and shaded her with his body. The angry mask was gone.

"A shite in knining armor!" Bob dubbed him from the tire carrier.

46.

Helmer and Martin bounced through semi-desert. Martin mouthed the words of his mother's letter to himself as he held the purple page in his hands:

If I have one regret in life, it's that I didn't take care of you before you were born, or after. Regret — that means I'd die to take back what I did. But I nearly died over you once already, and that's how I hurt you in the first place.

"So, what ya readin' thar, boss?" Helmer wondered.

He turned the letter away from Helmer.

"Whar ya headed then?"

"L.A.," Patsy answered from the sleeper.

"How y'all feelin' back thar?"

"Ooooh, it hurts real bad. I think it's broke."

"Let's see," he teased.

She poked a bare ankle through the curtains.

"Aw, that thang ain't barely swelled," he said as he tucked it under his arm and massaged it with his free hand.

"I'll require surgery."

"Mebbe I should come back and make it all batter." He winked at Martin.

"There's only a bunk back here for one."

"Y'all raid my mind." He dropped her leg.

He yanked his rig roadside and disappeared behind the curtain. There was quiet except for the squawk and squabble of the CB traffic. Helmer giggled and that soured Martin's lips. When she giggled back, he pinched his ears closed.

"Now stop that. What kinda woman you think I am?"

"The hitchhikin' kind," Helmer replied.

Outside, Bob climbed down from the tire carrier. He put his hands over his bladder and hopped up and down. He climbed up on the flatbed and tried the doors on the porta-potties. They were all locked. He jimmied one with a scrap of wood.

Back in the cab, the sounds of smooching made Martin squirm.

"Alrighty," Helmer said. "Next step, missy."

The air brakes hissed. "What was that?" she said.

"Just a little ayer bleedin' from the line."

"I been 'round these rigs long enough to know there was somethin' else in that sound."

"Something is burning," Martin said.

The sleeper rustled. Shirtless and shoeless, Helmer popped his head out and listened.

"You coulda had a tire blow. That could start a fire. I seen it happen," she said.

He buttoned up his pants, hopped into the driver's seat and jumped out the door. Patsy slid up front, her clothes intact.

"How could you do that with him?" Martin said.

"Relax. He didn't even hit a single." She settled into the driver's seat.

"You do not play baseball back there. I is not foolish."

"A single means kissin'. First base is makin' out with the girls, Martin."

She whiffed Helmer's garlic can and tossed it out the window. She looked out the giant driver's side mirror and saw Helmer stoop to inspect the undercarriage. She glanced at the control panel, a muddle of switches and gauges. A two-foot stalk sprouted from the floor. Three steel pedals punched out from the firewall. She wanted to pull or push something but didn't know which.

"This ain't anything like a bike," she muttered.

Outside, Helmer's ears pricked to the trickling of water.

"Could be a leak," he mumbled.

An octave lower, the echoes of a gravelly-voiced man sounded out an ecstatic prayer:

"Oooooh, God yeah. Ahhh, Lordie mama. Awww, ma ma ma ma wwwa."

Helmer cocked his head like a coyote locking in on a mouse and stalked the length of his trailer.

"Jesus, Lord, thank you so much for this," the voice echoed.

Helmer glanced toward the sky. Then his eyes homed in on one of the toilets. He hopped on deck and swung open the door. Bob was finishing up.

"Y'all git outta thar. Git!"

"Rainwater," Bob said as he zipped up.

"Thar ain't no friggin' rain 'round harr. Git off, you piece a —"

The truck lurched forward and tossed Helmer overboard.

Bob stepped out of the toilet.

"Live and let live. Evil tel DNA evil," he said. He began directing an imaginary orchestra.

The truck kicked into gear and inched ahead.

"What the heller ya doin'!?" Helmer screamed.

The rig jerked and wove all over the granny lane and Helmer chased it. The last he saw of his truck was Bob standing aft, bowing before his audience to applause only he could hear.

47.

The Route 66 Travel Center sprawled under a constellation of punishing white stadium lights. She didn't know if it was the desert that swallowed the truck stop or the truck stop that swallowed the desert.

The maxi-mart sold everything from oven mitts to the worldwide web. A gallery of restaurants and a gift shop opened up from an indoor mall off the maxi-mart.

Across an asphalt plain where dozens of torpid rigs idled in the night, a row of neon palm trees two-stories tall had been slant-drilled into the sage. They lit up in sequence along the path to the La Playa Casino. It flashed and dazzled like a giant keno machine.

Helmer's rig spasmed into the complex in a series of controlled jack-knifes. It staggered a few yards forward, the air brakes hissed, the tractor locked up and the trailer jammed behind it, again and again. They'd ridden five miles and it took them an hour and a half to do it. They'd laid down a torture of skid marks in the westbound lanes of I-40 for five miles. A bad wreck in the eastbound lanes had kept the troopers off their tail.

She nursed the rig to the back edge of the lot behind rows of leviathans and stacked it crooked next to a church-on-wheels. The doors to Helmer's cab opened and she and Martin dropped out and dragged themselves toward the hotel. Bob jumped down from the trailer.

"Aw Lord, why you gotta piss all over my plague?" she said as Bob caught up.

Martin glared at her liberal use of scripture. "Bob, is you okay?"

"I'm fine, Martin. Thank you. In need of a bowel ejecta, though."

"What does that mean?"

"It means he needs to take a shit. Comprende?"

48.

Walter nibbled at his white beard with an electric trimmer as Chad flew across the Oklahoma Panhandle. A storm cloud blunted Black Mesa, usually a sharp shape that punctuated the flat.

Chad had run out of tobacco so he lodged a purple Tootsie Pop in his cheek instead. In the backseat, Rachel studied a stack of psycho-socials and pre-sentence investigations, cutting and pasting together the several lives of Annie Amstead, AKA Patsy Pringle. On the dash, Walter had set down faxed copies of credit card statements along with a map that connected dots across the belly of the High Plains. They were on to her.

Just outside Guymon, Chad pancaked an armadillo and Walter's trimmer bit into his chin.

"Ow!"

"You know you're in Oklahoma when the roadkill turns from raccoon to armadillo," Chad said.

"Will you slow down!?"

"You just told me to speed it up."

He floored it now. Anything to piss Walter off.

"We should have the U.S. Marshal in on this. I don't like doing this alone," Chad said. "You thought about what you're gonna do if she makes a big stink back in Ukiah?"

Rachel's eyes shot up in a suspicious glance.

"They'll put her in jail wherever we find her, won't they? These are federal charges."

Chad shook his head.

"I thought that's the way they'd handle this," Walter said as he dabbed a hankie to his chin and checked for blood.

"Only 'til extradition. She'll stand trial in Illinois," Chad explained.

Walter cringed.

"And Mom wanted you to have the kids because you had all the brains," Chad remarked.

49.

They paid for the room from Martin's traveling bank. She popped the door and dropped her bag on the bed on the way to the bathroom like she'd done a thousand times.

"Know what it means to have the Y chromosome, boys?"

Bob shrugged at Martin. Their faces were caked with road dust.

"Means you get the shower last." She slammed the door behind her.

"But my bowel movement," Bob protested.

"Intestinal fortitude, Bob," she said behind the door.

The shower squirted on. Bob and Martin looked at each other.

"You and I should get better acquainted," Bob said.

"Okay," Martin replied, holding out his hand.

Bob shook it. They stared at each other for about half a minute.

"I should read," Martin said.

"And I should stare off into space." They retreated to separate corners.

"You should shave, Bob," Patsy said, muffled as she turned off the shower.

Bob felt his whiskers.

"Oh, okay," he said. He fished through Patsy's handbag and came up with a disposable pink razor.

Martin disinterred the Tallman Family Bible from the bottom of his duffel bag. He was on Isaiah now. He liked the way Isaiah sounded when he whispered the words. The bathroom door cracked open and steam drifted out along with Patsy's arm.

"Could you hand me my carpet bag, honey buns?"

Martin held out her bag at arm's length and the bathroom swallowed it. Through the crack, he made out the vague pink of her hips in the fogged-up mirror.

A few minutes later, she paraded out in jeans and a tee shirt. She primped herself in the dresser mirror.

"We can't stay long. Get some rest," she said.

Bob walked by, his jaw pecked with a dozen razor nicks.

"What did you do now?" she said.

"You told me to shave."

"Didn't you use a mirror?" she said. She ripped up a tissue and stuck the pieces on his cuts.

"Mirrors are useless artifacts to me. Useless," he said.

"You used to be able to see yourself in 'em," she recalled, dabbing under his chin.

"That was before we left Illinois. Whenever I leave the state, I become a vampire again. That's why the Illinois State Police put me in Hope House. The last time I crossed the Mississippi, I left a trail of mutilated cows that stretched over three states."

"Yeah, well, it'd be easier on us if you'd just stick with palindromes," she mumbled.

"Lack of red blood cells is interfering with my left hemispheric functioning. I am therefore unable to produce pattering palindromal pentameter. Only blood or alcohol can remediate this."

She slung her purse over her shoulder and did one last mirror check.

"I'm goin' out and get us some grub," she told Martin as he whispered Isaiah. "And stop readin' that. It's warped your mind. I mean it."

She grabbed the clicker, flipped on the TV, and shoved the remote in his hand.

"It's time you widen your horizons. Bob, you keep an eye on 'im," she said. "No, Martin, you watch Bob," she decided, then left the room.

Martin held the remote like a ray gun and surfed through the onscreen menu. He punched the wrong button and accidentally ordered soft porn that popped on in mid-scene. He couldn't change channels fast enough. He ended up on an infomercial and feigned interest in a diamond ring.

But then he surfed back to the porn. Bob pulled the Bible from Martin's lap and sampled Isaiah.

"'The city that was once faithful is behaving like a whore,'" Bob read. "Hey, this is some good stuff here."

Bob delved into Chapter 1, Verse 21. Martin delved into a man and woman in ritual foreplay. The man kissed the woman and squeezed her bottom.

The boy's eyes bulged.

50.

Walter and Chad were talking to a trooper, a young Native man. They stood under the canopy of a diesel island. Truckstop floodlights on high poles fooled moths and gnats by the thousands. The cop who'd nailed Patsy for speeding was in back of the State prowler, his foot slung out the window and bandied up like a homemade puppet. Rachel leaned against the trunk and read Patsy's file.

The Native trooper quizzed Walter. Chad had done most of the talking up until now, but the trooper sniffed something he didn't like. They were hiding something.

"Alright, let me get this straight: this crazy, old hooker kidnaps your son for no reason and brings him cross-country," the trooper said to Walter.

"Why are you interrogating him?" Chad asked. "He's not the suspect."

"I'm trying to extend you a courtesy, Sheriff," the trooper replied. "You're driving a patrol car from Illinois into my state. If you want my help, you just need to bring me on board, okay?"

Chad nodded and crossed his arms, following a moth with his eyes.

"Did your son know this woman?" the trooper said.

"No."

"Did you?"

Walter didn't answer — not with Rachel standing right there. It wasn't prudent to let one's current mistress know about the past mistress. But he could afford to say as much as he'd already told Virginia.

"I knew of her."

Rachel peeked up from her file.

"She used to live in our town," Walter said.

"How long ago?" the trooper asked.

"It was a long time ago. I don't really remember. Her family lived there."

"Did you have any connection to her?"

"She was in my congregation."

"But you weren't the minister back then," Chad clarified.

"That's right. I was in the lay ministry. I volunteered as youth minister. That's about all I remember about her."

"You're sure?" the trooper pressed.

Rachel walked back to Chad's squad, which was parked behind the trooper's. She got in back and closed the windows.

"Yes I'm sure," Walter said, studying her through the windshield.

"Wait here," the trooper said. He walked back to his vehicle, stepped inside, and punched Patsy's name into his computer.

"Let's go home. She ain't coming back," Chad said.

"She has Martin."

"What do you care? He's 18. Looks like he wanted to go."

"He did not. He was happy where he was. She put him up to this. And even if he did want to go, he's not able to decide for himself."

"She can do you a lot of damage if this gets out," Chad said so everyone could hear.

"Shhhh! We can handle it out of town. She's using my credit cards, right? We can get her for that on top of everything else. With the record you say she has, she's in deep trouble. But if I drop all charges, she'll give me Martin."

Walter looked into Chad's car and refrained Rachel's sad gaze with his winning smile. She managed a smile back.

"Yeah, and what if Annie Amstead won't budge? She's already proved she's crazy enough to do this. What if she calls your bluff?"

"He's my son."

"He's your ticket to sainthood."

"You don't know. You've never had kids."

"You tried erasing that ticket before it had a chance to slip out from between her legs," Chad said.

"She took the pills, brother."

"You lock him up in a fancy private jail because he reminds you maybe you ain't such a saint. Now I'm supposed to believe you really want him back?"

"Go to hell."

"Shit rolls up, in this case. Whatsoever seed you plant in a hole is gonna sprout right out of that same hole, know what I mean?" Chad said. They traded smirks.

"Just remember who's up for re-election this November," Walter reminded him.

"And what does that mean?"

"It means your votes are in my pews."

"You think that's why I'm doin' this?"

Walter turned to get in the car, but Chad clamped his arm and spun him back around.

"I'm covering for you, Rev," he said as he jabbed a finger in Walter's chest, "because I made a promise to our mother."

"You covered this up, too. If she talks, it's your job on the line as much as mine. So don't hand me that, Chad."

"I may be a lot of things, but at least I ain't no jailbait fucker."

"When this is over, I don't want to see you anymore. Not on Christmas. Not any time."

"Is that an excommunication? I sure as hell hope so."

The Native trooper stepped out of his car and caught the tail end of their tiff.

"Am I interrupting something?"

Chad glared into the desert black. Walter stared at an oil spot on the concrete.

"Here's what we're going to do," the trooper said, spreading a map out on his hood.

51.

Drivers stood in the aisles — heavyset loners with void eyes; thin, edgy guys with their eyes too beaming to look at head on. They had so many miles up high on wheels, they were like woozy sailors at a port of call still getting used to land.

Patsy stood in the snack aisle and snapped up a couple bags of Doritos, guacamole flavored. She'd read guacamole was healthy. Martin would like that. She liked the idea of buying stuff for him. It's what a mother did.

She glanced through the window into the parking lot. At one of the pump islands, the New Mexico trooper — the Native man — showed an orange WANTED flyer to the truck stop's security officer. The trooper whose foot she ran over sat in back of a prowler with a bandaged foot propped out the window. And Chad's squad was parked in back of that. Chad and Walter met with another trooper, a young woman with long blond hair. Chad showed her another fugitive sheet.

Patsy dropped the Doritos. She ducked her head and snaked through the aisles. She picked up some red hair coloring. She snuck into the back hall, lined with locked shower suites for truckers. A Latina woman scrubbed the washbowl in one. She slipped the woman a sawbuck, put her finger to her lips in a gesture of silence and danced the woman out as she slid inside, locking the door. She ripped open the hair coloring, punched on the clear plastic gloves and scrubbed her hair red, banishing the black to her roots. It took ten years off her. It was a perfect match with Martin's, and with Annie Amstead's. When she finished, she slicked it back like a greaser would.

She crept out of the stall. The Heat and the Light outside were gone — squads, crucifixes, and all. Then she spotted Chad chatting up one of the cashiers inside the mart. He showed her Patsy's WANTED poster. Patsy bent low and swiped a pair of reading glasses from a carousel. She duck-walked to the restaurant gallery.

She cut through the restaurants and waded out into the truck lot. On the other side, the La Playa Casino drizzled neon. It was 2:30 in the morning, but there were enough cars in the lot that she could use them for cover. She crossed under a stadium-sized jumbotron that flashed promos and ducked inside the casino.

The entrance hall was a dank and empty Pueblo heritage center with native pottery behind glass. She rushed through its quiet into a radioactive world. Armies of machines pulsed with psychedelic colors — poker machines, slots, keno. High-pitched whirs and hypnotic purrs blared like a marching band of robots. She waded neck-deep into a synesthesia that drowned the queasy warning in her stomach. In treatment, they'd told her that a place like this was an HRS — a High Risk Situation.

Patsy's HRS had a main pit in the middle of the building. The pit was fixed with Pension Pissers —white-haired RV couples playing blackjack. There were truckers dead-headed from the road and there were the locals, hooked on their own machines. No matter where they came from, they wore keyed-up masks. The ones on the machines tumbled toward trance. The ones at the tables leaned into mania. But underneath the masks, she knew, they were all the same: empty, looking to fill what Walter called the God hole. She twisted through the crowd.

The portal to the lounge beckoned like a black hole, utter and cool. Raunchy R & B staggered out the door in heavy stanzas. It was the kind of music that killed plants, she often said. After she got clean she refused to play it.

The icebox smells at the door knifed her: bar brand whiskey, whore lilac, the breath of ashes. She stumbled inside the cave, blind from the collapse of the casino nova. Bass beat at the walls. Truckers wobbled on the stools. Two lot lizards had tied themselves to different drivers.

One had a split lip and she might have to go down in price just to earn. Competition registered in that woman's eyes when she saw Patsy. Patsy had to think fast: who was providing protection? Who let the girls work here? That's where the danger would come from.

She needed a driver to smuggle them out of the truck stop. She slid in next to a pony-tailed Anglo about 25. The young ones were the worst, but at least this one didn't have a trick babe grabbing ass.

"Hi," Patsy wooed.

The man gawked at her reading glasses.

"There's somethin' ya gotta know," he mumbled in a half-stoned, Chicago slurry.

"Ya from Chicawgo?" Patsy said just the way a South Sider would.

"Yup."

"Me, too. Sout Side Irish." She pinched a few strands of her red.

"I'm occupado," the man replied. A skinny hooker with a cracked face stepped out from the Ladies room.

"Aw shit," Patsy whispered as she took off her glasses.

"You got a permit, bitch? I don't think so. Luis!" she called. "This one ain't in our stable."

A heavy-set man swaggered out from a corner booth. Patsy had missed him in her initial scan. The bartender was probably getting a percentage, so he let it play out. Luis grabbed Patsy's scalp in back. But with her hair so short, she twisted out, grabbed a beer mug, and smashed it over his head. Luis moaned and withered down to the floor.

"See ya," Patsy said.

She grabbed Chicago's money off the bar and ran out the side door.

52.

Martin sat on the bed, memorizing Patsy's letter. Bob watched C-SPAN and counted a House floor vote. Patsy burst back in and didn't bother to close the door.

"You hair," Martin said.

"We gotta go," she said, jamming clothes in her handbag.

"What we do is wrong: stealing, running from the police, going places where womens take off they clothes."

"Get your things."

He held up the letter.

"This says those things lead to a life of regret."

She grabbed the letter on the way to the bathroom, crumpled it, and dropped it. He rushed over and snatched it up.

"You has no respet for peoples. So peoples has no respet for you." He smoothed out the letter.

She threw his Bible and jacket in his bag.

"I is going to L.A. alone."

"On what, a wild ass?"

He ripped the duffel bag away from her and headed for the door. She went around him, slammed it and blocked his path. He cocked a fist.

"Go ahead, pardner. It's been done."

"Get out my way, Patsy."

"You're so pissed? You think you're the only one been life's chew toy? Go on, unload."

He rolled his fist in circles.

"Get out my way, and my life!"

"No." She held onto the door frame.

"Yes!"

"You couldn't kill nobody."

"You could not either. So I do not need you."

"I couldn't?"

She held out her suicide scars.

"Got the guts to do this?"

His mouth fell open. She knew he'd never seen them before. But she also knew the two of them were just between rounds. He went for the door handle. She locked her heel against the bottom of the door.

"I know what it's like to have nobody on your side, to be locked up," she said.

He picked her up and tossed her over his shoulder.

"You don't wanna kill nobody, and you don't want her locked up!"

He dumped her on Bob's lap and strode out.

"They're lookin' for us out there!" she shouted.

In the lot, two troopers checked the plates on the lone motorcycle at the far end. Walter and Rachel stood there too, with the security guard. Another two police, flanked by Chad, walked toward Patsy's room. Martin looked away and tried to play it cool. Patsy spilled out after him and crooked her arm around his, pretending they were a couple. They strolled toward the wall of black where the desert started. In seconds, they'd be untraceable. Then Bob popped his head out. He opened an imaginary trench coat and pretended to expose himself to the police.

"That's them," Chad said.

"You! Stop, arms wide!" a trooper screamed. Bob ran.

Martin and Patsy bolted in lockstep.

"Martin!" Rachel called out.

He froze and Patsy fell off his arm. Bob caught up. Patsy pulled at Martin until he ran with her. In a leap it seemed that they dissolved into a black hole. They stumbled over clumps of Mormon tea and bunchgrass. A bat chirped as it zigzagged through a diagonal sheet of moon that sliced the clouds. Bob chased after it.

"My ex!"

53.

They trudged a good 300 yards from the interstate. A squad's road lights strobed the highway. Its search beam scorched a narrow margin of range beyond the road.

Martin tried to leave them both behind. The sand murdered Patsy's high-heels.

"There's scorpions out here. I can handle roaches, 'n rats, but if it's one thing I can't abide, it's scorpions."

Bob picked one up by its tail.

"Probably the first creature to venture forth from the sea," Bob observed as he let it crawl up his arm. "Maybe it could give you personality lessons."

Patsy saw it and screamed.

He slipped it in his shirt pocket and patted it.

Martin ran up against a stretch of range fence and vaulted it with a scissor kick.

"Martin? I can't see you no more!" She hit the wire. "Martin, I can't get over this thing!"

He picked up the pace.

"Please, honey. Oh, I forgot you can't handle that word. But I mean it like you 'n I were related."

She stumbled into a sheep and screamed. It baaed back, a little indignant. Up ahead, Martin halted, the moon freezing his breath.

He hiked back to the fence, grabbed the wire and held it down where it broke from the post. His taut fists wrung out a stream of moon-washed blood as Patsy and Bob stepped over.

"Thank you," she said. "Martin, we can't go on. They're gonna tag us, so you gotta know…"

She wanted the words to come up. They had to. She'd feel sick forever if they didn't. Spilling out that secret was like kicking her last drug.

"You may think you know who I am," she trailed off.

A talon reached up into her pipes and strangled the words, dragging the cracked syllables back down to the hole where a person hid things they hoped would die. But there the secret festered and gnawed and turned into the part of her that wanted to see her dead. She'd pick up again one day unless those words came out. She just wasn't ready and she didn't know why. Maybe it was self-preservation or the fear that if she told him who she really was, he'd run right back to his father and have the second half of his life ruined too. So she reached for other words as he waited for her to say whatever it was she needed to let out so bad.

"I wanna show you things," she wheezed. "Like how to get a job, how to know when you're in love…"

"My dad already 'dopt me."

"But I won't have to."

There. She'd said it. She'd finally let the dog out. Did he get it? Was it too nuanced for him? He red-eyed her with a familiar snarl instead of unfamiliar shock. He hadn't gotten it. She tried again from the other end of the tale.

"I never did tell you 'bout your daddy."

"He takes me in. From his doorstep in swaddling clothes in a basket, like Moses floating down the Nile. He takes me in."

He seemed to be heading her off. He seemed to know she was going to tell him a secret about Walter. He read *those* thoughts well enough, she observed.

"No one else cares to give up they lives. He sacrifices his happiness. For me."

"So did your mother, but in the opposite way."

"No, she is off happy somewhere."

"She left 'cuz she thought it was best for you. And she's paid by bein' unhappy."

"She does not pay. I do."

"You know what remorse is?"

She tickled his cheek with her fingers and that seemed to calm him.

"Remorse is achin' to change somethin' that's past. It's dyin' all over again every time the sun comes up 'cuz you can't change it."

She brushed his hair out of his eyes and he closed them.

"Remorse is the worst prison there is. It's worse than a jail cell. People can say you ain't guilty. They can tell you you did your time. But you know better." She let it sink in. "Your mother has to carry 'round what she did the rest of her life."

"Me too."

He marched on.

"How do you know so much about her?" Bob asked Patsy as the two of them followed.

"She told me," Patsy said.

She decided to make up a story, a story she knew Martin would devour even though he'd pretend not to hear.

"I was — I *am*, I should say, somebody who's known Martin's mother since she was as old as Moses was when they found 'im floatin' in the bulrushes. When she was little, Martin's momma tried to be her own mother's best daughter, to be the most behaved little girl on Glass Factory Road. But she never measured up," she said. "Not in her own eyes. And when she couldn't be the best at bein' good, she decided to be the best at bein' bad. She became the Prodigal Daughter, goin' off and squanderin' her good looks on wine, 'n wickedness 'n …oh, whatever else it is that makes people go prodigal. Then she'd come to in the morning and she'd feel so horrid 'bout all the things she did the night before, she drank 'n drugged 'til she drooled. She was pronounced dead twice at the hospital."

"That's nothing," Bob said. "I'm pronounced dead every morning at sunrise."

"It took 'er a long time to come to 'er senses. Years. I was the one who finally helped her with that. One morning, after a real bad bout a boozin',

I came and had a talk with her. I made her some real good apple pan-cakes, and I asked her, I said: 'Patsy, I mean, Annie, you know why you been sufferin' and destroyin' yourself all these years? It's 'cuz you can't live with what you done to Martin. But feelin' shame and callin' yourself a whore and a terrible mom is just an excuse so you don't have to own up and face him.' That's what I told her."

They scrambled down an arroyo and followed that for a while.

"Then what happened?" Bob wondered.

"Then, I nursed 'er back to health, and helped 'er write those letters to Martin," she explained. "She wanted to come to Ukiah herself, but she knew as soon as she set foot in that town, Martin's daddy woulda had Uncle Chad arrest her for Abandonment and Irresponsibility. So, she sent me to deliver the message instead."

"Well you know, it's often cathartic to kill the messenger," Bob replied.

54.

Martin stared at his palms, crusted with blood from where the fence wire had cut in. Patsy limped on one heel and one pump without a heel. They dragged themselves down a deserted, two-lane road. No road signs, no billboards. Nothing but rangeland. Bob hadn't seen 'rainwater' since somewhere back by I-40.

They'd turned north and crossed under the interstate through a drainage ditch before sunrise. She knew they were on Navajoland, a tawny and rusty and piney green region that sprawled over parts of three states for 22,000 square miles. Spider Woman had scattered the first ancestors of about 170,000 Diné in a nation that vast.

Not one vehicle had come up behind them since sunrise. They'd passed a few trucks heading south on the way down to Gallup but nothing heading toward Shiprock. Patsy figured they could hold up there until their trail went cold. Walter might look for them in L.A., but he'd never connect her to a place like Shiprock. Ink's people lived there and Patsy knew them well. She'd detoxed there.

"You need to get away from old playmates and old playgrounds," Ink had said before he rode her there from L.A. just eighteen months before.

They wandered a Sinai of mummified dunes and the whittled bones of volcanoes. The only man-thing for 360 degrees was a hogan shaped from earth and timber and corrugated metal. It slumbered in the shadow of a mesa.

She glanced at her watch. Only 8:30. She stopped to wipe her face and Bob bumped into her.

"You got a million square kilo-miles of desert. That ain't enough room for you!?"

"Sorry."

Martin kept trudging. She and Bob needed water. She wondered if Martin did.

"You can't just keep walkin' forever. You'll get desert sick."

She didn't even know if there was such a thing. She hustled to catch up and they walked abreast. After a while, they got a rhythm going.

"Game clock, game clock, game clock," Bob muttered with each step.

"What does that mean?" Martin asked.

"Every time my left foot goes down, it says 'game.' And my right foot sounds like 'clock,'" he said.

A vehicle popped over a hill behind them — a black pickup. Patsy cocked her thumb like a pistol hammer and wagged it. The F-150 jetted by, whipping up a dust devil behind it.

"'Land of Enchantment,'" Bob coughed as he read the New Mexico plate.

An hour passed before another pickup did, but it was headed the wrong way. Heat shot through their soles from the tarry road. Even Martin panted. They spotted the carcass of a minivan off the road and headed for it. It was a pretzel of metal filled with owl shit and old beer cans, but they climbed inside anyway and hunkered down in its shade.

"We need water," she breathed. "Would you agree?"

Martin fingered salty jewels from his forehead and lanced them with his tongue. He nodded.

"We could always kill Bob," she panted. "Drink his blood."

Bob shot up and nodded.

Martin sent her a sick look.

"A joke," she said.

Bob seemed disappointed.

Martin's ears pricked. He looked toward the road. A pillar of dust rose in the south. Bob sat up.

"Let's go," Bob said. They scrambled out of the wreck and ran for the road. Salvation clarified through the mirage — the fuselage of a battered, baby blue school bus, a mini-bus, mounted on the bed of a grease truck with a bullnose cab — all of it forty years out of the factory. Its exhaust pipe scraped sparks up off the pavement.

Patsy waved and it slowed.

Maybe back in the 60s, someone had painted KNOW-PLEASURE-KNOW-PAIN-NO-PLEASURE-NO-PAIN-KNOW-PLEASURE-NO-PAIN across the side in a circle with a yin-yang filling its center. Martin and Bob hitched up ahead, but the truck-bus stopped in front of Patsy. She beamed her trademark smile at the driver. He gassed it and stopped in front of the men.

"This one's gay. I'll put money on it," she said as she listed on a single heel toward the sick and trembling people mover.

The driver cranked the door open with a jury-rigged lever. His wrinkles had wrinkles and taut pigtails dangled to his waist. He'd combed out his Amish beard like an apron.

"This thing got air?" she asked.

55.

The ceiling on the inside was white and it was signed in black paint with dozens of well-wishes like an old leg cast: *Good luck, Matthew. Matthew, nice knowing ya! Thanks for the ride, Matthew.*

"Where you headed?" Patsy asked as Matthew levered the door closed and coaxed his vehicle back on the road.

He considered her question, mulled possible responses. "Forward," he decided.

"Well, if you make it as far forward as Shiprock, you can let us off there," she said, disguising her sense of entitlement as best she could.

Her nose sniffed the scent of curry powder. The back wall of the truck's cab was punched out so the bus's body and the cab shelled one living space, if it could be called that. Rosaries of dried dates and ristras of wrinkled chili peppers draped the back window, swaying with the turns and jittering with the bumps. Jars of black beans were taped into gray wooden shelves built below homemade benches with mismatched couch cushions from across the ages. Bob held up a burlap bag filled with salt.

"Would it be alright, Captain, if I filled my main, multipurpose orifice with this fungible commodity, lest I rend the flesh of all hands aboard come nightfall?"

"It all depends on what your main, multipurpose orifice is," Matthew replied.

Bob opened his mouth and pointed at it.

Matthew shrugged and nodded.

"Wish the sun would just knock you off like it does every other God fearin' Nosferatu," Patsy grumbled as she fell back on a Mexican blanket and closed her eyes.

"My dominant human genes permit me abroad during the day," Bob explained.

He poured an ample heap of salt in his mouth. He stretched out on the floor, crossed his arms over his chest and went to sleep. Martin rode shotgun. Matthew pulled out a Meerschaum pipe with half the stem broken off and packed it with rose petals and white sage. He fired up, filling the bus with a wavy blue pall. Martin coughed.

"So, you're going to Shiprock," Matthew said to him.

"L.A.," said Martin.

Matthew glanced at Patsy in his rearview mirror. With a shake of her head, she pleaded him with him not to tell Martin that L.A. was in another direction.

Matthew savored the silence with thick pulls on his Meerschaum. After about half an hour, his curiosity finally piqued.

"What do you plan to do in L.A.?"

"Find my mom."

More silence, ten minutes' worth. Outside, the neck of a dead volcano pierced the red dunes that were fixed into place by prickly pear and century plants.

Martin saw Patsy's reflection in the windshield, caught her tricolored fingernails wandering to his duffel bag. They tried to snatch the lilac envelope in which she'd slipped her last letter to him. He spun around.

"Quit doing that Patsy," he scolded. He turned back ahead. "She steals," he told Matthew.

"That's alright. I don't have much of anything back there but an overabundance of head lice," Matthew said.

They rode up highway 491. Old green highway signs tacked over the new ones identified it as old route 666. They flitted past villages so small they seemed to be just names for things they could spot along the road: Sheep Springs or Little Water.

The billboard oracles, silent since Kansas, reemerged from the desert. One showed a pregnant Native American woman — *CARE FOR THE GIFT INSIDE. DON'T WAIT UNTIL IT'S TOO LATE.* They passed a Navajo double-wide church with a portable marquee: *JESUS IS COMING. ARE YOU READY TO MEET HIM?*

Martin stumbled back over Bob and yanked his duffel bag and envelope from Patsy's reach. She pretended to sleep. He took in her lithesome body as it hiccupped with every bump in the road. She snuck a peek as he swayed back to the front, hugging his personalty close: the family Bible, some underwear, her letter to him. She wondered what meant more to him at that moment — the Tallman Bible or the letter she'd written him.

Matthew never took his eyes off the road.

"Has it been a long time since you've seen your mother?" he asked.

Martin nodded. "Is it a long time since you see you mom?"

"She died."

He whispered his condolences and waited a polite interval. Then he pulled Patsy's letter from his bag and smoothed it out as best he could.

"Could my mom change? And not want to see me again because she gets a new life? New kids? A husband who does not want me? A real family?" His face was wrinkled like the letter.

Matthew took a minute formulating a response.

"What do you think she'll be like?" he asked Martin.

Martin dipped into his bag and came out with a glossy paper folded twice in meticulous quarters. He unfolded it, liberating the red-haired woman he'd framed like an altar Madonna at Hope House. She was Rachel in a vague way. He handed it to Matthew.

"Where'd you get this?"

"The magazine."

"Moms don't come from magazines," Matthew said as he handed it back.

"They sure don't," Patsy yawned, rising and stretching. She spotted an old Gibson steel-string leaning in the corner. She picked it up.

"You mind?" she asked.

"Uh-uh," said Matthew.

She strummed some chords from Van Morrison's "Into the Mystic" and didn't miss a note. Patsy never did. She could hear a song once and play back a perfect rendition. It didn't matter whether it was classical or heavy metal blues. And the music she chose always fit wherever and however she was. She'd always thought of "Into the Mystic" as a leaving song, one she wanted played at her memorial. She had everything all picked out for that. But she never wrote any of it down.

Gentle chords merged with Matthew's pipe smoke and then went their own way again. Mountains without names swaddled the high desert plains. Mesas tilted into the earth, sewn in by pink graveyards of talus. Further north, across the Colorado border, the La Plata Mountains were distant, blue plans in her future. To Patsy, they were the roof of the church Ukiah always thought would save her.

Matthew's hybrid vessel squeezed through sandstone spires with badland finish on either side of the road. She wondered what her boy thought of this raw plateau. What was it like to see this place for the first time? She was his age when she'd first seen mountains. Back then, an MDA trance transmogrified Sleeping Ute Mountain into a warrior god raised up on behalf of his people. A village, Towaoc, slumbered on the slope of the mountain. The five-mile god wore it on his shoulder like a talisman. While she'd watched, Sleeping Ute rose from the earth and vanquished an army of giants made from mesas to destroy the Utes. And she knew that the god had fought for all peoples and won. Seeing that battle had been a primeval ecstasy, but she hadn't earned the right to the experience.

This time, she'd earned her right to it. Salvation didn't only belong to people like the Tallmans. And she hadn't come to it out of virtue like they had. She'd gotten lost believing she needed to be good before she could stand inside paradise. But that wasn't the way it worked for her. She had to need rescue first. She was driven into its arms by pain, not goodness. She'd earned the goddamned right.

It didn't matter she saw it all through so much bug juice on Matthew's windshield. That didn't make her deliverance any less profound. If she focused on the windshield, all she'd see were dead bugs. But if she set her eyes on the red temples outside turned umber by the sun, the distractions fell away. She hoped Martin could look past her track marks and suicide scars and see the monument in her.

Up ahead, a shark's tooth erupted a thousand feet above the plain. Patsy crept over and crouched by Martin's ear.

"That's Shiprock, hun," she whispered so as not to bridle the awe. "The Navajo people who care for this land call it the Rock with Wings."

"It looks like it can fly. Like a rocket ship," he whispered back.

"They say it brought them here from the North. Those are the wings," she said, pointing to fantails of dark lava that spread like castle walls from the monolith itself.

Even Matthew took his eyes off the road and glimpsed it. They shared solitude. What was it Daddy told her as a child? Whenever two or three were gathered in God's name, there God was.

Then two lanes divided into four, and the billboard gods picked up their relentless chant. Bob sat up, salt crusted around his lips.

He pointed to the old highway marker. "Do you mean to tell me all this time we've been on highway 666, and I slept right through it?"

"That's right," Matthew said. "We also passed Dead Man's Wash and Many Devils Wash."

Cliffs, tie-dyed in pink and bone, brooded beyond the highway as their bus-truck approached a dusty, sprawling town. They crossed over the San Juan River with galleries of cottonwoods on its banks.

They rode into Shiprock proper. Crows scattered from a carcass in the middle of the highway and dogs roamed the shoulder with noses to the sand. Kids played basketball in the dirt. A giant billboard Jesus glowered down at a porn shop's comers and goers. *JESUS IS WATCHING.*

They passed the lots where the Begaye Flea Market set up shop each Saturday morning, offering mutton and fry bread, Navajo rugs and heavy metal CDs. Matthew clattered into a gas station. Patsy begged some money from Martin to pay for gas.

Matthew got out and pumped the tank full. Patsy, Martin, and Bob watched through the window as a busy woman with California plates rushed to fill up. A speckled dog with sharp ribs cowered up to her from the lot's edge, but the woman didn't notice.

"Folks come 'n go, but no one wants to be in places like this, 'cuz they think their lives are somewhere else," Patsy said as the woman jabbered on her cell. "So there's no eyes, no alms. Just hurry in, get it done, hurry out. Wam bam. What people don't see is that how they show up in places like fillin' stations is just about how they'll show up in the rest of their lives."

"A philosopher whore," Bob remarked.

She raised her leg to kick him, but then thought better of it. "No, just a whore," she replied.

Matthew paid up and climbed back in. Patsy scanned the lot. No police. "Boss, I think we'll get out here," she told Matthew.

"I'm going to Oregon," he said. "You're welcome to come along."

She smelled the air. A rain was on its way and it didn't rain here often. The offer might change everything, if Martin would go along.

"Martin, why don't we take Matthew up on his offer and go on up to Oregon with 'im? You haven't seen the ocean 'til you've seen it from Oregon, and we can get off anyplace we like."

He squinted like he was considering it.

Please please please say yes! she pled from inside.

He shook Matthew's hand.

"Matthew: that means gift from God," Martin told him, and Matthew smiled.

Martin stepped onto the pavement. She gulped hard, watching Oregon evaporate out there in the sun. Matthew handed Patsy his old six string.

"You'll get more out of this than I will."

"Why, thank you." She teared up and pecked him on the cheek.

Bob followed Martin out onto the tarmac and she watched them move into the shade.

"When that boy finds out I'm the one he's lookin' for, he plans to do me in," she choked.

"He may scare the hell out of you and take you just as you are," Matthew said.

She looked at him, surprised, scared, delighted by what he said.

She stepped outside. Her boys followed her out of the shade of the fuel island and down one of the few streets off highway 64. A pink cottage shrouded by a silvery canopy of cottonwoods and wreathed in Manzanita bushes stood by itself behind a school bus lot. She maundered to the door and knocked.

56.

Nellie stood under the awning in back of her clapboard house, which was denuded of the fresh coat of paint an Easterner might give it. She was sunny and plump and so nearsighted that it was hard to see her eyes behind her thick glasses. Nellie's jowls disappeared with her modest smile and gray weeds poked out from her black ponytail. She and Merissa, her only daughter, laughed as Patsy rolled around in their backyard dirt like she was one of the dogs attacking her.

"Brains, you bitch!" Patsy screamed at the heavyset chow-mix.

"Don't you mean 'bastard,' or whatever?" Merissa said. "He's a boy."

"Cassidy!" Patsy shouted, scratching the other mutt's ears.

Cassidy had a burnt-auburn freckle hanging over each eye. The rest of her was sleek and raven black. Like a lot of the pariah-dogs on the rez, she had some Aussie sheep dog in her. The third animal, 7 2 11, had been so riddled with ticks before Patsy found him, he'd almost bled to death.

Patsy slapped the dog pack off her and stood up. "Oh, it is so good to see you." She squeezed Nellie and Merissa one more time. "You kept your promise. You kept the dogs."

Martin and Bob stood against the fence. They saw the salt in Patsy's eyes, her nose moist as the dogs'.

"And you kept your promise too," she told the pack. "You're alive." She sobbed and knelt in the shit-infested yard, where rawhides slathered in dog spit ruled the late afternoon. Her arms hooked around the dogs. Brains' tawny hide was still riddled with old BBs where kids had used him for target practice.

Patsy gazed up at the cottonwoods and smiled as the sun filtered through to dappel her cheeks. This was where she'd kicked a year-and-a-half before. Ink had ridden her out from L.A. on his Hog. Nellie was his older sister. She and Merissa watched over Patsy until the termites had worked their way out from under her skin. Patsy had left that old skin in their hands.

"Let's go inside and eat," Nellie said.

She made them Campbell's cream of mushroom soup and tacos.

"Sit down boys," she said to Martin and Bob, who were glued to the kitchen wall.

They took seats around the table. Tacos rotated in the clunking microwave. She pulled them out and set them steaming on a red checkered tablecloth. Patsy's boys stared at them with eyes unable to contain hunger, but they looked at Nellie like dogs waiting for permission.

"Go ahead. It don't bite," she said.

Their hands lunged and their jaws snaked around the huge shells of fried flour stuffed with mutton, sinking down, crunching. Nellie glanced at Patsy.

"They haven't ate in a couple days," Patsy explained.

Nellie nodded. She understood hunger. She and Ink had been born deep in the rez, where you went to school hungry sometimes, and if you were lucky and had a good teacher, she'd bring you snacks to eat. They moved to Shiprock when they were kids. When their parents died, Ink left home for the Marines. But he never forgot his sisters. He still sent Nellie a money order every month. She was his favorite.

Merissa, 16 and bored as hell in an outpost like Shiprock, shot questions at Patsy: How was Ink? What was Patsy doing? What was Illinois like? How did she know Bob? Bob looked a little homeless. Was he?

"How do you know Martin?" she finally asked.

Merissa really didn't know how Patsy knew Martin. Nellie looked down at the table and waited for the embarrassment to lift. Nellie knew about Martin. Patsy had left every single john and pimp and scam in Nellie's ear one night a year-and-a-half ago. Shiprock was a place where secrets seemed safe. And at the bottom of the pile of dirty little tricks was the big secret that had fathered them all. And Nellie hadn't told a soul. Ink was the only other person who knew.

"Martin's a friend, right Pats?" Nellie said.

"A friend, that's right," Patsy agreed.

The moment passed, and Patsy filled them in on the last eighteen months. She'd made Nellie and Merissa promise to keep the dogs, who circled the table looking for scraps. Some Navajo didn't understand the Anglo regard for strays, but Nellie did.

"Did Patsy tell you how she named these critters?" she asked Martin.

"No, ma'am." Martin shook his head with a chewy smile.

Merissa tried to capture his eye with the interest in her own. She had a cherub's face framed by shimmering hair and she tried to charm him with both.

"Patsy found Brains just after she detoxed," Nellie said.

"Got well," Patsy corrected.

"Oh, y-yeah," Nellie said. "She found him wandering the desert just north of town. She tried herding him into the truck, but Brains hid under the front axle. So Patsy takes this burrito she got at Taco Bell and sticks it in front of the dog's nose."

Brains fell onto his front paws, delighted in the tale of his own salvation. Martin's eyes were sucked into the story. It was just like Moses floating down the Nile.

"Then she puts the taco —"

"Burrito!" Patsy said.

"Taco, burrito, whatever. She puts it in the back of the Toyota, keeps the hatch open so the dog could follow it in. Sure enough, after about a minute, Brains sniffs on up to the gate and jumps in. So I'm standing outside watching this. I refused to have anything to do with it. Patsy runs out and slams the back gate. But she forgets to close the driver's door, and Brains runs out the truck with the burrito! That's how a dog outsmarted a woman," Nellie finished, laughing.

Everybody laughed. The ache in Patsy's chest and the chatter in her head had been tailing her ever since she left Hope House, but the laughter chased them away. Her insides had hit home. No matter where she was, she'd never feel home. No matter who she was with, she'd never feel like it was family. She'd spend weeks chasing a guy, and when she got him, it was somebody else she wanted, or nobody at all. When she was a girl, all she could think about was busting out of Ukiah. But when she was on the road, she longed for a place to lay her head down and call home.

Here, now, was finally good enough. As she cast her eyes across the table, she lapped up Martin's shy smile with her own. She thought about staying. Not on the rez — an Anglo couldn't live here unless she worked for the Navajo Nation. But nearby, maybe in Farmington. Her smile fluttered off. She knew Martin would never go for it.

"She lures Cassidy to my same Toyota just a week later from behind City Market," Nellie went on as she coaxed muddy coffee from an old tin percolator. "Cassidy was just a pup. She was so starving. We could see the bones sticking out of her rear. It was hard to look at that. But Patsy fattened her up in two weeks. There was a man Patsy had a crush on from our church."

"Manuelito Cassidy," Merissa teased.

"So we named her that," Nellie said.

Martin lost his smile for a moment and Patsy knew why. It was the fear that maybe, just maybe, she'd bump into this Manuelito Cassidy and he'd steal her away. She knew when a guy was long for her. Her radar was infallible that way.

"You know," Nellie said as she wrinkled Cassidy's scalp with leather fingers, "I thought you were crazy when you picked them up."

"What about 7 2 11?" Bob asked as he scratched 7's ears in an expert kind of way.

"Oh, that one's kind of obvious, Bob. The convenience stores. You know: '7 2 11,'" Nellie said.

"Seven. Eleven. Seven," Bob muttered as an old switch flipped back on for him.

"Don't you start, Bob," Patsy warned.

"But the equation, the Grand U.N.ified Theory —"

"Why don't you just 'game clock' on out into the yard, okay?"

"Patsy is kind," Martin said as he looked on her.

"Yes, she is," Nellie said. "She nursed these dogs to health. They would've died without her."

"They nursed *me* back," Patsy said. "They did more for me than I ever did for them."

"Finding somebody to help when you need help is the best medicine," Bob said.

"Why yes. Yes it is, Bob," Patsy said.

7 2 11 slobbered on Martin's lap. Martin looked into his eyes — one brown, one blue.

"His eyes is different colors," he said.

"That's a prophetic trait, isn't it?" Patsy asked Nellie.

"Some people think so," said Nellie.

"Oh, that's so rez," Merissa scoffed.

"He has to go to the bathroom," Martin said.

"No, he won't want to go out until two in the morning," Merissa said.

"I think he has to go now," he said politely.

"Is he letting you know, Martin?" Nellie teased.

"Yes."

"Let's go, 7!" Merissa said.

The dogs all launched toward the door and poured outside with her. She watched 7 from the door as he lifted his leg and muddied the dirt. In less than a minute, they all flooded back onto the old linoleum, their claws dirty. Merissa glimmered at Martin. "How'd you know?" she asked, more smitten than ever.

"Martin can… 'read' people. Animals, too, I guess," Patsy said.

Merissa's eyes burgeoned with questions.

"Everybody has it," he explained, anticipating her. "Animals has it, too."

"Everybody —"

"Some people forget they has it. It becomes weak."

Outside of Rachel, this was the most he'd told anybody about his radar. Nellie leaned into Patsy's ear and whispered: "You got someone special there."

They moved into the living room and talked late into the night, sponging up pots of Nellie's heavy crude coffee with cornbread. Nellie splashed them with a collage of Ink stories — about how he tried to rescue his family from a troupe of Boy Scouts he mistook for German soldiers after he'd seen *The Battle of the Bulge*; and how he got drunk, stole a biplane, and tried to fly to Chinle. The problem was he'd never flown an airplane before, so he drove it there instead. Patsy updated the collage with newer stories of Ink sober. He was still rescuing people.

Martin nodded off by one and Bob lasted until three. But Nellie and Patsy stayed up until five, their faces burnished with the amber bulbs Nellie put in all the lamps because she thought they made the room look like she had a fireplace.

"Where's your brother?" Patsy asked Merissa. She was talking about Delaney, Merissa's twin.

"Huffin' gas at the bottom of some arroyo," Merissa said with disdain.

"Merissa!" Nellie scolded.

"Why lie? It's true," Merissa yawned. "Where you heading, Patsy?"

Patsy gnawed on her cuticle. For a few hours, she'd forgotten all about Abandonment and Irresponsibility and whether that crime was punishable by death.

"I don't know," she said softly, so as not to wake Martin.

Merissa looked back and forth between Nellie and Patsy. "Obviously, I've hit classified information," she said.

"Nighty-night, Merissa," Nellie agreed.

"Good night." She bent down and hugged Patsy.

"How long are you in town?" Nellie asked as soon as Merissa went to bed. Patsy knew what she meant. It was a follow up to Merissa's bomb. She really meant: "What are your plans? How did you get Martin? What the hell are you doing with Bob?"

"I…ran into some trouble back in Illinois, Nell."

"You can stay as long as you need to."

"I know. You 'n Ink — you're like my only family." She held back grateful tears.

"Does he know who you are?" Nellie whispered, nodding at Martin.

Patsy shook her head.

Nellie looked at Martin slumbering in the easy chair, his head leaning on the chair's shoulder.

"The only reason I ask is, he looks at you kind of funny, Pats, ya know?" Nellie said.

"I just don't think he's ready to know," Patsy said. The worry lines in her forehead crunched. Patsy cried silent and dry.

"One day, he will be," Nellie said.

She smiled and clasped Patsy's hand.

Patsy leaned over and buried her face in Nellie's bosom, keeping her close for a long time.

57.

Nellie drove them as far as Kayenta, a town south of Monument Valley. From there, Patsy bought them a ride to Tuba City from a long-haul trucker who had an empty can. She felt safe as long as they stayed on Navajoland. You didn't run into people out here who cared about a white person's crimes in the white world.

As they sailed southwest through the reservation, ossified reefs floated in sky islands and light fell like water through breaks in the clouds. They'd follow the rim of a cliff for miles. Outlines of soft-shouldered mountains stood in gunmetal cloaks on the far sides of wide, bottomless valleys.

Baby bangers cranked house and did grinds with their skateboards along the curb. If she blurred her eyes, they could've been Latino instead of Diné and this could've been L.A. instead of Tuba City. The kids didn't pay any attention to the reedy, red-haired boy towed by the older lady through the mini-mart parking lot. But Bob was aged cheese by now. They couldn't help but whiff a man who refused to bathe in anything but rainwater.

That night, they bedded down in a decent room for a change — one with two doubles. Patsy flicked on the tube. She wanted to catch the crime shows to see if she was still news. Melissa Pryne was on Court TV flashing stills of the latest missing, blue-eyed, blonde mother and the prime suspect: her handsome, preppy husband. Bob fell onto the bed and into a TV trance.

"I love TV. It gives me something not to think about," he said.

Patsy kicked him out of bed with an umpire's thumb. She plopped down and gawked at Melissa's thick pancake.

"Jesus, woman, give up 30," she said. "'Bout the only things holdin' that face together are Maybelline and bone." She turned to Bob. "I don't have to do that. I don't even wear base."

"I see her on TV. She use to be a procsecutor," Martin said as Melissa's *Be on the Lookout* segment came on.

"Prosecutor," she corrected him.

Her heart pounded. She didn't want to be the scumbag of the day.

"Okay, dodged that one," she sighed as APB segued into a teaser before a break. "Melissa's taken aim at a border-hoppin' bank robber instead."

"What is a prosecutor?" Martin said.

"Someone who's sexually frustrated and takes it out on others," she said.

Melissa voiced over her missing persons feature, to be shown on the other side of the break. A photo of Bob with a lusty smile and a sad one of Patsy flashed above a picture of Martin. A heart-and-question-mark graphic linked Patsy to Bob as possible lovers. Melissa fed the spot —

"In our Missing in Action segment, you help us connect the dots. Are this man and woman, mental escapees and kidnappers of an innocent disabled teen, lovers?"

"Look. That's us! That's us!" Bob hopped and pointed.

Patsy jerked the alarm clock from the socket and line-drived it at the TV. The clock shattered against the wall.

"Get your fuckin' story straight!" she screamed at Melissa. She glared at Bob. He wiggled his eyebrows for her.

"Get!" she launched up, pointing to the bathroom. He ran inside.

She flipped off the TV and steamed. Her and Bob? *Her and Bob?* What the fuck were they thinking?

She glanced over to see if Martin was watching. He was frozen in the corner.

"Sorry 'bout my temper. I work on it and work on it, and I don't seem..." she trailed off.

"Everybody gets mad. 'Do not let the sun go down on you anger,' Jesus says."

She nodded and chewed on his verse like it was a vegetable she hated.

"Resentment's anger that's more than a day old. I think that's what you're sayin'," she said, taking deep breaths.

"Never go to bed mad," Bob said from the bathroom.

"Thank you, Bob, for that contribution," she replied. "Three philosophers in a motel room maketh the room too small."

She looked at Martin and sighed. "I'll work on it, okay?"

He nodded and folded back his bedspread without wrinkling it.

"You too, alright?" she said.

He glanced up, nodded again, and smiled. He slipped under the covers without crinkling them somehow and took off his clothes. He pulled them up over the bedspread, folded them on his belly, and laid them on the nightstand in a careful pyramid.

"I'm a sleep needer," Bob said from the bathtub.

"I think that means he needs sleep," Martin said.

"For once, the Bob and I agree," she said. She buried her face in the pillow and drifted off.

Martin couldn't sleep. It wasn't his night to sleep. On those desolate off-nights, he'd just lay still. He wouldn't fight it. He'd let his body rest and feel his heart slow while his eyes adjusted to the dark. Then he'd start to pick up the sounds hidden by the day, and finally, when his mind got quiet enough, he'd snag the thoughts angling by like flotsam. But tonight, he picked up something else: cooing and scraping. His eyes narrowed. He couldn't figure out what it was. After a while, his face relaxed — there were pigeons in the air conditioner.

"There is seagulls in Kansas State. And pigeons in the desert," he whispered, and he listened to them knock and coo through the vent, sounding like old-time radio.

Then something happened that usually didn't when it wasn't his night to sleep. With Patsy snoring in one ear and the rock doves gurgling in the other, he drifted off.

58.

She grazed her fingers over her shins and dreaded what they told her: stubble. If it was one thing she couldn't stand it was whiskers anywhere on her body. So she set her feet up on the sink one at a time and lathered up her legs. Patsy pulled a disposable razor from her bag and shaved her calves. She tried to ignore the man in the tub wrapped up in the shower curtain, but she felt his eyes on her ankles.

"I prefer *au naturel* on the female of the species," Bob confided.

"Yeah, well, I don't. Beards are for men and menopause."

"I would've thought you were deeply involved in both those categories, Patsy."

She flicked some shave cream at him. The few strands of hair Bob had left poked out from his scalp like cat whiskers.

"Don't you ever get a whiff a yourself? You smell like you been workin' under cars too long." She dipped her razor under the faucet. "Why don't you at least comb your eyebrows or trim your nose hairs or somethin'?"

"No reflection, remember?"

"Kinda like bein' color-blind or tone-deaf I guess, huh?" She lit a Marlboro.

"Oh yes. It's very preoccupying," he agreed.

She nicked herself.

"Goddamn it, Bob. You dulled my razor."

"No refl—"

"Yeah, yeah, I know. 'No reflection.'"

She peered through the doorway. Martin sat on the bed mangling chords on her guitar. She smiled, and got an idea.

"Hey, boy. C'mere," she said.

He set the guitar down and walked up to the threshold. But he wouldn't cross over, not with a lady in the bathroom. She tickled the caterpillar under his nose and handed him a fresh razor.

"Grab that can," she said.

He held the shave cream can like it was mace.

"Go on," she urged him.

He pressed down and squirted shaving gel all over his shirt.

"Ready, fire, aim," she observed.

He wiped it off and tried to slather it on his face.

"No. You gotta wet your skin first. Like this."

She slapped water on her face like a man and bearded herself with shave cream. He copied everything she did, right down to the creamy whorls she made on her cheeks. She jammed the Marlboro in the corner of her mouth and smoke wandered up her cheeks. She shaved the space under her nose in smooth strokes as if she did it every morning.

He put the razor under his nose. His hand trembled. She held his wrist. Together, their hands pulled the razor down to his lip.

59.

One Ukiah Sheriff's vehicle to patrol all the aimless circuitry of L.A. Chad pulled into a strip mall, new but trashed with 7-Eleven garbage glued to the blacktop. Wrinkled movie posters from India were plastered in a video store window. Chad anchored his boot on the parking stripe and stepped from the squad. A Salvadoran banger sitting on a Chevy looked him up and down and decided Chad wasn't a threat. But Chad hadn't decided the same thing about him.

"You better come with," he told his brother and Rachel.

The three of them walked into the 7-Eleven. Walter and Rachel shopped for food. Chad addressed the Assyrian man behind the counter:

"Do you have a phone book?"

The man nodded and slid a White Pages over the counter for Santa Monica and Surrounding Areas, but it didn't cover downtown Los Angeles. Chad looked up 'Amstead' and copied the one Ann out of it.

"Thanks," he said, sliding it back.

They walked back to the car together. Walter gobbled a warmed-over breakfast burrito.

"There's one Ann Amstead in the phone book," Chad said. "It's from the Pacific Palisades. We'll need to get local law involved."

Walter chewed his customary twenty times and swallowed. "Not a good idea," he said, dabbing his mouth with a napkin.

"What if there's another Ann Amstead?" Chad said. "Are the Pacific Palisades even part of L.A.? We don't know. We need to check in with the locals. It's protocol."

"No." Walter was about to bite down again, but stopped. "We don't need them, do we?"

"Not if you have the guardianship papers," Chad said as they got in the car.

Walter wrapped up what was left of his burrito. He'd lost his appetite.

"You do have the order appointing you as guardian of Martin's person, don't you?" Rachel asked.

Walter reached down into a leather satchel and pulled out a handful of ripped up court documents.

"Did he do that?" Chad asked.

Walter nodded.

"Well, you can explain that," Chad said.

Walter turned back and addressed Rachel: "You'll back me up if we need an affidavit or something, won't you?"

"Of course," she said. "I just need to get my facts right. For the affidavit. You know her personally, right?"

She'd been pretty quiet since the Native American trooper interrogated Walter back in New Mexico.

"I was youth minister. She came to me a couple times. She was in trouble," Walter recited.

"And that's all?"

"That's all," he promised.

She smiled the kind of diluted smile a person gives to show good faith. Her hand slid up to the top of the seat and Walter's reached out to cover it. He turned to his brother: "What do we do now?"

"Well, we need to get paper, and I'm not talking about a torn-up order of guardianship, for chrissake. I'm surprised at you, bro. It's not like you to come unprepared."

"You're the one who should've come better prepared," Walter snapped. "Fugitives aren't my area."

"Well they're not mine either. See this badge? It doesn't say 'U.S. Marshal.' But with her as an affiant," Chad said, nodding toward Rachel, "we should be able to get what we need on paper to bring them back over state lines."

"Excuse me, but what's an affiant?" Rachel said.

"Somebody who swears out an affidavit. You know, a document they use in court," Chad explained, taking a more patient tone than he used with his brother. "And we will check in with the local PD and the U.S. Marshal. They can do a name search in case this Santa Monica address is a dead end. Then we find out where the ol' girl might be and stake it out."

Walter nodded, unwrapped his burrito, and took a bite.

60.

Pros worked the strip, a couple of them shadowed by a man in a silver SUV Caddie. Every once in a while, a woman and a man would drive up in a little white Dodge and pick one of the girls up to collect.

A shelter and a clinic jostled with two liquor stores on one side of the street. On the other side, a Rottweiler and a German shepherd paced back and forth behind the chain link of a used car lot like pent-up lions. It was late Saturday afternoon. Sun glinted off the glass of downtown, an Emerald City just west. Everyone down here lived outside its walls.

Patsy, Martin, and Bob walked past the used car lot. The Greyhound terminal had spit them out a few blocks away. Down the street, a one-story cinderblock building with narrow, prison windows stood out like a pillbox, flanked on either side by empty lots with rattlesnake grass and shards from uncountable bottles of MD 20/20, Night Train, and Thunderbird. The heat cooked the broken glass into gem fields. Bob took off his shirt.

Across the façade of the blockhouse, in red and black graffiti, someone had painted:

NITTY GRITTY DIRTBAG SPITTOON MAGOON SALOON

The front windows were glass block, but they had bars on the outside. A heavy-duty door seemed meant to keep people out, or maybe in. The door was painted black like the rest of the façade. At the curb out front, four Hogs left their marks — a '79 Low Rider Shovel Head, two softails, and an '88 Sportser XL — all shimmering and anointed with war paint and get back whips. They leaned in formation.

"I know this looks a little scary. But it's not a strip club, I promise," she said. "I used to live here."

"When you is in jail?"

"Not everybody gets to grow up in a house with heated toilet seats and walk-in fireplaces," she said. "I called this place home. I had to."

They stepped up to the security door and Patsy tugged on it. It stayed plugged like it didn't want anybody inside, but finally it gave in. A draft of old, cold air moaned out, flattening her hair. Martin shivered in a blast of booze and ash. Bob couldn't wait to get inside.

In the main part — the Pit, they called it — where it seemed like night no matter what time of day it was, people stood or sat; some at the bar and a few around the giant wooden cable spools they used like tables. Everyone was in various states of undress except for the bikers playing pool over in the corner. These were beaten-down, wooden-nickel people. They were people that ended up at Hope House sooner or later. And they were playing strip bingo. In the back of the place, a man groaned behind a black curtain.

Milton stood behind the bar in his underwear. He grabbed a slip of paper from an old Hills Brothers coffee can.

"B-10!" he shouted over the moans of the man behind the curtain.

A fat woman, too big for her piss-stained panties, stripped off her bra. Bob dropped his pants. Patsy slapped him across the head. "I'm just trying to fit in with the natives," he protested as he pulled them back up.

Milton spotted Patsy.

"Patsy! Game over!" he said to the people.

Whines floated up from the Wet and the Weary. That's what Patsy called Ink's crowd. They tossed down the Chinese coins and slugs they used as bingo chips and started putting on their clothes. The grand prize, a bottle of Jack and a Big Book from Alcoholics Anonymous, sat on the bar unclaimed. Milton hurried his pants and shirt back over his gray skin, rushed out from behind the bar, and hugged Patsy.

Behind the curtain, the moans became shrieks. Everyone stopped and listened. Back at the pool table in the corner, Dean Dealish, a jockey-sized man in biker cuts, unpatched, sewn up with flash patches where they'd taken his colors from him, wearing thick spectacles, listened and smiled. Then he banked the eight-ball in the side pocket and collected a sawbuck from another rider. Some of that iron out front belonged to Dean.

Martin stood behind Patsy. Bob grabbed a half-finished mug of beer from the bar and slurped it down.

The cries behind the curtain stopped.

"You're finished!" an old, hardy voice behind the curtain said.

"What is this!?" a weaker voice whined.

"He still in trouble with the Main Cop?" Patsy asked.

Milton nodded. "Last week he did a Jackson Pollack on a guy's ass. All the guy wanted was a lousy damned bull's eye."

"I wanted a fucking swastika!" little voice screeched.

"You don't like it, well, don't show it to nobody," big voice said back.

"Don't show it to nobody!?"

"I do what I see in you," the big voice said. "This is what I see in you!"

Glass smashed and furniture tumbled behind the curtain. Two figures bulged from the black drape and thrashed and tore at each other and brought down the shroud. It hid Ink's unlicensed tattoo parlor from the law.

Ink whacked the young skinhead on the side of the head with his tattoo gun and tossed him on the bar like so much meat. He'd needled an = sign between the man's shoulders in the colors of the rainbow. The man climbed down from the bar and ran for the door.

"I'll be back, you FUCKING buffalo nigger!"

"Make sure you bring the Panzers," Ink said as the weasel left. Ink glanced over and saw the tall, red-haired kid staring at him from behind Patsy's shoulder.

She walked up, joined the fingers of her hands around Ink's neck and kissed him on the cheek. To sputtering applause, Ink gave a reluctant hug back in front of the whole bar. He managed the hint of a smile.

"They are gonna shut you down again," she said as she released him.

"They shut me down every week. Next week, I open back up again.

I did what I saw in him."

"Ink, I can't believe we made it. I saw Nellie!"

He gave Martin the once-over.

"Who's this?" he asked.

"This," Patsy said, putting her hands on the boy's shoulders, "is Martin."

Martin cleared his throat. "Hello," he said.

Ink took Martin's hand and shook it softly. "You must be Navajo," Martin said.

"Why, yes. Yes I am. Let me take your things," he offered.

Martin stepped back. He knotted his knuckles around the handles of his duffel bag. He stared at the insides of Ink's forearms, thick like bridge cables, where angular, masked Navajo figures danced.

"Know what these are called?" Ink asked.

Martin shook his head.

"They're Yei Figures. They take away worry."

Dean snuck up from behind and slithered hairy, spider's arms around Patsy's middle.

"Hey, babe," he whispered.

Her face shrunk to a grimace. She dug her nails in his forearms. The arms withdrew.

"Got some chronic," he said.

She pulled away from him and shivered.

"Where you staying?" Ink asked her, scanning Bob.

"Here?" she asked.

"You get the master bedroom," Ink said, nodding toward a cot in his tiny tattoo parlor. Martin saw that the back room, if you could call it that, was frescoed with graven images that didn't come out of the Tallman Family Bible.

Milton cleaned up the mess from the fight and Ink helped.

"Then I gotta start lookin' for work," Patsy said.

Ink looked up from his dustbin as Milton swept glass into it. "Tell you what. Until you get something, why don't you play here like you used to?"

"Uh-uh. No more hand to mouth," she said.

"Last call," Ink told Milton.

"Last call!" Milton barked.

His customers grumbled, but at Ink's, last call could be five in the afternoon or it could be one in the morning. It was whenever Ink said it was. Milton stepped behind the bar and took care of the small crowd that lined up to get their drink on. Bob was first in line. He looked in the mirror that lined the wall behind the bar and read the fire occupancy bulletin reflected from the opposite wall. He read it the way he saw it in the mirror, backwards.

"snosrep 07 naht erom on yb deipucco eb yam sesimerp siht taht ed-nimreted sah lahsram erif ehT. GNINRAW"

"What was that?" Milton said as he handed Bob his beer.

"Your occupancy permit shows characteristic indications of structural entropy. It's coming out backwards," Bob explained before he downed the mug in one long swig.

"Is this guy for real?" Milton asked Patsy.

"Oh you have no idea."

Milton turned to Bob. "Can you talk backwards that fast, too?"

".tnaw I emityna ti od nac I. esruoc fO," said Bob.

Martin excused himself to use the bathroom. That's when Dean moved in again.

"How you feel?" he said, stroking her back.

"Clean."

"You're lookin' it."

"You're lookin' like shit."

"I got some tar. Wanna cook?"

"Ink's not gonna like it when I tell 'im you're bringin' that shit in here."

"Just tryin' t'share the glory, that's all."

"No, you're tryin' to resaddle the mule," she tossed back.

"Aw, c'mon Pats. If I ain't yo nigga?"

She ignored him. She wasn't 28 like last time. But free H? Hell, it'd been a year-and-a-half since she'd mained. What was just one time? She could use him like he used her — use his shit and then dime him to Ink. That'd be revenge. By taking his heroin, she'd just be getting Dean back for tricking her out along with about a dozen other joy sisters.

She looked over at Martin. He stared at her from in front of the john. She thought she saw him shake his head, just a trace. He seemed to know what she was thinking. *What was she thinking?* That by using, she'd be doing whoredom a favor? She shook the grip of that lie from her back along with Dean's hand.

She leaned into Dean and growled low and slow:

"I am warning you, you goddamn pimple: you stay the fuck away from me and especially from that boy over there. You don't, and I'll have Ink curb kick your motherfuckin' ass before he shoves that heavy soul you're slangin' up your goddamn manhole. You remember what a curb kick feels like, dontcha Dean?"

Dean remembered. Some outlaws had caught him in Moab one day a few years back before the jeepers and rafters got hold of the town and crowded all the one percenters out. Dean had been running 66, alone and unpatched, through town. The MC caught him doing a moonlight mile with one of their broads. A big no-no. They stomped him, made him open his jaw and bite the edge of a street curb, then kicked the back of his head until his front teeth leaned into his mouth like a funnel. That was how Dean lost his smile.

"And you know he'll do it," she finished.

"What happened to the girl I knew?"

"She picked up too many admirers."

"Admiration pays, baby."

She shoved passed him. Dean sized up Martin.

"You'll crawl home," Dean grumbled. "Skank always do."

61.

She'd spent the worst eight years of her life with Dean, whose road name was Beak because somebody thought his long, skinny nose looked like one. She'd thought it'd been rough before she'd met him. She'd been a call girl and she'd had to take it up the servant's entrance raw in a couple pro-am films. But being an escort and featuring as the backdoor girl in movies for drugs was near the top of the sex trade pyramid. Being a pavement pounder, where she finished her career, was absolute bottom. She always said that the Dean years were her sentence in the netherworld.

He'd met her at a party at the Playboy mansion. He and his crew had been hired for security. Some people in Hollywood liked consorting with edge players like Dean. It was hip to be seen with men who didn't always take baths or have straight jobs.

Bikers were different today. Ink would say that most were bolt-on week-end-warrior wannabes polluting the purity of the old rallies. *Waxers*, they called them. Ink and Dean were passing into history. The clubs themselves were more sophisticated today. Even one percenters went semi-legit. A lot of them didn't wear rags anymore and they lived in houses they actually owned.

Dean moved Patsy from L.A. to Barstow and hooked her on crack when crack was king. She was his top earner for seven or so years. That was a long time to keep a girl hooking, to keep her from aging twenty years, to keep her breathing. Dean believed in preservation of capital. He wasn't a beater. Bruising the merchandise was old school and it didn't fit

Dean's style. Not that he was a lover. He'd just been in the right place at the right time. He found a beautiful woman on her way down. He knew a good thing. He stuck to her. She'd kick once in a while, but she'd always come back. Until she met Ink.

Ink had never ridden with any chapter. He was that rare animal — an independent. He'd given up the life years ago. And when he came to, he had this bar on his hands. He'd been running it since a knee injury forced him out of roofing. He wanted to dump the Nitty Gritty but didn't know how else to make money.

He'd let people detox on the cot in his parlor. Or he'd pick up drunks off the sidewalk out front and cart them to the mission down the street. He tolerated guys like Dean, who hustled pool and made deals in back, because they were muscle against the street gangs who'd moved onto skid row to sell drugs. The gangs would want protection money otherwise. As long as two or three scoots were parked out front, the gangs let Ink alone.

62.

The place cleared out pretty quick after last call. Milton bolted the door and they were alone.

"I figure your mom gets the queen —" Patsy gave Ink a big kiss so he couldn't finish his sentence. She grabbed his face and shook her head 'No.'

Martin looked away when he saw the kiss. She could tell he was jealous.

"Ink ain't my boyfriend," she explained.

"Boyfriend? Hell no. I'm her personal savior. When I met her, she was still needling," Ink said.

"Sewing," she said, nudging Ink's bad knee.

"Ow!" He glared at her, rubbed the knee. "Why don't you unpack your stuff, Martin?"

He pinched Patsy's elbow and towed her to the corner of the bar, where the pool table and juke were separated from the Pit by a couple of inconvenient posts that forced shooters to use the short stick. Ink spread his own bedroll out on the table's felt. A POW/MIA flag was his blanket.

"You didn't tell him who you are?"

She squirmed. "Things ain't set up yet."

"'Set up.' What do you plan on setting up? A goddamn trust?"

"He ain't ready."

"Who ain't ready?"

"Lemme do this my own way. I waited half my life."

"He waited his whole life."

"Look, he wants his mom. I'm it," she whispered.

"Then tell him."

"If I do, he's either gonna grudge whack me or turn me in. That's what he says. I got two states wantin' my ass. I picked up an agg bat on a trooper in New Mexico. I stole a semi. Walter's on his way out here with his brother the law. He's got me on kidnapping, theft of charitable funds, credit card fraud, false impersonation. Haven't you been watchin'? I'm all over the goddamn tube." She tried to keep her voice down, but she was scared. "Man, I been in trouble before but not like this. This is my third strike. I could be in for life."

"It can't be kidnapping if he consented," Ink whispered back.

"He can make that kid say anything, believe anything."

"So, you're gonna lie to him the rest of his life."

"He'll come 'round."

"When?"

"He just needs somebody to show 'im things."

"Like honesty."

"I'm workin' on it, okay?" She bit her cuticle.

Ink grabbed her wrists and turned them toward the ceiling. He showed her her own track marks and suicide lines. She tried yanking them away.

"I hope you know what you're doing this time," he said.

Bob wandered up and Patsy pulled her arms free. Ink surveyed his place and planted his arms on his hips.

"I don't know where I'm gonna put you, my man," he said to Bob.

On the other side of the saloon, an old tanning machine with a closable lid stood in the corner. Ink tried it to make the white tattoos stand out on his customers, but it didn't work.

"I know where," she said.

She grabbed Bob's hand and led him over to the tanning machine. Bob smiled, climbed in, closed his eyes, and crossed his paws over his chest. After a while, he sat up.

"Got any limes?" he shouted to Milton who was washing glasses behind the bar.

Milton nodded and walked over with two quartered limes left over from his shift.

Bob bit down on one and closed his lips as far as they'd go. He looked like a parrot fish with a green beak.

"Uhm allerthic thew lemonth," he explained before he closed his eyes and drifted off.

Milton unleashed a wheezy laugh that lapped the walls. It was rare to hear that in a place like Ink's.

"I like this guy," he told Patsy. "If that's how they're minting 'em back East these days, bring back more like 'em next time. Left Coast could use a little funkspiel."

Milton went back to dunking glasses. He giggled and shook his head. The trace of that smile stayed on his face the whole afternoon.

63.

She flipped apple pancakes on the coffee maker's warmer behind the bar. They were the size of sand dollars to start with, but once she'd burnt them to a crisp, they shriveled up into half-dollars. She served them up to Martin at the bar with a phony smile that turned into a wince.

"They're good like this. Cajun style," she decided.

He slid them over to Bob who wolfed them down. Martin glowered at her and folded his arms.

"Give it to me," he said, holding out his hand.

"What?"

"The envelope from my mom."

She opened her mouth to deny knowledge.

"I see you go through my bag last night."

"I was lookin'—"

"I has no lighter. I do not smoke."

"Will you lemme finish my thought so at least *I* know what I'm thinkin'?"

She reached into her jeans and produced the letter. He snatched it and held out his hand again.

"The envelope."

"I threw it out."

"Why do you protect her?"

Ink had been inventorying bottles behind the bar. He stopped and waited for her answer. She sighed, beat by the double-team.

"Look, hun...I think we should get a place where we could grow tomatoes and peppers. I can teach you to cook."

"I know how to cook." He glanced at the pancake ash. "Without smoke."

"You waited all your life to get back at 'er. Can't you just wait a few more days?"

He turned to Ink.

"Do you has a phone book?"

Ink handed over the White Pages for downtown. Martin stared at it. He'd never seen a phone book thicker than a hymnal back home. He opened it and eventually found 'A.' It took him a while, but he found AMSTEAD on his own, too. Patsy felt a wave of pride that he could do that. Then she yanked the book away. But he held onto the page and it ripped out in his hand.

He gasped. "I am sorry, Mr. Ink."

"It's alright, Martin. It's just paper," Ink said.

Martin set the page on the bar and ran his finger down the names, mouthing them silently until he found AMSTEAD, ANN again. There was only one. She knew where that address would take him.

She asked herself why she hadn't paid for an unlisted number. But people like her didn't have the money to do things like that. She was lucky she had an address even if it was the Nitty Gritty Dirt Bag Spittoon Magoon Saloon. In the days when the homeless couldn't afford cell phones, Ink convinced her to list the bar as her phone number. She'd decided on club singing as a career, and she needed a number for callbacks. What a joke that'd all been.

"Well, y-you don't know that's her down on that page. Ann Amstead's a common enough name. And honey, L.A., it's got a maze a towns and a mess a phone books to go 'long with 'em. Ink, you got other phone books for the boy here?" she asked, trying to lead Martin down a colder trail.

"Could I use the phone?" Martin asked.

Ink handed him the phone and Patsy punished Ink with a heated frown. Martin dialed the number, not knowing he was ringing himself up. The busy signal pulsed in his ear.

"What about it, Ink? Phone books, not phones," she said.

Ink searched behind the bar and came up with a book for Santa Monica and Surrounding Areas. Why he had a book for the well-heeled Westside, she didn't know. But it let Patsy breathe a little. It would throw Martin off track. He found one listing for an Ann Amstead in that book, in Pacific Palisades. The closest she ever got to living there was a bachelor party for some producer's son where she'd been the main course.

"I figured I'd get myself a job," she announced to no one in particular.

"Could I get a pen?" Martin asked Ink.

Ink handed him the old ballpoint behind his ear. Patsy steamed at Ink for collaborating with the enemy.

"And you're goin' back to school," she said.

Martin studied the two Ann Amstead's from the pages of different phone books and different worlds.

"Can I has a paper?" he asked Ink. "I need to print her name and phone number."

"Just take the page out," Ink suggested as he went back to checking bottles. Martin's eyes bulged at the permission granted to rip the page from a book. Ink might as well have told him to rip a page from the Bible.

"It snows up in Pacific Palisades. And there'll be devil worshipers," she warned.

He creased the page and excised it like a surgeon.

"How'll you get up there? This first address is way up by the ocean, for Chrissake," she said.

"I want you to come with," he said, and grabbed his jacket.

"You do?" He nodded. She was flattered. He wanted her to meet his mother.

"I could keep these papers?" he asked Ink, who knelt behind the bar, counting bottles. "Both papers from both books?"

Ink inched his face above the bartop and nodded.

Martin folded each white page up in quarters two times until they were neat little squares.

"You need to call the police when I is done," he explained.

"What?"

Patsy looked to Ink for backup, but he wasn't about to help.

"To turn her in to the police, right?" she said as Martin headed for the door. "But, but not to call the police on you."

"Martin, should we get you a public defender or a real attorney?" Bob asked as he licked his plate clean.

She didn't want to believe Martin had it in him to lay hands on her. But she couldn't stop thinking about that woman on his front lawn. Then she realized that Bob, Ink, and Martin were looking at her. It was her serve.

"Well, there's just no way to get to Pacific Palisades, least 'til I get a job 'n...'n money for a cab."

"We take a bus then," Martin said.

"Crosstown L.A.? You ain't testin' too well for reality, there," she said.

"You could take my *new* bike," Ink said.

"I am gonna go out there and look for work today. Got that, Ink?" Martin undid the deadbolt on the door.

"I'll go with you tomorrow. I promise," she said.

He considered her offer and redid the latch.

64.

It was late afternoon, and the crowd was thin: a few late-stage boozers hunched over the round wooden tables varnished dark with spilled beer and liquor. They stared off into space like they were already Hope House people. And like Hope House people, their disability checks weren't due 'til Friday. Until then, the streets would be emptier and the shelters and detoxes a little fuller.

Milton smoked a raw Camel and worked a crossword by the daylight that battled its way through the maze of security bars and glass block in the front window. Martin helped Ink unload a case of Tecate into the cooler. Bob mopped the floor, drawing water pictograms of stick figures peeing and squatting in a palindrome array.

Patsy stomped into the bar with a scratched-out want ads under her arm.

"Do you find a job?" Martin asked.

She swiped one of the beers from the crate and popped the cap off on her heel.

"I never held a straight job in my life. Howda I explain seventeen years of crash and burn to some cherry-cheeked child in personnel —"

"Human resources," Ink said.

"What?"

"That's what they call it now," he told her.

Bob took Patsy's beer from the bar before she had a chance to take a swallow and swigged it all down in a few seconds.

"No trabajo," he summed up in a toneless belch.

"I don't even have a goddamn high school diploma. How the hell do they expect a woman to support a kid?"

"It is okay. Because I could," Martin said.

"What're you talkin' about?"

"Mr. Ink makes me his worker."

"Ink, I don't want 'im workin' this place. It's bad enough we gotta sleep here."

Ink shoved beer into the cooler, a little piqued. Martin pulled out two $10 bills.

"Ink already pays me. I take you out for dinner."

"No. I'm s'posed to be takin' you out for dinner."

"You want money, you know what to do," Ink said.

She ignored him. She knew what he meant. She pulled out a pack of job applications and walked over to the bar, grabbing the pen from Milton's hand.

"Hey, do you mind?" he said.

"You ain't s'posed to do crossword puzzles in ink anyway, unless you're God," she said.

"That's math you're not supposed to do in pen unless you're God," Milton said, swiping the pen from behind Ink's ear.

"C'mere," she told Martin.

"What is they?" he asked. He leaned over the bar and looked at the papers.

"Job applications. You learn these, it'll change your whole life."

"That's finishing school that'll change your whole life," Milton said.

"I know how to write these," Martin said.

He pulled away the application and started filling it out. It was from a carniceria a couple streets over.

"Who taught you?" she wondered.

"I has a job coach. Rachel."

He printed in tiny upper and lower case. He was careful to stay in the boxes.

"Is there anything that anatomically incorrect Barbie doll didn't do for you? Honey, print bigger," she said.

He paused and glanced up at her when he came to the box for his address. "What should I say? For the place I stay?"

"Just put down 'early modern apocalyptic,'" Bob said.

"Shut up, Bob." She turned to Martin. "Just put '7th and Wall.' That's the address here. This is where you live."

The application asked for references. He looked up at her.

"There's…" she stopped herself.

She had a felony record. Her eyes wandered over to Ink. His record was even worse even if he hadn't had a conviction in more than ten years. She looked at Bob and got that idea out of her head quick.

"…Milton," she decided.

Milton looked up.

"M-i-l-t-i-n." He whispered the letters, scrawled them in meticulous script.

"God, we should get you up to bat as a sign painter," she remarked. "But that's M-i-l-t-*o*-n. Not 'i,' hun."

He glanced up at her like he'd committed a mortal sin. "I has to start a new one."

"No, that's alright. You just write an 'o' around the 'i,' like this." She did it for him.

"But my dad say I has to start again unless I can erase it good."

"Your daddy has a little problem holdin' on to the world too tight with his sphincter. Fixin' mistakes is a helluva lot easier than he lets on. Mistakes like these anyway."

He seemed mystified by the new rules. "What is you last name?" he asked Milton.

"Fishback," Milton replied.

"F-i-s-h-b-a-c-k," Martin whispered. "Where do you live at?"

"The Ford Hotel."

He finished up the application.

"Have you ever had a job before?" she wondered.

He shook his head. "I like to work," he said.

"And your daddy never —"

"He say I is not ready."

"Well you know what? I declare you ready," she said. "Ready for that, and for a lot of other things."

She shagged his red shag. She couldn't mess it up any more than it already was.

65.

They sat in the only booth in the whole place, next to the back door that Ink bolted with a railroad tie. She held the resume in her hand. It was handwritten in Martin's ideal block letters. It took him a week to finish. He wanted it perfect.

"So, Mr. Tallman, what is your job experience?" she inquired.

"I help in school, cleaning erasers." He fidgeted, tapped his foot.

She waited for more, but he was waiting for the next question. She gave him the time out signal.

"Remember what I told you? Keep talking. About all your experience."

"Oh, sorry."

"It's okay," she said. "Time in."

"I also visit the sick —"

"— as a volunteer —"

"— as a volunteer for church. And I sing in the church choir."

"Oh, very interesting. Do you have any references?"

"Yes."

She waited for him to go on, but he didn't.

"Honey —"

"I has a man I help with the name Milton Fishbeak."

"U-huh," she nodded.

"I graduate from high school. I has hobbies. I sing good. I win metals for track," he mumbled, staring down.

"Medals," she corrected. "And eye contact."

"Medals. I know how to work hard and I do physical work and I read and write well and —"

"No, don't answer 'yes' or 'no,' but don't lump it all together like that either," she said.

They'd been working on the interview for a week. She'd made a deal with him. If he'd put off finding his mother until after he found a job, she'd give Walter back all the church money she stole, including what they'd spent. Martin didn't want either of them going to hell, so it was worth it. He seemed antsy today, like he wanted to confess something but couldn't.

"Hun, is there somethin' troublin' you today?" she asked.

He held off a few moments. "You could not find a job for youself. You try for a week."

"Oh. And if I can't get work, then maybe I'm not the best person to be teachin' you howda interview."

He nodded, apologetic.

"I think you're onto somethin' there, babe."

"Mr. Ink says you could work for him like I do."

"Mmm-hmm."

"He says you could keep all the moneys you make for youself."
She nodded.

"Maybe…" He wouldn't finish. He clasped his hands between his thighs.

"You can say it."

"Maybe you is embarrass to play music here," he let out.

"Why would I be embarrassed?"

"Because you is a loose harlot."

His face said he hated saying it, and the Great Red Spot rose between his eyes. She didn't get his logic, and he seemed to know she didn't even without looking up.

"I think that because once a woman is a harlot, she could never go back…"

"…and be like Rachel," she finished for him.

He nodded.

"Boy, that explains a lot," she sighed. She drummed her fingers on the table.

"Can I tell you a little story?"

He nodded.

"There's this girl. She's 16-years-old, and she has to run away."

"Why?"

"'Why' s'not important now. She has no high school diploma to help her get a job — no one to show her howda write out a resume, or howda interview for work. In fact, no one wants to hire her because she has no address. And even if they gave her a job, she couldn't make enough money to live on — you know: to buy food and pay rent."

He peeked into her eyes for a moment.

"What's a girl like that gonna do to survive?" she asked.

"Become a harlot with sex for money?"

"Well, that's what a lotta girls do who run away."

"Okay."

"These are girls who are good girls, too, most of 'em. But they don't think they are for long. Remember when you ran away and your dad found you eatin' garbage out of a dumpster?"

He stared up at her. Then she remembered she'd netted that bit of gossip during an eavesdrop over Martin and Walter back at Hope House. But she didn't care now.

"You were pretty hungry that time, weren't you?" she asked.

He nodded.

"When you get hungry enough, you'll do just about anything for money."

"But I do not," he paused, "I do not give sex for money."

"Some boys, they do end up so desperate that they'll give their bodies up for a meal or a man's spare bedroom."

He pictured that. His eye glistened with a tear for a boy who'd have to do that, but the eye wouldn't let the tear go. He looked around. No one else was here on a Saturday morning to see it.

"And then a girl, who was a good girl, she starts thinkin' of herself as a bad girl. And pretty soon, she just doesn't care anymore."

"That is what happens to Mary Magdalene," he surmised.

She took his hand. They were quiet for a while.

"But Jesus saves her," he said. "He changes her back to who she is before, pure like Rachel. You should pray to Him so he changes you back, too."

A hoary animosity climbed up into her throat and squelched her voice. Jesus hadn't done a damn thing for her but send her a messenger who got the whole trick started off in the first place. Walter had been her first pimp. But she held back saying any of it. Still, her fingers could speak for her.

She walked over behind the bar where the beat-up old Gibson Matthew had given her was tucked in the corner. She dragged a wobbly stool over to Martin and perched on it. She thrummed a few sad chords from a song she'd written maybe eight years back, when Dean had brought her up to Seattle to work Cherry Street for a few months.

In her whisky voice, she creaked out the words as she picked:

If you ask her,
She'll understate her age,
And she'll lie about her weight.
Even though she's 25 and 110.
She assumes this is her role.

Assign the part, Do the dialogue
In which the lines are blown and broken
By an actress hired
For what she'll do instead.

Consummating her audition
She walks away, her head hung low.
But she'll laugh,
If you ask her.
The handsome bouncer wants her,
But this is not her consolation.
Many hunger for her thighs,
Others dive into those hazel eyes.

'Make some babies, ma'am?
Or should we marry first of all?'

She sees her long-shot dream is broken.
She does what she is told instead.
Assign the part,
And do the business,
In which the words are conveyed spoken,
But by the eyes are said.

She gives away her flower
And decides to change her name,
Moves on to just one more town,
A step ahead of that dogging shame.
But still, she'll laugh,
If you ask her.
She'll do anything,
If you ask her.

She wound down her strumming with swollen eyes that finally dropped the tear his couldn't.

"That's what L.A.'s like for some girls," she said.

He stood and kissed her tear. He held her and wouldn't let go.

66.

That night, she played guitar to a fraction of a house. Ink sat on his stool behind the bar and did needlepoint. Milton had the night off. He'd taken Bob out to show his friends his new prodigy and to win some money. He'd bet seven people Bob could recite the U.N. Charter backwards. Milton came home fat.

Martin was Ink's barback. He swept up and washed out glasses. He moved like a machine, focused and fast. Ink had tattooed Navajo Yei figures on Martin's arms. Every once in a while Martin would stare at them and ripple his arms, make them dance. He would smile.

Getting tattoos was a baptism for Martin. At first, he was afraid they were sacrilege. Ink explained that the Yei were holy people. When Martin found out that he had to bleed a little, Ink told him that the pain gave you the right to wear the tat.

Martin thought about all that blood and sacrifice. "If it be good enough for Jesus…" he concluded.

Between numbers, Patsy looked over at him. She smiled, too. He seemed happy. Maybe, just maybe, she thought, things wouldn't break shitty for her. Everything seemed in place.

She played "Fire and Rain." Her handwork was flawless. Her singing wasn't. She was ashamed of that, especially with Martin there to hear. When it came to music or food, she was impossible to please. But she figured these people were target practice. It was hard to feel rotten in front of two bikers, an aging painted mama who threatened to split her jeans, and a pale obese man with a grease stain for hair who picked his nose with the cap of an old Bic pen.

Patsy cringed her way through the lyrics. When she was done, the only applause came from Martin, Ink, and the heavyset man, who hooted and whistled. And he was the only one who tossed bread in her fishbowl: a sawbuck. Later that night, she scooped out everything from the tip jar: $10, some change, and a pair of earplugs.

The next night, she played but gave up the singing. They were instrumentals bequeathed to the Wet and Weary. They were a different crowd tonight except for that big man. The man wasn't street and he didn't drink much. He was the one object that didn't belong with the others. Dean Dealish was there too, waiting for her to stumble over a chord.

Milton had made so much money off Bob the night before he decided to take him out to the movies. They went to see *Rocky Horror Picture Show* at the Nuart on Santa Monica. Bob was in full vamp drag.

While Patsy picked "From the Beginning" by Emerson, Lake and Palmer, the chubby man whispered to Dean and slid him some cash. That explained it, Patsy thought: the heavy man was in buying product. Dean supplemented his disability check moving whatever weight he could lay his hands on.

Martin wiped down the bar, polished the glasses, and emptied the ashtrays. But after every number, he stopped whatever he was doing and clapped like cymbals. Ink applauded too but never looked up from his needlepoint.

She finished her 10th number of the night, "La Rosa Negra," by Ottmar Liebert. She felt it was way over their heads, but she played it anyway. When she finished, a $50 bill wedged in her fishbowl. She fished it out and approached her patron.

"Y'know, you are really somethin' on that guitar," the large man gushed. "Name's Stuart."

He held out his hand. The fingers were pink and fatty, just like a baby's, she thought. She held the fifty in front of him.

"For a private lesson?" she ventured.

Stuart shrugged.

She stuffed the bill in his shirt pocket.

"I renounced music therapy," she said, glaring at Dealish. *She* was the White Lady he'd been pushing.

Stuart took out the bill and threaded it through the strings on her guitar. "Just a down payment," he promised with a yellow smile.

"Thanks, but I'd like to find a place to live before I start dating again."

"I got an empty trailer in Anaheim," Stuart offered.

"I'm broke."

"You could have it for free."

"Forget it."

"I own the whole park."

"I look like a trailerite to you?"

Then her old instinct kicked in. Why not take the guy for a ride? Take his fat ass for as much as she could without putting out? That would show Dealish, that maggot. Besides, they had to get out of the Nitty Gritty eventually. What kind of mother let her kid sleep in a place like this? She stood there deciding. She was in control; she took as much time as she needed. But what would the boy think if it even looked like she was shacking up? She peered over at him. He was filling out a job application. Stuart watched her watch Martin.

"I could always use a kid to keep the place up. I pay a buck above minimum," Stuart sweetened.

"Then let's go check it out," she decided.

Ink had been leaning over the bar chatting with a Latino man in an expensive suit who was out of place here. The man slid his business card across the bar.

"Patsy, there's somebody I want you to meet," Ink called over.

"Not now," she said.

Stuart took her hand in his and kissed it. A curious, flattering maneuver, she thought.

She smiled.

She and Stuart took their time getting to the front door so he could finish his scotch on the way. Martin looked up just as Stuart draped a baggy arm around Patsy's waist. She undraped it. Stuart whispered in her ear and she shook her head.

"Where is she going?" Martin asked.

"Looks like she got herself a new boyfriend," Ink said.

Martin let a hopeless gaze fall into the glaze of the bar varnish.

Ink whispered to him: "If you don't like that, then you go over there and let her know."

Martin set his job app down and marched to the front door.

"She is taken," he said.

Martin grabbed her away, kissed her on the lips, and squeezed her on the bottom; the exact moves he'd seen in the skin flick back at the La Playa motel. She pushed him off.

"What is wrong with you!?" she said, wiping her lips.

"I is ready. It has to be sometime," he said.

"You gotta wait your turn, chief," Stuart said, amused.

"You is having no turn."

"I just paid fifty for my cock wash. How much you pay for yours?"

"How dare you say that in front of him," Patsy said. She dunked his fifty in his scotch.

"He could always watch," Stuart snickered.

She took a swing at him but he feinted back. He was quicker than he looked.

"Get away. You is too fat for her," Martin said.

"*'Cuz I want her. You can't have her. I'm too fat for her,*" Stuart sang to the tune of "The Too Fat Polka" while he danced in a circle around them, snapping his fingers over his head.

He goosed Patsy. Martin cracked him in the nose with a cobra's strike.

"Ah, fuck!" Stuart moaned. He tried to pinch the blood back.

He socked Martin in the breadbasket and Martin doubled over.

"You never, ever touch him!" she shrieked.

She grabbed her guitar and swung it by the neck and broke the body off on Stuart's chest. He wasn't fazed. He mashed her in the eye with a corkscrew punch.

Ink grabbed a giant cast net from under the register, vaulted the bar, and threw the net over Stuart. He planted his back boot and yanked all

250 pounds of the man to the floor. Stuart thrashed as Ink dragged him across the sawdust while his audience clapped and cheered. They'd seen it all before. One of them opened the door for him and Ink hauled his catch onto the street. From inside, they heard the sounds of fists slapping into a side of beef. Ink never needed a bouncer.

67.

Martin dabbed Patsy's eye with a wet bar rag. Ink handed her a bag of ice. "Does it look bad? Oh I hope it don't look bad?" She fixed on it in the backsplash mirror.

Milton and Bob were back from the show and Bob threw quarters into the juke and played "Hey Hey What Can I Do" by Led Zeppelin. Customers came and went as Milton tended bar.

"Not my face, Lord, please. It's all I got left," she whimpered. The eye pillowed like a ripe banana.

"You look…beautiful," Martin said.

"Oh, sweetie, you are the most thoughtful young man."

She stroked his tidal wave of red, combed to one side.

"You deserve so much better than this," she said.

"I love you."

She eyeballed Ink, who scolded her with a coppery stare.

"I love you, too, Martin. But it…may not be the same way you love me."

He fell on his knee and took her hand.

"I wish you to marry me."

She knew their eyes, Ink's and Milt's and Bob's, weighed in on her.

"Do you really not know who I am?"

"Yes or no."

"Honey —"

"Then just say 'no.'"

"If you can read my mind, why don't you know 'bout me?"

"You do not care about me either." He tossed her hand down and shot up.

"I'd die for you, Martin."

"Because I hypnotize peoples."

"That's your gift."

"Because I is a freak."

She reached out to him but he knocked the hand away.

"You right. You could never get like Rachel again. You is just like the ladies on hotel TV — a lousy, stinky whore."

She slapped him. The house hushed and their gawks fell on his raw cheek. His unrequited eyes shot their numbness back in their faces.

"Why you all look at the weirdo in me!? See the weirdo in you-selves!"

He picked up a barstool, spun in a circle, and smashed it into the mirror behind the bar. Everything froze. His face turned away, unable to take their watchfulness, their disbelief. Oh, the scene he'd made. The scene, Reverend Tallman had taught him, it was better to die than face. The boy naked in front of his own congregation.

He dashed out the back door. Ink followed him, but Patsy grabbed his arm. This was her job.

In the alley, a light over the door poured black light on an allegory of war etched into the Nitty Gritty's decayed brick. It was Ink's apocalyptic masterpiece: warriors from all eras clashing in one final battle.

Martin hunched on a slab of broken concrete against the chainlink boundary between the alley and the empty warehouse behind. He took out her crumpled letter and pored over it for guidance:

You have to go back to the beginning of something to find out what it really is.

The words shook in his hands. She crept out the back door not know-ing what to expect.

"It is not fair," he muttered.

"No, it isn't," she said. "Life isn't fair. It isn't fair to anybody, so it's fair to everybody."

"It is not fair that, she end up, a harlot, like you is. When she is, like Rachel, 'long time ago," he spit out in pieces.

"I know," she said, afraid to touch him, afraid of the meaning he might give it.

"And it is not fair that I end up a crazy retard like Bob."

"Oh, no. You mustn't say things like that." She hushed for a moment. "If you weren't a little different, you might not be able to read people. Would you really trade that gift in?"

"Yes!" he splattered back. His eyes pleaded purple in the black light.

She crouched down. "Then you'd just be tradin' in a rare kind a smarts for a common kind."

The heat and hum of the L.A. motherboard sizzled the air. She nestled in next to him on the curb. The shiner filled the hollow of her eye. She looked at her letter and caught a few lines:

Maybe at the center of yourself, you felt like you were no one, like no one was there, not even you. It may have felt dark and icy and empty. I've been in that place. I've felt that same emptiness without you. That's how a mother feels without her son, like she has no soul.

"Her handwriting looks an awful lot like my own," she said.

He rose, towering over her. "I hate you. I hate you like I hate her."

She stood and faced him.

"You can hate me. You can hate me and hate me and hate me. That's alright. It won't change what I feel for you."

"Ooooh. You so much confuse my mind, Patsy."

"Then read mine. Go ahead. Find the truth."

"You say I is ready."

"Not for me. Not like that."

"Am I not good lookin' enough?"

"Oh, you are so damn handsome you could make your livin' under the bleachers. But even if I wasn't... 'who I am' to you, I'm all old and used up."

She reminded him with the scars on her arms.

"Can't you see?"

"We is both damage goods."

"I may be a floor model, but you? You're just under construction."

He clutched her shoulders. "It is okay that you is. Really."

"That I am what?"

"One of those women."

"I did what I had to. It didn't always feel like a choice."

"I could help you."

"No, I could help you."

"Take away you pain."

"Nobody can do that. For anybody." She tried to free a puff of dandelion seeds with her toe but missed. "I came to free you, and you wanna free me. How crazy is that?"

"But I has to get her first."

"Goddamn it, Martin. Why don't you get this?" She lit a cigarette, and the flame bronzed her puffy eye. She was struck by the knowing that his crush on her blocked him from understanding who she was; he couldn't fathom that the woman he had doe eyes for was the same woman he wanted to do in. It was too much for him to hold that they were the same person. "You'll pulverize your heart grindin' out that hate. Look what that did to me."

"You?"

"Yeah, me. You think I got this way by accident?"

"Who do you hate?"

"A man. The man who got me pregnant. With you."

He shook his head.

"I gotta forgive 'im, don't I? If I expect you to forgive me."

"You is not my mom."

"And I gotta forgive myself, too."

"You is trying to protect her."

"Not anymore."

She wished she'd kept some ID, some shred of the past to prove she was Ann Amstead. But it had all gone roadside years ago. All that was left of Ann Amstead was a line in the phone book.

"I forgive that man. I forgive Walter Tallman," she said.

"Shut up!"

"You been hypnotized by him. All this time."

He shoved her into a pile of paint cans stacked against Ink's masterwork.

"I do not want to see you ugly face again! Ever!"

He launched himself in long strides down the glass alley. She struggled to her feet.

"In the latter pages, that Bible of yours says nobody can throw the first stone!"

She hoped that would call him back from the powdery dark.

"Martin there ain't nowhere left to go!"

She fell back into the Nitty Gritty.

"I did it this time. He ran off and I won't find him!"

Ink slipped on his rags.

"He hates me. I told 'im the truth and he hates me."

"Quit looking at you," Ink said. "Which way's he headed?"

"Pacific Palisades maybe. He called me ugly."

He grabbed his keys and Patsy's arm and they headed out the door.

Out front, he kicked up his Hog as Patsy slid on back and they rumbled off. Across the street, Stuart camped out in his old model Lincoln with a bloody Kleenex jammed up his nose.

68.

Chad's back bumper scraped the gutter as his patrol car turned out from the lot of the U.S. Courthouse. He had everything Reverend Tallman needed and more: a federal warrant issued by his other brother, the federal district judge in Peoria; state warrants faxed from New Mexico and Illinois; and a writ of habeas corpus to deliver Patsy up to the State of Illinois. And that was just for Patsy. It took one whole week to get all this paper lined up. Walter used to tell his congregants that God was old and slow. Well, he was learning that the criminal justice machine was even slower.

Riding shotgun, Walter skimmed a fresh emergency order of guardianship from the Logan County Court in Lincoln, civil orders of commitment for Martin and Bob, and a removal warrant from the Illinois Supreme Court directing California to return Patsy's boys "forthwith" under Chad's escort, pursuant to the Uniform Act for the Extradition of Persons of Unsound Mind. Judge Tallman in Peoria had arranged for most of it. Dr. Hope chipped in by filing a petition claiming Martin was a danger to himself and others. It wasn't hard to convince a judge about dangerousness when a mental patient had fled cross-country.

"When I'm right, I'm right. Tell him I'm right, Rachel," Chad said, and he looked back and smiled. "Two Annie Amsteads in the metropolitan area."

"This first address is on Wall Street," Walter told Rachel as he fed her the address on a slip of paper. "The other one is in the Pacific Palisades. Is that a surburb?"

Chad snickered at the mispronunciation.

Rachel studied a map with the overhead on. They'd lost daylight.

"I think…we're closer to the address in Pacific Palisades," she yawned. "I can't be sure."

"Chad, we should stop for directions," Walter said.

"Go here. Go there. All my goddamn days. You know something, Rachel? I've been a Bobby Kennedy to his JFK as long as I can recall."

"We need to stop for directions," Walter insisted.

"It's alright. Wasn't your doing. It was ol' man Joe Kennedy, after all, who raised Bobby to have his brother's back. Same as our mother raised me to have yours."

"Whatever it is that may be on your mind, this isn't the time. Please," Walter said. "Stop for directions."

"In other words, not in front of other people, right?" Chad said.

"Nobody wants to hear about your childhood, Chadwick. Even if it is still going on."

"How do I get to Pacific Palisades, Rachel?" Chad asked.

She folded the map over and showed him.

Chad found the freeway and gassed it down the ramp.

69.

Trapped between the pavement and a thin film of rain, street lighting shimmered like a sheet of new pennies. Slow traffic splashed the water endlessly, peacefully. A sinewy, B Model V-Rod with a blacked-out frame cruised the streets west of the Nitty Gritty. It was liquid cooled. 109 horses could spin out from the rear wheel and propel it from a dead stop past just about anything in the next lane. Ink had named it Scimitar. Its riders searched for a raily, red-haired boy trying to become a man. But Patsy knew how fast and far their quarry could move on foot.

"We gotta find 'im, Ink."

"We will."

"He's never been outside bumblefuck his whole life, and now this?"

"We'll find him."

"How's he gonna make L.A. if he couldn't do Alton? They found him dumpster diving for eats back there!"

"He's a survivor."

"I'm a shit."

"You are."

"Shut up."

Ink threaded his scoot down alleys mulched with dirt and rubble and through streets flaked with shattered vials and half-pints. They froze the stares of the streetwalkers, this Navajo ink-slinger two-up with an Anglo woman, the fire in her hair undampened by the murky L.A. sauce of smog and drizzle.

"If you would've been honest with him from the beginning…" Ink told-her-so.

"Quit pissin' down my back. I tried!"

"It's not rocket science."

"I know. I don't know why he won't listen."

"I know why," Ink kept on.

She winced. She knew what was coming — the truth, or something close to it.

"You haven't changed," he said flat out.

It pained her to nod, but she did.

They canvassed east as far as the River and then went north to the freeway, motoring slowly as Patsy scanned from side-to-side.

"You led your own boy on."

"I did not!"

"You didn't really want him to know the truth."

"You wanna throw it down, Ink!? Huh? Why dontcha just stop right here and let's have this out!?"

"Now who doesn't want to listen?"

She fell quiet and watched the street.

The city was shedding its scabs. Gone from 6th and San Julian, from 3rd and Main, were the porta-potties that doubled as stalls for half-and-halfs and drug trades. Gangs had moved in and hired day laborers to sling rock and meth and H. But now City Hall was shutting them down, too. Condos and Starbucks were squeezing out the halfway houses and street missions. Sometimes the cops raided the hobo camps under the expressway slabs. The City Council was even talking about putting in cameras. What was the world coming to?

Patsy almost missed the purity of the old skid row and what it used to be in every city she'd ever worked. Ink hated the changes. He called it *gentri-fuck-cation*. There was something real about the street, about being cut so close to the bone it made you feel primal. If you survived it, skid row had a redemptive quality. It was nearer hell, so it kept you on the Red Road to Recovery, as Ink called it. You had to have lived the street to understand that.

Ink idled while she jogged up to the doors of the Cathedral off Hollywood Freeway, thinking back to those quiet times Martin would spend in small town churches on their way out. Maybe he'd be inside, she hoped. But the doors were sealed like coffin lids. Down Temple Street, she spotted a tall man with a red mop-top leaning into his step, carrying something, moving fast.

"That's him!" she pointed.

Patsy saddled up, Ink revved it and pulled a U. The Scimitar's roar drew the man's attention. He was just a corner hustler.

"Shit!" she cursed at the guy, who wondered what he'd done.

Ink throttled it until they were beyond the whine of the freeway.

He toed the tar at a redlight. "If Martin knew who you really were, he'd probably go back home to his father," he tossed back. "You'd lose. You just don't want that man to win."

"That is just pure bullshit!"

"You're not ready to be his mother, Pats."

She chewed her cuticle.

They decided L.A. was too big and that Martin could cover too much of it. They'd never find him this way so they gambled and decided to try Pacific Palisades. Ink jacked it into fifth whenever he could. On a bike he could make good time even in the city. The fast punch meant he could beat any car off the mark. And he could split lanes when there was gridlock. So it wasn't long before they made it up to the putting green exclusivity of Pacific Palisades. Patsy read from an address she'd dashed off on a Post-It note at a liquor store where she'd borrowed a phone book.

"Go right," she said. "There he is!"

She saw him stepping out of a car. He must've hitched.

Down the street, Martin seemed out of place, walking past the sculpted topiary hedging the front lawns. The air wafted with virgin scents; the unfamiliar linger of salt. He couldn't know the ocean was only a block over his shoulder. He matched addresses with the one he had on one of his phonebook pages.

Ink parked his sled a half-block away. He kept it idling as Patsy stepped off.

"Tell him everything. Don't stop until he hears you," he said.

She nodded.

"How you gonna get back?" she wondered.

"Oh, no. I'm not walking."

"But we'll be three up."

"It's nine o'clock Saturday night!" he hollered.

She pressed her palms together and pleaded. He kneaded his hands into fists. Fury rippled through his bulldog body, but she just waited for it to pass. She knew he'd relent.

He whipped her the keys. "I wanna see my bike this time!" he said and pointed a finger. "Goddamn it, Patsy! Fucking Pac Palace." He gusted off, his curses fading along with his silhouette as he kicked a bottle down the street.

Night quieted the streets, and a sea breeze tousled the fronds of the royal palms. She turned the corner and their paths met in front of 120 Buenaventura.

"My real name isn't Patsy. It's Ann Amstead."

Martin ignored her, headed up the walkway, scrutinized the address on the house, then moved like a mailman back down the walk to the next one. She followed.

"I know you were born sixty-two days too soon. At 3:15 a.m. At the Presbyterian Hospital."

He trudged down the walk to the next house, careful to avoid the lawn, and checked the next address against the one in the phone book.

"I know your middle name's Gabriel. I named you that 'cuz you were my little angel."

They stood in the driveway at 124 Buenaventura. His phonebook page said Ann Amstead lived at 128. He whispered the number on the garage.

"And I know you didn't have red hair when you were born. It was all black."

She grabbed his arm and pulled him face-to-face. He jerked away and bumped past her up the walk to 128. He approached slower this time, like he was treading up center aisle to the altar of his father's church. She was his usher.

"And after you were born? Your daddy threatened me with the law 'less I left town."

He stopped, strafed her with his look.

"He always says: 'Sometime, for what they say, for what they stand for, a minister is a target.'"

"So are girls with big boobs in small towns."

He strode up to the door, tried to flatten his hair with spit, and rung the bell.

"My father would not pick someone like you to have his baby."

"Exactly."

"You fool around too much."

He rang the bell again, pulled out the letter, and rehearsed his line in a whisper: "You send this to me. I is you son."

The door, appointed with a brass knocker and a stained-glass transom, creaked as someone unbolted it from inside. Martin's head shuddered. His hands rattled. She hated seeing him set himself up like this. In a few moments, he'd be dragging himself back down that walk more disappointed than he'd been his whole life. And she hated herself for letting it all happen. She was sorry she ever busted him out of Hope House.

The door swung open. That's when Patsy spotted that white letter opener in his back pocket. *He was going to kill whoever stood on the other side of that door.* She tried swiping it but he slapped her hand away and pushed her back.

An elderly, light-skinned African American woman waited at the door in a muumuu. She had a freckled nose just like him, and her relaxed hair was a dark shade of red.

"Is you Ann Amstead?" he asked faintly.

"What?"

"Is you my bio mom?"

"Say that again. I'm a little slow at my age."

"Me too!" He was excited or enraged or terrified, Patsy couldn't tell which.

He pulled out Patsy's letter. He had all his lines down.

"My name is Martin Tallman."

Patsy tried grabbing the letter opener again, but he kept her at bay with his arm.

"Did you write this letter," he quivered, "saying you is — saying you is my m-mom?"

"I certainly don't think so," she said, and slammed the door.

Patsy worried what he'd do next. She waited for his tremors to die down. Hers, too.

"Honey…"

She pulled out the envelope addressed to him back in Ukiah and gave it to him.

"…it's got a Ukiah postmark."

"Get out!" he said.

She explained fast before he could rabbit again.

"I reached out when I was mixed up, and your daddy was there."

"Leave him be. He is a good man!"

"And after he got me quickened with you, he was the one who asked me to get rid of you."

"You lie! He preach 'gainst 'bortions."

"But I waited and waited 'cuz I was sure he'd change his mind."

"I warn you." He whipped out the letter opener.

"But he didn't. And I just didn't care no more. So I got stoned."

"Stop talking to me!"

"And after you were born, he paid me. He paid me, and I took it. I been a whore ever since!"

He yanked her into a hostage pose and jabbed the tip of the letter opener in her throat. She locked onto his wrist with both hands, kept it from going in with all her might.

"You ain't spendin' the next twenty in the state hospital at Lincoln," she gurgled.

She twisted his wrist and broke the hold. He gaped at the bleeding tip in his hand and his eyes crested white. He flung the letter opener into the hedges.

She dabbed the smidgen of red from her neck.

"You ever hypnotize him?" she panted.

"No."

"What're you afraid of?"

"He is innocent."

"Then I must be guilty."

"He raises me up, takes me in."

"Either him or me is lyin'. Is it me?"

He looked away.

"Look at me!"

The old woman whose bell he'd just rung slid open a second floor window and watched.

"You're the lie detector," Patsy said.

The raw grind of bad brakes punctured her moment. The rasp of a juiced engine revved up the block. That meant LEO's.

"Go!" she shouted.

She grabbed the letter opener from the bushes. "Run! Now!"

The squad screeched to a stop in front. The corner of her eye snatched the word UKIAH on the door. Walter jumped out. Martin hurdled the hedges. Walter chased. Nobody had the lungs or the legs to catch him on foot but she'd use herself as bait just to make sure.

She ran between two houses. Chad cornered her at a backyard fence. On the other side of the yard, a mastiff snarled. She jumped onto the chainlink and hopped it. The dog ran for her but she grabbed a yard hose and smacked it on the nose. It yipped and ran in a circle. She turned on the water and hosed the dog until it took off. Chad stopped on the other side of the fence. He wasn't about to chance the dog. She tossed the hose, raced the dog for the far fence and beat him to it. She climbed it, then another and another, porpoising through the yards until she spilled out at the end of the block where Ink parked the Scimitar.

She mounted it, keyed it, kicked it, and rode off in a blue cloud.

"I'm badder than a dog and smarter than a cop!"

With an APB out on her, riding a standout machine like the Scimitar with ape hangers and get back whips fluttering in the blowback, she knew she was easy meat. And she figured the Nitty Gritty would be staked out by now. She had to think, and she needed a place to do it.

Squad lights torched up a few blocks ahead. She only hoped that didn't mean they'd caught him. But then she realized their backs were up against the ocean. She and Martin had run out of land and she'd run out of ways to tell him. There really was nowhere left to go. And now there was nothing left for her to do.

She'd lost. That's what Ink had been trying to say. She hadn't lost to Walter as much as she'd lost Martin, lost to him. Game over. She didn't bother to take any secret way.

She hopped on the Santa Monica and rode east. She didn't care if she drove double-5's or 10 miles over or 10 miles under. It didn't matter.

She dumped off the freeway, motored through some beat-up Valley and pulled up to the rear of a rundown California bungalow with terra-cotta tiles chipped like a broken smile. She parked the Scimitar in the alley and stepped through a weedy yard with a fence that leaned. She knocked hard on a door long past its paint.

A slight, bony woman answered. She was in her 70s with sharp, high cheeks that hinted at Cherokee blood. She stared at Patsy for an endless moment.

"I told you I never wanted you here again," the woman drawled in a dry, woody timbre.

"I just want you to know somethin'. I want you to know what I know now. Once you have a child and make mistakes with that child, you can understand the mistakes your mother made with you, even if they were different mistakes."

Her mother stood fixed like a headstone. There'd be no invite.

"I'm headin' back to Ink's bar. It's called the Nitty Gritty Saloon, east of downtown. They'll be waitin' for me there. This time, I'm gonna face it. I'm not lookin' for a thing from you this time."

Not a wrinkle flinched on the woman's bunched face. Her granite eyes pinned Patsy down in the doorway.

"Your grandson'll be there, and they'll be takin' 'im back to Illinois. I just thought you might like to see 'im before he goes."

She wheeled like a soldier and marched back to the Scimitar in small, fast steps.

70.

The bus clattered and Martin straddled the seat that rode the rear wheel well. It bucked him like a mechanical bull every time they hit a pothole.

He had $18.65 in his pocket. It was the money Ink gave him in the morning, minus bus fare. His chameleon eyes darted around, drawing the glances of people who had to ride the bus on a Saturday night: cleaning ladies, fast food workers, night watchmen. His whole life, he'd heard nothing but Midwestern twang and Little Egypt drawl, and now on one bus ride back from the Palisades, he'd heard colliding riffs of Farsi, Russian, Armenian, Tagalog, Korean. His ears picked up the chatter of a Latina, no more than 18, scolding her two hijos in Spanish. She had a third child on the way. He kept glancing at her, trying to make if she was safe. She finally smiled, and he leaned over to her.

"Is this how I go to the Nitty Gritty Dirt Bag Spittoon Magoon Saloon?"

The bus hit a bump and jostled him.

"¿¡Que!?" she shouted over the motor.

"Is this how I go to the Nitty Gritty Dirt Bag Spittoon Magoon Saloon!?" he yelled.

"No entiendo." She apologized with a kind shrug.

He squinted out the window for clues about where he was, but the icy bus lights sealed out the night. All he could see were reflections of the people inside.

An African-American man with an eye patch babbled to himself across the aisle. Uncle Chad had warned him about Black men — they usually went to prison, he said. But the man seemed stricken, not dangerous. He looked like he might've belonged in Hope House. Maybe he was the kind of person Patsy had been talking about before she sang her last song back at the bar. Maybe when he'd been a boy, that man had to live out on the street, give his body up for money or food, and that made him the way he is now. Maybe Uncle Chad wasn't right about everything just because he wore a badge and a gun.

Martin watched the man's reflection in the window glass, but a double reflection off the man's window planted one of Martin's eyes in the middle of the guy's head like a Cyclops. When he blinked, it blinked back.

"You hear the music, too?" the man asked.

Martin froze.

"You hear the music, too," the man concluded. He got off at the next stop, riffing about see-through notes of baby jazz crushed by a neutron star.

Martin's eyes moved over iterations of Our Lady of Fatima stickers plastered on the back of a seat, prophesying the End of Days. He whispered its warning: "Avoid hell for your sins." Graffiti blotted out the rest of the warning.

Each stop, more people slid off. The expecting mother readied her children and stood by the back door. She wished him well in English. The driver pulled curbside for her and the back doors unfolded. The bus hummed and shuddered up his bones as it idled. City heat invaded. The heat simmered the rain into a subtle steam, melded with asphalt and monoxide. She stepped out the back door. The doors screeched shut and the bus droned on like a rickety metal animal, maybe held together by twine and wire. He was the last rider.

He cupped his hands on the window and the Nitty Gritty's black façade flitted by. He jumped up. "I need to get off!"

The brakes squealed and he staggered. The rear door opened.

"Thank you." He waved and stepped out into the ginger haze.

71.

The frigid cave dark of the Nitty Gritty welcomed him in. Rick Derrenger wailed out "Rock and Roll, Hoochie Coo" from the juke. In back, Martin spied Dean Dealish shooting pool with Stuart. Martin tried to back out the door, but it was too late. Stuart spotted him and waved. He and Dealish strolled over with their pool cues. Milton watched from behind the bar.

"Heyyy, it's the thin man," Stuart said with a back slap. "Am I still too fat to be your lover's lover?"

They walked him to the bar and sandwiched him in on either side like old buddies might. Stuart ordered three fingers of Southern Comfort. Milton laid the whiskey down in front of Stuart. Stuart slid it over to Martin.

"Go on. It's on me."

Martin shook his head. Stuart leaned in real close so Martin could see the blood scabbed in his nose.

"It'll put some weight on you," Stuart said through his stuffed-up nose.

"If you tap this kid, when Ink gets back, he'll tear ya both into pieces too small to sew back together," Milton warned.

"Oh mind your own goddamn business." Stuart said. "Get your drink on, kid. Go on."

Martin pretended to sip it. Dean shook his head.

"Uh-uh-uh," Stuart clucked. He held the glass up to Martin's lips. Dean grabbed Martin's hair on the back of his head, yanked his head back and they made him slam the whole thing down in a second. He choked.

"We're just trying to make a man out of him," Dean explained to Milton. "How can we help you with that, son?"

A stupid stare plastered itself on Martin's face.

"We're going to make a man out of you, if it kills you. Now answer him," Stuart said.

"Find my mom." His head bobbled as the booze fizzed his blood, batted his eyes for him.

Stuart grabbed Martin's elbow to stop his fall. "Steady, steady. What's mommy's name?"

"Ann Amstead," he mumbled.

"I knew a woman with that name. She changed it though," Dean said as he stacked his fingers and held them out for another whiskey.

Milton shook his head and crossed his arms.

Stuart leaned over the bar and whispered to him. "It's either this, or we take him out back and bottle his fuckin' throat." He sat back down.

Milton's eyes pictured the image. He poured the drink.

"You know where this woman lives, Dealish?" Stuart said.

"Yup."

Milton set down the whiskey in front of Dean who slid it to Martin. Martin gurgled it down.

"Let's do it," Stuart said. He and Dealish each grabbed an arm and dragged Martin out the front door.

72.

Martin swayed in the back seat. He'd puked on his shirt. Outside was as bad as L.A. got. They were in Wilmington, in Harbor Hell, as Patsy called the refinery district. Fractionating columns piled into the sky and the air was sick with carbon.

They drove down a side street lined with shacks, rotting Royal palms, and dirt yards. Someone had blown out the streetlight so it was hard to see what lurked down the street. An abandoned Olds was parked in the middle of the block, stripped and up on pallets. Every once in a while, a car would slow ride down the street and stop by a shadow that hovered by the curb. Then the car would inch up to a figure in a hooded sweatshirt farther down, who took something from the driver. The hoodie made a signal to a runner, who jogged to the Olds, hunched down in the back seat, and sprung back out. He'd lope up to the car and hand something off. The car would speed away. It happened like that about four times in fifteen minutes.

Stuart kept his foot on the brake at the beginning of the block.

"She lives right over there, Marty," Stuart said, pointing to a house somebody had torched.

"This is not the street," Martin slurred.

Stuart turned toward Martin and pointed at his own nose. "Next time maybe you won't be so goddamn nosy. Out."

Martin bumbled out the back door of the Lincoln. Stuart zoomed off, almost running over the front man who took orders at the drive-thru.

Martin wobbled into the darkness. Even in the unlit night, his hair

smoldered like embers. The order taker, the mule, and half a dozen figures slid like cats from porches and gangways, coiling around him. They
were 15, 16 years old. One boy sat on the hood of a jack-chassised SUV.
He wore a white Starter jacket and matching silk sweats. A white do-rag
smoothed over his shaved head. He moseyed over last like he was in
charge, dragging an aluminum ball bat along the pavement. A deep scar
hooked out from the side of his eye in a sickle. He lifted his jacket to
show Martin his ink, from a Latin crew. Martin tried to read the street
tag written across his belly: SUGAR BEAR.

"What you gazin' at, white boyyy?" Sugar Bear said as he poked
him in the shoulder with his bat. Martin teetered and fell.

Sugar Bear's crew swarmed him, pulling his pockets inside out,
moving slow, methodical, the way police searched a suspect. One found
Patsy's letter. He lit a Zippo and started reading by its light:

"'A mother needs her boy, as much as the child needs his mother.'"

They laughed. The mule found Martin's two White Pages from the
phone books and unfolded them. Sugar Bear snatched them, studied
them.

"What's this, your Terminator list, holmes?" Sugar Bear said. He
slipped the pages in his pocket.

"It's from a telephone book," his mule explained.

"Yo se lo que es," Sugar Bear red-eyed his mule and barked back. "I
know what a telephone book looks like." He turned back to Martin. "I
asked the white boy."

"I try to find my mom with them," Martin burped, fighting through
the booze.

"Boy is on a radical pipe rage," somebody said.

They all laughed, except Sugar Bear, whose finely-honed sense was
trained on the street, on a blue sedan idling at the beginning of the block.

A lookout, a baby banger about 12, was cradled in the bough of a
tree. He shot Sugar Bear a complex hand signal. Sugar Bear signed back
a short burst. Sugar Bear couldn't read, but he'd taught himself and his
set American Sign Language.

One man, a chunky enforcer in his twenties with a simple-minded glare, dug the heel of his boot into Martin's Adam's apple.

"Tito here's in a mood, man. Soon as this coche feeds, you bought yourself some skull screws, esse. That's known," Sugar Bear said. "Up, let's go." He snapped his bat in along his arm like a switchblade.

His boys dragged Martin to his feet.

"Reyito, two red caps," Sugar Bear told his mule.

Reyito jogged toward the stash car.

"They is the police," Martin warned, sobering up fast.

Sugar Bear studied the car, its plates. He let out a whistle, clapped his hands twice, and stopped Reyito before he reached the Olds.

"You dime us? Eh, esse?" Sugar Bear shoved Martin.

"They is pretending to buy drugs from you!" Martin said.

Sugar Bear rammed the core of his bat in Martin's belly. Martin fell against a parked car and folded over on the curb.

"How would a vato like you know shit like this? Huh?" Sugar Bear kicked him.

"You friend get 'rrested. He tells the police on you's. He tells them where the drugs is."

Sugar Bear signaled his lookout, who climbed down from the tree, snuck low behind some cars on the curbside, and pulled the package from the junked Olds.

Sugar Bear delivered a few soft shots with his bat to the back of Martin's legs.

"How you know? Huh? You workin' for Puerco? You workin' off a debt? Eh?"

"I can see you thoughts! I hypnotize you!"

"Leash 'im up," Sugar Bear said.

Tito ripped off his own belt, lashed it around Martin's neck. "What'm I thinking now, bitch?" Sugar said.

"You is scairt. You worry about… 'Five-Oh.' You wonder if you could hide in you auntie's house."

Tito notched the belt as tight as he could. Martin gagged.

"Pleazz, I could not breath."

Something Martin said put worry in Sugar Bear's face. His crew dragged Martin behind the cranked-up SUV and shoved his head down. Martin's fingers dug at the belt but there was no wiggle room. His face swelled with blood.

"Loosen it," Sugar said.

Tito let the belt out a couple notches. Martin sucked in air.

"Do not go…to you auntie's," he panted. "The police…is there."

Sugar Bear waved for his crew to bring Martin out into the middle of the street. He created a diversion — shoving Martin around — while his lookout snuck through a gangway with the package and ran down an alley. The idling sedan squealed down the alley after the lookout.

"If that ain't the world. The bitch's a snitch for the People," Sugar Bear said. "Let's get ghost!"

They hauled Martin into the SUV and screeched off.

73.

Old school Latin techno thudded the windows. The elbows of Sugar Bear's crew were an iron maiden holding Martin in place. Tito drove and Sugar Bear rode shotgun, standing his bat up like a scepter between the seats. It was his SUV even if he wasn't old enough to drive.

"Hey X-Ray, you know what a Milagro is!?" Sugar Bear shouted over the bass as they shot over the bridge to Terminal Island.

Martin shook his head.

"Means 'miracle.' Mi tio used to say everybody's entitled to one miracle in their life. I don't mean just a lucky day. I mean like where the Holy Mother comes down and scoops your ass up, takes you out of the oceans so you don't drowned. I think you need to ask Her for that miracle to come to you right now."

Sugar Bear turned and faced him.

"You know, I heard that back in the day, boys like your age used to swim the channel to the Island out here just so they didn't have to pay a nickel for the ferry. A fucking nickel, X-Ray! Can you believe that shit!" He slapped Martin's thigh and laughed. "Know how to swim?"

"No," Martin said.

Sugar turned to Tito. "Right here."

The Chevy skidded to a stop on the bridge. A back door swung open. Reyito unloaded Martin with a kick and his head nicked the street.

"This is your miracle, X-Ray."

The Bear signed him 'goodbye' in ASL and flipped Martin's two White Pages at him. The truck burned its back wheels and squealed off.

As the trance music faded, he felt the scrape over his eye. He gathered the White Pages from the street and dabbed the blood with them.

74.

He sponged his face with a soggy hankie and massaged his chest. "Could you please just go a little faster?" Walter said to his brother.

"Are you alright?" Rachel asked.

"We have to beat them to the other address," Walter replied as he popped a pill. "We should've checked the other place first and waited for them. Just waited is," he breathed, "what we should've done."

Chad started a reply but held it in. An oily varnish shined up his scowl in the morning sun.

"I prayed on that and that's the answer that came: to just wait," Walter panted.

"Alright, lemme ask you a question, Reverend? You the Chief of goddamn Detectives or just God's little helper?" Chad said.

"Jesus Christ," Walter whispered.

"Thought you weren't supposed to use that name in vain," Chad replied.

"And when was the last time you set foot in a church?" Walter clicked his silver pill box shut. "You've exacerbated a bad situation."

"'Exacerbate.' Rhymes with 'masturbate,'" Chad observed, flicking his eyes toward Walter. "I like playing word games. For instance, the word 'therapist.' You know what I learned about that word, Rachel?" Their eyes met in his mirror.

"If you hyphenate it, it's 'the-rapist.'"

She closed her eyes. Walter turned toward him.

"That is enough. You leave her out of this, Chad!" He faced away.

"You're such a…" he mumbled.

Chad flicked on the A.C. "Such a what?"

"I told you the recycled air's no good for my allergies," Walter said. He popped a Claritin from another compartment in his pill box.

"Such a deviant? That what I am?"

"Will you please, both of you?" Rachel intervened.

Walter pouted out the window and they were quiet for a while.

"Back at the truck stop in New Mexico, why did they ask you all those questions?" she asked Walter.

"I hope you know where you're going, Sheriff," Walter said.

He folded his arms and shivered. He flipped off the air conditioning. Chad turned it back on.

"Walter?" she prodded.

Walter turned to the back seat and squared with her. "When this is over, I'll be happy to go through the sordid history of every person I ever had to reach out to when I was a youth minister. And there are a lot of them. And sometimes, you get burned if you try to help people in crisis. Sometimes, they've got problems because they're problematic. Sometimes they muddle up their feelings for you. They stop seeing you as an emissary of Christ. They see in you what they want to see. They see *you* as their savior."

"Hah," Chad grunted under his breath, and Walter shot his gaze upon his brother, before turning back to Rachel.

"They can accuse you of things if you refuse to give in to their demands," Walter explained. "It can descend into blackmail. I'd like to tell you all about Ann Amstead, but right now I'm trying to save the life of my son."

She glanced down, peered out the window, looked anywhere but at Walter, who stared her down with his glacial blue eyes.

"That's it. That was the street," she alerted Chad. "You just passed it."

Chad pulled a U and then a hard right onto Wall. He slowed down and they checked out the addresses.

"What does Martin know about her?" she asked.

"You know everything he knows. You're his therapist."

"No, bro. She's talking about what you might've told the boy," Chad said. They stopped at a light. Chad's cheek turned just a little toward her. "Nothing good grows in the dark," he said and smiled.

When the light changed, he rolled slowly so they could see the street numbers.

"A boy, especially one without a mother, one with...deficits, you can turn a boy like that awful easy. You can tit feed him the scary chapters from the O.T. You know, the stuff about how God laid Man low because Adam let a woman screw with his head," Chad said. "You spoon him all the holy propaganda about how women are a dangerous ruination and how some of them are harlots and how men should steer clear. And you tie it all up, weave all that in with the story of how his mother was one of them whores and how she sold her child out like Judas sold Jesus."

"Lies!" Walter said.

"You do that in private. You do that to inoculate the boy against her in case she ever shows up to claim him. You do that until he starts to hate, until he starts to act on that hate. Then you try to hold him back from doing it. In public, you talk to him about forgiveness. You bait and switch. You wean him off the fire and brimstone, and you start feeding him the same Gospel you been reading to your congregation the whole time," Chad said. "By then, your monster's done. Time to take him out of the oven."

The smooth bridge of her nose peaked between Rachel's chocolate eyes. Her breath was unsteady. She seemed like a child who'd just put together a horrible truth. Walter ground out a prayer between his teeth. The cityscape eroded into lower forms, open lots, clinicas.

"Do you know, Rachel, that the-rapist can assume a lot of forms. I nabbed my share of them over the years. Nowadays, they call rape 'criminal sexual assault.' Or even 'aggravated' criminal sexual assault if you do it with a minor. Statutory rape's what they used to call it," Chad said.

"What is he talking about, Walter?" Rachel begged, her voice cracked and soggy.

"Himself, I'm sure!"

"Do you know what it's like to grow up behind a saint and have to hold his robe while he waltzes down that aisle?" Chad said.

"You shame this whole family. Stop the car."

"And then have to go back and clean up his shit like the elephant keeper at the circus?" Chad's voice was brittle with hate.

"Stop the car!"

"You wanna walk? Fine, be my goddamn guest." He slammed the brakes.

"No, you passed it," Walter said.

Chad backed up the squad to the Nitty Gritty. Before he even stopped again, Rachel opened the door.

"You should wait here," Walter told her.

"I'll take a plane back."

He grabbed her elbow but she yanked it away and got out. She was crying.

"I'll tell you what went on," he promised.

"You don't need to anymore." She slammed the door and skittered away.

Walter got out and chased after her. He grabbed her by the hands.

"No matter what you think of me, we all need to focus on what's best for Martin. Do you believe he'd be better off with her in a place like this…"

"Don't worry, Walter, you look great." She smiled wicked through tears, pushed past him and stalked away.

"He needs you," he said.

She stopped and wiped her eyes.

"*You* need me. As bait. And I won't let you use me again."

She walked off but he followed her, reached into his pocket, and came up with cash. He caught up and tried to give it to her.

"You'll need this to get back."

"Not every woman goes that way. But don't worry, Reverend, your secret's safe with me. Your son's reputation needs protecting."

She crossed the street. She'd be long gone from Ukiah by the time he got back.

Chad stepped out of the car, leaned back on his door, folded his tawny arms, and shook his head.

"Past always falls due." He grinned.

He looked up at the Nitty Gritty. He crossed the sidewalk out front and glanced down. Handprints were set deep in one of the squares. Ink had promised to let anyone who'd been sober more than a year stick their hands in fresh cement. But there were only three sets — Ink's, Milton's, and Patsy's. Chad crouched down and traced his finger along the fingers in one of the hands, scooping out the dirt with his nail. ANNIE AMSTEAD, she'd scrawled under her palms along with her dry date.

"Past always falls due," he whispered.

75.

Chad tried the front door but the Nitty Gritty was closed, so he went around back. Ink usually propped the back door open to air the place in the morning. Chad stepped in from the alley and appraised the place. Milton did the New York Times Sunday crossword behind the bar. Cigarette smoke drifted like white nylons through early morning rays that filtered through the front window.

Chad meandered around. He loitered in front of Ink's tattoo parlor. Samplers covered the wall; images Ink had borrowed from Navajo blankets and sand paintings. Chad inspected the cracked mirror behind the bar, covered with a slab of cardboard from the bottom of a case of liquor. IMAGE TOO DIFFICULT TO CONTEMPLATE, Milton had written on it.

"Interesting place you got here," Chad remarked.

Milton never looked up.

"I'm looking for Ann Amstead. She also goes by Patsy Pringle. I have a warrant for her arrest."

He sat down across from Milton. He pulled a photo of Martin out and held it up.

"You seen this kid?"

"Nah," Milton said, without looking up.

"What about this man?" Chad asked, holding up a blown-up photocopy of Bob's state ID picture.

Behind the bar under Chad's elbow, Bob lay in state. His hands were crossed over his chest. A quartered lime fixed him with an unnatural

Joker's grin. Milton looked at the picture, pursed his tarred lips, and shook his head.

"You the boss?" Chad wondered.

"I look like it?"

"I'll wait."

Chad settled in on a stool, tapping his fingers on the bar gloss.

"What's a seven-letter word for 'anus?'" Milton asked as he stared down at his puzzle.

"That a clue in the puzzle?"

"No. Just wondering." By the time Ink strode through the back door, Chad had helped Milton finish about half the puzzle. Chad nursed a sweaty bottle of Miller. Ink slid behind the bar and hung his citizen's cut on the hook next to the register just like he always did. He uncapped a bottle of Fiji water with one hand just like he always did.

"You count last night's receipts?" he asked Milton.

"You don't seem to do much business," Chad addressed him with a grin.

"You want a tattoo?" Ink asked with his back to Chad. He still hated cops.

"Actually, I'm here to execute a warrant."

Ink glanced at Chad's beer.

"You know we're closed, right?" Ink said.

"Then you're in violation," Chad concluded, belching in Ink's face as he walked by.

"And you drove all the way from Illinois to write me up," Ink said as he popped the register.

"You mind if I look around?" Chad asked.

"That paper you say you got — it entitle you to?"

"It wouldn't sit too well with your liquor license if you held a fugitive," Chad said.

"Or with my illegal tattoo parlor. Get the fuck out of here, Illinois."

Chad nodded and walked out.

Milton set a piece of paper on the bartop filled with a grid of hundreds of dots aligned in rows. He and Ink started a game of dots. Whoever got to complete the fourth wall of any square wrote his initials in the box and pulled a scrap of paper from an old cookie tin. Milton made the first square. He pulled a slip from the tin and read a question:

"What's the name of the 1948 film noir classic starring Robert Mitchum and Kirk Douglas?"

"I thought we agreed," Ink carped. "No old movies."

Milton just held out his hand without looking up, and Ink frowned.

"I have no fucking idea," Ink admitted.

He turned to his register, pulled out a fin, and slapped it in Milton's palm.

76.

Patsy fell in through the back door about an hour later, as Milton added his initials to the last completed square in the game of dots he played with Ink.

"Uhm, I'm afraid you've lost again, Ink," Milton informed him, counting his money.

"They have paper on you," Ink warned Patsy. "Some Illinois badge is looking to enforce it."

She paraded up to the front door, unlatched it, and opened it. "I'm right here, Chad!"

"Did you find Martin?" Ink asked.

"Yeah. I told 'im. He hates me."

"What do you expect? Pulling johns down in front of his nose," Ink muttered.

"We needed a home."

"You don't go out and get a home. You make one."

"Not in a place like this."

"To do that, you had to act like a mother, Pats. But you've just been acting like something else."

"I just wanted to teach 'im to be on his own," she shot back. "You know what? Fuck off."

"He might not like you as a mother. But as a whore, you can always keep him coming back."

She picked up an ashtray and flung it at Ink, shattering what was left of the mirror.

"There's 49 more bad dog years," Milton said.

Ink stamped over and grabbed her.

"This is your third strike. They pop you now, you're no short timer like before. You parole out the back door. You understand that?"

"Let 'em come. I won't run for 'em anymore."

77.

Martin hiked down Alameda, negotiating wide rivers of boulevard that flowed between concrete shores. Morning smog burned his misty eyes. He seemed to search for a theme to the architecture, for a hue or style that linked one block to the next. Ukiah was an atoll where red brick and white frame repeated like parking meters. Out here, too many points of view all flooded into the same moment competing for his attention. He lost his heading.

He stopped at a taco stand for directions and ended up buying a tamale and a Diet Coke. Regular Coke had too much sugar. A man sprawled on the sidewalk next to the taco truck. He had no legs. His face was blotted and pink and raw with old skin peeling away before the new skin was ready. His thigh stumps squeezed a coffee can, the begging can. Martin peeped at the half-doll figure but he did it from the side of his eye. You weren't supposed to step on the trampled by gawking at them. Walter had taught him that. But that didn't mean you couldn't offer the man your tamale and Coke.

"No, thank you," the man said in a weak, displaced voice.

The man's eyes were someplace else. Martin stared into the can. A little lonely change scattered at the bottom. Martin was down to $13, but he leaned over and dropped in a ten and change.

"Thank you. God bless you," the man said. It sounded like a recording.

Martin saw the man's fold-up wheelchair parked by a meter down the street.

"Could I carry you somewhere?" Martin asked.

"No, thank you," the voice replied.

Martin nodded and glanced up and down Alameda. He finished his meal, wiped his mouth with his sleeve, and walked to the curb. He stuck out his thumb. Traffic thundered by in pulsing rapids. Finally, a Honda Civic dropped out of warp and puttered to the curb. It was rusty and dented. Martin looked it over. Mother Tallman drove a Civic even though she could have afforded a fleet of them. She used to parade him around town in it, showing off her 'adopted' grandchild, concealing his bloodline against all those small town questions. "My son thinks there are enough unwanted children in the world," she'd brag. "He's chosen to call one of 'em his son."

The man inside the Honda reached over and rolled down the window.

"Hi," the driver said over the traffic.

He had a silver beard, a little patchy on the jaw. He wore a blue sweater vest over a short sleeve shirt and blue jeans. He was about as old as Walter but thinner and less prosperous. He pushed the door open and Martin stepped low into the seat. Fast food wrappers and gas station receipts cluttered the floor, and the ashtray brimmed with nail clippings and floss rolled into tiny balls. Martin slammed the door and it clanged. The inside panel was stripped off.

"My name is Martin," he said. He flickered a nervous smile.

The man hesitated.

"Lloyd," he said finally. "You go down?"

Martin strained his eyes at Lloyd.

"Give head?" Lloyd asked.

"Head, down," Martin repeated.

He tucked his head under his shoulders like he understood. Lloyd seemed to think it was a joke. He drove a few blocks and turned into a warren of boarded-up factories.

"Is you going by the Nitty Gritty Dirtbag Spittoon Magoon Saloon?"

Lloyd smiled with curious eyes. "Sounds too rich for my blood."

He backed his hatchback down the loading dock of an empty factory. The dock dipped below ground level and swallowed up the Honda in both directions. The street was empty.

"I'll drop ya off in Compton." Lloyd held up a twenty. "This okay?"

Martin felt the dollars in his pocket. "Yes," he said with a puzzled grimace.

Lloyd stuck the bill in Martin's hand.

"I has money," Martin said, pulling out his three ones and showing them off. "I work for this."

"Okay," Lloyd sniggled, a little confused, a little intrigued.

They each pocketed their cash. Lloyd lifted up his vest. His jeans were already unbuttoned. Martin's eyes shot around the car. The Great Red Spot rose between his eyes. Lloyd unzipped himself and pulled out his junk.

"You wanna smoke this?" he invited.

Martin fumbled for the door handle but he couldn't find it.

Lloyd yanked his pants up. "Didn't you know what this was?"

Martin kicked at the door.

"Just pull the fuckin' handle. There," Lloyd said, leaning over to unlatch it.

Martin shoved him back and popped the handle.

"This is all I need," Lloyd muttered and pounded the wheel.

Martin launched out, stumbled, and ran.

"You're 18, right? You were 18?" Lloyd called after him.

Lloyd started up and squealed off past him. Martin found the alcove of a shuttered factory door and dipped inside. He leaned on his knees and gagged.

78.

Alone hooker, about 17, with stringy, dishwater hair, worked the deserted strip in front of Ink's in the fresh light of Sunday. She swung her arms up and down in a tweaker trance.

A junk truck chugged down the street. It was crammed with copper tubing, metal casement windows, and Martin Tallman. It squeaked to a stop by the Nitty Gritty and Martin jumped over the tailgate. He waved to the old man who drove it and walked toward Ink's.

Inside, the bar was clean and empty. The chairs rested upside-down on the round tables, making neat pinwheels. The sun ricocheted off the remains of the mirror behind the bar, penetrating the jade or dusky bottles of liquor like beams through stained glass.

She sat at the far end of the bar. She'd pulled her hair back in a prim bun and she wore a pristine, white blouse buttoned to the neck. She composed herself into a serene and deliberate pillar. Patsy savored her cigarette as if it was her first and her last. The skin around her eyes was resolved and firm. Through her black eye, she gazed at slivers of herself in the bar mirror. Martin's duffel bag was zippered on the stool next to her. On top, his jacket was folded without a wrinkle, and his plastic letter opener was set on top of that, polished bloodless in the cathedral light.

He swung open the front door. He stepped in but lingered by the door, skewering her with his eyes.

"I has to be sure," he told her.

She held her poise.

"Take out those phonebook pages you've been carrying around."

He pulled the pages from his pocket, wrinkled and damp like hankies.

"The second page, the one you haven't been to yet — what does it say?"

His eyes wandered down the page until they bumped into Ann Amstead.

"Go outside. Look up at the door."

He walked outside and the door closed. When he came back in, he wasn't the same.

She picked up the letter opener, walked over, and offered him the handle. She didn't ever eye him.

He took it in his hand. She waited.

The seconds trickled by but nothing kept the time. The world waited on him. The traffic waited outside while he made up his mind, holding its noise back.

He let the white blade drop to the floor.

"I is never going to kill her. I just want to find out why."

She picked up the letter opener, and teased its tip with a finger.

"I never could use it. I never want to kill you. Just to know why."

"And that's what you came all the way out here for?" The words hung low.

He nodded.

She nodded too, and drew in her thoughts with a breath.

"All this time, I've been trying to tell you why," her voice shriveled. "But you weren't ready to hear it. If you weren't ready to hear the reasons why, then you weren't ready to hear them from your mother who spoke them."

She pricked her finger and drew a red drop of dew.

"You sparin' your mother's life, or your girlfriend's?"

"You could not be my woman."

She nodded.

"You could not be my mom either."

"What you want me to be doesn't change what I am."

"I kiss you, feel you bottom."

"You didn't know."

"I is ashame."

"I led all the way, Martin."

"But I still love you."

She wedged the letter opener behind her ear.

"There was this boy named Freud. Had cigar breath. You ever heard of 'im?"

He shook his head.

"Well, he said that a boy's first crush? It's usually his mom."

"Okay," he said, his voice still in his throat.

"But they get over it."

He glanced over her shoulder and spotted his things packed on the stool.

"Your daddy's outside."

His head dropped a little. She noticed that.

"He promised me a last cigarette with you. We worked out a deal: no more Hope House. He says you got an auntie in town with an empty room over her garage. You're gonna get your own place. And a job." She didn't even try to sound excited. "You'll find that cheery cheerleader and start poppin' out little Martinets."

"What happens to you?"

"He won't have me arrested, if that's what you mean." Her eyes went back to the past. "Why should he? His ghosts won't come back ridin' in on a Harley to spook 'im." She smiled, sad and slight. "Fits nice, don't it?"

"Yes."

"I just want you to know, I'm not tryin' to save my own skin like last time I left you with 'im. The truth is, you were right: I couldn't be a mother to you." She took in the room. "Look at this place. Maybe you weren't ready to hear who I was 'cuz I wasn't ready to be who you need-ed me to be."

Their eyes fixed, each into the other, as the walls soaked up the last of morning. "C'mon. Your daddy's waitin'."

"I want to say goodbye to Mr. Ink."

She shot a teary nod toward the pool table, where Ink slept swathed in his POW/MIA flag. Martin walked over. He barely tapped Ink's shoulder. Ink pulled the flag tighter.

"Mr. Ink?" he whispered.

"Mm," Ink grunted, waking. "Oh, Martin. What's up?"

Ink sat up on the table and pinched the sleep out of his nose.

"I is going back to Illinois."

"Oh?" He perked up.

Martin nodded.

"You really want to go back?"

"Yes."

Ink hopped down and folded his flag military style.

"What'll you do?"

Martin shrugged.

"I won't find anyone to replace you. You're the best barback I ever had."

Martin's Great Red Spot glowed proud.

"You sure about this?" he asked Martin as he looked beyond him to Patsy.

She nodded. Martin nodded.

"Well, if a man's sure…"

Ink rolled his neck until it cracked, a morning ritual.

"Hold on," he said. "I got something."

Ink walked behind the black curtain into his branding parlor. He came back with a Navajo blanket. There were eight figures on it, standing in a ceremony. He presented it to Martin with both arms.

Martin gulped. "It is beautiful."

"My grandmother made it. It's called Ye'ii Bicheii. That means 'Gods for Grandfathers.'"

"Where is you grandmother and father from?"

"A place called Many Farms."

"There is many farms where I come from, too." Martin took the blanket and folded it in a perfect square. Ink held out his hand. Martin shook it soft, then looked back at Patsy who waited in enforced solitude.

"Please take care of her," Martin asked him.

"She'll be alright, Martin."

Martin walked over to the tanning machine. He stood there for a moment, not sure how to wake a vampire. Finally, he touched Bob's brow, his heart, and his shoulders with his fingers, making the sign of the cross. Bob came to and sat up, palming the gooey lime that had been in his mouth.

"What goes, Martin?"

"I is leaving."

"Ukiah, is it?"

He nodded.

Bob dropped the lime and stuck out his fingers for a stiff handshake. Martin winced.

"Oh, sorry," Bob said, wiping his hand on his shirt. They shook hands.

"Did you tell her you've always known that your dad didn't have to adopt you to be your dad?" Bob whispered.

"No," he murmured back.

"Hmm. It sounds like you want that to stay *our* secret," Bob said.

Martin nodded. "I hope you find the world's largest palindrope," he said.

"I've given up on palindromes for the time being. I find that I can only be possessed of one delusion at a time if I really want to excel at it. My focus from now on needs to be on matters vampirical."

He gave Martin the Vulcan salute and went back to dead.

79.

They stood like chess pawns — two U.S. Marshals guarding the street corners on either side of the Nitty Gritty. Chad parked in front and stewed behind the wheel. In the back seat, Walter sat next to Patsy's mother. They stared straight ahead, seated as far apart as dignity required and as the back seat allowed. Patsy couldn't bring herself to speak to him, so Walter had found another woman to handle the details for him: Patsy's mother had brokered the deal between Patsy and him.

As soon as Martin and Patsy stepped outside, Walter sprung from the squad and landed in his son's path. Old Mrs. Amstead listened through an open window.

"I just want to tell you how wrong I've been. I know the reason you ran away is because I was keeping you out."

Patsy saw the tears in her long-ago lover's eyes that had built up over 2,000 miles. They came out all at once. Walter had always been a blubberer. But people were watching, and all the wrong people — Patsy, her mother, his brother, the Government. So Walter gathered his face and turned his tears off. He took off his glasses to dry them. He smoothed his hair and took a deep breath. Patsy leaned against the brick of the tavern and lit her next cigarette with the butt of her last.

"You *are* part of our family," he said. "You always were. We're going to treat you like you were our own flesh and blood."

"Ha!" Patsy grunted.

"I've spoken to Virginia. She promises you that. Virginia is your mother from now on too, not just little Walter's."

That was all Martin needed to hear, Patsy figured as she snorted out smoke. Walter had managed to offer the one thing the boy couldn't pass up: the perfect stand-in mom. Patsy smiled and shook her head.

"You've got a little brother now who needs you." He took his son's hand and squeezed, but the hand stayed limp. "You're going to get your own place. Aunt Sue has that suite over the garage and we're going to fix it up real nice for you. Or you could come live in the house on Magnolia with us. Whichever you choose. But no more Hope House. In the Lord's name, I promise you that. And I want you to work in the church with me. I want you to have a job there, a job that pays."

And no one has to know the truth, Patsy reflected. But just like when she'd been 16, she tried to think about what was best for her child, not herself. She pocketed glances at Martin. He seemed impassive. Shouldn't he be more excited? But he was so stoic anyway. She would've almost tricked herself out to know what he was feeling right then.

She sensed an awkward poverty of words in Walter's immaculate mouth.

"Have — have you said goodbye?" he asked Martin.

His son shook his head.

"You'll need some time alone with her, then."

"How very generous," Patsy whispered.

Walter retreated to the backseat of the squad. He'd never once looked Patsy in the eye.

Martin approached her. They stood in an awkward face-off, with Martin at an angle to her. She flicked off her Marlboro and rubbed the corner of her eye. She couldn't look at him. And with the window open, Walter would hear everything.

"You can write if you want," she told him. "If you still want my address."

He pulled the envelope from her letter out of his bag.

"I has it," he promised.

"If he sticks you back in that Hope Hole, you get a hold a me," she said, looking into him with a promise of her own.

His sunny eyes smiled back.

"Take care a that singin' voice a yours, you hear?"

He couldn't peel his eyes off her. They were wet just like hers.

"You'll be better off with him. You'll see."

He nodded and looked down.

"Please don't take this the wrong way," she whispered.

She pecked him on the cheek, hugged him hard, and let him go. He picked up his bag and walked to the car. Momma pulled herself out of the backseat and she and Martin crossed paths. They stopped and took each other in for a moment. It was the first time she'd seen him since he was six hours old. Her back hunched down with so much that remained unsaid, but to tell him who she was now? It wouldn't have been right.

"Take care of you daughter," he said. Her eyes widened in surprise after he said that. But then narrowed in understanding.

"I-I will," she stammered. "I promise."

He set his hand on her shoulder, and then ducked in the car.

Chad signaled the Marshals and they left. Patsy waited until Chad pulled out. She hoped Martin would turn his head and look at her one more time. Just then he did. He smiled — a sad smile, she thought. She waved. She watched until the Ukiah Sheriff's car dissolved in the tide of exhaust that made everything fuzzy and grey. A crooked, distant smile attached itself to her face.

"It's hard having lost a child," Momma said.

Patsy's spray-on smile carried like a kite down the street as if she could follow him all the way back to Ukiah with it.

"But sometimes they come back," Momma soothed in her gentle drawl. "Sometimes, they come home."

Patsy's cheek dropped onto her mother's head. Momma embraced her, and Patsy's muffles found a home in those brittle, gray strands. Momma stroked her daughter's back, and shed a tear, too.

80.

Time seeped out in dribs and drabs the first few weeks after he'd gone. Day or night, no matter what time it was, she called it A.M. time: After Martin. There was so much room inside her now. He'd taken up all her space inside. Pre-Martin had been P.M. time, when the demons would dial her up any time, day or night, and remind her of the worst thing she'd ever done. Most of those fiends had moved out now. This was the first time since before Daddy died that her attic wasn't cramped with squatters dissing her and advisors dosing her with bad advice. The attic was empty. The Borderline Personality Committee may have been torture, but at least it wasn't lonely. The new silence disquieted her. She needed company. She moved in with Momma. She got her first straight job — working intake at a woman's shelter down in South Central. She paid her mother room and board, and she paid with clean money. She'd drop by Ink's now and then, but not as much as before. Some of her demons had stayed on at the Nitty Gritty after she'd left. Why risk being repossessed, she figured.

But Bob didn't mind demons. The deal Patsy had worked out with Walter included getting Bob's commitment order dismissed. He was free. Milton signed on as his rep payee and had his disability checks mailed to him. That paid for Bob's room at Milt's hotel. And Bob made a few extra bucks as Ink's barback. The delusions tapered off. He even gave up vampiring.

For Patsy, the new normal eventually gave way to terminal restlessness. That lust for the road, for something or someone different, had tracked her down in every town she'd ever called home. Boredom burrowed back under her skin. It was worrisome, and Patsy's mother felt the worry. It was dangerous, and Ink sensed the danger. But this time, the roots of her rootlessness weren't the same. It wasn't the man she complained about not having, then about having. It wasn't the city that made her long for open fields or the empty country that made her jones for action. And she wasn't carping about money. That was the worry. She wasn't saying anything. She didn't care enough to moan.

The job was about the only thing that kept her going. Then she'd come home, flick on the little TV on her dresser, smoke in bed, and eat Ben & Jerry's Strawberry Shortcake ice cream until the sugar helped her nod. She gained 10 pounds. In the old days, gluttony was the only Deadly Sin she wouldn't have to the party. Now, she didn't care.

"For you to lack a phrase for anything is the same as that Tom Cruise gettin' humble, Ann," Momma remarked one cool September morning in her kitchen.

Patsy didn't reply. She just thought about how Martin had suspected Tom Cruise was the Antichrist. All references referred back to Martin.

She stared out the lace-curtained window, the kind he would've wanted Rachel to hang in their kitchen. She strummed on a 12-string that Bob, Milton, and Ink — the Scarecrow, the Tin Man and the Lion, as she called them now — chipped in and bought her a few weeks back. Her chords wove themselves into a dirge, sounding out what she couldn't say.

She kept thinking back to the last words they'd had. Not the talk outside the Nitty Gritty. The words they'd had inside. The same phrase kept up in her mind, playing out like the sad tune she couldn't shiver off:

I'm not tryin' to save my own skin, like last time I left you with him.

She remembered the words exactly. It was terrible sometimes, having a memory like she had. And it was terrible that those words had been her own.

"He's better off with them," she muttered. "I'm damned unfit."

"What was that, Ann?" Momma asked, enthused Patsy finally flashed a vital sign.

"Momma, you remember what you always said about regret?"

"I do. At the end of life, you regret not what you've said so much as what's been left unsaid; not what you've done, as much as what remains undone."

An Amstead aphorism. Patsy first heard it the morning after she'd forgotten to kiss her guinea pig goodnight. Daisy died that night.

She fell quiet again, lost in her fingers, wandering in her strings and frets, rambling all the way up to the nut, back down again. The music was aimless and bruised like those storm clouds they'd seen together on the Panhandle.

"I don't know that I like that music," her mother said as she shuffled over and served up Patsy's egg-in-a-basket. "Play something that's got a happy ending."

She returned Momma's worried furrows with a fretful frown of her own, scrutinizing the advance of years in Momma's face. She'd been shocked to see that when she first saw her again. But what could she expect after ten years gone? Patsy ignored breakfast.

"Eat something besides ice cream. You'll get the sugar diabetes."

But Patsy didn't seem to have an ear for anything anybody said. She could only hear her guitar. Momma was so worried she'd even called Ink and asked him to stop by. She didn't care for Ink, but she knew her daughter trusted him.

The kitchen door stood open, but Ink leaned against the railing outside, waiting to be acknowledged as was the custom of his people.

"Come on in, Rainer," Momma said, addressing him by his given name.

"Mrs. Amstead," Ink said, greeting Momma with a respectful nod.

His old snakeskin boots scuffed up the floor as he stepped in. Patsy tried to smile but only managed a quick grin. She kicked out a chair for him. Ink spun it around and squatted on it backwards like he always did. He draped his smooth, heavy arms over the back.

Momma poured them coffee.

"What brings the big man anywhere near the Valley," Patsy wondered as she lit a smoke.

She was down to Marlboro Lights now, which she made by poking pinholes in the filters of Marlboro Reds.

"I got a surprise," Ink said, putting on a rare smile as he fished a letter from his vest.

Her fingers froze. Her heart drumrolled. *A letter from Martin!?*

"I'm turning the place over to Milton for a couple weeks and making a run out to the Keys," he said. "You could ride as my fender."

There was a new rally in Key West this year and it promised to be big. But Patsy's eyes faded. She didn't want any part of it.

"If that's all you came down here to tell me, you might as well turn tail and head right on back to the Nitty Gritty," she said.

But she couldn't even keep a good head of displeasure going for very long. She lapsed back and strummed those blue, off-chords that worried her mother so much.

"Actually, Queen Ann, I have more tidings," Ink said.

He looked at a photo of Martin enshrined on the table, set in an expensive silver frame that shouted down the cheap Special Olympics picture inside. Every bit of Walter had been eliminated from the picture except for the hand wrapped over Martin's shoulder. These last few weeks, Ink had been just as assiduous in excising Martin from all his conversation with her. So had Momma.

"Can I address you now? I mean, you look pretty busy," Ink said.

She shrugged and strummed.

He made a big deal of flattening the letter out and presenting it to her.

Guillermo Robles, the letterhead read. *West Coast Hospitality, LLC.*

"Remember that Marine buddy I tried to get you to meet the night you and that trick mixed it up?"

"He wasn't a trick," Patsy sighed. She expressed no indignity over the fact Ink would say something like that in front of her mother.

"He owns eight clubs all across the state," Ink said.

Patsy homed in on Martin's picture. She kept seeing him the way he looked when she told him he was going back to Ukiah.

"These are nice places, Pats. Clean, $30 covers. You work for tips, and he promises a base," Ink went on.

The boy didn't really want to go back to Ukiah. That's what his crestfallen look had told her back at the Nitty Gritty that last day. She strummed a little harder.

Ink and her mother traded glimpses. Ink laid fingers on the fretboard and squelched her music.

"He wants you to play," he said.

She nodded like she understood and started strumming again. It was soft and mournful at first. Then she wrung the blue out of it and picked up the pace.

"Damn me, I'm a coward. Damn me, I'm a coward," she sang quietly.

She played faster and louder, gathering fire in her hands and stoking the Great Red Spot between her eyes. She dug hard fingers deep into the wires, spinning out the machinated thunder of a locomotive, strumming so violent it shocked Ink's fingers and he yanked them off the strings. He had to let the music come out. It was twisted and powerful, splashing pain in Momma's face. Ink reared back.

She stamped her foot to the crazy, atonal piece that flew out of her hands, raising the hair aback Ink's cowhide neck.

"Damn me, I'm a coward. Damn me, I'm a coward! DAMN ME, I'M A COWARD!"

She shot up, raised the guitar like a sledgehammer and slammed its back on the table, shooting out breakfast plates and hot coffee underneath. The dishes shattered but her instrument stayed whole as it chimed a final chord from the soundhole, deep but hollow. Momma and Ink froze.

"I'm goin' back," she declared.

"Aw, man, you've already been," Ink groaned, flicking a broken cup handle off his lap.

"You are not going back there," Momma said.

She looked at her mother, then at Ink, back and forth again.

"Don't you get it? I sold him out. Again. I told myself I was sendin' 'im back 'for his own good,' but I was still too busy tryin' to save my own worthless ass!"

"Well it won't do a lick of good going back!" Momma shouted. "Not where he is now!"

Stillness jacketed the room. Ink and Momma didn't dare join eyes. A truck shuddered by out front.

"'Where he is now.' What does that mean?" Patsy said, unnaturally calm. Momma glanced at Ink, looking for a lifeline.

Patsy picked up the guitar by the neck and readied to clear the counter with it.

"I mean it," she hissed.

"It means you can't break somebody out of the same place twice," her mother confessed.

Patsy bowed her head, ready to charge. Her irises stabbed out from the tops of her eyes, riveted on Momma. She accused her in a cold, measured rumble —

"Do you mean to tell me…you knew…my boy…was locked up in Hope House…………and you said nothing?"

She turned on Ink.

"You knew 'bout this too?"

"You're like candy glass. We thought you'd try to kill yourself," he said.

"Oh bull —"

"I'm not going to leave this earth with my daughter in prison!" Momma said.

"But it's okay if Martin is!?"

"He isn't in prison. He's in a home," Ink said.

"The only thing worse than livin' the kinda life I've had to live is to not live it at all," she said. "Thanks to your Judas ass, that's what he's got now!"

Ink ground his jaw and swallowed his fury. No one ever accused him of being a traitor.

"You wanna know something? What you just did to me is worse than anything Walter ever did. When he kicked me outta town, at least he did it to my face," she said. "I'd rather let him fuck me again than spend another minute with either of you."

"Yeah, well you sold your kid, not us," Ink replied.

She flung herself at him, sinking her fists in his chest, slapping his face. He held her off, until she pulled his ponytail. Then he tossed her seat first on the table.

"Did he write me? Did he write me!?"

She squalled over to Momma, grabbed her wrists and turned them over, exposing her mother's veins, gnarled and blue.

"Gimme the key to the goddamn breakfront," Patsy said.

Patsy flung the arms down. Momma backed over to the silverware drawer and pulled out a skeleton key.

Patsy swiped the key and rushed to the dining room and over to an antique cupboard that housed a small secretary desk. She jammed the key in, jerked down the desktop, and pulled out a false back. All the important papers, all the Amstead family secrets, had always been stowed back there. And there it was, an envelope addressed to her at the Nitty Gritty in Martin's perfect upper and lower case, almost as if the words had been typeset.

Jittery hands reopened the envelope and unfolded the letter inside.

Dear Ann and Patsy, I call you both names because I is not sure which is you real name anymore. You tell me if I ever is in Hope House again, I should let you know. I do bad. I try to run away to see you again, but I get caught and dad locks me up. I belong here. But I would like you to visit me. Maybe you could take a vacation and stay in Hope House again. I has to go now. Dr. Hope is coming down and I do not like him to see my writing.

It is Martin.

PSSST:
My Dad sees my tattoos and makes me get rid of them. I did not know tattoos could be derased like phone messages.

In the way that Martin had done, judging from all the creases, she folded the letter back up into quarters two times and slid it back in its envelope. She walked back to the kitchen.

"I need your bike," she told Ink.

81.

Bells chimed midnight in the little white church at the end of Hickory Street. They'd fall silent until morning. She puttered into town and nudged the Scimitar along the curb, and made sure it was in the tow zone. She'd spent her life running from the law. This time she wanted them to run into her. She walked down the empty street.

It had been a nonstop haul all the way from the coast. Patsy yawned. She made her way to Presidents' Park, Ukiah's one and only. She nestled in behind some rose bushes in back of the bandstand. She tried to nap in the rose petals, but she was cold and the thought of aphids mining her scalp made her itch. She stretched and decided to walk around town. Her first stop was Glass Factory Road.

The houses along Glass Factory Row were all gone. Somebody plowed them under in favor of a nursing home and a parking lot. Old people seemed to be the only growth industry left in Ukiah. She stood on the asphalt where her house used to be. She closed her eyes and smelled the small town night, the sweet winds of cows drifting in from the farms. For this moment, she'd never left.

They still lived in this spot, her and Dawn sleeping on the foldout couch, Daddy and Momma in the only bedroom. She heard Momma whisper for Daddy to stop snoring. She tasted the cold, coppery water she used to sip from the yard hose and heard Daddy peal out that piercing whistle he could do with no fingers — the one that called her home from games of ditch on summer evenings. She heard her cousin Margie call out "Olee Olee Olson Free Free Free!" after Margie gave up when she was the one who was It.

She heard Momma playing "Jimmy Crack Corn" on the record player, ghosting Mitch Miller's all-male chorus with her sweet, soft hum. She pedaled her Big Wheel down the sidewalk, the panels of the concrete heaving from the roots of the cottonwoods and elms in the parkways. Mr. Hoffman two doors down asked Annie how old she was, and she held up four fingers stained purple with Popsicle.

There were no such things as dying and longing. She didn't know there was a world outside Ukiah to be exiled to. And she wasn't old enough to know she was Glass Factory people.

She opened her eyes, expecting all the inequity and iniquity of what her life later became to hose her in the face like cold, autumn water. She expected the ache that came with trying to hang onto someone already passed on or someone who didn't want you the way you wanted them. But the ache didn't come. The place where her house had stood wasn't hers anymore. She didn't live on this street. Ukiah wasn't her town. But it wasn't anybody else's either. She realized then that the pain came from trying to hang onto something you couldn't own.

When she'd do lines with faded, second-string rock stars or hand out drinks in her bunny suit at preview parties, the BP's would ask where she came from with a funny "accent" like she had. She'd laugh Ukiah off. "Even the roadkill go off and die somewheres else. They wouldn't be caught dead in Ukiah," she'd crack. But she'd spent every moment since she'd left time-traveling back to 16 and trying to fix what went wrong. She ran and ran, but she'd never been able to leave town until just now, when she was standing right in its middle.

She walked past Washville School. All those junior high resentments — when Willie Newborn tossed a jar of spit at her; getting slapped in the ass by a row of boys before a volleyball game and Mrs. Nillson calling her a tramp for it. She could still remember these things, but they didn't carry a charge anymore.

She walked out along the highway to Gretta's, where some outlaws had tried to pull the train on her. She could always call that one back in an instant. The images would flood in like it happened this morning in flashbacks only an eight-ball could fade. She stood on the highway in front of the bar and tried hard to invoke that shame, but she couldn't. She remembered falling in the mud in the parking lot, but she couldn't feel the dirt on her anymore. It wasn't that she was numb. She was over it.

Everywhere she walked, there'd been a memory that could jolt her long distance, 2,000 miles and 20 years removed. She couldn't help it — it was part of her disease: borderline, histrionic, PTSD, whatever you wanted to name perfect recall coupled with a heart as sensitive to feeling as her ear was to pitch. That Dialectal Behavioral Training group at the hospital told her she couldn't be cured of a personality disorder. But now, recollections that had stored incapacitating voltage for decades lost their shock. All the melodrama winnowed down to a final *So what.*

And this night, she felt Daddy standing beside her for the first time since he'd died.

"I gotta give it one final test, just to be sure," she whispered to him as she walked back into town.

She treaded down Magnolia Street in the darkness, the boulevard parkway sheeted in cool, silky breeze overlain with cricket chorus. She waited for her heart to thrum, for her stomach to kink, as she closed in on it. And then she stood in front of it — the home, the Tallman home, with the Tallmans still in it, the ones she hated anyway. The ones she used to hate. But there was no gnaw in her belly this time, no taste of vomit on her tongue. No snake coiled itself around her ribs tighter with every breath. It was just a big, old plantation house with tall windows curtained and dark. It even looked peaceful, she thought.

She didn't know why it had happened, but she knew what had happened. She finally learned that the facts were outside her, beyond her grasp as they slipped into the past. But the feelings had been inside her all along. Now she could separate the two. Her ideas about things were all she owned and the only things she could choose. Long ago, she'd fallen under the spell that her anger and her agony were inflicted by a town and its people. She thought the world had pained her, but she'd wounded herself with the world. She thought the world owed her, yet she only owed herself. How many shrinks and social workers and PO's had tried to get that through her head? And now it came all by itself without suffering. Maybe that's what grace was — unexpected ease. Maybe there was something in Martin's God she'd missed.

Grace wasn't something God gave you even though you didn't deserve it. It was something you didn't earn because there's no way to earn what you already were. There was no way to work for it, to improve yourself to become worthy of it. You never lost it. You didn't need to add anything to yourself to convince God you deserved it. You needed to take stuff off just to see it for yourself. Each of us were and are and always will be innocent children, no matter how many welts and bruises and scars we pile on top to hide it from ourselves. That's what Martin had reminded her of; that knowledge of who she really was, which she'd forgotten after Daddy died.

She wandered behind the house, to the yard. The swing where she and Walter sat that night she fell in love with him was gone along with the Mulberry tree that had stained it. She waited for the electric shock as she stood where they'd sat. But she wasn't in love with him anymore, so she couldn't be in hate with him either.

It was still dark, but the east stirred with its first light. That was her cue. She slipped off her boots and walked back up the parkway in the center of Magnolia Street, cleansing her soles in the dewy grass. She wandered down Hickory to the Bun-on-a-Run Eatery. The sign showed a hotdog with legs chasing a bun. Patsy snickered at the unwitting, small town double entendre. At the same time, she savored the innocence of it.

The diner was closed. A pudgy woman with a washed-out face and an unlit cigarette stuck on her lip cursed as she huffed up to the door and jiggled the wrong key in. She looked about ten years older than Patsy, who waited while the woman found the right key.

"Uh, breakfast won't be ready for a while, but you can come in and wait 'til Auggie shows," the woman said.

"Okay," Patsy replied.

The waitress flipped on the icy fluorescent lights, blinding Patsy, and tossed her big bunch of keys on the old Formica counter. She flicked on the coffee maker plied with fresh roast readied from the night before.

She glanced at Patsy.

"Do I know you?" the woman asked.

"No. Yeah. Yeah, you do. Ann Amstead."

"I know that name. I do and I don't, ya know?"

"Wacky Annie," Patsy said.

"'Wacky Annie?' *Ohhhh!* Wacky Annie," she remembered. She fingered her nametag and smiled. "Bunny. Bunny Bower."

"You were a cheerleader," Patsy recalled as she puckered a Marlboro. She glanced at Bunny's puffy eyes and double chin and hid a satisfied grin.

"And prom queen," Bunny swanked in self-mockery. She poured Patsy a quick half-cup.

"I was long gone by senior year," Patsy reflected.

"You were big as a house. I remember."

Patsy lit the cigarette and kept the match going for Bunny's.

"So, did the asshole make you an honest woman at least?" Bunny asked.

"There were ecclesiastical complications."

Patsy looked at the church through the window as Bunny studied her.

"It wasn't one of them Tallmans, was it?"

She topped off Patsy's mug.

"Those Tallman boys bagged about half the virgins in Ukiah. Didn't seem fair to the rest of the stags in town," Bunny said.

Patsy smiled. She didn't feel like talking now. She just wanted the sun that had begun to break through the old storefront glass to warm her up and bring her back to life. That made her a lizard, she supposed. She smoked, nursed her coffee, and waited for the church doors to open. When they did, she paid her bill and left a $20 for a tip.

82.

Chad loved the Sunday morning shift since there wasn't much to do. He'd take it for himself and putter around the office. He'd left his Egg McMuffin half-finished on its paper wrapper, and his coffee still steamed through the plastic lid. In the chaste morning light that poured through the old-fashioned metal blinds, he worked an X-rated crossword puzzle.

Chad could hardly believe what he saw when he peered up: Annie Amstead strutting by on the other side of the street, in a black bomber jacket and matching harness boots, on her way to church.

83.

The brakes squealed. The sun pounced off the hood. Chad's wheels straddled the highway's midline just inside Tazewell County, the next county over. Dent corn walled his patrol car in on both sides, nearly ready for harvest. His boot struck the blacktop with purpose. He yanked open the rear door.

"Out!"

She uncoiled herself from the back seat. It was hard getting out when you were manacled.

"You gonna seize my second bike too?"

He unlocked the cuffs.

"Maybe you could impound it for yourself, Sheriff. I hear the soph-omores really get wet when a big, strappin' man such as yourself rides 'round town on a Harley. Except they wouldn't be able to tell who the Hog was."

He shoved her against the hot metal trunk and stuck his lips by hers so she could smell the onion from Saturday night's pizza.

"You come back to my jurisdiction, you get natural life. Do you under-stand? You have two felony convictions behind you already, so you're on your third batch, bitch. You're wanted on outstanding felony warrants in two states. One of them's aggravated kidnapping. That's Class X."

He twisted her arm behind her back and wrenched up the arm.

"Ow!"

"When my brother, as complaining witness, and myself, as arresting officer, decided not to execute those warrants, that didn't mean they went away. The statute's open. Somebody with your legal experience oughtta know what that means."

He marched her to the shoulder.

"Sad Chad. You'll always be Big Brother's little brother."

He shoved her into a ditch and she rolled into some thistles.

"And you stay away from Hope House," he warned.

He jumped back in his squad and scorched a violent three-point turn.

"Such a powerful man. But where's the love, Sheriff?"

He flipped her the bird, then roared back to Logan County. A crow landed by the ditch and cawed.

"You again, senorita? Last time I saw you I was bustin' out. This time I'm bustin' in."

She picked herself up and pulled the burs from her hair. The crow cawed three times more.

"That a welcome or a warning?"

She headed back toward Logan County.

84.

The church was cozy, more like a parlor, anointed with red oak timbers that ribbed the knave like the boughs of the elms on Magnolia Street. The long, clear windows were framed with cherry wood and swathed in burgundy satin sashed to the sides to welcome in the last Sunday before autumn. The window frames matched the burnt sienna lacquer gleaming from the pews. The carpet was smoky red wine and the walls shone soft morning white with a breath of cadmium yellow. The altar was unadorned, except for an intricate 17th century pulpit rescued from a bombed-out church in Dresden, Germany, just after the war. The pulpit was an incongruity, relieved with panel carvings of lions and lambs and the faces of the Gospel writers. Fed by a winding staircase, it stood too high for such a small church. The people in the first few pews had to crane their necks to get a good look at the man who'd mount its stairs.

The only stained glass in the place was the simple rose window over the choir loft, where a small pipe organ accompanied the singers. The choir's red satin robes matched the drapes. Mr. Nicholson, Patsy's old music teacher, led the choir and played the organ. Their chorales were locally famous because of one young man. In the insular celebrity of small town church choirs, Martin was a Sunday morning cynosure.

Packed pews listened to him render a solo of "Simple Gifts." With his eyes closed, Walter floated on the altar, robed in a green cassock overlain with a seamless white surplice. His lightsome wife and his namesake nestled in the first row. Dr. Hope sat behind Virginia with his own wife and teenage twins, identical girls. Mr. Kantwell was there, retired from the League of Ushers due to pulmonary fibrosis. Cammy, the cheerleader who made Martin sign her yearbook, hunched hungover in a back pew. Her mother made her come.

The last of Martin's baritone floated out the windows. A final chord from the organ found its way into the oak and satin, and the church was wrapped in silence. Walter climbed the stairs to the pulpit to read the day's reading, from the Second Letter of Paul to the Corinthians:

> "'I have to boast, even though it does me no good. But I will now talk about visions and revelations given me by the Lord. I know a certain Christian man who fourteen years ago was snatched up to the highest heaven. I repeat, I know that this man was snatched to Paradise, and there he heard things that human lips may not speak. So I will boast about this man — but I will not boast about myself, except the things that show how weak I am. If I wanted to boast, I would not be a fool, because I would be telling the truth. But I will not boast, because I do not want anyone to have a higher opinion of me than he has as a result of what he has seen me do and heard me say.
>
> "'But to keep me from being puffed up with pride because of the many wonderful things I saw, I was given a sting of the flesh, which acts as Satan's messenger to beat me and keep me from being proud. Three times I prayed to the Lord about this and asked Him to take it away. But His answer was: 'My grace is sufficient for you, for in weakness, power reaches its perfection.' I am most happy, then, to be proud of my weaknesses, in order to feel the protection of Christ's power over me. I am content with weaknesses, insults, hardships, persecutions, and difficulties for Christ's sake. For when I am weak, then I am strong.'"

Outside, Patsy marched up Hickory Street. She spied Chad sitting on the bottom church step, smirking at her. She stopped in front of the pharmacy, shuttered for the Sabbath. Through the pharmacy window,

Chad grinned at her from an election poster that tendered him as THE ONLY TRUSTY CHOICE for Sheriff.

She picked up a newspaper box and heaved it through the window, knocking the smile off the real Chad as she knocked his image out of the window. An alarm rang, but the real Chad didn't budge.

She crossed the street and saddled up, the Scimitar tagged with a fresh ticket. She ripped it off the handlebar and keyed up. She pawed her boot on the asphalt and revved the machine. She upshifted — 1st, 2nd, 3rd, 4th. She coiled her head in her shoulders, her eyes homed in on the hunter a block down.

He stood, and set his hand on his gun. She set hers on the throttle, and poured it on wide open in a burnout. Her thunder swallowed the shrill drugstore alarm. Her pipes shook with thrust, and she used every ounce of muscle to gag its launch.

She went into an extreme crouch, speared her arm forward, popped the clutch, and unleashed the front brake.

"Yahahhhhh!"

The Scimitar's black flew like a heat-seeker down Hickory at the man who drew his gun. It was him or her. If he didn't fire, she'd run him down. It was her or him. If she didn't run him down, he'd fire.

She streaked so fast he couldn't keep a bead on her. The hunter held his ground. She sprung the curb and soared over the steps. He fired, and the bullets crisped her mane. He dove in the bushes as she landed.

She crashed through swinging doors and that slowed her run. She worked the front brake, easing the rear brake as she chewed up center aisle and counter-steered, leaning her bars left, turning right. She almost low-sided, but her front wheel caught the altar step and she came upright like a skier braking to a stand. Rubber side down.

The Reverend gawked down from the pulpit. Virginia squeezed Baby Walter. Dr. Hope fainted.

Patsy stared at all those horrified eyes through acrid rubber that rose from friction tracks still smoking like a slow fuse down center aisle. They all had a bad look out for her. She downshifted, flipped the kill switch. She stepped off her machine, toed the kickstand down, and faced them with her hands on her hips.

"It's the attention-seeking again," she said.

Martin leaned at the balcony's edge.

"I RiSViP to your invitation," she called to him.

Walter stumbled down from the pulpit and whispered to Mr. Mack, the burly usher with a jarhead cut. With a finger crick, the Reverend summoned Hope, recovered from his swoon, and murmured instructions. Mr. Mack and the doctor whooshed down the side aisle and Mack left church. Hope ran the steps up to the choir loft.

Walter cleared his throat as he approached her. He stayed on the altar two steps above.

"You need to leave," he said.

"This really ain't about you and your family, Walter. It's about me and mine. So far as they overlap, I s'pose you do have an interest."

"I feel so sorry for you, Ann," he said.

The choir roiled as Martin fought off Hope's hands. A loud thump echoed through the organ pipes and Hope screeched like a cat.

Martin flew down the stairs and up the side aisle. Chad tripped up the outside steps and pushed through the doors, blown off the upper hinges. Cuts from the rose bushes marred his tanned election face. Walter held his brother off with an outstretched palm, and Chad nodded. He blocked center aisle with an unrequited rage heaving in his chest.

Mr. Mack came back into church with Chad's deputy, Greg, and four big men. The deputy handed Chad a fistful of warrants on Patsy. Then Mack and Deputy Greg fanned out up the side aisles and clogged the side exit. Martin was bottled up in the side aisle. The other men held back with Chad. Deputy Greg took out his cuffs. Whatever would happen, would happen here.

"You can haul me away, gentlemen, but you can't stop my words from landin' on you. I'll just wait on the judge and tell it to him, and it'll be all the worse on you for havin' waited longer," she said.

Chad dispatched the men up all three aisles. She had to tell it fast.

"My name's Ann, of the Amsteads. I don't know you gave us much thought, but I remember most of you. I was known by people in this town. You know what I mean."

The men advanced on Martin, who stumbled through a pew. Virginia held Walter, Jr. close.

"I was 15 and you tried to know me, Mr. Kantwell. I mean, I was goin' on 16, and Mr. Dobson, you knew me, too," she said to a heavyset old man who'd taught her gym, and some other things.

"That can't be, as I am married AND HAVE GRANDKIDS!" Mr. Dobson shouted her down.

"And I won't let you ruin my name or the good people of this town," Mr. Kantwell wheezed through his O_2 cannula.

"Get her out!" somebody shouted.

"I was 16, and you knew me, Reverend. You knew me best of all." She turned and faced him.

"All I ever tried to do was help you," Walter insisted.

She turned to Martin.

"Martin, what seems like a lifetime ago, you asked me why I left you. But I only gave you half an answer," she said as the men closed in. "Most people can't stand the blank slate the universe is 'cuz they can't handle the terrible freedom that comes with choosin'. So they let other people tell 'em how wide their ties should be, which rascal to vote for, who to marry. They even let other folks tell 'em what God's will is for 'em. But they gotta have reasons behind it, excuses for everything they choose. Your reasons'll kill you, Martin.

"When I left you behind, I had all kinds of reasons, and they were good reasons: I was 16. I was crazy. I'd just OD'd to prove it. I was in love with a solid man from a powerful family. He'd take care of my son. He'd make sure you were okay."

Dr. Hope walked up center aisle. From opposite ends, he and Mack penned Martin up in the middle of a pew. Martin parted shoulders and stepped over pews to get to the altar.

"But that man went back on his word, not once, but twice," she accused.

"I never 'knew' you and I never went back on anything. Please, let these men take you to a place where you can get help," Walter said. "I won't press charges if you seek help now."

"Make me the crazy one, huh, Reverend? With the threat of jail if I won't play the part. The strategy worked once before."

"It's in your record, Ms. Pringle or Amstead or whatever your real name is," Dr. Hope said. "You've tried to kill yourself. And you either faked crazy to get into Hope House or you really do hear voices. So that makes you a scam artist or a psychotic." He threw the labels down as Chad's men walled her in, squeezing the vise. "You've been in jails and psychiatric wards half your life. You've prostituted yourself in order to weasel old men out of their fortunes. I think that makes you both."

"Currently wanted in two states! For stealing this church's money!" Chad shouted, holding up the paper on her.

"Yeah, I took it. But it was money from this same church you paid me off with when I was 16, wasn't it, Walter?" she said.

Two men grabbed her and Deputy Greg cuffed her.

"No!" Martin shouted. "Leave her 'lone!"

He fought his way to the altar, but Mack and Hope sandwiched him and grabbed his arms.

"You leave him alone!" she shouted. "That boy didn't do nothin' wrong but be born to the wrong woman. And the wrong man!"

The church stilled. A senate of shocked eyes set on her. They were her jury. And Walter's, too. But Walter's centurions were dragging her away before she could make her case.

"Please!" she yelled. "Make him let me prove it."

Walter laughed. "There are no proofs of lies."

"I know how to prove it, Reverend. You take a paternity test," she said.

"I am not going to accede to a demand fed by your delusions," he said.

"Prove it ain't a delusion!" she said as she grabbed onto a pew so they couldn't haul her off.

"You come back after all this time to make these… 'accusations'? Martin's 18 years old. Have you ever heard of the statute of limitations!?" Walter yelled.

"Then you got nothin' to lose," she replied.

He wiped sweat with the sleeve of his robe.

"This is insane," he said.

"But it's gettin' saner."

She and Martin kicked and clawed just to stay in church. Walter appealed to his jury:

"Sometimes, for what they say, for what they do, a leader becomes a target." But she could tell from their faces there was reasonable doubt about him now. "And sometimes, the character of a leader is assassinated for failing to appease an imperious demand of the flesh," he preached.

"The cover up's always worse than the crime," she said.

"You heard her say it — she was in love with me. And when I wouldn't return that love in the way she wanted, she swore she'd get me back. I just never thought she'd hold on to her hate for eighteen years."

"DNA, Rev, Does Not Alter. Not even after eighteen years."

He quoted Paul: "'I am content with weaknesses, insults, hardships, persecutions, and difficulties for Christ's sake. For when I am weak, then…I am strong!'"

"But you seem to think it stands for 'Does Not Apply.'"

She was winning the war of words, but he was winning the war of muscle and law. Cammy ran up the aisle and stopped them from taking Patsy any farther. The resolve of Walter's forces was weakening. They felt the jury's ambivalence. The men held her in place, waiting for something to sway them. For the first time in her life, the balance was even between her and Walter. She needed something, someone to give her the weight.

Instead, Chad proceeded up center aisle and ceremoniously presented her with warrants for her arrest. "Ann Amstead, also known as Patsy Pringle, I place you under arrest for the crimes of aggravated kid —"

"Let her finish," a voice said. It was a young father with a wife and kids in the pew.

Chad glanced at his brother, who backed him off with his hand again. Walter had to convince his people. What a jury in Peoria would do to her later didn't matter. This was the one that could do him in now.

"As your counselor in faith, I invite you to strengthen your trust. I ask you to take my word," and then he turned bitter, "against the word of a woman who has been certified a danger to others and to herself, with a tortured history of fraud and imprisonment, who, though unfit to mother, is trying to turn my own adopted son against me."

She didn't care what Walter said. She didn't care what Ukiah thought. She wanted acquittal from her son, not them. So she turned to Martin:

"He's right about one thing, Martin. I had the right to fuck my own life up, but I didn't have the right to ruin yours."

"Shut up you dirty mouth!" Martin said.

"Don't you see what he's done to you? He's made your sky just a little tiny pinhole, made you make a Grand Canyon out of a gravel pit. He's your warden, son. Not your savior."

She watched his eyes flit back and forth between his father and his mother. She watched him pant as the pressure built to a temblor that rocked him.

"All your life, you've been waitin' for God to tell you what to do. But God's been waitin' for you to whisper in Her ear your wildest heart's desire," she said. "Don't be afraid of your own desire. Choose!"

"I'm his guardian," Walter said. "He doesn't choose."

"Oh, yes you do, Martin."

Martin shook like temple pillars about to crumble. "He is not guilty. He only make that one mistake. His whole life, he only make one mistake," he said.

"Martin, what mistake —"

"You have sex with her then pay her money. I look inside you, s- s- see the lie."

That stoned Walter to silence.

"I can't take any more of this," he finally said. "He needs to go back to Hope House," he told Hope. "You need help, son," Walter said to Martin.

"Can two people be crazy?" Patsy asked the church.

"Yes, they can," Dr. Hope replied. "There's something called shared psychotic disorder. Two people can suffer from the same delusion, usually a psychotic belief created by the more powerful personality of the two."

"Chad, could you, please?" Walter asked with a long-suffering sigh.

Two tousling bundles of men dragged Patsy and Martin down center aisle toward the door.

"I see it in my dream! She tells the truth!" Martin hollered.

"You can't see things in dreams. You can't possibly know things like that, that happened before you were born. God only gifted the prophets with that," Walter insisted. "And the age of the prophets is past."

"These things happen! I do not know how I know, but I do!" Martin fought against the furious tears that needed to fall.

They escorted Martin out in gentle lockstep. But Patsy, the blue denim prophet, they dragged in cuffs. Only Cammy pushed against them.

"I'll go! I'll go and face all your charges on one condition!" Patsy offered them. "Make him take a paternity test! I can't force him to, but if he won't, then at least y'all will know why."

Walter sweated.

"'Cuz if you can't ask him to do that, then you're accessories after-the-fact. Then you all conspired with him," Patsy argued.

The men had her as far as the back pew.

"Let her talk!" Cammy yelled.

The young father stepped out into the aisle, walked back and blocked the men.

"Again, I ask you to have faith in me as we have faith in Christ," Walter said to his people.

"You're not Christ," someone spoke from the pews.

"Jesus gave His blood, Reverend. Are you too good not to give yours?" Patsy asked him.

Walter's lips parted, but there were no more words.

Martin gazed at his father and sobbed. The surges of his body forced the men to let him go. They couldn't hold him, not in the way he needed to be held. But Patsy was still chained. She shook off her jailers, approached him, and managed to nudge her son's head onto her shoulder.

The rains came, throaty crests, years of them, wept onto the column she became, more resolute than any that held up the roof of the church.

Mr. Kantwell slipped out quietly. So did Mr. Dobson, her old gym teacher. Dr. Hope made a show of looking at his watch and abandoned the pew with his family. The choir loft drained. The church emptied by ones and twos, the oldest first.

In the end, the only congregation Walter had left was Virginia, little Walter, and Chad. Chad unlocked Patsy's cuffs and left the church.

The drapes along the side windows fluttered in a velvet breeze. Virginia stared at her husband for a long time. His gaze pled back. She shook her head, and a tear dribbled down her nose. She slid out the pew with her baby and rushed out.

Patsy rocked her own child in her arms with a deep peace, a peace she hadn't felt since her father had held her like that.

Martin hushed. The hum in his body ceased. He unclasped his arms and moved back from her. He assured her with a nod and stepped up the altar until he was even with his father.

"I come by to pick up my things," Martin calmly told him.

Walter looked around his church, at the lacquered beams that held his roof in place; at his pulpit, where the pages of the Tallman Family Bible flapped in the breeze drifting through his front door. He looked out over Hickory Street where he'd led the parade. A train waited in the station — an Amtrak.

"All this," he said. "I really believe in it. Even though I couldn't live up to it." He unhooked his vestments and they dropped to the altar like things heavier than clothes. He seemed relieved. Over his polished black wingtips, he wore slacks torn at one knee and a yellowing tee shirt.

"Don't judge it by what I did," he said to his boy.

Walter left the church out the front door just like everyone else.

They stood in each other's silence until a wind reminiscent of spring gusted through the doors and chased the last of the perfume and dirty diapers out the windows.

"How long have you known? That your daddy didn't adopt you?" Patsy asked.

He stared down at her square toe boots.

"Deep insides, my whole life."

"I see."

"He is all I have."

"Yeah."

"He stick by me."

She tried to swallow the feeling that he'd betrayed her.

"He wasn't guilty of Abandonment and Irresponsibility," she concluded for him.

She felt her whole life had completed a great circuit that moment.

"It's easier being Jesus than Judas, even though something inside you has to die either way," she thought out loud.

He glanced up, surprised by the remark.

The Amtrak train called out one more time before it left town. He remembered something in his wallet. He pulled out the phony arrest warrant naming her she'd made way back in Kansas. He unfolded it, ripped it up and threw the pieces to the breeze.

"I'll help you find a place in town before I leave, get you set up. I'll bet your auntie still has that room over the garage."

His eyes were steady on her. She thought he looked awkward in that carmine cassock, with one shoulder up and the other pulled down from the tussle.

"I got a job now. I'll send money. Maybe we can even get you a job. I hear the pharmacy needs some fixin'," she said.

"Do not run away from me again."

And she looked at his hair and knew she'd never be able to tame it.

"I came back to set you free, not to keep you for myself," she said.

She couldn't resist. She straightened out his cassock.

"With a little help, you'll make it on your own alright. You'll see. I have faith in you."

"You never show me the gorgeous tear in the world."

She didn't get the reference.

"The Grand Canyon," he explained.

"I've done a lot of thinkin'. I'm no mother. I tried, but I'm not ready. And if I'm not ready now, I never will be."

"The only way you get ready to do some things is to do them before you is ready. For some things, that is the only way," he reminded her.

"Just so we're clear —"

"I no longer think you is my girlfriend," he said.

"Just so we're clear," she started again and smiled, "I didn't come outta no magazine."

"But you is my real mom."

And she felt it, all at once. Cocaine never brought her as high.

She tucked in the kickstand and they walked her bike out of church.

85.

On a highway hemmed by forest, they rode with the wind. She poured it on, following the signs and the gravel roads to the Vista Points. His choir robes rippled like crimson flags. They vroomed past ponderosa higher than anyplace else on earth, past logs fallen across the road. Only two-wheels could weave around them, dipping into dark forests where the wind roared for dozens of miles, becoming a vast instrument moaning its one long song.

As the sun dusted the tops of the ponderosa, they pulled into Parasawampitts Point. He asked her what that name meant, but she'd never figured it out.

They reached the edge of the plateau, the edge of the world. Like the first time she rode here, she rode until she ran out of land. Only this time, they'd reached heaven. They'd landed at the Rainbow Rim.

She parked the Scimitar, leaning their iron under a spruce that shuddered and swayed with the violent wind. She led him to the head of the Rainbow Rim Trail. Crimson, flecked with rust the color of their hair, flowed along with veins of blue and chrome in the heart of the Grand Canyon. The colors set their eyes afire.

They walked together out to a headland surrounded by cubic miles of air. The aspen quaked and the ponderosas thundered in the wind. Out across a gulf of sky stretched a vast plateau, forested with high crowns, its sheer bronze walls a citadel.

In all directions, towers and steeples soared as he whirled in his gown. The far rim was a distant horizon, and beyond, sprawling plains poured over it. Mountains floated on mist, islands in the sky.

He held up his long, long arms. She stripped off the satin like an old skin. Even in the wind, it clung to his hair in an electric way. But the wind wanted it. He let it sail. They watched until it dissolved into the cliffs above the river.

AUTHOR BIOGRAPHY

Michael Just is a former attorney, actor, psychotherapist and adjunct professor with an amateur background in science, mythology and storytelling. Born and raised in Chicago, he now lives in the Four Corners region of the American Southwest. A hiker with an interest in geology and natural history, Mike expresses his interests in his writing.

His writing has appeared in *The Chicago Sun Times*, and he received an honorable mention award from *Writer's Digest* in 2011 for short fiction. He was a semifinalist in America's Best Screenplay Competition for best screenplay, and a quarterfinalist in *Fade-In Magazine's* screenplay contest for two screenplay entries. He has edited book-length historical fiction and served as a script doctor for dramatic works.

He posts new essays on his blog, *The Accidental Naturalist,* every two weeks at: https://justmikejust.substack.com

His short story anthology, *Canyon Calls*, was published by Zumaya Publications in 2009. Mike's novel, *The Dirt: The Journey of a Mystic Cowboy*, is available in softcover or eBook formats through Amazon.

Mike's other titles, including his novels, *The Crippy* and *The Mind Altar*, as well as *Canyon Calls*, are available through his websites or Amazon:

https://justmikejust.com
https://canyoncallsthebook.com
https://www.amazon.com/stores/Michael-Just/author/B002LFMX-AW?ref=ap_rdr&store_ref=ap_rdr&isDramIntegrated=true&shopping-PortalEnabled=true

Five of his short stories have recently been published online:

"Lies, Ltd." has been published by *The Mystery Tribune:*
https://mysterytribune.com/lies-ltd-literary-short-fiction-by-michael-c-just/

"The Obligate Carnivore" has been published by the *Scarlet Leaf Review*:
https://www.scarletleafreview.com/short-stories47/category/michael-just

"I See You, Too" has been published by the *96th of October:*
 http://96thofoctober.com/articles/i-see-you-too/

"Offload" has been published by *The Worlds Within:*
https://theworldswithin.net/offload/

"You Get the Two" has been published by Hellbound Books in the anthology *Kids are Hell!* and is available in print, eBook, kindle, or audio format:
https://hellboundbookspublishing.com/kidsarehell.html